The Torch of Triumph

The Torch of Triumph

Sally Laity
&
Dianna Crawford

Tyndale House Publishers, Inc.
Wheaton, Illinois

Library of Congress Cataloging-in-Publication Data

Laity, Sally.
    Torch of triumph / Sally Laity and Dianna Crawford.
        p.   cm. —(Freedom's holy light)
    ISBN 0-8423-1417-2
    1. United States—History—Revolution, 1775–1783—Fiction.
  2. Indian captivities—Fiction.   I. Crawford, Dianna, date.
  II. Title.   III. Series: Laity, Sally. Freedom's holy light ; v. 6.
  PS3562.A37T67   1997
  813'.54—dc21
                                                                    96-47576

Printed in the United States of America

02   01   00   99   98   97
7   6   5   4   3   2   1

To the valiant souls who paid the ultimate price
to obtain liberty for all who came behind
and to the faithful readers of Freedom's Holy Light,
this book is lovingly dedicated.

The authors received a wealth of invaluable assistance in acquiring the various research materials needed during the writing of Freedom's Holy Light, and much of it was used in this final book in the series. With heartfelt gratitude we express our thanks to:

Edgar Hughes, John Comitz, and Coach Walter "Chip" Sorber, of Lake Lehman High School, Lehman, Pennsylvania, for historical data regarding the Wyoming Valley Massacre, the Six Nations of the Iroquois, and the Sullivan Campaign.

Barbara Cragle, for numerous trips to the Wyoming Valley Historical Society and Osterhout Library to obtain additional historical details on the above subjects, on colonial Wilkes-Barre, and on Colonel Edward Hand, whose First Pennsylvania Riflemen played such an important part in the Revolutionary War.

Brian Leigh Dunnigan and Susannah Allen, of Old Fort Niagara, Youngstown, New York, for forwarding detailed information on Fort Niagara and the surrounding area.

Susannah Rich and Lynda Carpenter, for critiquing the manuscript along the way.

Penelope J. Stokes of SilverFire Editorial Services, for bringing out the best in us.

May the Lord bless you all.

December 1776

Evelyn Thomas stirred and roused to wakefulness as fingers threaded the long, thick curls spilling from her nightcap and gently toyed with them. She smiled and relaxed with a sigh. The warmth of the quilts added to her euphoric state, and tender fantasies of smiling blue eyes drifted into her consciousness . . . eyes belonging to brave, sandy-haired Christopher Drummond. Fate had brought him across her path not once but twice. And both times, the handsome young Knight of the Realm had proven himself Evie's stalwart champion by valiantly taking a position between her and impending danger. How easily all memories of her previous suitors vanished. . . .

A second tug on her locks brought Evelyn fully awake, and the enchanting reverie gave way to reality. Instead of a soft feather bed, she lay on a straw pallet with Emily MacKinnon and the young widow's two small children. Evie turned on the hard padding and disengaged her hair from the grip of the slumbering two-year-old, Rusty, then lifted the blankets and eased up. In the dim predawn light of the loft bedroom, it was hard to make out the forms of the other two little ones—the Haynes children, dozing under down quilts on a second pallet a few feet away.

Dan and Susannah Haynes, who occupied one of the two

downstairs bedchambers, had not in the least been put off by Dan's sister's unannounced arrival, despite the fact that she had not come alone. They welcomed Emily and her children warmly, along with Evelyn, her sister-in-law Prudence Thomas, and friends Christopher Drummond and Robert Chandler . . . plus a large herd of horses.

Evie smiled at the thought. What an astounding spectacle they must have made when they rode up to the little farmstead! When she and Prudence had joined the party in Princeton, the herd—over sixty sorrel-colored Narragansett Pacers—had already been driven all the way from the Haynes family farm in Rhode Island, barely escaping the British forces poised to swoop in and confiscate or destroy everything in their wake. The great drive had been accomplished in less than a fortnight—the last leg of the trip in a blizzard. It was nothing short of miraculous, even to Evelyn.

Even more amazing was the fact that she and Prudence, also fleeing from the redcoats, happened to be in Princeton at the exact moment Christopher came riding through town! Circumstances could not have been better if she had planned them herself.

Evelyn tingled at the realization that at this very moment, Christopher and Robert shared the room directly below the loft. Even knights succumb to weariness, especially after managing to stave off the enemy and endure a raging snowstorm during the harrowing journey. She hoped last night had provided them with some well-earned rest.

Chris was so competent for one only eighteen, so . . . manly. Though somewhat lanky now, his form already bore promise of shoulders that would broaden deliciously above his trim waist, and arms that displayed fine muscle definition. A light smattering of freckles across the bridge of his nose added a captivating appeal to his countenance, and his infectious grin had the power to reduce Evie to mush.

Evie felt herself beginning to blush just at the thought of him. She had to get control of herself. After all, this was the last precious morning they would have together. In a few hours, Christopher had to leave with Robert to rejoin General Washington's army.

The war was all but lost—everyone knew it. For a brief moment Evie considered trying to convince Chris to stay rather than go back to his rifle battalion . . . but she could not bring herself to ask him to choose between her and the cause. Besides, it wasn't as if he had given her the right to request such a thing. Though he had been more than attentive on the trip here to northeastern Pennsylvania's Wyoming Valley, he had made no profession of the affection she was certain he felt toward her. Nor had she revealed the secret feelings blossoming within her own heart for him.

But what if he did this morning?

She sprang up and snatched her dress off a crate. She had to get ready—quickly. He might awaken before the others and . . .

Shrugging out of her flannel nightdress, Evie dressed in haste, ran a brush quickly through her hair, then tiptoed to the ladder. She fixed her gaze on the door to his room as she descended the rungs, willing him to join her.

Christopher hurriedly fastened the buttons on his shirt and tucked the tails into his breeches. Everyone had stayed up late last night getting reacquainted, catching up on one another's latest news, and nothing as yet disturbed the morning stillness. Even Robert remained sound asleep. Yet he hoped against hope that Evelyn might also rise early.

What a treat it would be for him to share a last few *private* moments with her, perhaps over a cup of coffee. To feast his eyes on her exquisite beauty and carry the memory with him when he left. To have that vision to warm him on the cold, lonely nights ahead, once he and Robert were back in the thick of battle.

Chris released a rueful breath. His dreams would likely be all he would ever have of Evelyn. Somehow, someway, he would resign himself to it. He had to. Only the war had brought them together in the first place, and once the conflict ended, she would be out of his life forever. Evie's station was too far above his. There was no point even hoping for a future with the pampered sixteen-year-old daughter of a rich Philadelphia merchant.

That stark reality sank like a stone into his heart. All too well Christopher remembered his own father—a disreputable character known all over Princeton as the town drunk—and the memory made him cringe. Despite God-fearing foster parents who were proprietors of a fine coaching inn, and the fact that he had been attending the College of New Jersey before the war with Britain broke out, Chris knew it would be many years before he could earn the engineering degree he coveted and find himself in a financial position to court someone like Evie. If ever.

But for these last few sweet hours, he would put those sad circumstances out of his mind. If only the Lord would grant his fervent prayer for some time alone with Evelyn. . . . If only she would merely come downstairs before the others awakened. . . .

Picking up his boots, he moved silently to the door, trying to imagine climbing the ladder and rousing her without disturbing Emily and the children. What would Evie think of such boldness?

The hinge gave a light squeak as he opened the door. Chris held his breath and glanced over at Robert. Seeing no movement, he backed out and closed it carefully behind him.

When he turned around, Evelyn's smile was the first thing he saw.

"Good morning," she whispered, her face aglow.

Christopher's spirits soared. "Good morning to you," he whispered back, returning the grand smile.

Evie, too, carried her shoes in her hand. Taking them from her, Chris set them beside his on the hearth. Out of habit he knelt to stir the banked coals to full flame—he scarcely noticed the chill. His prayer had been answered. Here they were, the two of them, alone in the quiet of morning while the household slept.

He looked up. Evelyn's eyes, a shade of blue so pale they appeared almost transparent, gazed into his. Was it possible that she felt as he did? Christopher hardly dared believe it. But all the same, he felt more alive than he had ever been.

Once the fire blazed to life, Evie took the lamp from the mantel, and he lit the wick with a fire stick. A golden glow illuminated the interior of the cozy dwelling . . . a house meant for a young family—or a young couple.

Chris reached for the lantern, and his fingers brushed Evie's, sending a shock clear through him. Not daring to look at her, lest she see how profoundly that brief contact had jolted him, he turned toward the kitchen and went to fetch the water bucket from the sideboard.

Evie, only a step behind, picked up the coffeepot and held it out. Christopher hoped his trembling hands wouldn't betray him as he poured water into it. Their eyes met for a heartbeat . . . long enough for him to see that she also had been affected by that touch. With difficulty he forced himself to stop staring, and the two of them returned to the hearth.

The coals were glowing brightly now. Chris shoveled them toward the front, and Evie leaned down to place the coffeepot on the trivet above them.

Their faces almost collided.

Evelyn drew a quick breath and whirled away, returning in a matter of seconds with the ground coffee beans. She smiled demurely and lowered her eyes.

Christopher held his breath as he lifted the lid of the pot for her. Never in his life had he imagined the small chores of first light could be so . . . stirring . . . so intimate.

But he had to keep a grip on himself. He steeled himself against his racing heart and offered his hand to help her rise.

Evelyn looked at it, then raised her head and met his gaze. Without hesitation, she placed her fingers in his.

As Christopher assisted Evie to her feet, the wondrous realization dawned on him that no one in the house had yet been disturbed. He bent to retrieve their shoes, then nodded toward the front door.

Evelyn plucked her woolen shawl from a peg near the door, and the two of them stepped outside into the bitter December air. Chris took it from her and wrapped it about her slender shoulders with infinite care. He stretched out the simple courtesy for as long as possible, then they sat down on the porch step to put on their shoes.

For a moment or two Chris allowed himself to marvel at her trim ankle and foot, but he dared not let his gaze linger too long. She was a lady, after all, and he must behave like a gentleman.

At last the time came to help her stand again, and he was only too glad for a legitimate reason to touch her.

Remnants of the recent snowfall crunched beneath their feet as they walked in the direction of the privy. Normally this was a journey one took alone, but it was such a joy to have Evie at his side that he shrugged off thought of their destination.

Several horses stirred and milled about when they passed the corral, but none betrayed the moment by whinnying. Snow-covered hills, in the delicate lavender blue of morning, added a peaceful backdrop to the pastoral scene.

Suddenly Evie broke the silence. "Do you have any idea how many sprawling arms and legs I had to climb over to reach that ladder without waking anybody?" She laughed lightly and tugged the shawl more closely around herself.

"I can only guess." She probably had not the slightest idea how radiant she looked. Carved ivory combs at the sides of her hair held back a riot of shining curls in tumbling disarray across her shoulders, and a mischievous sparkle shone in her eyes. He tore his gaze from her cheeks, already rosy in the chill temperature.

"I was so pleased to see you coming out of your room."

"Were you?" Chris's heart pumped crazily inside his chest.

"Of course. Heaven only knows what Robert might have thought of me if he'd awakened to find me in there shaking your shoulder."

"You'd have done that?" The very concept sent a thrill through Christopher's whole being. Evie's desire to be with him was as strong as his own desire to be with her. He turned to her . . . and discovered they had reached the outhouse. "I'll, er, be back in a minute." With a discreet tip of his head, he veered away toward a small wooded knoll. But he couldn't stop himself from taking one backward glance to watch her walk the remaining steps to the tiny structure. Her graceful movements enchanted him.

Once she disappeared inside, however, the sharpness of the Pennsylvania winter finally registered. Christopher wished he'd had the presence of mind to grab a coat on his way out. He blew on his hands and rubbed them together, picking up the pace in order to keep warm. Only sheer determination kept his teeth from chattering.

By what miracle had he and Evie been brought together this second time? It had to be more than mere chance that had her running from the British for spying, hiding out at his foster parents' coaching inn when he arrived at the Lyons' Den. And what other explanation could there be that he and Robert Chandler would take leave from military duties at that very time to help Emily move her father's horses to safety?

But even as he marveled over those wonders, Christopher couldn't suppress a sigh of resignation. He'd best enjoy these moments while he could. In all likelihood, even if he didn't get killed in the patriots' last desperate attempt to defeat the English forces, all too soon Evelyn would remember that the two of them came from different worlds, that he was far from suitable for her.

On the other hand, stranger things had been known to happen over the course of time. What if the feelings he had for Evie weren't hopeless after all? What if she turned out to be the very one God had chosen for him? She had been a real trouper during the trek through the wintry mountains, never complaining about hardships . . . or blizzards. She had helped with the animals, and not once had she treated him as less than an equal. A warm glow infused him, despite the brisk gust of wind that whipped by.

Turning away from the woods once more, he saw Evelyn waiting for him, and his heart leaped. She could easily have gone back to the house ahead of him but had chosen to wait. The realization meant as much to him as her sweet smile had when their eyes had first met early that morning.

Christopher lengthened his stride and caught up to Evie. Gaining confidence from another of her fetching smiles, he boldly took possession of her hand. He'd have preferred to take a few more liberties as well, but cold or not, he refrained from venturing even so far as to put an arm around her as they walked back toward the dwelling. Slowly. This time they gave a wider berth to the corral of milling animals.

The plume from the chimney reminded Chris that by now the coffee would be done, and he and Evie could share another tantalizing—and private—interlude. He took her elbow and assisted her up the slippery step. They tiptoed across the hollow boards of the narrow porch, and he reached for the latch.

But the door swung wide from inside, and there, attired in winter flannels, his somber glare darting from one unchaperoned young person to the other, stood their host, the Reverend Daniel Haynes.

2

Evelyn's best efforts could not overcome the flush creeping into her cheeks, but somehow she resisted the impulse to giggle. So often during her life she had encountered an identical reproving expression directed at her by her older brother Morgan. Dan Haynes had deep sable eyes rather than Morgan's cobalt blue, but he apparently shared her brother's need to thwart her happiness. Right now the minister was intruding on her special time with Christopher, and with no little dismay, she felt Chris shift uneasily and drop her hand.

"Is, er, the coffee boiling yet?" he asked.

The minister's gaze flicked to him. "As a matter of fact, the aroma is what woke us up."

Us? Evie's heart plummeted as Dan stepped aside to allow her and Christopher to pass. The remaining adults were, indeed, present in the kitchen . . . Dan's wife, his sister Emily, and Robert Chandler, all of whom were not only awake but fully dressed as well. Susannah looked especially rested and efficient, her tawny hair in a chignon beneath a crisp ruffled house cap as she fussed about in the kitchen.

"We hope you've saved some for us," Evelyn said as brightly as she could.

"Of course." Susannah's lilting British accent complemented the soft tone of her voice as she removed two more cups from the sideboard and set them on the dark walnut table. "It was rather a pleasant surprise, actually. We do thank you for making it." She locked her blue gray eyes on Christopher. "And you, Chip, for starting the fire."

"My pleasure," Chris mumbled, darting a sidelong glance at Evie as if embarrassed by the reference to his childhood nickname.

One would think the two of us had shared more than a paltry few morning chores, Evie thought with chagrin. But then a far more gratifying notion came to her. If Christopher were to commit himself to her so she would not have to doubt his sincerity, this would be merely the first of a whole lifetime of mornings together.

But Chris was a man of few words. He had absolutely no gift for the shallow, fanciful conversation favored by the young British officers who had vied for her attention in the past. But after the many months she'd been obliged to entertain the glib English aristocrats while ferreting information for the patriots, Chris's company was quite refreshing. And if her brother, Morgan, had not gotten caught spying himself, Evelyn would likely still be stuck in New York in the middle of the intrigues, right along with her brother and his wife.

"I was reminded of those delightful bygone days when you and I both worked at the Lyons' Den in Princeton," Susannah was saying. She handed Christopher a steaming mug, gave a second to Evelyn, then served coffee to Robert Chandler and Emily.

The two exchanged meaningful glances, then rose, coffee mugs in hand.

"We'll go see to the herd now," Emily said, brushing a lock of honey blonde hair back over her shoulder. She glanced up at the tall, compelling man whose glossy brown hair and blue eyes were a marked contrast to her coloring. "I know you men would appreciate getting an early start."

"Thanks, Emmy." Dan smiled, then turned and accepted a refill from his wife with a tender peck on the cheek. "I should go, too, and pack up."

Susannah blinked back tears but said nothing. Her forlorn gaze followed her husband to their bedchamber.

"You're coming with Robert and me?" Christopher asked Dan, heading to the room he'd shared with Chandler.

"I have to if I can help make any difference at all. The cause is so very near lost, I must try. Susannah understands my convictions."

His wife turned away and busied herself by pouring flour into a large bowl.

Evie looked from one to the other. She knew that Washington's army was close to defeat—as close as it had ever been. The patriots had been run out of New York and foiled at every turn since then, and at the present time were being chased across New Jersey with General Howe's army close on their heels.

A flush crept over the Englishwoman's face. Chagrined, she blotted a tear with the hem of the long work apron protecting her indigo dress. "Dan and I discussed the matter at great length last night, but I could not bring myself to ask him not to go. He's believed most strongly in the cause since the very first. I knew in my heart that with the need so dire, he'd not find it in himself to turn his back."

The pain in Susannah's eyes cut through Evelyn's own defenses. The Americans had struggled so long and hard. The idea of defeat before the British dogs was unthinkable. Hoping to gather her own ragged emotions, Evie glanced out the window overlooking the barnyard and the corral teeming with horses. There she was met with another shock—Robert Chandler, with his arm around Dan's recently widowed sister, tugged Emily close and bestowed a kiss on her forehead.

Evelyn quickly drew back. Dropping onto the bench, she took a sip of her coffee, then set down the cup. "I realize it's not my concern, but have you noticed how . . . friendly . . . Emily and Chandler have become?"

"Rather like another pair I've observed of late," Susannah teased over her shoulder as she kneaded the biscuit dough.

Evie bit off a flippant retort. How could Susannah possibly compare her and Chris to Emily and Chandler? The older pair had both been immersed in mourning their lost loves—

that is, until the last day or two. Or had Evie just been so preoccupied throughout the journey that she hadn't noticed their budding relationship? Recalling that long trek northward, she found herself smiling, as she did so often now, at every tiny remembrance of her and Christopher's time together.

Chris returned, taking a seat next to Evie. In spite of her hostess's knowing comment, she broadened her smile to include him. "But it seems . . . I don't know . . . improper," she continued. "Emily's husband was killed only a few months ago."

Susannah drew a thoughtful breath, then paused and wiped her hands on a towel. "A person's grief isn't something the rest of us should judge," she said kindly. "Dan and I are both happy that God has allowed Emily to reach beyond her pain and loss so quickly. And Robert lived with the death of his Julia for far too many bitter, empty years. Seeing new life in his eyes is a true blessing. I trust that if he and Emily take things slowly, they shall do well together—particularly now that he's finally resolved his dispute with God. And who can ignore the way Emily's children have taken to him?"

"Or the way he's become enamored with them," Christopher added. "I agree with Susannah. Emily and the children are good for him. Even among the men in the battalion he keeps pretty much to himself."

"Robert will be a fine match for our Emily," Susannah went on, rolling out the dough and cutting biscuit rounds. "His family, you know, has quite the prosperous plantation in North Carolina. He'll have no trouble providing for her. She and the little ones will want for nothing, I'm sure."

Evie felt, rather than saw, Christopher lower his gaze. He seemed to draw away from her, and she felt certain she knew why. He had no family or wealth to offer, and that fact, no doubt, weighed heavily on his mind. She reached beneath the table for his hand and covered it with her own. "The value of a person's worldly goods is of little consequence in the grand scheme of things."

"That's very true." Susannah turned with a pleased smile. "The most important consideration is for the couple to be equally yoked, both having the same desire to follow the will of God. And now that Robert has rededicated himself to the Lord as well as to Emily and the children, I'm sure they'll find great happiness together."

Evie maintained an even expression as she assessed her simple surroundings. While not especially grand or bespeaking worldly wealth, the Haynes home exuded loving warmth and a peaceful sort of homeyness, with sturdy handmade furniture and Susannah's colorful touches in the needlepoint cushions and crocheted throws. The only unpleasantness about the place, in Evie's mind, was the excessive number of religious platitudes that issued from Susannah Haynes's lips. Evie shrugged. No doubt that came from being married to a minister.

"I'd venture to say," Chris added, the low timbre of his voice sending a thrill through Evelyn, "that Robert shall have more regard for his own safety now that he has someone besides himself to consider."

"Well, let's just hope you have equal regard for yours." Evie laced her fingers with his under the tabletop and smiled. "In fact, why don't I go along with you and see that you do?"

"You jest, of course!" Susannah returned with fervor as she and Chris both gaped at her.

The words had just popped out, but Evelyn liked the sound of them. A lot. She tossed her head. "I don't know why I shouldn't go. My sister-in-law, Prudence, did just that— dressed up like a man to fight at Bunker Hill. And I'm taller than she is. Surely I could—"

Christopher pulled his hand from hers and took her by both shoulders, his expression somber. "That's the last word we'll hear about such a notion. It's completely out of the question."

It seemed to Evie that everyone in the world had banded together for the sole purpose of telling her what to do, where to go. Yet she could not ignore the passion in Chris's voice. It revealed how deeply he did care about her and brought her some measure of comfort. "It was just a thought," she finally said.

"Let's keep it that way," Susannah added with finality. "I'm afraid the men would be so concerned over you, they'd not be cautious enough with their own lives."

Evie had never considered that possibility, and she began to feel foolish. She lifted her eyes to Christopher's. "I hadn't reasoned it through. But you must promise to write me at least once every week so I'll know you're all right. Will you do that?"

He hadn't relinquished his hold on her shoulders, and she was more than conscious of the warmth and strength in his fingers. It lingered even after he eased his grip. "If you'll do the same for me," he murmured, a tentative, hopeful question in his face.

"Every single day," she whispered back.

He drew her a little closer, renewed joy and hope washing over his countenance. His gaze dropped to her lips, and he dipped his head slightly, his warm breath feathering and mingling with hers.

Evelyn's heart skipped a beat.

"*Ahem.*" Dan emerged from the bedroom. "Your things ready to go, Chip?"

Nodding, Christopher released Evie and scooted a few inches back on the bench, his neck reddening by the second.

Even with the minister's interruption, Evie wanted to shout for joy. Chris had wanted to kiss her. He had.

"We need to ride out as soon as Morgan gets here."

As Dan's words finally sank in, Evie regarded her host with alarm. "So soon?"

"Winter days are short," he reminded her gently. "We must take advantage of what daylight we have."

"I suppose." Turning away before anyone could witness her disappointment, Evelyn trained her gaze on the window. Silently she begged her brother not to come. Not just yet.

Morgan and Prudence had spent the night nearby, with Christopher's sister, Mary Clare, and her husband, Jonathan

Bradford. Not only had the invitation helped relieve the overcrowded Haynes house, but it had provided Morgan and Prudence privacy and a room of their own for their blessed reunion. For over a week after his capture by the British, everyone had feared for Morgan's very life, until even Prudence had to accept the possibility that he'd been hanged as a spy. But Evie's brother had always been as lucky as he was charming and clever. He'd managed to escape his captors, and when he finally reached Wilkes-Barre yesterday, he was welcomed with both relief and abundant joy.

Evelyn focused on some movement outside.

Robert Chandler stepped into view with Emily at his side. And for all the world to see, he drew her into his arms and kissed her full and long on the lips.

Some people were so fortunate, Evie mused wistfully, touching her fingers to her own deprived lips. If she and Christopher had the luxury of a few more days together, she could convince him she cared not a whit about being the daughter of a prominent Philadelphia merchant. If he believed her, there would be nothing stopping him from asking her to wait for him. If only they had more time.

Suddenly she became aware of his shallow breath warming the nape of her neck. Chris had turned with her and was watching the newly proclaimed lovebirds. An unaccountable shyness overtook her, and she jumped to her feet. "Is there anything I can do, Susannah, to help with breakfast?"

"Thank you, Evie, dear. That would be most helpful." The Englishwoman motioned to the worktable. "You might start cutting off slices of bacon."

Serves me right for asking, Evie scolded herself. *Greasy, slimy bacon.* Forcing a smile, she left the bench to help out. Dared she hope Chris would offer to help her?

"I believe I hear horses," Susannah said suddenly.

Christopher and Dan went to the window.

"Morgan and Prudence," Chris announced. Then he stared more closely. "With Jonathan and Mary Clare, leading a packhorse. Think Jon's planning to come with us, too?"

Susannah exchanged an eloquent glance with Dan. "It would seem you weren't the only one making a midnight plea to your wife."

With a rueful smile, the minister crossed the room and hugged her. "And we won't be the only men to leave the valley. Most of the fellows who helped build the corral said orders had just been received from General Washington. Both local militias are to report to him for active duty. They'll head out on the first of the year."

"But that will leave the valley without defense!" she blurted out. "And one can never be certain about—" She cut a glance to Evie.

Dan quickly took her into his arms. "I don't want you to worry, love," he said comfortingly. "Another regiment of five companies will be formed under Nathan Denison to protect our valley. He may have a game leg, but he can shoot with the best of them. Chip—" He turned to Christopher. "We'd better go saddle a couple of mounts before breakfast."

Tossing a wistful look at Evelyn, the younger man grabbed his greatcoat off the wall hook and followed Dan out.

Evie's stomach knotted as her time with Chris came to an abrupt end. There wouldn't be a chance for another minute alone. Not even for the briefest of kisses. And he'd be gone for months and months—with only the promise to write. What if, when they were separated by distance and time, he came to the conclusion that the two of them would never be suited for each other? Her last beau had done just that when he'd gone off to war—forsaken the grandiose promises he'd made her. Not only had he failed to write, but he'd taken up with a farmer's daughter near his encampment. Still, Evie assured herself, Christopher was made of sterner stuff. A noble knight. And a knight was true to his word . . . she hoped.

❧ ❧

Christopher, collecting his horse, watched the foursome approaching. Morgan Thomas, tall and solemn, held a special place in Chris's heart for befriending him years ago when he was an unhappy young man in Princeton—and ashamed of being the ragged child of a mean, drunken lout. Beside Morgan rode his lovely wife, whose exotic beauty appeared all the more fragile now that she was with child. It was hard to believe she and Evelyn had, along with Morgan, actually risked their necks to become spies for the patriots. When the plot was exposed, the two reckless lasses barely escaped New York with their lives.

Chris shifted his attention to Jon Bradford, his sister's husband. Jon, one of Morgan's fellow classmates at the College of New Jersey, had also befriended young Chris—and not only him, but timid Mary Clare as well. Over the objections raised by his family, Jonathan and Mary grew to regard one another deeply. Jon's love proved strong enough to commit himself heart and soul to Mary, in spite of the loss of his parents' approval or financial assistance.

Chris would always owe his brother-in-law a great debt for his selfless sacrifice on behalf of Mary, who had been deeply shamed by their worthless father when he sold her into servitude. The young couple had carved out a life in the frontier country of the beautiful Wyoming Valley. Their strong faith in God and their love for each other saw them through the lean beginnings and even yet bound them together. They hadn't been apart for more than a day or two since they wed.

Jon and Mary's oldest daughter, Esther, perched in front of her father on the horse, and their youngest, Beth, was tucked in front of Mary Clare. Mary's reddened eyes matched her wind-chafed cheeks and swollen nose. Obviously she'd been crying for some time. Christopher's heart went out to her at the certainty that Jon would be going to war with him and the others.

His thoughts drifting to Evelyn, Chris looked toward the house just as she came out, her own expression as bleak as Mary's. Was it possible she might consider giving up her privileged life in exchange for one with him? Could the two of them find the same kind of happiness Mary and Jon knew?

Evie came straight toward him, which he took as a good

sign since everyone else was converging on the newcomers, extending greetings and hugs and tearful good-byes. The pacer Chris was saddling stretched its neck over the corral fence, and Evelyn stopped just outside the rail, near enough for Chris to catch the scent of the soap she'd used to wash the smell of bacon from her hands. Lowering her lashes, she reached across the top rail and raked her fingers through a tangled spot in the animal's mane.

Christopher's hold on the cinch straps relaxed as he paused to watch her rapport with the animals. How at ease she seemed with them . . . *and with him.* He could almost feel those tapered fingers twining themselves into his own hair. Quickly berating himself for such wild imaginings, he looped the strap tightly through the ring, then led the mount out of the pen and joined Evie. "You have a wonderful way with horses."

She smiled up at him. "I always enjoyed grooming the ones in our stable . . . whenever I could sneak out without Mother knowing about it." Evie wrinkled her nose and laughed. "Odorous, Mother termed them. And of course she always maintained a very safe distance."

Chris let his laughter blend with hers. "Can't say I ever had to sneak out to a stable. One of my main tasks at the coaching inn was to help hitch and unhitch the stage teams, feed and groom them. I got to know quite a number of the horses by their first names."

"That sounds ever so much more interesting than the *gentle endeavors* that occupy the life of a proper young lady," Evelyn returned, softly stroking the pacer's muzzle. "The most important being, of course, that of perfecting the art of tiresome and useless conversation. Oh, and one must not forget stitchery."

Christopher couldn't help wondering if she was referring to her own life before becoming a spy. "I'm sure it was much more cultured than the life I hope to lead," he heard himself say. He couldn't have been more surprised to be revealing his secret dream—up until now, he had told no one. But having said that much, he decided to trust her with all of it. "I plan—after the war, that is—to finish my engineering studies. Western Pennsylvania is in dire need of good roads and bridges. But I'd like to build a place of my own, too, as Jon and Mary have done. I hope to do some crossbreeding . . . develop a better breed of coach horse with increased strength and stamina."

Evelyn's brows knitted in a frown, and she looked away.

Chris felt his spirits sag. *She hates the very idea.* But then, what could he expect from a girl who'd had all that wealth could offer?

Evie's gaze returned to him, her frown still in place. "A name. The new breed should have a very special name, don't you think?"

Wonder of wonders, she didn't sound displeased after all! There was even enthusiasm in her tone. Christopher quickly regathered himself, then inclined his head toward the herd of sorrels. "These Narragansett Pacers were named after the biggest bay in Rhode Island. Guess I could call mine Susquehanna Coach Horses, after the river that runs through this valley."

"No." A sprightly grin displaced her frown. "Drummond Coach Horses. They should bear the proud name of their breeder. It sounds ever so much better, if you ask me. Much more . . . striking."

Proud? He echoed silently in amazement. *She thinks the name Drummond is of value? of worth?* Recalling how she'd taken hold of his hand earlier and even teased about going back with him to the rifle battalion, he felt a rush of courage. He tugged his mount forward, blocking the two of them from the view of the others. "I'm really going to miss you, Evie. Not an hour will pass that I don't think about you." Reaching out, he ran fingers through the soft brunette curls framing her brow.

She placed a hand over his, her pale blue eyes luminous, sparkling. "And I will count every minute until you return. You will come back to me, won't you, Chris? Promise?"

Her lips, sweet and full and tantalizing, were so close. He needed only to lower his head. He brushed his mouth across them, and found them to be as soft as he'd dreamed. His pulse thundered in his ears.

Evelyn sighed and pressed nearer.

Dropping the reins, Christopher encircled her with his arms and pulled her closer, deepening the kiss. Even in her heavy cloak, her slender form molded to his. He could feel the thrumming of her heart against his as she slid her hands up his chest and around his neck. A sense of awe overwhelmed him—she cared as deeply as he did!

But even in the tenderness of their embrace, reality intruded with an ache of its own. With the uncertainties of war, their different backgrounds, the aspirations of her family, he knew this first sweet kiss might very well be their last.

With everything that was in him, he hoped it was not.

3

Their mounts plodded onward in the mild, clear winter air, the rhythmic clopping over the thawing road echoing amid the wooded hills. Christopher glanced at Jonathan, riding alongside him, and then at Morgan and Dan, directly ahead. Hardly a word had been uttered since they'd left Wilkes-Barre, the glum silence a testimony that all thoughts were on tearful partings and loved ones left behind.

A vision of Evelyn, misty-eyed as she'd tried bravely to send him off with a smile, drifted to the fore, blotting out the wintry, rolling countryside. Chris revelled in the bittersweet picture and the memory of the kiss they had shared. It was his first, and he knew he would never forget it. A girl with Evie's background probably had suitors by the dozen, but he had been caught up in his studies and had no time to dally with the silly town girls who giggled and nudged one another whenever he walked by. Still, he was not sorry to have waited. Evie was special. Far beyond his dreams. Suddenly aware of the simpering grin plastered all over his face, Christopher cleared his throat and straightened in his saddle.

From the opposite direction, a wagon piled high with household goods rounded a bend and rumbled toward them. This one, like so many others they had passed since turning onto this road to Easton and the Delaware, bore a contingent of solemn-faced women and children, families forced to flee the onslaught of British plunder and terrorism. Chris sent up a silent prayer of thanks that Mary Clare, his only remaining family since his father passed on three years ago, was tucked safely away in the Wyoming Valley, far from the towns and farms of New Jersey. And that Evie, too, was out of danger now. Thank heaven she had not been caught spying. The thought of a rope around the dark-haired girl's lovely neck was too abhorrent to ponder. But surely the king's puppets had more than enough to pillage along the seaboard without venturing into the mountainous reaches of northeastern Pennsylvania.

Finding comfort in that slim hope, Chris noticed the growing number of houses and business establishments, which indicated that they were nearing the town of Easton. He turned to his brother-in-law. "Time's running out, Jon. We'll soon reach the ferry crossing. You'll have to decide whether you're going to cross the Delaware with Chandler and me and ride on to Peekskill on the Hudson or go downriver with Morgan and Dan to join General Washington."

Jon gave a noncommittal shrug. "I reckon you'd prefer me to go with you, but I can't help thinking it's too far into winter for the British to sail down the Hudson from Canada. If I wanted merely to hole up someplace till the cold weather's over, I'd just as soon have done that at home with Mary and the girls. You did say it's Washington's force that's in dire need of help."

"True. But you've never yet had any military encounters. You could get thrust into the fray before you've been given any training. Morgan will probably be returned to his old duty as quartermaster, and Dan's postriding experience will most likely get him assigned to courier duty like his brother, Ben. You would have no one to see you through your first battle."

Jonathan's eyes narrowed in thought.

"I wasn't supposed to tell you this," Chris added, "but Mary made me promise to look after you."

"Oh, she did, did she?" Jon rested a palm on the Pennsylvania rifle in its sheath. "I've been tracking deep into the woods, risking confrontations with Indians to put meat on the table ever since your sister and I moved up on the Susquehanna. And I've always managed to get back home . . . *with* our supper."

Chris nodded, but he wasn't to be deterred. "I'm not implying that you aren't a capable shot. But when cannon-balls and grapeshot are exploding, setting trees and houses ablaze all around you, the noise and smoke are unbelievable. Then, suddenly—too late—the smoke will clear, and there'll be a line of redcoats charging right at you, every one of them intent on killing you. And they won't be taking aim with just muskets, either. Their Brown Besses are fitted with bayonets, ready to gut a man. First time you're in the middle of a ruckus like that, it's impossible to think, let alone dodge." Jonathan made no reply.

Dan and Morgan, who had gained a little distance by this time, reined in while the two caught up. "There's a fairly good tavern just ahead," Dan said. "What say we take a last meal together before we go our separate ways?"

They stopped at the simple two-story mughouse, hitched their mounts, and entered, doffing their heavy coats to settle down at a vacant trestle table. An inviting fire glowed in the huge hearth.

The noisy common room held quite a few patrons, mostly traveling women and children. Jonathan grinned and waved at the proprietor.

"Well, well," the short, slight owner said as he came over. "Jon Bradford, as I live and breathe! What brings you down from the hills?"

"I reckoned you were missing me, Mr. Jeffries," he answered with an almost straight face. "Actually, I heard the folks across the Delaware have been overrun with a plague of lobsters. Thought I'd see what I could do to help out."

Jeffries shoved his wire-framed spectacles a notch higher with his thumb. "Well, you boys won't be lonesome, I'll say that. Militias from down Philadelphia way have come upriver to lend General Washington a hand, too. And just yesterday, Lee's army finally made it as far as here—but without their leader. Seems they lost quite a few of their comrades when their fort across from Manhattan Island was taken. We ferried 'em over to this side of the river. General Sullivan's taken charge of the couple thousand that's left of 'em. And thank the good Lord, General Gates brought another six hundred from Fort Ticonderoga, up north. Took every last boat we could scrounge, and all day, to get those men over from the other side."

"What about General Heath, at Peekskill?" Christopher began to wonder if he and Robert would find themselves going down to Washington's camp with the others after all. "Did he and his men come down the Hudson with Gates?"

"Nay. He was left behind, in case the Brits try to send ships up thataway from New York City."

Christopher whacked the table. "Blast!" He turned to Jonathan. "Well, will it be two of us, or three, crossing the Delaware to rejoin the First Pennsylvania Riflemen?"

"That's Colonel Hand's battalion, isn't it?" Jeffries piped in. "They crossed yesterday, too. Gates brought them down with his men."

Beside Chris at the table, Dan broke out with a smile and looped one arm around Chris's shoulder and the other around Jon's. "What do you know? Looks like we'll all be going downriver together!"

Some of Christopher's fears for his brother-in-law began to lessen. And he had to admit, the thought of being closer to Wilkes-Barre was attractive, too. Maybe he'd be able to get leave now and again to go see Evie. She had, after all, shown more than a little interest in his dream of living on the frontier and breeding horses.

※ ※

Chris stood next to Robert Chandler as he conducted a reloading drill at their camp directly across the Delaware from Trenton. "You've got to be quicker." Chandler glared at the new recruits. "Try again. And this time, do it as if your life depended on it! Soon enough, you'll find out it does."

Christopher leaned his rifle against his leg and rubbed his hands together to generate warmth. The last several days had been growing steadily colder, and the icy wind whipping through the trees held the promise of an imminent storm. Even the mud and brown grass on the frigid ground crunched underfoot as he walked behind the firing line facing the wide river.

"Look yonder," Chandler drawled, pointing toward the hundred or so houses that made up the town of Trenton across the dark water. "See those soldiers marching up the river road? That headgear indicates they're Hessians. German mercenaries. Hardened professionals, whose muskets are fitted with bayonets. They are one very good reason why y'all need to get lightning quick at loading. Before we realized what a deadly force they are, we lost a fair number of men to them last summer on Nassau Island."

A mumble circulated through the ranks.

Christopher grinned. "Don't let that put you off, lads. Colonel Hand's riflemen have gained a reputation of our own. The enemy knows the First Pennsylvania, too."

As Robert launched into a discourse on the proper procedure of firing volleys, Chris's gaze came to rest on Chandler's tricornered hat. A fragment of white paper sticking out of the band fluttered in the cold wind—the temporary designation of Chandler's newly commissioned rank.

Colonel Hand had made a wise choice in this North Carolina man, Christopher decided. Not long ago Robert had shirked even the thought of the responsibilities of being a commissioned officer. Odd, how the love of a good woman could change a man for the better, bring out the best in him. Emily MacKinnon had done so for Chandler, that and more. The previously morose widower laughed often now, and even amid the hardships of war, he was beginning to enjoy life again.

And so am I, Christopher thought as his mind wandered, as always, to Evelyn.

The sound of running footsteps broke into his reverie as an

officer's aide approached. "Lieutenant Chandler, sir. The colonel wants the entire battalion to form up in front of his tent. Now, sir."

"Corporal Drummond," Robert said. "March the men back to camp. And step lively."

Within moments, Chris and the others reached the outskirts of the encampment. Chris saw Dan astride his pacer in front of the large tent bearing the dark green regimental flag with the motto, *Donari Nolo, Nothing will stop me.* Dan had been assigned to courier duty—official word must have come from Washington's headquarters, four miles inland from the river.

He waved to catch Dan's eye as the men jogged into camp and took Dan's returning smile and wave as an encouragement, however dubious. The British were still on the New Jersey side of the river only because Washington had confiscated every boat within seventy miles. But with this cold snap, the water would soon freeze solid. Then the Crown forces could converge and merely walk across . . . all twenty thousand of them.

Chris knew that the Continental army, even with recent reinforcements, numbered only around seven thousand soldiers. Washington's army had retreated across all of New Jersey. Would they have to retreat across the breadth of Pennsylvania, too, leaving the colony—Philadelphia and all—to be plundered by the redcoats? If the beautiful City of Brotherly Love, the richest jewel of the Colonies, fell to the English, it would ring the death knell for the whole rebellion. Such a prospect was too dark to contemplate.

Robert walked away to join the cluster of officers. His promotion from the ranks had put an end to their fraternizing and sharing a tent, as they had done when Chris had first joined up.

Glancing among his men, Chris spotted Jonathan and went to stand beside him while they awaited the news.

Colonel Hand lifted a hand for silence. "Men, General Washington has requested that an article published in the

Pennsylvania Journal be read to the troops. Lend your attention." He nodded toward Dan.

The men quieted while, atop his mount, Dan spread out a broadsheet. "This is an essay entitled 'The American Crisis,' written by Thomas Paine, aide-de-camp to General Greene, published on December nineteenth, four days ago." His voice rang with the distinct modulation of a practiced minister as he looked down at the newsprint and began reading: "These are the times that try men's souls. The summer soldier and the sunshine patriot will, in this crisis, shrink from the service of their country; but he that stands by it *now*, deserves the love and thanks of man and woman.'"

Huzzahs broke forth. When the enthusiasm finally died down, Dan continued: "'Tyranny, like hell, is not easily conquered; yet we have this consolation with us, that the harder the conflict, the more glorious the triumph. What we obtain too cheap, we esteem too lightly. . . . Heaven knows how to put a proper price upon its goods; and it would be strange indeed, if so celestial an article as *Freedom* should not be highly rated.'"

Whistles and cheers rose again, then quieted.

"'. . . that God Almighty will not give up a people to military destruction, or leave them unsupportedly to perish, who have so earnestly and repeatedly sought to avoid the calamities of war by every decent method which wisdom could invent.'"

As Dan read further, praising General Washington's leadership and character, Chris found himself in total agreement with the author's convictions. It was common knowledge that Washington spent much time in secret prayer. Christopher decided that if he had written the essay himself, he'd have added that in God's own goodness and wisdom, he had given the Americans a man *after his own heart*.

Chris's heart swelled with gratitude that he would be here to serve this great cause under the leadership of such an incredible man. The other soldiers, too, were standing a bit taller and straighter, despite their ragged condition. Some had even literally marched through the soles of their shoes.

But it didn't matter, nor did the fact that the British had a seasoned force across the river in New Jersey, one that stretched from one border of New Jersey to the other, nearly three times the size of the Continental force. Let the river freeze over. Let them come. God was with the Americans.

Yet even as convinced as he was that they would prevail, the fleeting memory of Evie suggesting she dress like a man to join him here for the fighting sent an added chill through Christopher. Overhead, the leaden sky was heavy with its burden of snow . . . pristine white snow, destined soon to turn to blood red.

4

Compared to the many happier holidays he had known, Christopher found the abbreviated Christmas service in the bitter cold less than satisfying. Half an hour later, he and Jonathan huddled in their drafty makeshift shelter of canvas and boards, awaiting the full fury of the storm that had been building since the day before. Easing an arm from under the blanket he'd wrapped around himself, he stretched out a hand to capture some warmth from the glowing coals in the brazier, where a small kettle of water for coffee was taking forever to boil. He was too miserable to make conversation, and his brother-in-law seemed equally untalkative.

The flap covering the entrance whipped open, admitting a frigid blast of air.

"Ho ho, lads," Morgan quipped with a wink as he and Robert Chandler entered.

"Thought y'all could use some good cheer," Robert drawled. The two of them stood there grinning, as if harboring a delightful secret.

"I've seen better Christmases, if you must know," Jon groused, hardly glancing up. "Feel free to bask before our grand hearth here."

Morgan chuckled. "Now, is that any way for you to greet good old Saint Nick? After all, we've come bearing gifts—or a gift, to be more precise. Dried apricots from Portugal."

"Let's see." Christopher smirked and snatched the sack

from Morgan. He took out a piece and bit into the tangy treat. Then, grinning his thanks, he passed the sack to Jon. "Coffee will be ready soon. You two are welcome to join us."

Chandler checked his pocket watch. "I suppose I can spare a few minutes." He clicked the elaborate watchcase shut, then returned it to his fob pocket and sat down on the square of canvas spread over the frozen ground. Morgan took the remaining spot, folding his long legs Indian fashion. Both men remained bundled in their heavy woolen greatcoats and tricorns.

"Where's Dan?" Jonathan asked, rubbing his hands together and blowing into them.

"Taking a message down to the Congress in Baltimore," Morgan replied. "All you two have to do is say the word—I could easily get you transferred to me. Mary Clare would certainly appreciate that, Jon. You'd be well behind the lines, instead of at the forefront. Hand's battalion has an uncanny knack of being wherever a fight breaks out, you know."

"Hm." Jonathan raked his calloused fingers through the unruly waves of his brown hair. "That's mighty tempting, but being a frontiersman turned me into a fairly decent shot. I reckon this is where I'd be the most help."

Christopher saw a disappointed grimace cloud Morgan's strong features. A buddy of Jonathan's from their Princeton days, Morgan was as concerned for the farmer as Chris was. He nodded to Robert. "Well, looks like he's all yours, then."

"We'll do our best to see that he returns to Mary unscathed, won't we Chip?" Robert said confidently.

Chris nodded.

"Which reminds me," Morgan cut in, branding Christopher with a stern stare. "I do believe I noticed some very— shall we say, affectionate—glances pass between you and my little sister when we were all together up north."

A warm rush rose from inside the thick collar of Chris's greatcoat, but then Morgan's expression softened.

"I think I owe you my gratitude," he added kindly. "From what I hear, you're the reason she's reverted to her old sweet self rather than the brittle miss she'd become while we were in New York. Outrageous flirting, traipsing around with Tories and redcoats in order to wheedle information out of them—" He shook his head.

"Y-you mean, you don't mind if I keep in touch with Evie?" Chris asked, astonished. "You won't oppose my writing to her?"

Morgan gave a good-natured shrug. "But I daresay, *if* the two of you become serious in your intentions, you'll have the matter of a very formidable adversary to contend with once this war is over. Our mother!"

A cautious smile broke free even as Chris did his best to smother it. "I'm just glad Evie's someplace safe." *From the redcoats and from her mother's influence,* his mind added.

Morgan nodded thoughtfully, and his gaze drifted elsewhere. "My wife, my Prudence . . . raised as a Puritan, she'll do just fine in a simple home and natural setting, having a spartan Christmas. But Evie!" He rolled his dark blue eyes. "She's accustomed to attending the rounds of parties, receiving elaborate gifts—lots of them. I rather think she'll find this holiday a disappointment."

"I wouldn't be so sure about that," Robert countered. "After spending time with your sister while we herded the horses up to Wyoming Valley, I'd say she's got a lot more grit than you give her credit for."

"That remains to be seen," Morgan replied.

A sad smile quivered on Jonathan's mouth. "This is the first Christmas Mary Clare and I have spent apart. We're about all either of us has, you know. My family has never really accepted her, and we moved far away from the Lyonses. With Chris so busy with classes, he seldom came to visit, so we've done what we could to make each holiday season as meaningful as possible for each other. I . . . miss her more than I thought possible." As if embarrassed by his confession, he swept a quick nervous glance around. "But say, we did all have a great get-together just before we left, didn't we?"

"Sure did." Chris draped an arm over his brother-in-law's

shoulder. It pleased him to hear his sister spoken of so tenderly. She had suffered such abuse after their mother had passed on and their father sought solace in rum. If the Lyonses hadn't taken the two of them in and showered them with love, he'd probably still be stuttering every time he opened his mouth, and Mary would still be bolting and running at the sight of any unfamiliar face. She retained a measure of shyness around strangers to this day, but Jonathan's love provided her with confidence she might never have known otherwise.

"And I pray Emily doesn't change her mind about marrying me before I return," Robert mused aloud. "That she will still allow me to court her when this whole mess is over."

No one responded to Robert's plea. Christopher wished fervently that he and Evelyn had made some kind of commitment to each other.

The tent had grown gradually warmer since Morgan and Robert had come. Jon shifted his position, loosening the blanket enshrouding him. "Let's pray for a swift return home. I try to convince myself there's no reason to worry. We've had very little trouble with the Indians since we've lived in the valley. But I keep getting this niggling feeling. A few months ago, a bunch of them came downriver from their settlement in Oghwaga to tell us they want to dwell in peace, that they won't take sides between us and the English."

He frowned and went on. "Just seems strange that a people with whom we were already at peace would send a delegation to state that fact all over again. Could be I'm just borrowing trouble, but I'd sure appreciate it if you lads would remember those concerns whenever you pray for the women we left behind. So many men will be gone from the valley, come the first of January."

"Personally," Christopher remarked, "I think the women and children are much safer there. The blasted Hessians haven't confiscated their homes and livestock yet, like those New Jersey families we passed on the road. Not to mention others in New York and Newport."

Robert grimaced. "I agree with Chip. It's likely the British will try to push their way down from Canada again next spring, encircling all of New England. Then there won't be a safe place for our women anywhere in the north."

Jonathan looked from one face to the next and gave a reluctant shrug. "I suppose we should stop fretting about next summer and just be grateful General Washington felt it would be unneighborly to exchange cannon fire with those Hessians on Christmas day. Maybe we'll get a good night's sleep tonight, at least."

Christopher, however, found himself infected by Jon's concern. He began to feel more uneasy than ever. "Who of us knows for sure where those king's puppets will strike next summer—if not before? We must keep in close contact with the women. You'll be dealing with a lot of civilians, Morgan. Can you find somebody willing to ride up to the valley at least once a month, to keep us informed of their welfare?"

"I, for one, would rest easier if you could arrange that," Jonathan added.

Morgan exchanged a meaningful look with Robert and shook his head. "Might as well forget about rest tonight. A plan of attack on Trenton has already begun."

"What?" Chris shot a glance at Jon.

"Washington," Morgan explained, "has already sent Colonel Cadwalader with his Pennsylvania militias to cross the Delaware at Bristol, then march on the two enemy garrisons below Trenton—Bordentown and Mount Holly. Afterward they'll return to cover our flank, if need be."

"We're attacking in this storm?" Christopher asked incredulously. "On Christmas?" He shook his head and picked up the coffeepot.

Robert accepted a mug of coffee and blew on it, parting the column of steam wafting upward. "The Hessians would never expect us to take action today of all days—which is most likely what the general is counting on."

"I've had my men hauling caissons of gunpowder and cannonballs up to McKonkey's Ferry since daybreak," Morgan informed them. "The Marbleheaders from Massachusetts are going to take us all across to the other side as soon as it's dark."

"Artillery, too?" Jon asked with alarm. "Have you taken a good look at that river lately? Aside from the rising blizzard, the Delaware is strewn with huge chunks of ice!"

Morgan met his gaze. "Washington is determined to win this one. He feels the men need a victory now more than ever before. A good three-quarters of the enlistments are up on the first of the month. If we don't strike a hard blow now, we may not have another chance. General Ewing's militia is going downriver just below Trenton. They're to cross right before dawn and take the bridge over Assunpink Creek, severing that avenue of attack. Then, with water blocking a Hessian retreat on two sides, and our lads closing in on the other two, the added element of surprise should provide us an easy victory."

"I'll drink to that." Robert raised his cup.

"Hear! Hear!" Christopher piped in. "Attack now. Much better than waiting and wondering when they'll come for us once the river ices over. At these temperatures, I doubt it'll take much longer to freeze."

Jonathan looked to Morgan again, his expression conveying his dismay. "We passed McKonkey's Ferry on the way down from Easton. A good nine or ten miles upriver, isn't it?"

"That's right." Robert handed back his mug, then checked his watch again and stood to his feet. "Have another apricot. There'll be no big Christmas feast today. We're to move out at noon."

5

One frail ray from the sun peeked through a narrow crack in the heavily clouded sky, briefly catching Jonathan's eye before slipping from view behind the forested hills. The numbing temperature plummeted even further.

Hunkering into his greatcoat, Jon ducked his chin into his scarf and inched nearer to Christopher as they and the rest of the Continental army crammed together near the McKonkey Ferry house. The structure offered scant protection from the bitter cold wind. With blankets wrapped around their outerwear, the men tried hopelessly to use one another as shields from the icy blasts.

Shivering, Jonathan nudged his brother-in-law with an elbow. "If it gets much colder, we'll be stiff and brittle as cheap tin soldiers, ready to topple in the next gust. Then somebody can come along next spring and just rake the whole army up like old cornstalks."

The lad emitted a mirthless chuckle through blue lips. "I'm beginning to think being a 'summer soldier' isn't such a bad idea. Just thinking of spending the long, cold months inside a warm cabin, cuddling with Evie before a crackling fire . . ." He let out a sigh. The reference to home fires did nothing for Jon's sagging spirits. He seriously doubted that Chris could find happiness with a girl who had been catered to and waited on by servants all her life. She was nothing like his Mary Clare, who even as a timid young serving lass at the Lyons' Den had been a diligent worker.

A mental picture of his sweet wife eradicated for a few blessed moments the bone-chilling shivers and chatters. He missed the sight of her perfect face with its fine features and eyes of summer blue, a smile that still sent his heart racing. He missed the silkiness of her golden hair. If he imagined hard enough, he could still feel it trailing through his fingers as they lay together at night. How could he have left Mary Clare's comforting presence for this? Hearing nothing but men's voices—muttering and griping, or worse, coughing and hacking—when he could instead be basking in the delicate tones of her airy laughter and singing.

And the little ones, Esther and Beth, barely a year apart in age and each a miniature of Mary, mimicking the fastidious way their mama had of keeping the house tidy. Thoughts of his precious wife and daughters flooded Jon with homesickness. He'd give six months' army pay to be back in Wilkes-Barre right now, with his family.

Beside him, Christopher shivered, his teeth chattering.

Jon exhaled a ragged breath as the winter cold seeped into every gap in his clothes, penetrating even his bones. He stomped his feet on the hard snowpacked ground to keep the circulation moving. His cheeks burned from the four-hour march upriver, and tromping through the ice-scabbed mud had taken a toll on his good boots. But one glance around at poorly clad fellows far worse off than he sent a stab of guilt through him. Some had shoes so worn that the soles flapped with every step. A few had nothing but rags rapped around their bloodied feet. At least his own boots were still sound.

Nearby a man coughed. "This ain't nothin' but balderdash," he griped hoarsely. "Hurry up an' wait. Hurry up an' wait."

Jon gave a commiserating nod. "I know, but Lieutenant Chandler said we can't cross until all the boats, men, and artillery have been assembled. Washington wants his force at full strength when we surprise them at Trenton."

"Full strength?" the man rasped. "It's all I can do to put one foot in front of t'other."

"Only half the artillery's made it here so far," another mumbled.

Christopher rolled his eyes and snorted, bouncing a fat snowflake into swirls as it and a multitude of others whipped about crazily in the gale-force wind. "The river was already starting to crust along the shoreline last time I checked."

"Nay," a burly man from another regiment piped in. "It's too turbulent to freeze very solid."

Jonathan caught looks of similar concern passing among the others. "They say if anybody can get us across in this storm it's Glover's Marbleheaders, from Massachusetts," he stated with more confidence than he felt. "I hear those amphibians face this kind of weather up north every day."

But the men around him only grunted and scrunched deeper into their blankets.

When the last of the force finally arrived and the tedious process of ferrying began, Christopher and Jonathan stood with their battalion awaiting their turn while General Washington boarded the craft at the head. Chris assessed the freshwater Durhams that would transport everyone to the other side. Sixty feet long and eight feet wide, pointed fore and aft, each of the shallow-draft barges could hold about two hundred men. When the first boats finished loading, the amphibians shoved off, poling and rowing and disappearing almost immediately into the snowy night.

Many anxious moments later, the sight of the Durhams returning with only their crews filled Chris with relief. The first bunch had made it. He, Jon, and their company, along with Colonel Hand, would be part of the second wave.

"Step lively, gents," a seaman ordered in his Massachusetts twang, waving the soldiers aboard. "Find a spot an' get down."

"Down?" Chris echoed, taking stock of the sloshing water

aboard. But with a resigned shrug, he dropped to a crouch with the rest, doing his best to keep his rifle and gear dry.

The loaded boat moved out quickly on the precarious three-hundred-yard journey across roaring, swift current. Large chunks of ice bumped and crunched against the sides, sending a chilling spray over the vessel as it inched across the treacherous Delaware.

Christopher felt his eyebrows starting to freeze in the wind-buffeted snow and sleet. He pulled his tricorn lower and clutched the soggy blanket, growing stiff with ice, around him and his rifle.

"Ice!" a Marbleheader yelled. "Aft!" He pointed off the upstream side.

Another crewman ran from the stern with his pole, but the slab slammed into the craft before he could fend it off. At the shuddering impact, many cried out in alarm and a few uttered choice oaths.

Jonathan leaned close, his face uncharacteristically serious. "May the Lord be with us."

"Amen to that." Chris relaxed a little. "I'm glad we only have to do this once," he added, struggling to talk around the chattering of his teeth. "If we were Marbleheaders, we'd face a whole night of this." He sent a quick prayer aloft for the brave Massachusetts sailors.

At last the boat bumped against the landing dock. The crew scrambled to jump off and secure the ropes.

"Stand up, men," Robert Chandler's voice called out from a circle of torchlight on the shore. "Unload quickly."

The half-frozen soldiers needed no prodding.

Seconds later the empty craft shoved off from the landing, and Chris stood swiping at his wet breeches as he watched it go.

"Isn't that General Washington?" Jon jutted his chin toward a tall man several yards away who had been supervising the procedure.

Even as Christopher nodded, the commander turned in a swirl of his great long cape and strode toward Colonel Hand.

The flickering glow of torches illuminated the set of the general's jaw and revealed his piercing eyes.

Chris stared with admiration at the forceful leader who had made the impossible a reality. By sheer determination, the commander would see his entire army amassed on the New Jersey side of the river, blizzard or no. Then he himself would lead the nine-mile march to Trenton, the town that commanded the upper reaches of the Delaware at the falls. Small wonder the ragtag men fighting so valiantly for freedom would follow him willingly, this great man whose very being exuded the steely confidence that had made him a hero during the French and Indian War.

Colonel Hand's back, also ramrod straight, was turned to Chris now. The colonel had the same effect on the men under his command as Washington had on the army as a whole. What a great privilege, Christopher thought, for him and his friends to serve under two such able leaders.

"Colonel," he heard Washington say, "move your riflemen down the river road about half a mile. Detain any traffic. It's imperative that the Hessians have no prior warning. On the odd chance they've been alerted and are marching here to intercept us, do your utmost to delay them. Remember the password, 'Victory or Death.' So it shall be this night for our brave army."

Hand gave a stiff salute.

Jonathan moved closer. "Glad we'll be getting away from this open water," he said quietly. "Now maybe we can find some shelter in the trees and wait out the rest of the storm."

"A traveler's inn would be more to my liking." Chris chuckled. "Yessir, those 'summer soldiers' Thomas Paine wrote about may be nothing but a bunch of cowards, but they're *warm* and *dry* cowards."

During the four or five torturous hours of guarding the road, Christopher thought the droll comment "Hurry up and wait" seemed much more fitting a password than "Victory or

Death." The storm had not relented in the slightest, and the winter-bare trees lining the way gave no shelter from the wind and sleet. Torches were not permitted for this advance party, yet their vigil had been fruitless—not a soul had ventured up the road that fearful night. The men were tired, wretched, and cold.

The following morning was no better. Moving on in the wee hours of morning ahead of horse-drawn wagons of artillery, Chris didn't know how much more of the miserable cold the men could endure.

"Halt!" came the shout down the line, and the long column stopped for the first time in two hours.

Peering through the sleet, Christopher could make out the front of a roadside inn. Just the thought of its great roaring fire, of being warm and dry again, made him want to break ranks and run for its shelter. But his commanding officers clustered near the front, their torches reflecting against the stone exterior.

Jonathan, stomping his feet, inched closer to Chris as Robert Chandler returned to the troops.

"Break out your rations, men," the lieutenant said quietly. "There'll be no time to eat later on."

So much for a dawn attack, Chris thought, eyeing the lightening sky to the east. Every stage of the march had taken far too long, and judging by the looks of the men, many would fall by the wayside before ever reaching the town, still four miles away. He could feel his own strength flagging. Hoping to renew both his energy and his sagging spirit, he munched on a hard biscuit.

"On your feet, men," Robert ordered a few moments later. "Eight abreast. There's a fork ahead. General Green's division and ours will veer to the left on the Pennington Road with General Washington's men. Sullivan's division will continue on the river road. From now on we maintain strict silence." He swung abruptly to a soldier.

Christopher wondered about his gear. Surely the cork plugging his powderhorn must be soaked and soft by now. He unhooked the swinging powderhorn from his haversack and tucked it inside his heavy shirt. Around him, others did the same.

The chances of Washington's desperately needed victory were diminishing fast. Frozen and exhausted men, wet equipment, dawn already on the horizon with Trenton still miles away . . . and icy sleet falling with blinding fierceness from the sky. A Hessian picket was certain to spot them coming and send a warning into a town full of dry weapons and powder.

Seemingly undaunted, however, the general rode his chestnut mount up and down the long line as daylight continued to gain strength. Tall, straight, and confident in his resolve to take Trenton, he presented an example of encouragement to his bedraggled army.

But over the next hour, the road grew increasingly slick with the icy rainfall. A difficult march was gradually becoming impossible.

Suddenly a shout rang out. Beyond the depleted regiment in front of Christopher's battalion, a blue-uniformed man in tall brass headgear ran for a house, waving his arms wildly. Several other Hessians burst out the door, two of them with raised muskets.

"Duck!" Chris yelled. He grabbed Jon's sleeve and pulled him down to a crouch. Shots whizzed overhead.

"Rush them!" General Stephens ordered from the front of the ranks.

As one, the leading regiment charged off the road after the Germans who'd emptied their weapons and needed to reload.

The mercenaries fled toward the town, shouting at the top of their lungs, while a dozen more Hessians in uniforms of both blue and green poured out of the house and tried to form a firing line. A few managed to get off a shot. Most ran, and those standing firm soon followed. One pair who hesitated too long were taken prisoner.

General Stephens rode to the forefront. "Halt, men. Reform! Reform!"

Then in the distance, Chris heard the sound of drums and bugles.

There would be no surprise attack this day.

6

Suddenly the ground beneath Christopher's feet shuddered. *A cannon!* He swung toward the direction of the sound, the river, just as another blast went off. Then another. It was impossible to tell which side had fired the huge guns.

Through the freezing rain Chris could see more Hessians fleeing from a nearby outpost. He let out a whoop and charged.

Jonathan and the others also cried out and followed him.

"Halt!" Robert Chandler commanded. "Company, halt!"

Christopher stopped in his tracks. "But, Lieutenant! The Hessians!"

"We're not infantry," he said flatly. "We're riflemen."

Even as Chandler spoke, another regiment thundered past, bayonets poised as they chased fleeing green-coated Hessian *jagers* toward Trenton.

"Our orders are to go up yonder and guard the road to Princeton," Robert said, eyeing his company. "To keep the Hessians bottled up and prevent any reinforcements that might come from their Princeton garrison."

Drummers struck up a swift marching cadence. Everyone in Greene's division scrambled into line and jogged in the sleet through the uneven, crusty snow. Even if the cannons were American, Sullivan would soon need assistance to close off the enemy's escape.

From the direction of Sullivan's force, a rider galloped out of the mist and headed straight for General Washington, who was riding alongside the column near the head.

The drummers ceased at once, and the soldiers came to a stop. Mounted officers rode to the front.

"Now we'll find out who's cannonading," Chris remarked.

Jonathan hiked a brow. "Yesterday Morgan told me that the Hessian commander views our army with such disdain that he hasn't fortified the town's perimeter at all. The fool is so confident he's even placed two of his cannons in front of his headquarters as mere decorations."

Christopher felt a slow grin break forth. "You know, there might be some truth to that. I haven't seen even one trench berm on their side, nor a single redoubt."

"Redoubt?" Jon frowned.

"Dugouts," Chris explained. "A sort of earthen fort with sides built up of excess dirt."

The leaders up front dispersed, and the rider sped away.

An officer galloped down the line. "The cannon fire is ours. Ours alone! Praise the Lord!"

Cheers resounded all the way to the farthest reaches of the column. Drums resumed amid the joyful shouting, and the men began quick-marching forward again with renewed vigor.

We will take the day! Christopher realized. *God is with us. We will take the day!*

Chris and Jon crouched behind a stone wall bordering the snowy road to Princeton, their breath vaporizing in the bone-chilling cold. The rest of the battalion was scattered throughout the fields and lightly wooded areas on either side of the roadway, keeping watch for enemy movement of any kind. Since the storm had begun to abate, it was now possible to see flashes and smoke from General Green's cannons at the crossroads, as well as to hear the *boom*s and feel the vibrations.

Christopher glanced at the indistinct figures of the artillerymen moving behind the line of cannon carriages and caissons. Among the mounted officers directing the firing, Washington's powerful presence on his long-legged chestnut horse stood out clearly.

The slope of the terrain hid all but the roofs of the buildings beyond the artillery position, but Christopher could tell that the cannon fire and grapeshot were aimed down the lengths of Trenton's two main streets. Reports from hundreds of muskets gave evidence that most of Greene's regiments had swarmed into town to join Sullivan's division on the far end of the village.

"I didn't expect being in the army would be like this," Jon commented dryly.

Chris dragged his gaze from the scene and observed Jonathan's weary face.

"I've had to endure cold before," his brother-in-law continued. "Danger, too, when I had to conceal myself from an Indian hunting party. I've held my breath watching them as they read my footprints. And I've tasted the fear of being discovered while hiding out in winter snow for hours on end."

"Well, then, you should be used to these conditions by now," Christopher chided.

Jon grimaced. "That's not it. What bothers me most about this is having somebody else make all my decisions for me. Telling me when to move or wait. Where to go. When to sit still. I hate this endless standing around, doing nothing."

"This hurry up and wait, huh?" Chris quipped with a chuckle.

"We joined up to fight for the cause, didn't we?" Jon said, still exasperated. "But look at us! There's fighting going on not half a mile away, and we aren't in it."

"Don't worry, we'll get our turn. We always do."

"You think we'll actually take them?" Jon asked.

"Of course. We now have them trapped on three sides. And if they try to go downriver, they'll run smack into General Ewing's men, who crossed just below Trenton. Cadwalader's regiments should be coming upriver to join us anytime now, too. The garrisons at Bordentown and Mount Holly are much smaller than Trenton's. Those probably surrendered without a fight. For once we have the upper hand—*if* the Hessians don't get any outside help from up this road. And we're here to see that they don't."

A rider galloped across the field from town. From his position, Christopher couldn't tell if it was an American or a Hessian dispatched to the Princeton garrison twelve miles up the road. He took aim.

Jonathan did the same.

"Wait," Chris whispered. "Until we're sure if he's friend or foe." Seconds later, he relaxed. "It's one of ours."

The horseman swerved toward them.

Christopher turned and recognized Colonel Hand's battalion flag being waved to the rider. He could see his commander peering through his spyglass. Robert and the other officers also ran toward the colonel from scattered positions.

"Perhaps this is it," Jonathan said eagerly. "Robert's sure to come back with new orders." He pulled out the tail of his woolen undershirt and wiped the flash pan of his rifle, then blew on it.

Chandler left the huddle and came running back through the snow as the messenger galloped past him on the return to town.

Chris and the others rushed to intercept Robert.

"Neither of our downriver forces thought the river was safe enough to cross," Robert panted, out of breath. "The left flank isn't covered. Our battalion and Haussenger's regiment have been ordered to defend the area between here and Assunpink Creek to the east. We're to take up a position behind the big orchard just outside of town. Grab your gear. Form up."

The battalion quickly crossed the farmland to the southeast, toward the backside of a large, leafless orchard that fronted the east side of Trenton. Nearing it, Christopher spied what appeared to be a regiment of green-clad Hessians, retreating past houses and into the trees. The *jagers* would have a partially shielded escape if they managed to beat the riflemen to the other side.

"Break ranks!" Colonel Hand yelled. "Run! Cut off the devils' escape!"

Jonathan exchanged a look with Chris. "God be with you," he said, then took off running.

"You stay with me, Jon!" Chris shouted, chasing after him. "Do what I do."

"Yessir, little brother," Jon retorted on the fly.

The cannons had ceased. Only the sound of musket fire now cut the stillness, particularly down near where the Assunpink Creek forked into the Delaware. Chris figured there were other Hessians trying to shoot their way across the stone bridge as they fled from the Americans. The American army had been on the retreat for the last three months; this time it was the enemy trying to quit the scene.

The backside of the orchard came into view.

Colonel Hand wheeled his horse and fired his pistol. "Halt! Form a firing line from here to the creek," the colonel bellowed, indicating the spot with the tip of his sword.

Now that the sleet had finally stopped altogether and the cannon smoke had dissipated, Chris had a clear view down two sides of the orchard. The trees were now within range of their long rifles but not within reach of Hessian musket fire . . . a deadly situation for the enemy. The riflemen would be able to pick off anyone emerging from the orchard.

Robert Chandler signaled for his company to follow him toward the creek, keeping a safe distance between his men and the orchard.

Christopher checked to make sure Jonathan was keeping up, then kept an eye peeled for any lurking enemy within the rows of trees.

They were halfway to the creek when rifle fire sounded from not far behind them. Slowing enough to glance back, Chris saw his comrades shooting at Hessians who were now retreating back into the leafless orchard, dodging from the cover of one tree trunk to another.

"Drop off and load," Chandler commanded, "one man every two yards."

Christopher quickly found his spot.

Jonathan, who had stopped a little before him, already had his rifle aimed into the trees. He remained tense, poised to shoot.

"Relax, Jon, we're out of range of their guns. Take careful aim before firing. Let the *jagers* know what they're dealing with."

Robert directed a look of concern toward Jonathan, then met Christopher's eye with a nod, as if entrusting Jon's well-being to him. Suddenly it came to Chris that he'd have done better to sign on with Morgan when he'd had the chance. If there was any hope of wedding Evie, it was her brother's respect he needed, not Robert's. But it was hard to give up being one of Hand's Men, as others were starting to call them.

"Listen!" Jonathan hissed.

Chris strained to hear. "What?"

"That's what I mean. It's too quiet."

The puzzling silence after so much noise and smoke and confusion was more than a little disconcerting. Trees blocked all view of the creek bridge, the town, and the Delaware River.

On the other side of the orchard a cheer began. It grew louder, then was picked up by men at the bridge. Chris looked back to where Washington and the now-silent Greene-division cannons were located. The generals and several mounted officers left the artillery and their tenders behind and rode into town.

It's over so soon? Impossible. Christopher told himself. *Trenton had a garrison of six full regiments of Hessian mercenaries and* jagers. *Professionals, every one.*

At the far end of the line, Colonel Hand also charged his steed toward Trenton. Scarcely had he disappeared from view before he returned at a full gallop, with a huge grin—one of the few Chris had ever seen on the Irishman's sensible face. "They've surrendered!" he hollered. "The devils have surrendered!"

The riflemen lofted weapons above their heads and let out a deafening cheer of their own.

Jonathan stepped in front of Christopher, his eyes narrowed. "That's it? We all but wash overboard into a swirling, horrific river, march day and night through a killing blizzard—for this? I haven't fired a single round."

Chris laughed and grabbed him in a bear hug. "Yes. Isn't it grand? We won. We won!"

Dozens of others joined in, turning it into one great hug, thumping and pounding one another's backs.

"Praise the Lord!" someone cried. "No king but King Jesus!"

The rallying cry echoed far and near.

It had been one very good day.

7

Evelyn positioned the chisel against the layer of ice that had formed in the horse trough and gave a sharp whack with the hammer. A large chunk sank into the brackish water, then bobbed to the surface. Some yards away, a few of the strawberry roans hovered, their velvet brown eyes glued thirstily to the trough while she repeated the procedure.

With this blow a shard flew upward, grazing Evie's chapped cheeks. She ground her teeth in frustration. *No less than I deserve,* she thought grimly as she stood in the muddy, hoof-mushed snow. *I was the one who came up with the feather-brained idea to learn as much as I could about the care and feeding of these stupid pacers.* But, she reminded herself, it was all for a very good reason—Christopher Drummond. Handsome and ambitious Christopher Drummond, who someday would be a renowned engineer whose new breed of coach horses would traverse the whole country over roads and bridges he had designed.

Remembering the way his smiling eyes had shone when he'd entrusted her with his secret dreams, Evie's heart filled to bursting. With renewed vigor she continued the task, stealing herself against the bitter cold. This winter felt twice as harsh as any she'd known in Philadelphia.

If only I had finished my chores earlier, she chided herself, *I could have gone with Emily and Mary Clare to the mercantile.* A while ago Mary had stopped by for someone to accompany her. She was leery of going all the way to Wilkes-Barre by herself now that so many able-bodied men from the valley had gone off to the war. *Oh, well. I'll be lucky to finish this before they get back!* She jabbed at the ice again.

Not far away, a barn owl hooted.

In broad daylight? Evie started. She'd heard tales that Indians often used birdcalls to signal to one another. The fine hairs on her arms and the back of her neck prickled in alarm, and a chill ran up her spine. She moved between two of the horses and searched in the direction of the noise. If only she'd brought a rifle outside. Susannah, in a house closed tightly against the weather, would not hear her if she cried out.

She watched. But no movement of any kind stirred the darkness beneath the distant line of snow-covered evergreens.

Suddenly a large bird flapped its wings and took flight.

Evie exhaled in relief. It really was just an owl. Silly of her to think otherwise. But she couldn't deny the uneasy feeling that refused to abate. No wonder the men of the valley had been so reluctant to leave and go serve with General Washington. It hadn't been a lack of patriotism, as she had originally suspected. They must have known their families would be truly vulnerable in a place where only a scattering of old or infirm men remained to look after the welfare of the women and families left behind.

The few days that had passed since Christmas seemed to Evie like a month. She sighed. If only Christopher could have stayed here.

Stepping back to the trough, she chipped away another slab of ice and peered westward toward the frozen Susquehanna River. There was precious little civilization on the other bank, and beyond that, nothing but endless wilderness fraught with mystery and danger—danger that could rage forth on the spur of a moment, in the form of murdering, farm-burning Indians. The very thought added to her disquiet, particularly since she could not shake the notion that unseen eyes were watching her every move.

Suddenly conscious of the racket she was making, Evelyn swallowed nervously and resumed working with gentler strokes.

From the corner of her eye she caught a flash of color and turned. A great wave of relief washed over her at the welcome sight of Emily and Mary Clare returning, still a quarter mile down the road. What a goose she was being, to allow her imagination to get the better of her.

But Evelyn knew she'd better finish before Emily saw her. Without regard for the icy splashing water, she quickly dislodged the last chunk and flung it out of the trough. Bending low, she dashed to the next container. Sounds carried easily across the snowy landscape on such a still day, so Evie swiftly dispatched the frozen layer on the last trough, stuffed the chisel into her coat pocket, and then hastened to the cross-rail fence and began pounding on one of the rails, pretending to wedge it back into place. Hopefully the women would think that's what the banging was about.

As the two neared, their rifles conspicuous in sheaths alongside their saddles, Evelyn waved. She administered one last blow to the rail, then hurried past the horses toward the gate. Her excitement mounted. Perhaps there'd be a letter from Christopher! She'd already asked Emily to post a second missive to him this morning. The first had been written hastily on a scrap of old paper and sent along with one of the departing militiamen she'd met at a Christmas gathering.

Writing parchment was hard to come by here, much more scarce than back home in Philadelphia. She almost had to beg Susannah for a second sheet. Even writing on both sides with tiny script barely allowed her to say all that was in her heart.

A lack of paper was only one thing about living on the frontier that had caught Evelyn by surprise. The unfamiliar physical labor was hard on her, but she wanted Chris to know she cared about him enough to become the wife of a horse breeder—even if he planned to stay in this area.

She never, of course, intended to become as unstylish and homespun as Mary Clare, Evie thought as she went out the gate and relatched it. Or like most of the other women she'd encountered at Christmas services held in a rude barn . . . just one more proof of how primitive this settlement was. Why, the townspeople had yet to construct even the simplest church building—rather odd, she thought, considering their never-ending Almighty-praising talk. Still, she could overlook just about anything—for Christopher. *Oh, please, let there be a letter from him!*

"Wait!" she called, seeing the two fair-haired women dismounting in front of the house. "Wait for me."

Emily, unhooking a tote from the saddle, shot an amused smile to Mary Clare. But Mary wore the expression of a suffering Madonna. Such a pity that there was no artist here to capture the benign sorrow residing on Mary's face since Jonathan's departure.

"Were there any letters from the men?" Evie asked, striding over to them.

Emily ruffled gloved fingers through her bangs and laughed. "I hardly think that even the most stalwart Cape Cod postrider would have braved the storm we've had the past few days."

A patient smile softly curved the Madonna's lips. "It's too glorious a day to think about anything but the blue, blue sky, the sun turning everything to sparkles," she said in her whispery voice. "The ride home from the village was lovely, wasn't it, Emily?"

It was difficult for Evelyn to think of the slight, timid young woman as Christopher's older sister. But the resemblance between Mary and Chris was so close that Evie often found herself staring and had to remind herself to look away. Mary shared the same china blue eyes, with blonde hair a shade lighter than his, worn in a single braid down her back. Her feminine features were finer than her brother's, yet there was still much that mirrored him, from the way she held her head to the guileless smile that curved her lips up at the corners.

One thing she woefully lacked, however, was her brother's ability to hold a person's complete attention with a mere glance. Mary rarely looked anyone in the eye, or so it seemed to Evelyn.

Evie reined in her thoughts. "The ride must have been quiet for you," she said brightly. "Not a single child along."

As if on cue, the front door banged open. "Mama!" Copper-haired Rusty charged out and flung his arms around Emily's legs.

"You'd think I'd been gone all day," his mother said with an airy laugh. She swung her son up into an embrace. "You know better than to run outside without your coat, sweetheart. Where's your sister?"

He pointed toward the loft. "Playin' house. I don' wanna be baby. I be so'dier."

With an understanding nod, she settled the tot on her hip and led the way inside.

Evie, lagging behind, stripped off her outer garments and hung them alongside the rest, then smoothed the butternut dress Susannah had loaned her. Although not quite the quality she was accustomed to, it fit surprisingly well and was reasonably fashionable. At least it was a change from Evie's only dress—the one on her back when she arrived.

The roaring kitchen fire at the end of the big room beckoned to her. Susannah turned from the fireplace, kettle in hand. "My, haven't we all got rosy cheeks," she said, her wide blue gray eyes moving from one face to the next. "I thought you all might find a spot of tea rather tempting about now."

"Oh, my, yes," Mary Clare said softly. "And with your best dishes, too, I see."

Evie followed Mary's gaze toward the table. It was set with a crisp linen cloth and delicate King's Rose china. Raisin and cinnamon scones were arranged artfully on a lace-covered platter. Somehow, even in this wilderness, Susannah always managed to add a touch of grace to everything she did. And she always looked attractive, too—today especially so, in a gown whose dusty blue brought out her eyes.

"I hungry," Rusty announced.

"Me, too," his older sister, Katie, called, her dark head peering over the edge of the loft along with Susannah's two youngsters.

"Stay where you are, honey," Emily said. "We'll send some up to you." She set her son down, then gathered four scones into a napkin and tied the corners. When Rusty had climbed most of the way up, she handed him the bundle. "Be Mama's good helper and take these up."

Susannah measured tea leaves into the pot and hung the kettle back on its hook over the fire. After wiping her hands on the long apron covering her dress, she returned to the table. "Do sit down, everyone. Tell me, how do the townsfolk fare?"

The look that passed between Emily and Mary Clare troubled Evie.

"It was a lovely day for a ride," Mary hedged airily, in that strange tone she'd used earlier. "Don't you think?"

Emily arched an eyebrow. "True, but I hardly think anyone at the settlement took much notice of it this morning."

"Why ever is that?" Susannah asked, bending to check the tea before taking her seat.

Mary sprang up, her face ashen. "The refreshments look lovely, really. But I—um—need to get back home." She bolted for the door. "Prudence has been looking after my girls long enough, especially now that her morning sickness has been getting worse by the day. It's not right for me to add to her burden."

Susannah followed, staying her friend's hand before she snatched the coarse woolen cloak from the peg. "Mary Clare, I'm sure Prudence wouldn't mind your taking a few extra moments to warm up after the ride into town."

"I must go," Mary answered with surprising determination. She took down her cloak. "Perhaps if the weather holds, you could bring your little ones over to play soon." Without meeting anyone's gaze, she flung the wrap about her shoulders and fled.

"Well, do take care, love," Susannah called after her as she closed the door. "How very curious." She poured tea into the china cups and returned the kettle to the fire, then settled herself at the table. "Most peculiar indeed."

Emily took a sip of her tea. "She was fine on the way into town, talking about what a help Prudence has been to her despite the nausea, how she's insisted on doing half the work—even Jonathan's outside tasks."

"But—" Susannah's slender brows dipped in concern. "Mary just said Prudence—"

"A little nausea would never keep that Puritan from *doing her duty,*" Evie cut in. "The girl is absolutely obsessed about doing chores and her duty and that sort of thing."

"Speaking of chores, Evie," Emily said, "how's the herd? Did you pitch out plenty of hay for them?"

Evelyn lifted her chin. "Of course. I said I would, didn't I?" *Even if it wasn't the instant you issued the command,* she finished silently.

"Emily," Susannah said quietly, "please. What happened at the settlement that upset Mary Clare so?"

Appearing to gather herself, Emily released a long breath. Her clear green eyes rose to meet Susannah's. "When we got to the mercantile, everyone there was buzzing about some young woman. A Bitsy Jordan."

"Bettina?" Susannah echoed in distress. "Why? What ever is amiss?"

An unbidden shiver shot up Evelyn's spine as quickly as it had earlier, when she'd mistaken the hooting of an owl for Indian calls.

"It seems the young woman rode in from her place yesterday with her baby—both of them nearly frozen, and her horse almost ridden to its death. She was crazed with fear. According to her, Indians have been stalking her place every night since her husband left with the militia."

Evie felt gooseflesh break out on her arms at the frighteningly real image of a mighty hatchet-wielding red man with head shaved but for a strip down the center. She noticed that Susannah shared the same alarm.

"Oh, dear." Emily blushed. "I started all wrong. There's nothing to worry about. Several of the older men rode out to the Jordan place and found not a single track of man or beast—not even *one* since the storm laid down that fresh blanket of snow four days ago." She tossed her head in nonchalance. "Of course, no one can convince the Jordan girl. We heard she's refused to set foot on her farm again. The smithy's wife took her in, and someone else went out to fetch in her livestock."

Susannah's hand clutched her throat. "Oh, my. The poor child. Bettina's not more than sixteen or seventeen."

Evie tried to envision one of her society friends being married and already the mother of a baby at that age. She herself couldn't imagine taking on two such awesome responsibilities at sixteen, all alone in the wilderness.

"From what I heard," Susannah replied, dipping a piece of scone into her tea, "the Jordans came to the valley this spring with very little, and have been trying to make a go of an abandoned farmstead downriver. I have a feeling they might be a couple of runaways."

"It's clear she's far too young to be on her own," Evie declared.

Susannah tilted her tawny head. "She did choose to marry and take on adult obligations. I'm afraid her husband is almost as young as she is, but he seems a good sort. 'Tis likely he merely didn't understand how terrifying it would be for a young wife and mother to be left completely alone."

Evie couldn't help wondering whether if she and Christopher had been in that situation he would have gone off expecting her to survive on her own. How much was one supposed to sacrifice for a cause even as worthy as freedom? She sampled a warm scone and chewed slowly in thought. Perhaps she should regard Mary a bit more sympathetically.

"I shall ride in this afternoon and visit with Bettina," Susannah said. "Try to reassure her."

A new thought surfaced in Evie's mind. "If the Indians were all in Bitsy's imagination, why was Mary so upset?"

Emily answered without hesitation. "Because Mary Clare is having a difficult time being brave herself. She's always had Jon's love and protection to rely on. From what she says, he's never been gone more than a day or two hunting."

"I can understand her being lonely and missing him," Evelyn replied. "But she's not alone. She has my sister-in-law for company—and Pru is very brave and daring, for all her Puritan ways. She even taught me how to shoot."

Giving a brief smile, Susannah patted Evie's hand. "Certainly having Prudence there is the reason Mary has remained at her place, despite feeling very lost just now. We must all keep her in our daily prayers. Pray that she'll allow herself to find peace again in the Lord."

Emily nodded. "And while we're praying for her, we'd better add that she will begin to understand the patriot cause. Mary can't bear the idea that Jonathan might die for liberties she feels have nothing whatsoever to do with the people of Wyoming Valley."

Bristling, Evie looked at Emily. "I can't believe such a narrow-minded idea—particularly coming from one who was once a bondservant."

"War *is,* after all, a dreadful business," Susannah said gently. "Mary Clare confessed it took nearly every ounce of strength she possessed to refrain from begging Jon to stay home, and I might as well admit I share her feelings. If only people would talk over their problems, reach an agreement beneficial to both sides of a matter, instead of resorting to killing one another. I often remember the old tales of King Arthur. Might does not make right . . . might should *be* for right."

"Spoken like a true Englishwoman," Emily teased. She set her cup down on the saucer. "But Great Britain has been bullying us for money ever since we first started prospering as a people. The very audacity of their trying to make us pay for their last war with France—a war over some distant territory!"

All eyes turned to Emily as she continued even more forcefully.

"They only compounded their arrogance by pretending they'd been battling the French in order to save us from them and the Indians. Surely they must have known we'd remember there'd been no problems with the French Canadians until that conflict began. And we'd had a wonderful peace with the Indians all over New England for several generations. *Until the English made war.* Now, relations with the Indians may never return to normal. How dare the Crown expect us to pay taxes for that! We carved a life out of this new land with no help whatsoever from King George. Just because His Royal Highness puts pen to paper does not make any of this land his, when he's never so much as set foot on it." Emily abruptly stopped speaking, and her face reddened. "Oh, dear. I did get carried away. I do hope I haven't offended you."

Susannah smiled and shook her head. "Not at all, little sister, as long as you'll agree that violence is far from the best way to settle a dispute."

A light laugh bubbled from Emily.

Evelyn realized that Susannah's sister-in-law laughed quite often now that she and Robert Chandler had come to an understanding. And since Evie had nearly lost her brother, Morgan, to the war—and especially now that she'd met Christopher—she could see Susannah's point regarding violence.

"Speaking of audacity . . ." Emily rose from the table. "I brought back a newspaper—it came all the way from Philadelphia. I was told it contains an essay the storekeeper feels everyone in the valley should read. The old man actually said, 'Maybe then you women would stop whining about your men being gone.'"

Susannah's eyes narrowed. "Ha! If Mr. Jamison had a wife of his own, I rather doubt he'd have such a loose tongue."

"Go on, Emily. Get it," Evelyn coaxed, her interest piqued. *A weekly from home.*

Retrieving the paper from her tote, Emily returned to her

seat and opened it. "'These are the times that try men's souls,'" she began.

By the conclusion of Thomas Paine's "The American Crisis," Evie had to wipe tears from her cheeks. The portrayal of the army's desperate but valiant efforts, their suffering as they fought for not only their very lives but the lives of every freethinking person in America, inflamed her anew with the spirit of the cause. Their own dear ones were right in the middle of that hardship, suffering untold miseries in the name of freedom. Through watery eyes, she saw that the other two were no less moved than she.

Susannah caught Emily's hand, then Evie's. "It truly is a most righteous and holy cause. We must pray as we never have before. Almighty God shall surely see us through. He shall."

Evelyn, however, placed the success or failure of the American struggle in other hands. But she kept her opinions to herself; she didn't want to risk having Susannah preach those *believer* ideas to her, about God's being one's own personal everyday friend. As if God didn't have more pressing matters, with an entire universe to attend to! How could Susannah and Emily think the Creator had nothing better to do than be at their beck and call every minute of every day? They spoke about being humble, yet their very assumptions seemed to Evie the height of conceit. Why, Emily had lost her husband to a British musket ball. Where was that personal God of hers then?

No. Evie would put her faith where it belonged . . . in Christopher and Morgan and Robert and all the other brave young men out there right now, fighting for right. If it took might, they'd find it. No matter how hopeless things might seem at this moment, the Americans would win. And God, in his eternal wisdom, would see to it that right was done in this great cause. He didn't have time to listen to Mary and the other women whine and cry any more than the shopkeeper did.

And Evie was equally sure that Christopher would survive and come back to her. Her love would bring him home.

8

A tentative sun peeked through a break in the clouds and sliced between the winter-barren limbs of the maple, hickory, and black oak trees at the encampment on the Pennsylvania side of the river. Christopher and Jonathan, taking advantage of the first sunshine since they'd returned to camp, shook out their damp blankets and clothing and draped them over the bare bushes outside their shelter.

"A welcome sight to behold," Jon remarked cheerfully with an upward glance.

Christopher grimaced and checked the northern sky, already heavy with yet another bank of leaden clouds. "Won't last long enough to do much good."

"Always looking to the gloom, eh?" Jonathan said, chuckling. "Try looking on the bright side once in a while. We've had two whole nights of sleep uninterrupted by cannons dueling across the Delaware." He grinned. "'Course, they're all ours now."

"You're right," Christopher conceded. "It's great to feel rested again . . . *if not warm and dry.*"

In a tent nearby, someone coughed, a harsh, raspy sound.

Jon motioned toward the sound with his thumb. "And we can thank the good Lord neither of us has come down with the fever, as have so many after marching both directions in that blizzard."

Chris grunted. "As they say, we'd best not count our chickens just yet. I doubt this gear of ours will dry in the cold." He rearranged his wool blanket to catch more of the sun's rays.

"I reckon not." A worried frown on Jonathan's face vanished as quickly as it appeared, and he whacked his knee. "Of course! I should've thought of it sooner. Morgan is bound to have some dry ones. They took quite a few from the Hessians." He whipped one soggy cover off the rigid branches and began rolling it up.

"Hold on," Christopher said with a reluctant shake of the head. "He can hardly give some to us without doling out the same to everybody else."

Jon barely paused. "Ah yes, if we merely requested extra blankets. What if we made a trade? Wet ones for dry?"

"I see what you mean." Suddenly more hopeful, Chris ripped his from the bush. "Come on, man."

On the way to the supply center, they passed a group of men trying to dry their own sodden blankets before a small campfire that billowed more smoke than heat from the damp wood being fed it. "I just learned a little ditty I think will cheer you lads up," one of them said to the others. He whistled a few notes, then began to sing:

> *"On Christmas day and twenty-six,*
> *Our ragged troops with bayonets fixed,*
> *For Trenton marched away. . . ."*

Chris and Jonathan exchanged grins and joined in, Jon whistling along with the singer, and Chris beating out the peppy rhythm on his thigh.

> *"In silent march we passed the night,*
> *Each soldier panting for the fight,*
> *Thought quite benumbed with frost. . . ."*

Several others started clapping to the cadence, and one pair even hooked elbows and danced a jig:

> "*Twelve hundred servile miscreants,*
> *With all their colors, guns and tents,*
> *Were trophies of the day.*
> *The frolic o'er, the bright canteen*
> *In centre, front and rear was seen*
> *Driving fatigue away.*
> *Now, brothers of the patriot bands,*
> *Let's sing deliverance from the hands*
> *of arbitrary sway. . . .*"

Much guffawing and back thumping accompanied the end of the tune, and spirits seemed noticeably higher in spite of the coughing and wheezing that abounded throughout the camp.

"That truly was some morning," Christopher remarked as he and Jonathan resumed their walk. "This ragged crew of ours not only defeated the dreaded Hessians but did it without losing one life to the mercenaries."

Jonathan nodded. "Amazing. Especially considering the enemy losses—twenty-two dead, eighty-four wounded, over nine hundred taken prisoner. God was with us in that battle."

"According to Colonel Hand, though, the record shows that another five hundred or so Hessians escaped. A pity the downriver regiments weren't able to join us. We might have encircled them sooner."

Jon's jovial smile faded. "I'm sure word has reached British headquarters in New York by now."

"Can't help wondering how much vengeance those mercenaries are wreaking as they retreat across New Jersey." Christopher turned to Jon. "I worry about Ma and Pa Lyons in Princeton. As of a few weeks ago they and the coaching inn had been left pretty much unscathed, despite the enemy's presence. But now—" He frowned.

Jonathan gave a hopeful shrug. "Jasper's an irascible old cuss. I just hope he has the good sense to keep his opinions to himself . . . for once."

"That's a mighty tall order. Never in my life have I heard

anyone who could out-bellow him." Chris chuckled at the thought, then sobered. "I do love that old tyrant, though. Who can say what might have become of Mary Clare and me if they hadn't taken us in when we were kids?"

"Well, hopefully Esther can wrestle the old bear down and lock him away in the attic for now," Jonathan said with an encouraging squeeze to Christopher's shoulder.

"It's possible. She does have the twins to help her."

"Twins?"

Chris grinned. "Oh, that's right. You wouldn't know. Remember those redheads of Mort Spaulding's?"

"The barn painter west of town?"

"Right. Well, when his wife passed on a few months back, he decided to join the army. He left his gals with the Lyonses, to work there in exchange for being looked after until he gets back."

"They can't be old enough to be put out to work," Jon said dubiously. "They were such little things, coming to Sunday services."

"Well, they're a bit more grown now," Chris said, breaking into a slow grin. "About fourteen or fifteen, I'd say. Taller than Mary Clare . . . and downright fetching, even with all those freckles."

"That's not very good news, with those devil Hessians and the British nothing but a scourge in the countryside. We'd best keep the Lyonses and those innocent young girls in our prayers."

Christopher nodded. Then, coming into a clearing, he saw Morgan directing the unloading of supplies from a wagon fitted with snow runners.

Their friend waved and hurried over to them, grabbing them both in an exuberant hug. "Praise the Lord! From the injury report, I was fairly sure you two weren't hurt, but it's good to confirm it with my own eyes. I've been so busy collecting all the supplies we captured from the Hessians, plus all the loot they'd taken on their march down from New York, I haven't had time to come by. Is Chandler well, too?"

"I reckon," Jon said. "We haven't seen much of him either. He's been spending most of his time at brigade headquarters in meetings with the other officers."

When Morgan's gaze lowered to the sodden burdens they carried in their arms, Chris grinned and held his out. "I suppose you're wondering why we've come bearing blankets."

"You don't think the two of you are the first, do you?" Morgan grinned. "We had a big run on dry ones yesterday."

"Oh, then we're too late."

Standing between them, Morgan draped his arms over their shoulders and walked them toward the supply tent. "I had a feeling you might come by, so I saved back three, just in case."

"What a buddy," Jonathan said lightly.

"We Princeton lads must stick together, and all that." Reaching the entrance, Morgan raised the flap and waved the pair inside, where he took dry blankets from under a tarp. He gave one to Jon and two to Chris. "The other's for Chandler."

Christopher nodded, his good humor restored. "It does pay to know a quartermaster."

"Which reminds me." Morgan looked from one to the other. "I've found someone who's packing supplies up to the Wyoming Valley tomorrow, if the weather holds. So any letters you might have for Mary, Jon, I'll need by this evening."

"Splendid!"

Chris felt a flood of emotion wash over him. Not only would he be able to send his own missives to Evie, but he might also receive some from her on the man's return.

"I miss my little family," Jon mused. "More than you know. Worry about them, too."

"As I do about Prudence," Morgan confessed. "She always tries to act so self-sufficient, but with our first little one on the way . . ."

Christopher cocked his head. "My sister is with her. And she has Susannah and Emily close by. She couldn't be in better hands."

"Quite," Morgan said with a nod. "One of these days, however, when you've a lady of your own, you'll understand."

It took considerable effort to hold his tongue, but Chris managed. Morgan had accepted the idea of Chris's corresponding with his sister, but mentioning marriage might be pushing his luck a bit too far. When he looked up, Christopher caught Jonathan's knowing smile. He couldn't help wondering exactly how often he'd mentioned Evelyn to his brother-in-law.

Jon glanced away rather abruptly, and so did Morgan as the *rat-a-tat* of drums came from the encampment of a nearby regiment, calling the men to parade.

"Wonder what that's about?" Morgan started for the exit. "According to what I was told, the men were being given a few days to rest up. General Cadwalader returned last night from downriver. He reported that when he finally got his men across the Delaware down near Bordentown, he found all the small enemy garrisons along that side deserted. The English dogs heard about Trenton and have all run for their lives back to New York."

The three emerged from the supply tent to find Morgan's workers already gravitating toward the gathering across the clearing. Near a flapping regimental banner, Christopher spotted General Washington, sitting erect on his tall horse.

The general rode past the entire length of the front row, viewing the troops, then returned to the center, where he reined to a stop. "Men, I have come personally to thank each and every one of you for the great service you performed for our people in the Battle of Trenton. I am certain this siege will go down in our annals as one of the great victories of this war—a war which I am determined we shall win. You have all proven yourselves to be of the highest caliber. The difficulty of crossing the river on such a severe night, your march through a violent storm of snow and sleet did not in the least abate your ardor in pressing forward during the charges, adding greatly to our success."

He paused and cleared his throat as he searched the sea of

faces. His booming voice contained a humble quality when he spoke again. "Now I must come to you with yet another request. Many of your enlistments will expire a few days from now, on the first day of January. I know you are looking forward to rejoining your loved ones after a year's absence. But your country needs you now as never before. I have come to entreat you to volunteer for one extra month . . . at which time you will be given a bonus of ten dollars."

A raft of groans and grumblings broke the solemn silence.

"Will all those who would volunteer please step forward?" the general asked, his voice steady.

Christopher, astounded at the lack of discipline in the disrespectful outburst, watched the commander ride his mount down the line once more to the accompaniment of the drums.

Not a single man stepped out.

General Washington wheeled his horse and returned to the center. "My brave fellows, you have done all I have asked you to do and more than could be reasonably expected. But your country is at stake. Your wives, your houses, and all that you hold dear." He nodded toward the drummers, who filled the tense stillness with another insistent tattoo as men directed their gazes anywhere but to their great leader.

He lifted a palm to silence the instruments. "I will guarantee the bonus out of my own pocket."

The drums took up the cadence once more.

Christopher turned to Morgan and Jonathan. "This is appalling. Colonel Hand's men would never shame him this way—*or* Washington, let alone themselves."

At last, one man stepped forward, head high. Then another, and a handful more. The drums throbbed louder, and soon at least two hundred soldiers had accepted the call.

The general raised a hand for the instruments to cease.

An officer approached him. "Sir. What date do you want on the new enrollment papers?"

"None." The commander waved him off. "No papers. Men who will volunteer in such a case as this need no enrollment to keep them to their duty." He turned to the soldiers. "I know what a sacrifice you are making. I *and your country* thank you."

As General Washington turned his mount and cantered away, Morgan raised an eyebrow. "Well, I haven't received orders to pack up the supplies for a march, so my guess is the good general is expecting company. And I rather doubt our guests will be coming for tea."

9

After a six-mile march from Trenton the day before, Colonel Hand's men had taken positions on either side of the Princeton road just past the village of Maidenhead. Waiting halfway up a wooded hillside while their comrades were out of sight in the fields across the way, Jon, Chris, and many others had cut boughs from the trees and spread them with blankets. At least the makeshift beds got them out of the wet snow during the long, freezing cold night.

But all for naught, Jonathan thought bitterly as morning dawned, then stretched toward noon. No enemy had yet ventured forth. Disgusted, he glanced once again along the half-mile stretch of road that climbed a rise and disappeared from view.

He whacked the lumps beneath the blanket he sat on with Chris. "I said it before, and I'll say it again. This is an utter waste of time. There's no reason for us all having to stay out here and freeze. And it's sure no way to spend the first day of a brand-new year. Two or three sentries could keep watch for the British. The rest of us could be out of this weather, warming our feet down below at the Maidenhead town hearths."

Christopher leaned back against the tree and stared at him. "If I were you, I'd wait until I had a little experience before I tried to out-think the officers."

Having his younger brother-in-law talk to him as if he were

a green kid was more than a little irritating. Jon jerked his head toward another soldier down the line. "I'm not the only one who feels this way. That moon-faced lad, Phelps, says General Howe will never order a winter campaign, not with the weather so unpredictable. The fellow next to him agrees. He says Howe's been gun-shy ever since Boston, when he led the attack on Bunker Hill. Seeing so many of his men slaughtered there has made the general plan every maneuver with extreme caution. Now he never attacks without an overwhelming force."

"Yes, well—" Christopher stopped as he saw someone heading their way along the ridge. "Robert's coming."

Jon turned to see the tall lieutenant trudging toward them through the trees and snow. Chandler would certainly agree with him. With lifted spirits, he stood with Chris as Robert approached.

"Sir!" The two stood at attention. Friendship aside, he was an officer and deserved the proper respect.

With a nod, Robert motioned them to sit down. "Just thought I'd check and see how y'all were getting along."

"Word in the ranks is that General Howe won't even consider mounting an attack unless he's assured of victory," Jonathan said.

The lieutenant gave a noncommittal shrug. "True."

Jon shot Christopher a smirk.

"*Except* for one thing," Robert drawled. "Up until now our people feared the British army—especially those foreign-tongued Hessians. But now that we routed them all along the river and have them on the run, we've got volunteers pouring in from neighborhoods on both sides of the Delaware to join us. That resounding victory of ours has inspired many to fight—even those who formerly doubted our chances. I think the general will force Cornwallis out of his warm bed to march forth with his division and stamp out this new threat."

"You say we're getting more recruits every day?" Jon remarked incredulously. "In this weather, yet! The good

Thomas Paine won't be able to term these new men 'summer soldiers,' that's for sure."

Christopher snickered, inching deeper into his coat. "No one would call *this* summer."

"Take heart," Robert said with a grin. "I've got two men stirring up a big hot stew on the back side of the hill. Should be ready in about half an hour. Come down and eat then, one at a time. I don't want everyone leaving the hill at once."

"Surely no entire division of soldiers could sneak up on us," Jon retorted.

Christopher and Robert exchanged cryptic glances.

"No," Robert assured Jon. "Nevertheless, stay alert. Our battalion is all there is up this far. De Fernoy's brigade is behind us a good four miles, and it's another mile or two back to the rest of our army at Trenton."

The news stunned Jonathan. "The brigade hasn't moved any farther since we left them yesterday?"

"Like I said, keep your eyes and ears open." Robert raised his hand in a parting wave, then turned and tromped off through the snow toward some riflemen positioned about fifteen yards down the line.

Watching after him with a frown, Jon got up and scanned the top of the ridge behind the hill. In the sound-deadening snow, it would be entirely possible for a swift cavalry troop to descend undetected upon them. But then he glimpsed a sentry perched in the branches of a tree near the highest point. Somewhat comforted, he relaxed a little.

Christopher dug deep into his pocket and retrieved a coin as he came to his feet. "Flip you to see who eats first."

"Don't bother. I'm not all that hungry right now." Jonathan scanned the road in both directions, then the area across from them. He knew riflemen were picketed behind stone walls intersecting those newly whitened meadows.

Glancing to his right, at the buildings of Maidenhead, Jon noticed a woman hanging clothes on a line behind her house. The scene seemed suddenly ludicrous. "Would you look at that! Doing laundry as if nothing is amiss."

"And in this cold, yet," Chris remarked. "Those wet things will do nothing but freeze—along with her bare hands."

"My Mary wouldn't dream of taking such a risk . . . casually putting herself between two lines of fire."

Christopher tipped his head in thought. "But to an unknowing eye, it looks as if it's just an ordinary day. I take my hat off to her for that brave act."

Jonathan continued to stare at the stocky woman. "I don't think it's bravery. She reminds me of old Mistress Bisset, up in the valley. If it's wash day, she washes. Someone told me that a few years back, an alarm went out that hostile Indians were on the way. She wouldn't take one step toward the fort until every last thing in the house was in perfect order. Far be it from her to have those 'heathens' think she was untidy."

Christopher chuckled. "Speaking of the valley, I wonder how our gently raised Miss Evelyn has been faring." A smile spread across his mouth. "She'll do just fine, I'm sure. I'll never forget the first time I saw her. She had dragged Prudence up to the battlefront, searching for some young man who hadn't written home. Nothing would keep Evie from coming to find out for herself if he was all right."

"Sounds like something a spoiled little rich girl might do."

"Maybe." Chris's voice conveyed a measure of doubt, but he seemed to shake it off. "Anyway, unhappily for her, he'd deserted. Run off with a local farmer's daughter, to boot. Believe it or not, that happened to be the very day the British launched their attack against us at Throg's Point in New York."

Jonathan hiked his brows. "You wrote us about that battle. Prudence and Evelyn were there in the thick of things?"

"Well, almost. Since Chandler knew Prudence, we were ordered to escort them to safety. We hopped on the backs of the ladies' horses and had barely ridden a mile when a party of mounted redcoat officers gave chase. I hid with Pru and Evie while Chandler rode away with the horses to divert the patrol."

"I reckon that would make a first meeting rather memorable."

"Ah, yes." Chris's eyes took on a faraway look. "But what really stayed with me was the way Evie clung to me. I can still see those huge, gorgeous eyes of hers, such a light blue they—" He stopped abruptly, then cleared his throat, obviously self-conscious. "Anyway, I knew right then that I would have died before I let one of those lobsterbacks touch a hair on her head."

Jonathan managed to contain his amusement at his smitten brother-in-law. Apparently the lad had no idea how often he worked Morgan Thomas's sister into the conversation. But there was more about this particular liaison that plagued Jon. "Chip, there's quite a lot about that Thomas girl that's different—more than you might realize. Aside from the life of luxury she's led, her family is Anglican. High Church, as I recall."

"So?"

Uncomfortable, Jon shifted his weight to his other leg. Maybe he should have left the matter alone, but it was too late now. He decided to come right out with it. "Some Anglicans don't accept that salvation is a free gift from God, received by faith by those who believe in our Lord. They're taught that it's their good deeds, their own works, that earn them a place with God, and a large part of those revolve around being loyal to the Church of England, as well as to the Crown."

"Morgan's not like that."

"Not now. But he believed that way when his father first banished him to the strict Presbyterian college in Princeton. As time went by, he became a believer as well as a rebel. I reckon his father rues the day he enrolled his son at Nassau Hall."

Christopher's expression hardened. "Well, Evelyn has proven she's equally disloyal to the Crown. She was spying for us, you know. Maybe she's also rebelled against the king's church, the way her brother did."

Just as Jonathan opened his mouth to reply, the washerwoman below them suddenly dropped a piece of clothing in the snow and bolted for the road, where a lone rider on an ungainly farm horse was coming at a fast gallop.

The fellow hauled in on the reins when he saw her, and after a few seconds' exchange, she pointed up the ridge Jon and Chris occupied.

Was she betraying them? Before Jon had time to consider the possibility, he saw the rider nudge his horse up the hill.

Colonel Hand, behind Jon and Chris, gave a shout and rode down to intercept the newcomer. Robert Chandler loped along behind the colonel on foot, and other officers converged as well.

"The British are coming!" the man all but yelled. "The whole blasted army! Must be seven, eight thousand of them devils. Passed right by my farm. Cannons, too. Lots of 'em."

"How far back?" the colonel asked.

"They'll be coming over that hill anytime now, you'll see." The farmer peered back over his shoulder, nodding for emphasis.

The half-mile of visible distance seemed totally inadequate now. Jonathan's hands trembled as he grabbed his rifle.

"Any outriders?" he heard Colonel Hand inquire.

"Nope. Didn't see any, or they'd have shot me for sure."

The colonel turned to his mounted aide. "Ride for Trenton at once. Warn General De Fernoy on the way, then report to General Washington. Ask if he wishes to change our orders."

"Yes, sir!" The lieutenant spurred his horse and charged down the snowy hill.

"Gentlemen," Hand said to the remaining officers. "It is not possible for us to hold back an army of that size. We can easily be outflanked."

Three hundred against seven thousand? Jonathan wanted to shout. *We'd be more than just outflanked . . . we'd be annihilated!* But he held his tongue.

"The best we can do is hold them up," the Irishman went on. "Give Washington in Trenton a couple of extra hours. Order a delaying action. But stay well out of range of their muskets. Keep moving your troops so their artillery can't get a fix on us. Each of you will be responsible for your company's flank. Send five or six men to the top of the ridge to pick off any riders who attempt to circle behind. Now, get back to your men. We've got our work cut out for us this day."

As the officers scrambled, Jon gripped Christopher's sleeve in panic. "Delaying action? What did the colonel mean?"

"We'll be keeping just ahead of the enemy all the way back to Trenton, slowing them up by sniping at them as we go." Chris worked his coat out of Jonathan's grasp.

"For six whole miles?"

"Just stick with me," Christopher returned quietly. "And no questions. Do exactly what I tell you. We'll be moving fast." He took up his rifle and checked the load.

Watching his brother-in-law's calm manner and steady hand, Jon realized how much the war had matured Christopher. The lad had become a man, and that assurance eased some of his own edginess. Turning, he placed a hand on Chris's shoulder. "Thanks, Brother, for being here." Then, with a glance heavenward, he closed his eyes. "Dear Lord, may your protecting hand be upon us this day."

"Amen," Christopher whispered.

A subtle vibration rattled the ground beneath their feet. Jon shot a glance all around but could see nothing. The tremor continued to grow in strength.

Chris met his gaze. "They're coming."

Could there be so many soldiers on the march that the ground shakes before they even come into view? Amazed, Jon peered down the road.

"Think of it this way," Chris said lightly, hauling up his haversack. "The last half of this day won't be as boring as the first."

At the top of the distant rise, a thin line of scarlet appeared like a ribbon, then spilled down the snow-whitened road in a torrent of bright red. Slowly it took on distinguishable forms—marching soldiers, mounted men on strong, fleet horses, an army moving in cadence with the *rat-a-tat* of drums.

Horse-drawn cannon and ammunition caissons crested the road now as well, in the unending stream heading their way.

Jonathan felt his mouth go dry. There was no way in the world this pathetic battalion, divided as it was into a mere one hundred fifty men on either side of the road, could hope to withstand that awesome British presence. His heart started pounding almost as loudly as the enemy drums.

A quick glance at his brother-in-law revealed Chris crouching behind a boulder. Brushing snow off the top, Chris propped his rifle on it and took aim.

On wooden legs, the blood roaring in his ears, Jon dropped down beside him. He swung his weapon into position and pulled back on the hammer.

"Not yet," Chris said quietly with raised hand. "They aren't in range."

The comment added to Jonathan's feeling of stupidity. He knew the British were still quite far away. He inhaled a calming breath.

Christopher pointed to a spot some distance ahead of the oncoming army. "See where that stile goes over the stone wall? When they reach there, we'll shoot."

"Both of us? At the same time?"

"Right. The men closer to the British will have already fired and left to take up a position at the far end. We'll be their backup. Then we'll fire, and those farther back will do the same for us. Fire, run to the other end of our line, load, then wait for the enemy to come into range before we fire again. We'll do this all the way to Trenton."

"But what about their riders?" Jon asked at the sight of the scores of horsemen accompanying the troops.

"Keep a steady watch out for them. They'll take off and circle around behind us as soon as shots are fired." He paused. "Oh, and one more thing. Shoot low. Try to wound, rather than kill. They won't leave the wounded behind, and it'll take two men to carry one man off. That way one shot takes three men out of the action."

Struck by Christopher's matter-of-fact tone, Jonathan regarded his young brother-in-law. Chris, alert, possessed the deadly calm of someone confident in the assigned task. Jon had heard Hand's Men relating past battles, and until this moment had figured the talk was more exaggeration than fact. But now he had the sickening feeling that those stories were probably all true. He also understood that Christopher's pride in his battalion was well founded.

It was up to Jon to trust Chris. To place his fate in the hands of his 'little brother.' He glanced toward the enemy. Any second, red-coated soldiers would step within range of the closest rifles. Then all would be chaos. He had to trust Christopher's experience and calmness. And trust God to see them both through.

10

Evelyn found the ride through the woods to Mary Clare's a pleasant break in the routine on the first day of the new year. To ensure a few moments' peace and quiet, she lagged a bit behind Susannah, Emily, and their noisy broods. The endless chatter and giggles were tiresome enough to endure, cooped up in the house, when one wasn't accustomed to such nonsense. She wasn't about to waste this little respite from it all.

Golden afternoon sunshine drifted through the bare branches and lit the frosted ground like a million scattered diamonds. As Evie lost herself in winter's beauty, a bramble snagged the skirt of her dress. She tugged it free, then pulled her cloak more fully over the gown to protect the sapphire gabardine. It was the only one out of her extensive wardrobe she had with her. The rest had been left behind when she fled New York. Thank goodness it was her most serviceable and durable frock. It was also a finer gown than any she'd seen in this backwoods settlement . . . a fact that would mean very little if it were in tatters.

If you weren't such a goose, she reminded herself with chagrin, *you would have kept on the plain dress Susannah loaned you. After all, we're not calling on some village dignitary, only Mary Clare and her children.* But Evie was accustomed to dressing in her finest on New Year's Day. In Philadelphia there would have been afternoon festivities to attend, and in a horse-drawn shay, at that. At least she had her sidesaddle, but it didn't protect her from the elements. Spying for the patriots had certainly brought about a number of changes in her life, and no telling how many others were yet to be.

If only the Continental army could continue having successes like that surprising one in Trenton she'd heard about just this morning! Then her personal sacrifices and the loss of her parents' trust would be more than worth the price. She sorely missed the comforts she'd known living in their affluent home, but what bothered her most was what her parents must think of her now that they knew she'd betrayed them. Rather than dwell on the depressing thought, she forced the bothersome guilt aside and focused on the noble cause she served instead.

Evie thought back on the welcome and hospitality Dan and Susannah had extended to her. They had made her feel at home from the moment she arrived. And Susannah had done any number of other thoughtful things Evie appreciated—not the least of which was providing warm knitted undergarments for her to wear on this ride.

Running a hand over the many layers of skirts covering the cozy underthings, Evelyn inadvertently brushed the pocket that contained the treasured letter from Christopher, and a thrill ran through her. She had been daydreaming about him almost every waking moment since he'd left, so when the freight man brought the packet of letters from the men that morning, Evie's joy knew no bounds. Seeing words penned by Christopher's own hand, thoughts written from his heart to hers, seemed infinitely special. She started to draw the missive out and gaze upon it once more.

"There's Aunt Mary's house! We're here!" Miles hollered. "Giddyap, Firefly."

Evie noticed that her little group was coming out into a clearing, and she let her gaze wander from one end of the farmstead to the other. She saw that the Bradfords had much more land cleared than Dan and Susannah, but then Jonathan and Mary Clare had been established in the valley since long before the Hayneses arrived last summer. This farm had a sturdy barn, a springhouse, and numerous other outbuildings. The cabin also was more comfortably sized, with an addition built on one side. An inviting spiral of smoke curled upward from the chimney, a welcome sight after watching everyone's breath float on the frosty air during the ride.

Squealing and laughing, the older youngsters prodded their mounts ahead, loping across the snowy field toward the house.

"Children," Emily called after them. "Don't forget your manners—and when we're all in the house, remember to keep your voices down. *All* of you!"

Amid cries of "Yes, Mama!" and "We will, Auntie!" they charged onward.

The door swung wide, and Mary Clare waved a cheery welcome, barely snagging Esther and Beth in their attempt to bolt past her. Her braid tumbled forward over the shoulder of a coarse, olive green dress shaped only by the waistband of a worn apron. Her little ones, though clean, were dressed a little less shabbily in matching burgundy frocks.

Evelyn noted that Christopher's older sister took even less care with her appearance at home than when she was out visiting. But Evie knew it would be to her advantage to disregard Mary's utter lack of fashion sense. She would make a real effort to befriend the young matron without revealing her distaste.

"We have letters," Emily announced, waving them in the air as she hopped down off her pacer.

Miles, Katie, and Rusty, already off their horses, ran inside with the two Bradford daughters. A second later, ebony-haired Prudence appeared at the entrance. "Oh," she breathed, "tell me one's from Morgan. It seems forever."

She rushed to Emily and took the correspondence. "Here, Mary, this one's for you," Prudence said, and a rosy blush heightened Mary Clare's cheeks as she clutched her letter to her breast. "I'm sure you won't mind allowing us a few moments to read our mail, will you?" Pru said, encompassing

Evie and the others in her gaze. "Come in. Make yourselves at home."

Eventually everyone was inside and settled, the women with hot spiced cider at the table, and the children seated on a blanket in front of the hearth with games and toys.

Mary Clare, still flushed from reading her letter from Jonathan, brought an unfinished quilt to the table, unfolded it, and spread it out. "We need to finish the rest of the stitching. Seth and Laura's wedding is just around the corner. "You're welcome to help, Evelyn," she added, offering a spare needle to her. "That is, if you want to, of course." She blushed even more deeply and looked away.

Only with supreme effort did Evie manage to hide her aversion to stitching, the one "gentle pursuit" she loathed above all others. All her life she had balked whenever her mother suggested she embroider a handkerchief or the edge of a pillow slip, and here lay an entire quilt before her. "Why, I'd love to, Mary, dear," she heard herself gush. She withdrew her hand from her pocket—from Christopher's letter—and claimed the needle, then reached for the spool of thread.

"I hear you received a letter from my brother," Mary added in a slightly braver tone. "The only one he sent, in fact."

Evelyn felt suddenly uncomfortable. She flicked a glance to Prudence and met a knowing smile. Then, not certain how she should respond, since she hadn't spoken of Chris to any of them, Evie returned her attention to the section of quilt before her and began stitching in earnest.

A snicker from Prudence filled the void.

Evie, irritated, lifted her face. "I suppose he took pity on me, since he figured you'd all be hearing from your men."

"And rightly he should," Emily piped in. "Evelyn, in her goodness, has been kind enough to help me with the herd. She insists on learning everything there is to know about horses."

Any relief Evie felt at the change of subject was short-lived.

"Has she, now?" Mary tilted her chin, a peculiar smile on her lips. "Isn't that a coincidence. There are two things Chris wants to do when he completes his college studies—build bridges and raise horses."

Evie straightened and swept a glance around the table. Obviously, the cat had been let out of the bag. Just as well. "He sent you his deepest regards, Mary," she lied. Chris had not mentioned his sister once.

"Oh! I just remembered." Susannah leaned forward. "When the mail was delivered to us, the freight man also imparted the latest news. Our army had a great victory. With scarcely an injury, they managed to take the Hessian post at Trenton. Nearly a thousand men were captured in the process. That gives us something we can truly celebrate this New Year."

With the talk turning to further details of the battle, Evelyn's thoughts easily drifted away from the sounds of the children and the women's conversation and centered instead on Chris's letter. She had read it so many times this morning that she knew it by heart, and in her mind's eye she could see the words as clearly as if the paper lay open before her. She lingered on the memory of an especially favorite phrase after his warm greeting:

> *It seems a very long time since I departed the Wyoming Valley and your pleasurable company, though it has been but a week.*

Pleasurable company. Evie sighed. He missed her *pleasurable company.* And since he'd gone away, the days seemed interminably long. It was gratifying to know he felt the same.

> *Our tent, if one might call it that, leaves a bit to be desired where actual comfort is concerned. It is hardly more than a few odd boards with canvas nailed between and is so drafty Jon and I must huddle together to maintain the least warmth.*

It saddened Evie to picture the two of them in such horrid conditions. It was common knowledge that the Congress wasn't providing much in the way of comfort. But surely young men who gave up all to serve their country deserved proper quarters, good food, and warm clothing, at the very least.

> *Dan has been assigned duty as a courier again. He was once a postrider, you will recall, working for Sam Adams and the other patriots before he gave up his duties in favor of the ministry.*

Those impersonal details and others of only slight interest, her memory skimmed over, hurrying on to where, near the closing, Christopher included much more intimate remarks—all of which were imprinted upon her innermost heart forever:

> *Our last morning at the Haynes farm is never far from my mind. Every time I close my eyes I see your beautiful face. It makes the distance between us seem less vast, somehow, and I take great comfort in each thought of you. May God look after you in my absence. Until I return, I remain your ever admiring and faithful servant,*
> *Christopher Drummond*

Evelyn recalled the undisguised joy in his expression when he'd sneaked out of his bedchamber that morning and found she'd done the same. Everything she had wanted to see had been right there in his eyes. Everything. A warm tingle ran down her spine. She only hoped he'd caught a glimpse of the same promise in hers.

". . . but I still can't help it." Mary's near wail brought Evie out of her reverie. "I've felt an awful tightness in my chest for the last few hours—as if something is dreadfully wrong. With Jon, I mean. We've always been able to sense each other's pain."

One of Mary's little daughters flew to the table. "Is something the matter, Mama?"

Her mother swallowed and forced a smile. "No, sweetie.

We're just talking. Go back with the others. Mama's very proud of how quiet you're being."

With a thin smile, the child did as bidden.

Wondering if Mary Clare had some mysterious second sight, Evie experienced her own sudden feeling of foreboding. If Jon truly were in trouble, Chris could be in danger too. She glanced at Prudence. Her sister-in-law had paused in her sewing, her face almost as white as the crisp apron she wore over her dove gray gown. Only a few short weeks ago, Pru had thought Morgan was dead for many terrible days—a heartbreaking prospect made all the worse by her delicate condition.

Beside Mary Clare, Susannah reached to place a hand over hers. "Then I am even more thankful we came this day. Our imaginations can so often get the better of us unless we allow our heavenly Father to bear these heavy burdens for us."

"That's easy for you to say," Mary sniffed. She withdrew her hand. "Most likely your Dan is riding in complete safety between the Congress in Philadelphia and Washington's camp, toting nothing but a saddlebag full of messages."

Emily laid her needle aside. "Mary's right. There is reason to feel concern. If the Trenton battle was as successful as reported, the British will surely retaliate. But let's take comfort in the fact that General Howe is noted for taking ever so long in getting around to it. Especially in this wintry weather."

"Normally I would agree," Prudence cut in, her smooth forehead lined with concern. "But this is too great an affront to English pride. Howe will have to do something. And *because* the weather will only worsen as winter deepens, he must act, and swiftly."

Evelyn nodded. "Pru is right. One thing we can always count on is the arrogance of the British."

"Well said," Prudence added with a broad smile. "Evelyn and I had to abide more than our share of the braggarts in Philadelphia and New York gloating beyond our endurance about their superiority. And dear Evie has borne years more of it than I."

Evie thought back on the interminable social functions she had attended with her Loyalist parents every season. Tiresome and dreary. A life she would never return to, she vowed, fingering Christopher's letter. With him, life would always be new as they lived that romantic step beyond the edge of civilization while he forged roads into the vast wilderness. Such an exciting adventure would more than make up for any lack of conveniences. For him, she would learn to do without them. She would.

"I don't mean to frighten you, Mary. Truly I don't." Emily's serious tone cut across Evie's musings. "But the very moment my Robby was killed, I knew it *absolutely*, in my heart. Is . . . is that how you feel?"

Mary lurched to her feet, her knuckles colorless where they rested on the tabletop. *"Killed?* He can't be. Not my Jon."

Susannah, with a reproving stare at Emily, nodded calmly toward the children, then rose to place her arms about the younger woman. "Now, now, of course he's not. Let's put away such foolish talk."

But Evelyn caught the trapped-deer expression on Mary Clare's face. She hardly seemed brave enough to be a frontier wife. Jon must have sheltered her quite a lot. How different she was from her brother, the stalwart adventurer. *But then, I'm nothing like my simpering ninny sisters, either,* Evie told herself. *I'm much more of a daredevil, like Morgan.*

Emily got up and went to Susannah and Mary. "I'm so sorry, Mary," she said softly. "I shouldn't have spoken so. It's just that when Robby died, no one would believe me until word came . . . and I so needed their belief and their comfort."

Tears that had been brimming in Mary's eyes spilled over. She reached out to Emily. "That must have hurt you deeply. You probably felt all alone. I know how that feels."

"Well," Susannah said with assurance, "now that most of us are standing, this would be a wonderful opportunity to go to almighty God in prayer. Pru and Evie, please join us, won't you, while we beseech the Lord to renew our courage to trust him and his love in these harrowing times."

Again? Evelyn cringed inwardly and rose with reluctance. Susannah had to be the prayingest woman she'd ever met in her life. But then, who was to say? God might actually answer her petitions. If he didn't, she'd probably give him no rest! And it might just be that kind of persistence that would keep the men safe . . . keep Christopher safe.

11

Early morning sunshine tinted the fragile coating of hoarfrost a delicate pink. Overhead the sky deepened to a brilliant blue, beauty that seemed completely at odds with the realities of battle marches and sleepless nights. Nevertheless, Christopher and Jonathan's footsteps blended with the muffled sound of hundreds of feet tromping the snowy road to Princeton.

Stretching a kink out of his back, Chris noted his bedraggled brother-in-law's trudging step. He doubted he looked any better himself, with rumpled clothes and several days' growth of whiskers scratching annoyingly against the collar of his greatcoat. In the bitter cold, the few pitiful hours of sleep the company had been allowed had been anything but restful. He slapped an encouraging arm around Jon's shoulder and grinned. "Tired? Feet aching, are they?"

Jon shot him a sour glare.

"Hey, aren't you the one who reminded me not long ago to look on the bright side? We're still alive, aren't we? Which is saying quite a lot, after yesterday."

"I reckon so." Jon perked up a bit. "We did it, didn't we? Hand's Men. Didn't matter what they threw at us—cannonballs, grapeshot, light horsemen—we held them up long enough for our entire army to cart themselves and all their baggage across the Assunpink Creek Bridge."

"That we did. Those lobsterbacks are always underestimating us. I just wish we were headed someplace else now, though, instead of Princeton. I can't stomach the thought of waging a battle in my own town. Pa Lyons is such a stubborn coot, he'd stay with that inn of his no matter what. Cannonballs could slam clear through the walls, and he wouldn't budge."

Jonathan gazed toward the quiet village. "Surely old Jasper would see Esther and the twins to safety, wouldn't he?"

"I sure hope so." Chris released a pent-up breath. "Who knows, maybe the Princeton garrison came with Cornwallis's troops to Trenton."

Jon nodded. "Sure seemed that way yesterday. I haven't seen such a horde since the days when Reverend Whitefield used to come through here on one of his preaching tours."

Reaching a fork in the road, Mercer's regiment swerved to the west, marching eight abreast.

"We must be going to attack from two fronts again, like we did in Trenton," Christopher remarked. He knew that the route the others were taking would cut over to the main post road, which also ran from Trenton to Princeton. He turned to scan the distant rise over the heads of those following behind. "From the looks of it, it'll be just our army and whoever Cornwallis left here. There's still no sign that the Crown's main force is trailing us."

Jonathan nodded. "General Washington's ruse worked."

A grizzled frontiersman on the other side of Christopher chuckled and turned to look as well. He spewed a stream of tobacco juice from the corner of his mouth. "I can just see old Cornwallis. About now, somebody should be shakin' him awake in that nice warm bed of his. *'What's that, me good man?'*" he said, mimicking an English accent. " 'Those cowardly rebels, gone? We left them right there last night. Right there, across the creek.'"

Christopher jabbed Jonathan with an elbow. "The old fox gave them the slip one more time."

"What tickles me," the other fellow said, "is that we're not just runnin' away this time. Pity you got folks in Princeton,

Drummond, but we gotta attack. An army loses heart if it ain't doing nothin' except tuckin' tail. And this is one fight we get to pick for a change. Not one them fancy redcoats decided for us. I like that a lot."

"I reckon what I like best," Jon said in a gentler voice, "is knowing the good Lord is watching out for us, even in this frozen countryside. With all the odds against this little army of ours, he's kept us alive to fight one more time. The entire British army was just across the creek from us when we slipped off last night. Just a cannonball away. It's as if God struck the enemy deaf and blind."

Chris gave a thoughtful nod. "Well, leaving some of our men behind to keep the night fires burning probably didn't hurt."

"Nor did wrappin' rags around them wagon wheels and horse hooves," the frontiersman added.

"Say what you will," Jon declared evenly. "But remember we were trapped between the Assunpink and the Delaware, both of them too frozen for the boats but too thin to walk across. We had but one route of escape, and that could easily have been blocked."

Christopher, too, could sense the hand of God in the matter, but he kept silent. Some feelings were too deep for words.

The fringe-coated fellow stiffened and squinted into the distance. "Look yonder. A lobsterback!"

Glancing through the leafless trees lining Stony Brook, Christopher spotted a light horseman. Chris stepped out of line and uncorked his powder horn.

At that instant the rider wheeled his mount and galloped toward Trenton, the horse's hooves clattering over the frozen field as if it were made of cobblestones.

The easy chatter up and down the line ceased. Without an order, the pace picked up.

No one knew whether or not the Crown garrison in town had been warned. A low hill blocked the small college town from view, and a second rise just to the west hid any glimpse of Mercer's troops or the post road into Princeton. The sooner this column reached town, the better.

Within moments, sporadic musket fire could be heard on the other side of the hill. Mercer's command had encountered the enemy.

General Washington charged up the western hill. His aide rode swiftly down the line to relay orders to the men.

"Halt!" Robert Chandler called to his company. Then he and other brigade officers ran toward the aide.

Colonel Hand, on horseback, reached the man first.

Within seconds, Chandler raced back to the troops, sword raised high. "Over the rise, men! We're to back up Mercer's brigade! Charge!"

Christopher, in a surge of excitement, took off at a dead run as the order carried down the ranks. Suddenly he remembered. *Jonathan!* He swung back to check on him and caught the encompassing glance Robert swung over the whole group. Chris was suddenly grateful his only concern was Jon.

Colonel Hand and the aide crested the sparsely wooded rise soon after General Washington disappeared down the other side.

Most of the musket fire had subsided already. Most likely they were reloading, Chris conjectured . . . *or fighting hand to hand.* His legs pumped harder, faster, taking him to the front of the pack. As he reached the top, Colonel Hand halted the company with an upraised arm.

Chris, panting for breath, steeled himself for a bloody scene of hand-to-hand combat below. But instead, he saw Mercer's men running pell-mell for an orchard at the south end of the shallow valley. A single British infantry regiment gave chase, their ruthless battle cries sounding as lethal as the outstretched bayonets. Disgust burned through Chris for his fellow soldiers and their cowardly panic.

Then he spied General Washington bravely riding back and forth between the opposing regiments.

A couple of the enemy noticed him, too. They stopped and took aim. Fired. Their weapons belched flashes and smoke, but the gallant leader remained unscathed as he swung his sword in a desperate attempt to regroup his fleeing men.

More redcoats leveled their muskets on him.

"Please, God," Chris breathed, looking heavenward. "Protect him."

Brown Besses discharged, one after another.

Still the general kept mustering his men, without regard for personal danger.

A commotion behind Chris drew his attention. Their own six-pounders were being drawn up the hill by teams of horses.

Colonel Hand raced by. "Form a firing line! Prime your loads! Prime! Be quick, lads!"

The British were almost within range. Chris grabbed a paper cartridge, burst it, and poured a small measure of powder into the pan, then rammed the rod up his barrel. When he had replaced the ramrod, he took a bead on one of the redcoats charging on Mercer's men. He held his breath, waiting for the order to fire.

Below, two of Washington's officers galloped out to the general, pistols in hand. They grabbed the bridle of the general's horse and led him to safety.

Christopher was sure those officers would be reprimanded by Washington when the battle was over. Nonetheless, he was relieved that their commander was now in far less danger.

"Pick your target," Colonel Hand cried the instant the general was off the field. "Fire!"

Chris squeezed his triggers. When flash and smoke cleared, a number of redcoats had fallen.

"Down the hill!" the colonel yelled. "To the right. Wheel to the right!" He then galloped in that direction, his horse's hooves breaking up the icy ground.

Hand's Men took off after him to flank the redcoats, leaving the other regiments to rush straight down on the British.

Artillery roared.

It's turning out to be another Trenton! Exhilaration flooded Chris. The blackguards would be surrounded in no time. He let out a whoop and ran all the faster. Others took up the battle cry.

Cannonballs from the Crown line exploded into the orchard where many of Mercer's men had retreated.

On all sides, regiments ran down the hill, their musket fire adding to the roar and smoke that now filled the bowl-like valley. Christopher and his battalion kept going, closing off any British route of escape.

Suddenly Colonel Hand raced across his men's path. "Halt!"

Chris stumbled to a stop and snatched a paper cartridge from its box. He and the rest began loading their barrels.

"Right oblique!" the colonel yelled as Chris rammed the load. "Enemy reinforcements coming from Princeton. Cut them off!"

Chris looked up to see redcoats pouring over the rise separating the town from the battlefield.

The colonel charged toward the new threat every bit as recklessly as General Washington had done. The rifle battalion followed on foot right behind him.

Hand swung his sword. "Don't let the devils join forces! Forward, men! Charge!"

"Charge!" the ranks echoed. They barreled ahead toward another regiment of British infantry.

Christopher tried to ignore the niggling detail that the riflemen had not a single bayonet among them. On they ran. A hundred yards. Two hundred.

Again the colonel galloped across their path, hand raised. "Halt!"

The riflemen spread into a firing line, grabbing their powder to prime flashpans.

A few feet away from Christopher, Jonathan struggled for breath. But his now experienced fingers worked steadily.

"Count off, men," Chandler ordered. "One, two, one, two."

This was where they'd make a stand.

The king's men knew the limited range of their Brown

Besses. They rushed forward to close the distance with savage, blood-curdling yells.

Christopher swallowed, maintaining his aim. From the corner of his eye he watched for Colonel Hand's sword to fall.

The signal came. The riflemen fired a deafening volley.

Chris dropped back to reload while Jonathan and the other alternates stepped forward and fired. He rammed in his load.

Red-clad soldiers raged ahead, stepping over their fallen comrades.

Jon's group quickly dropped several paces behind.

Christopher raised his rifle and took aim.

The British, coming into range now, did the same.

He pulled the trigger.

A musket ball whipped past him, knocking his tricorn off. Undaunted, he retreated several paces behind Jon to reload.

In the midst of the shooting melee, a horse whinnied.

Chris glanced toward the sound just as Colonel Hand's mount reared. A bright stream of blood poured down the right side of the colonel's face.

12

Just as Jonathan aimed his rifle, Colonel Hand's horse staggered clumsily into his line of fire. The animal snorted, dull-eyed, and came to a stop, blood streaming down its right shoulder and foreleg.

The colonel, bleeding profusely from a facial wound, reeled in the saddle. *Our leader's been hit!* The sounds of battle dimmed, lost in a strange fuzzy sensation inside Jonathan's head while he stared, frozen.

Robert Chandler appeared out of nowhere and caught the injured officer as the horse collapsed.

"Shoot, Jon, shoot!" Christopher yelled, bursting past him.

Jonathan, jarred back into action, fired at the nearest redcoats, the advancing scarlet horde a mere seventy-five yards away.

Musket balls zinged all around Robert and Chris as they carried the colonel to the rear.

Jonathan retreated quickly behind the line to reload. Out of preassembled cartridges now, he poured powder from the horn into the flashpan and down the barrel, then a ball. Ripping a strip of paper with his teeth, he jammed that in with his ramrod, trying to will his fingers to act nimbly while bullets and musket balls whistled all around him. The men in front moved behind him as he finished up, leaving him in the firing line.

The king's men weren't stopping to reload. With blood-chilling cries they charged madly ahead, bayonets thrust forward, determined to slash their way to victory.

Jon could almost feel the cold steel running him through. Heart pumping, he pulled both hammers at once, firing into the knot of scarlet rushing at him. Then he fell back at a run to prepare another shot.

At his side now, Christopher did likewise.

"The colonel," Jon blurted. "Is he dead?"

"No." Chris rammed a load into his barrel. "Looks like a nasty graze near his eye. Hasn't stopped him, though. He's still barking orders." Chris snapped the rod back into place.

The swath of red uniforms facing them had many gaps, but they pressed onward despite their tremendous losses. Bayonets gleamed in the sunlight, mirroring the deadly resolve in the British faces. One of them lunged for Jonathan, blade pointed right at him.

Suddenly a roaring cloud of smoke swallowed the redcoat, along with those near him.

Cannons! Two more explosions followed swiftly, decimating the charging British. Those still standing in the thundering confusion turned and bolted in hasty retreat.

Uncocking the two hammers of his rifle, Jon expelled a breath of relief and glanced around.

The second enemy regiment was also fleeing up a hill toward the post road and Stony Brook Bridge. American soldiers led by General Washington stormed after them in pursuit.

The British would be routed soon. Surely God had been with the patriots again.

❧ ❧

At first, the fact that both British regiments had surrendered within half an hour of the attack sent a wave of exhilaration through Christopher. Then he learned that most of the British Seventeenth, which had sent General Hugh Mercer's men fleeing, escaped down the post road to Trenton. In their wake, the brave general lay dead. Nearly half of the British

Fifty-fifth, who had tried to come to the aid of their Crown comrades, had fled through the far end of town. They were making haste for Amboy, unpursued. The American army was too weary to give chase.

Still, a victory was a victory. But Christopher's spirits plummeted when he heard that Nassau Hall, the massive building that held so many fond memories of his college days, was now occupied by the Fortieth Royal Regiment. He cringed as American artillery rolled up to the front of the three-story structure. Blasts to the walls of uncut native stone did damage enough, but cannonballs directed at the front entrance ripped through the huge doors.

Redcoats came pouring out of the splintered remains, their hands above their heads.

An unrestrained cry of victory rang through the ranks, and Princeton residents came pouring out of cellars and from behind stone walls to congratulate and thank the valiant patriots.

Christopher searched the gathering faces earnestly. "Do you see the Lyonses anywhere?" he asked Jonathan.

"'Fraid not. No sign of them yet."

Worried, Chris latched on to a townsman. "Mr. Appleton, please . . . Ma and Pa Lyons. Have they left town?"

The clockmaker ran a hand through his thinning hair. "Nay, lad. You know old Jasper. He wasn't about to leave his enterprise to them thievin' lobsterbacks."

"Maybe they're still down at the inn, then." He sought Jon among the crowd. "Come on! Let's go check the Lyons' Den!"

They raced past the snow-covered shrubs and up the graveled front walkway of the stone coaching inn, then burst through the heavy door.

"Ma!" Christopher hollered, his voice echoing through the long common room. "Pa Lyons! Are you here?"

No response.

Chris met Jonathan's gaze and shrugged. The fire that would normally be blazing in the wide hearth had burned down to embers, leaving an uncharacteristic coldness in the unlit common room. "Try upstairs. I'll take the kitchen."

Without wasting a second, Chris darted into the workroom. "Ma! You here?" But that, too, was deserted. Meat that had been left in the pans on the cooking hearth was burned black as coal.

A heaviness flooded through Christopher. Overhead, sounds of Jonathan's clomping echoed through the ominous quiet. He held his breath, waiting, listening to his brother-in-law's footfalls and calling.

Perhaps Pa Lyons did have the sense to take everyone to safety. Then Chris remembered the root cellar—the one spot that would have been safe from the cannonade. Tearing out of the back door, he went directly to the slanted trap door. The outside bolt was not in place. "Pa?" he hollered, pulling up on the handle.

It did not budge. Chris frowned and tugged harder. It was being held closed from inside. "Ma! Pa!"

Chris hoped it was his family, but he couldn't be too rash. Hundreds of redcoats had fled the battle, and some of them might still be in hiding—in this very cellar. He moved cautiously to one side of the opening.

Jonathan came out to join him. "Are they down in the cellar?"

"*Somebody* is, that's for sure, but they're not answering." Unslinging his rifle from his shoulder, Chris removed the powder horn.

Understanding registered on Jon's face, and he began loading his rifle as well.

"Barry! Grimes!" Christopher snapped in a distinct voice to nonexistent comrades. "You two cover the door from the sides. I'm gonna shoot through it. Jon, when I swing it open, you and Cooper stay low. Cover me."

"We may have a few more lobsters to add to the pot," Jon announced, joining the ploy. "Out of the way, Grimes, so I can get a clear shot."

Chris pointed his weapon at a crack in the slats beside the handle. He clicked back the first hammer, then the second.

Sounds came from below, as if someone had scurried away from the entrance to go deeper into the cavernous room.

Figuring that the door would swing open easily now, Chris stayed clear of the opening. He used the barrel of his rifle to reach across, sliding it under the latch.

"No!" a young female voice screamed. "Don't shoot!" But her next words were muffled in grunts and scuffling sounds.

Christopher recognized the voice as belonging to one of the twins. The enemy definitely had found the root cellar . . . and now held dear old Ma and Pa Lyons and the girls hostage! With a mighty jerk, he swung the squeaking door open wide.

Light flooded the rough-hewn stairs. The rest was a dark yawning void.

"Come out! Now!" he ordered. "We've taken the garrison. None of those puppets will come to your rescue. Toss up your weapons and come out with your hands up."

There was some whispering, some milling about. But no one complied.

Chris wasn't about to duck his head inside and have it blown off. He met Jonathan's troubled gaze.

Then feet clunked on the steps.

"Hey! Back here, or I'll shoot," a heavily accented voice commanded.

But a white mobcap kept coming, and beneath it the drawn face of Mrs. Lyons emerged. "Thank the good Lord!"

Christopher gasped and reached over to yank the short, plump older woman clear—this woman who had been the nearest thing to a mother that he and Mary Clare had ever known. The thought of how close she had come to having her life snuffed out angered him. "You could have been killed, Ma Lyons!"

"By them?" With a huff, she narrowed her small hazel eyes. "They can't afford to waste their loads on the likes of me."

"It was still foolhardy," he chided. "Move back." Hearing his own bossy tone, his ears reddened as warmth rose from his collar.

"The rest of you come on out," Jonathan ordered. "Weapons first."

"I ain't about to die down here like a rat in a hole," an English voice answered. A bayonet-tipped musket sailed out of the root cellar, followed by a soldier.

Jon picked up the weapon and crooked it under one arm, then took aim at the redcoat with his own rifle.

Next came a young redheaded girl, her green eyes wide with fright. She dashed straight to Chris and clung to him. Then, spying Mrs. Lyons, the slender redhead let go and flew into the older woman's waiting arms.

Further sounds of scuffling issued from the darkness. The innkeeper came barreling up the steps. Then another musket, followed by its owner.

Jonathan tossed Mr. Lyons the Brown Bess.

The white-haired man looked about in momentary confusion, as if surprised to find Christopher and Jon alone. Then he recovered. He lowered the musket toward the second redcoat and backed him farther away from the entrance.

"Comin' out," another voice hollered, and a third weapon sailed forth. Jon collected it while the uniformed man appeared, hands clasped above his head. Anger flared when he, too, realized they'd been outwitted. He glared at his cohorts.

One of the Englishmen shrugged, his eye ever on the sharp bayonet tip pointed at his midsection.

The latest arrival turned his head toward the open cellar and drew a breath as if about to yell down a warning.

"Go ahead," Christopher muttered menacingly. "It'll only take one shot."

The thin lips clamped shut. Meekly he moved to his countrymen's side.

"Sit!" Chris commanded. "The three of you. How many more are down there?"

"One."

"Don't take your eyes off them, Pa." He moved closer to the root cellar. "Come on out, or we'll blast you out."

"'Twould be most unfortunate," a cocky voice responded, "for this comely little sparrow, here. Wouldn't it, my pet?"

A harsh feminine gasp could be heard.

"Selina!" Mrs. Lyons cried. "Don't let him hurt our Selina!"

13

"Rather astute of you, old woman." The eerie British accent from the shadowy root cellar was even more frigid than the wintry air. Then the voice hardened. "The wench and I feel this hamlet is a bit too crowded and noisy for our taste. Right, my pet?"

"Ouch!" Selina's voice caught.

Her twin echoed the cry and buried her face against Mrs. Lyons's neck.

Rage overwhelmed Christopher. "You've no cause to hurt the girl. Let her go."

"—Or I'll run you through, you filthy British dog," Mr. Lyons finished gruffly, moving closer to the entrance. His wild shaggy brows met in an angry glower above his craggy face.

"I'd back off, if I were you." The officer moved into the light, one hand holding a pistol to the terrified fifteen-year-old's head, his other arm clenching her shivering form in front of him like a shield.

Selina's feet groped blindly for the steps as he forced her upward, his sheathed sword banging each rise of the stairs.

"I said back away!" the Englishman growled. "Unless ye'd prefer I blew a hole through this comely little head o' hers."

Chris could do nothing but stand helplessly by. He ground his teeth and waited.

The redcoat did not release his captive when he gained the top, but continued to hold her in front of himself. He glanced at the other soldiers huddled on the snowy ground in Mr. Lyons's impressive shadow. "Reclaim your Besses. I believe we've overstayed our welcome."

Jonathan's fists coiled in a moment of indecision.

"No!" Christopher yelled. Even an arrogant lobsterback would realize his only bargaining power lay in the single unspent bullet in his pistol.

The officer glared menacingly at Chris as if he might actually risk it. When Chris returned the glower with equal fervor, the man's face went slack. He inclined his head at his comrades with an offhanded shrug. "Methinks I'll not be able to take ye lads with me. Ah well, another time, perhaps." Dragging the terrified Selina along with him, he backed toward the big barn that normally housed stage teams.

Christopher slid a glance toward the thick forest directly behind the inn. Not only would it provide good cover for a fleeing man and his hostage, but the acquisition of a horse would make recovering the girl even harder. Men of the king's army were notorious for their callous misuse of maidens. The villain would have to be stopped—now!

Moving forward pace for pace with the retreating Englishman, Chris stayed within ten feet of him.

"Back!" the redcoat demanded, gesturing with his pistol. "Back, I say!"

Tenaciously, Chris kept on. Neither of them could afford to shoot as long as the twin was between them.

The girl's fright-filled eyes pleaded eloquently with Chris. At the edge of his vision he could still see Ma Lyons restraining the quietly sobbing Sarah within her heavy wool shawl. He bolstered his own resolve and pressed closer.

"Stay back, or I'll kill her, I swear." The officer backed through the wide doorway into the gloomy confines of the horse barn.

Since Princeton was the overnight layover between Philadelphia and New York, Christopher would have expected to find at least two coach teams put up until morning. But only Pa Lyons's old gelding Dandy occupied a stall. Chris figured the Crown must have confiscated all the coach horses the same way they had everything else in New Jersey that wasn't fastened down. But if the Englishman made good his abduction of Selina and escaped with their one and only horse, he could easily disappear before another mount could be located.

Numb with fear now, Selina went limp, coughing and gagging as she was dragged onward.

Her abductor bumped inadvertently into something behind him.

Christopher ducked in reflex, expecting a shot to ring out, but the man glanced over his shoulder and saw that the obstruction was merely a stack of supplies for the inn. He elbowed some of them over, scattering crates in his wake as he headed for old Dandy.

Chris's only hope was that Jonathan had thought ahead and circled around to cut off the officer's escape out the rear door.

A shriek pierced the tension. Christopher froze.

The redcoat swung his pistol toward the sound.

Chris saw his chance. He flung his rifle aside and dove for the man's weapon.

His own rifle discharged when it hit the ground at the same instant he and the Englishman thudded to the packed earth. They grappled for the man's pistol. That, too, went off.

A sharp pain seared through Chris's upper arm. *I've been shot!* He tried in vain to move. Clutching the man with his other hand, he glanced wildly down at his injured arm.

The tines of a pitchfork pinned it to the ground!

The officer broke Christopher's hold, but crashed backward. Jon loomed over him with a bayonet, and the redcoat spread his arms wide in defeat.

"Girl!" Jon told the other twin. "Get that blasted hay fork out of Chris's arm."

A small foot pressed lightly on his pinned arm, and Sarah gave the fork a hearty yank.

"Aaahhh!" A shower of stars exploded before Chris's eyes.

For a moment he could not catch his breath. He inched up and sat clutching the wound.

"I'm so sorry," the girl whimpered. "I-I was trying to get that awful redcoat." Biting her lip in dismay, she tore her apron off and wrapped it around the wound, coat sleeve and all, to stem the flow of blood.

It took Christopher several seconds to get beyond the burning pain enough to conclude that the scream that had distracted them had been hers.

"Hey!" Pa Lyons boomed as he came into the barn. "Everything all right in there? Anybody shot?" His beefy fingers raked hedgerows in his thatch of white hair.

Chris quickly located Selina, sprawled where the Englishman had dropped her, still trembling and weeping in dazed shock.

"No one's been shot, but we got *him*," Jonathan replied, jutting his chin. "Up, you no good miscreant."

Ma Lyons rushed straight to the sobbing twin, her round face mirroring the girl's distress. "Oh, my dear child. Are you hurt?" Bending down, she gently helped the distraught girl stand, then wrapped her shawl around Selina's shoulders.

Christopher managed to gain his feet and took over holding the wadded cloth to his arm. On the verge of berating the other twin for the attack, he saw that her face had turned as red as her hair. Neither she nor her sister had ever been able to look him clear in the eye since their first days at the inn, and now her lashes were even more downcast. He shook his head. "You might have gotten yourself killed," he chided.

She looked up with a grimace, almost meeting his gaze. "He . . . he was going to hurt my sister."

Chris knew it would serve no purpose to demean the girl's bravery—even if it was more than a little reckless. Someone had once told him twins shared a stronger bond than most other siblings. It must be especially true for a pair such as the redheaded Spaulding sisters, who were mirror images of each other, freckles and all.

Suddenly someone barreled into him from behind. Girlish

arms tightened about his neck in a near stranglehold. "I'll never—forget—what you did," Selina managed between sobs. "Never ever."

Despite his throbbing arm, it was all Christopher could do to keep a straight face. He'd be some time forgetting this day himself . . . the battles, balls whistling past his ears, cannonballs and grapeshot exploding all about—none of which singed a hair on his head. Then to have his arm run through by a mere slip of a girl—and have her sister well on her way to choking him to death. And all this in his own backyard.

From outside came shouts of other arriving Continental soldiers who'd heard the shots and come running. Chris relaxed and smiled as stout Ma Lyons peeled her young charge from around his neck. "Let's get inside, where it's warm," she said firmly. "We haven't even greeted each other yet."

Christopher allowed the older woman to sit him down in the kitchen and fuss over him in her usual motherly fashion. It brought back so many memories, watching her bustle around the room, filling a basin with water, taking out a clean rag, returning to see to his wound.

"Tsk, tsk." She wagged her head, new lines of concern blending with a myriad of others crisscrossing her face. She pushed the droopy ruffle of her mobcap out of her hazel eyes, then gingerly unwrapped Sarah's bloodied apron and helped Chris shed his ruined greatcoat. "Well, at least it bled good," she said in her practical way, assessing his arm. "That likely washed out most anything dirty from the hay fork."

"What if it didn't?" Sarah asked, her guilt accented by her speckled blush as she hovered near enough to peer over Ma Lyons's plump shoulder. Selina watched from afar, her green eyes bright.

The older woman shrugged. "Then I suppose it'll swell even more than it would otherwise."

"Oh, dear." With a sigh, the girl turned away.

"Stop your fussin', child, and do something. Get the fire going and set the kettle to boil. Selina, this basin isn't big enough. Bring me the biggest cauldron you can find, then go fetch some clean towels and a fresh sheet. And after that, one of you go and bring down Chip's old coat from the attic. This one's in need of mendin'."

"Yes, ma'am," they said in unison and hurried to comply.

"There's still a bit of hot water on the embers, Mistress Lyons," Sarah announced from across the room.

"Good. We'll use that," Ma Lyons said. When Selina set the large pot on the table, the older woman filled it with the water. "Bend your elbow, Chip," she told him, then plunged his arm into the pot so the entire wound was submerged.

The water made the open gashes on either side of his arm smart, and the blood flowed freely, reddening the fluid in the bath. The sight made him feel a little light-headed—and ten years old. Chip, his childhood nickname, seemed to fit again. He gathered himself together little by little.

"That will do for now." She gently eased his arm out and wrapped it in a towel. "Hold this in place with your other hand. Tight, so the bleedin' will stop. I'll whip up some herb salve real quick, now that the fire's goin' good."

"Thanks, Ma." Christopher grinned after her as she hustled away to the herb cupboard.

"Does it hurt much, Chris?" Sarah asked shyly, coming closer and staring at the reddening spots on the towel.

"Not as bad as when I broke it as a kid."

She smiled, revealing a dimple in her right cheek, then set about slicing cheese and smoked ham onto a plate.

Her sister poured milk from the clay jug into a glass and set it before him. "Mistress Lyons is mighty good at making sore things heal. I hope your arm gets better soon. It was so brave of you to risk your life just for me."

"Thanks." Flicking a glance from one fidgety lass to the other while he bit into the ham, Chris saw them exchange secret smiles. A dimple in Selina's left cheek reflected her sister's exactly. The two slyly feminine expressions added to Chris's discomfort. "It was Sarah who really was the brave one, you know," he told them. "If it weren't for her, that soldier might have gotten away." *With Selina,* he refrained from adding.

"Oh, yes, wasn't she daring?" Selina moved at once to give her sister a hug. "I was so proud of you, Sissy." But even in the embrace, she swept an adoring glance over Chris.

He looked away and gulped some milk. Hadn't it been a scant year past that those two were young enough to be toting dolls under their arms?

Heavy footsteps clomped from the common room, and the door swung open to admit Pa Lyons. "The place is fillin' up with hungry patriots. Best we set out some victuals to feed 'em."

With a sigh of relief, Chris watched the girls scurry off.

The familiar aroma of the concoction Ma Lyons was stirring over the fire drifted around the kitchen, the scent and sounds taking him back to his childhood. He glanced at the alcove under the stairs, where he'd slept as a boy after his own father had sold him and Mary Clare to the Lyons couple for a few bottles of rum. What a bedraggled pair the two of them must have been then!

All things considered, he thought with a smile, life with this old childless couple had more than made up for their rude beginning. Between Ma Lyons and the newly bonded Susannah Harrington from England, plus the friendly jests of the students from the college, he and Mary Clare had both come to understand the love of true friends as well as the abiding love of God. Eventually, through everyone's faithful prayers, even their drunken father had been touched by the Lord's grace and forgiveness. That knowledge meant nearly as much to Christopher as his own deep faith.

Yes, he thought, his heart filling up, this kitchen was a place of true love and kindness. It was home. His home.

Suddenly a shiver of fear ran through him when he considered what could have happened to this place and the people he loved. It was one thing to march proudly off to war, to encounter the enemy on an open battlefield—but seeing the conflict brought home was quite a different matter.

Suddenly Chris understood in a new way how desperate the

settlers on the frontier must have felt years ago when their farmsteads were attacked during the French and Indian War. Those who weren't killed outright—men, women, even tiny babies—suffered unspeakable tortures. Small wonder so few frontiersmen back then agreed to leave their families behind and go fight for the British. They had too much at stake to get caught up in another European squabble over vast territories neither French nor British leaders had ever laid eyes upon. Their refusal had earned the colonial men a reputation as cowards. Well, after this past week of valiant fighting, that old reputation would be changed.

"Now, then," Ma Lyons said, returning with the little pot of camphor mixture. "Let's see how you're doin'."

Christopher winked at her despite the throb in his arm.

"From that look on your face, it appears you're glad to be home, anyway." A warm smile belied the worry creases in her forehead as she carefully unwrapped the towel and studied the mean gashes. She sobered. "This must be kept real clean. Puncture wounds can fester quicker than most." With a wooden spatula, she slathered some hot goo over the gaping sore on his inner arm.

"Ow!" A quick intake of breath hissed through his teeth.

The older woman paid no heed. "Quit squirming. Here. Hold this." She placed a clean folded cloth over the gash. "Best not to let these scab over. Any poison that sets up will need to drain." Then she applied some of the foul-smelling ointment to the wound on the outer side and covered that, too, with a square of cloth. Finished, she wound long torn strips of an old sheet around his upper arm. "See that you keep these sores clean, y'hear?" She gave a playfully firm tug to his ear.

"Yes, Ma."

"And put some of this camphor salve on it every day without fail." She scooped the remaining ointment onto a square of oilcloth. "There's enough here to last a couple weeks. In fact," she added, "maybe you'd just better stay here, where I can look after you proper."

Two fair freckled faces turned from loading trays with food and eagerly glanced his way.

Chris cleared his throat. "You know I can't do that, Ma. I've signed on for a year with Colonel Hand. I'm sure Jonathan will help me take care of it well enough."

She regarded him steadily, then gave a grudging nod. "Well, I just better not hear about you losin' this arm over a hay fork. Understand?"

Christopher craned his neck and gave her plump cheek a peck. "I want you to take care of yourself, too. I wouldn't want a repeat of what happened here today."

The door to the common room swung open again. "Sarah, girl, get a move on, will ya? There's gonna be another uprisin' if these lads don't get something to eat soon."

The redheads picked up the trays loaded with bread and sliced ham, then with a last longing glance at Christopher, disappeared through the doorway.

Pa Lyons remained behind. "It's mighty good to have you home again, Son." A sudden narrowing of his faded blue eyes added more crinkles at the corners. "But let me catch you *ever again* acting as almighty foolish as you did today," he added, jabbing the air with a thick forefinger, "and I'll take a horse-whip to that backside of yours."

Chris averted his gaze.

"Speakin' of the *Almighty*," Ma Lyons interrupted, "get them old bones of yours over here, Jasper. Let's put our hands on this arm of our boy's an' ask the good Lord for some swift healin'."

The suggestion amused Christopher, but he didn't let it show. The innkeeper had a strong faith in God, but he wasn't one to talk about it much—and even more, not one to make a show of it. But some things were plain as day about the old man—including his devotion to his aging wife.

Pa Lyons hesitated, scrunched up his weathered face, then shut the door with a huff and came to the table. He covered Ma Lyons's hands as they held Chris's bandaged arm.

"Say the words," she urged him.

He glared at her.

Ma Lyons held her ground.

With a deep breath, the old blue eyes closed, and the shaggy head bowed. "Lord, you know what we be wantin' here. Take care of this boy, will ya? We'll be mighty obliged. He's the only son we ever had."

Christopher's heart leaped at those last words, and he felt a stinging behind his eyes.

Just then Jonathan burst into the room. He went right to Ma Lyons and seized her in a hug, then pumped Pa's big hand. "Just now rid myself of the prisoners, so I'm afraid it's how do you do and Godspeed. We gotta go."

The sound of drums could be heard in the distance, calling the soldiers to parade. Scuffling feet and chairs scraping back over the plank floor in the next room added to the growing ruckus.

"Ya just got here!" Pa Lyons said, clearly disturbed. "What's the hurry?"

Jon glanced at Chris. "Cornwallis is on his way. That mounted redcoat we saw on the road earlier must have high-tailed it straight to Trenton, just like we figured. I hear the whole army is fast-marching toward us, all ten thousand of them. Cornwallis is puffing and blowing and swearing about being outwitted."

Chris had been relishing the comforts of home, and he wasn't looking forward to the prospect of being on the move so soon. But one thought helped energize him. "That English general is fit to be tied, for sure. We whipped them real good. Again."

"Please, boy," Ma Lyons said, grasping him by his shoulders. "Don't go."

Pa Lyons gently pulled her away.

Chris looked from one loving face to the other. "You two do something for me, all right? Those miscreants will be here soon, and they'll be tearing mad. Promise me you'll leave this place for a few days."

"But they'll wipe out my stock!" Pa Lyons protested.

Knowing he could plead all day without changing the innkeeper's mind, Chris maintained a steady gaze. "Do what you have to, but at least make sure Ma Lyons and the girls go someplace safe."

"That I'll do. Esther, go get Sarah and Selina and take the path through the woods to the Bentleys' farm. I'll send for you when it's safe."

"I can't leave you here by yourself."

"Sarah!" Christopher hollered. "Selina!"

The pair came running.

"You're to take Ma Lyons and go over to the Bentleys'." He nudged the older woman firmly toward them. "And don't let her talk you out of it. I'm counting on you two to keep her there with you, hear?"

Two pairs of puppy-dog eyes grew soft.

"Go! The British are coming—and this time there's too many to stop." Chris yanked open the rear door and waved them through, all three snatching heavy shawls on their way. Then he clutched Pa Lyons's callused hand. "Take care of yourself. Please."

"You too, Son. And you, Jon. God go with you both."

Christopher gingerly slid his bandaged arm into the sleeve of the worn greatcoat he'd left behind when he'd joined the army. Then tucking the ointment into his haversack, he and Jonathan, rifles in hand, dashed out to join their battalion.

Partway up the road, Chris turned and took one last look at the coaching inn. His boyhood home was in jeopardy once more. *Please, dear God, keep your hand of protection upon the Lyons' Den and all who dwell within.* A story from the Old Testament flitted through his mind, encouraging him. . . . *And cause the Angel of Death to pass over this house.*

Jon also glanced over his shoulder. "I'm so glad my Mary is up in the valley right now, out of all this madness. The kids, too."

And Evie, Chris added silently.

14

April 1778

A year and a half had passed since Evelyn had seen Christopher—a year and a half since she'd first come to the Wyoming Valley. A year and a half of worrying, wondering, waiting . . . and trying to make the best of a difficult and uncertain time.

But now bright spring sunshine pushed the temperature higher, melting the leftover patches of gray white snow in the shade of trees and rock crevices. Evelyn and Emily were taking advantage of the mild spell to exercise a pair of green-broke horses.

Evie, astride a spirited two-year-old, laughed lightly. "Now that I've got this mama's boy out of sight of his mother, all he wants to do is go exploring." She tightened her hold on the reins to prevent him from bolting off into the groves lining either side of the path leading from the Haynes farm.

"All my filly wants to do is run," Emily replied good-naturedly, doing her best to restrain her own prancing mount.

"Well, we're almost to the river road. Maybe a race would run some of this energy off them. What do you say?"

Emily's lips curved into a challenging smile. "How about it, Penny? Think you can take that lazy Comet?"

"Ha! When I give this little fellow his head," Evie said, "the word *lazy* will be the last one you'll apply to him."

Her friend's green eyes sparkled as she swept a glance toward the Bradford place. "Let's race to Mary Clare's cutoff. We could drop in for a quick visit with her and Prudence."

The very suggestion made Evie wince. "The last thing I need on such a pretty day is to endure more of Mary's whining and complaining. You'd think we lived on the very edge of the wilderness with Indians lurking behind every tree and bush, instead of in the middle of a peaceful valley with three thousand other settlers."

"There's nowhere near that number, and you know it," Emily reminded her as they neared the road along the Susquehanna. "It's been well over a year since almost all the able-bodied men of the valley—including our own—went to join the war. And you know folks across the river have found moccasin tracks near their places, as if they're being watched."

Evelyn ran a hand over the stock of the Pennsylvania rifle in her sheath. "I'll wager I can hold my own with any Indian who dares to come around here." Christopher, when he returned, would be very proud of how hard she'd worked this past fifteen months to turn herself into the kind of wife he needed. *If* he ever returned.

"You've become a real frontier woman, I have to admit," Emily said. "You could probably outshoot and outride even Daniel Boone himself!" She glanced toward the river, high and swift now from the spring thaws, and laughed. "Just don't let me catch you going into town and trying to outdrink the men!"

Evelyn hooted. She reined her young horse around in the direction of Wilkes-Barre and gave a swift kick to its sides. "Race you there!"

"Hey!" Emily cried, left behind in the dust as the other pacer lurched ahead. "That's not fair!"

Evelyn didn't even look back. The wind tossed her curls, and the glorious feeling of freedom all but blotted out the memory of winter's long, stifling confinement as she flew along the road.

Finally she turned and saw that Emily, leaning low over the neck of her fleet-footed filly, was closing the gap. "Come on, Comet. You don't want that prissy little girl to catch you, do you?" Evie urged her horse faster around a bend.

Ahead, no more than a few rods away, she spotted two horsemen coming slowly toward her.

Evelyn pulled hard on the reins but to her dismay felt Comet turn his head and try to ignore her. She jerked harder, forcing him to obey. He slowed reluctantly, snorting and prancing wildly the whole time.

Having similar problems bringing Penny under control, Emily drew up even with Evie, and both of them automatically straightened their spines to more ladylike postures.

Evelyn gave a demure nod to the gaunt strangers and averted her gaze.

"Evie!" one of them gasped. "Emily!"

"Robert!" Emily wheeled her mount across Evelyn's path.

Comet reared, and Evie had to struggle to keep her seat.

One of the bearded, painfully thin men swung to the ground. He came up beside her and put a hand on Comet's bridle as the horse settled down. "Evie. It's me."

At the familiar glow of love shining from the depths of his blue eyes, Evelyn felt her knees grow weak. "Chris!" she squealed, flinging herself down to his open arms. "It's you. It's truly you! Oh, I can't believe it!" Laughing and crying and smothered in his embrace, she clung to him, loving the outdoor smells that adhered to his doeskin coat, the pounding of his heart against hers, the strength of his arms.

He smiled tenderly down at her for a breathless eternity, then lowered his lips to hers.

Evelyn had dreamed of this moment a hundred times, had longed for it every time she reread the seventy-nine letters he'd written. But the reality of it was far beyond her imaginings. She gave herself up to the glorious expression of his love.

Finally Christopher eased away a little and brushed a lingering tear from her cheek with his fingers. "Evie, Evie," he whispered, searching deep into her face. He drew her into another hard hug, and she felt him shudder.

"I can't believe you're home," she breathed. Pressed so tightly against his lanky frame, she began to realize how the war had ravaged him. He was little more than skin and bones. Her heart contracted as she thought of all the hundreds of hours it had taken her to perfect the art of caring for horses. She should have spent some of that time in the kitchen learning to cook.

Well, there would be time enough for that. She nuzzled closer and kissed him tenderly.

Suddenly Evie remembered that they were not alone. What would Emily and Robert think of her kissing Christopher right out in the open for all the world to see? She braced herself for their expressions of shock and peeked over Chris's shoulder.

But Emily and Robert were lost in their own reunion. Evie doubted either of them cared about anything or anyone else. She relaxed in Christopher's arms once more.

"I missed you so much," he whispered against her temple, then leaned to bestow a kiss on each eye. "I've thought of nothing but being here with you again."

"Me, too." Rising to tiptoe, Evelyn pulled him closer and raised her lips to his.

❧ ❧

Evie knew she'd never feel the same about the barn or its pungent smells again. She had volunteered to help Christopher unsaddle the horses, and they had taken a very, very long time to finish. But they would have to return to the house soon. She closed the gate on the last stall and turned. His intense gaze brought a flush of warmth to her cheeks.

He grinned. "You look . . . different."

"Different?" she asked breathlessly, suddenly conscious of the old split skirt she wore to work with the horses, her windblown curls, the calluses on her hands. She probably *smelled* horsey, too. Her blush heightened. If only she had known he was coming, she would have dressed in her finest gown, dabbed lemon verbena toilet water behind her ears, and welcomed him as a proper lady should. He must think her such a tomboy.

Chris leaned back against one of the pens and propped his heel on the lowest board. He nodded slowly, his blue eyes roaming her face. "You've done a lot of growing up while I was away."

Evelyn's heart skipped a beat.

He reached tentatively to brush the backs of his knuckles over her cheekbone, and Evie swallowed, pressing slightly into his touch. When he cupped her face in both hands, she had to close her eyes for the briefest second against a bittersweet ache in the center of her being. "Jonathan didn't figure you'd be apt to sacrifice your privileged life for one of hardship. And Ma Lyons told me I shouldn't set my sights so high, that I'd only be hurt." He paused. "I wish they could see you now. My beautiful Evie. . . ." He drew her near and brushed her lips with his.

Evelyn all but melted as she swayed against him, feeling the rapid throbbing of his heart, dizzy with the wonder of his kiss. When it ended, tears flooded her eyes. "Oh, Chris!" Her voice caught, and she could not go on. At last she collected herself. "We've got to go to the house now, before someone organizes a search party."

He flashed another grin. "You think they might figure we should have finished tending all four horses by now?"

"Those and the rest of the herd."

With a nod, he gathered her close to his side, and they strolled out of the barn. Halfway to the house, he bent to kiss her cheek.

Evelyn knew they were in direct view of the kitchen window, but she didn't see Susannah or anyone watching. She giggled and let herself enjoy the moment. "You know," she teased, "it really isn't proper for us to be doing this out in the open."

"Oh, really? What about this?" They had almost reached the porch step when Chris leaned down and nuzzled her neck.

Evie gasped and broke away. She quickly straightened her clothing and patted her hair into some semblance of normalcy. It wouldn't do for anyone to think the two of them had spent as much time kissing in the barn as they had unsaddling and feeding the horses. But recalling the suspicious look that Emily and Robert had turned her way when she and Christopher had volunteered to see to the mounts, Evie had to admit that at least two of the people inside would guess the truth. "Fix your shirt," she told Chris. "It needs to be tucked in better."

Chris, with a devilish grin, complied, then reached for the door latch.

"Wait!" Evie pulled him aside. "Do I look all right? Is my face flushed?" It felt warm to her hands. She moistened her lips.

Christopher's forehead crinkled as he studied her. "Hm. I'm not sure." He hauled her into his arms. "One more good kiss should set that to rights."

Evie didn't have it within her to care about propriety—especially during a kiss that curled her toes and left her breathless.

Then before she realized it, he yanked open the door and pulled her inside after him.

Susannah looked up from the sideboard, where she'd been preparing food. "Chip!" she cried, rushing to him. But she slowed to a stop a few feet away and pressed her fingertips to her mouth. "I rather expected Robert to be thin . . . but you're a rail." With a disturbed shake of her head, she came the rest of the way and hugged him. "Well, don't you worry, we shall see that the two of you get some proper meals while you're here."

It suddenly dawned on Evelyn that she had never gotten around to asking Christopher why he hadn't been eating—or even how he managed to come home after all this time without even a letter of notice. But they'd had other things on their minds out in the barn. She sighed and turned to him.

"Come, sit down at the table. You, too, Robert. You must be hungry."

Robert, across the room with his arms around Emily's son and daughter, smiled and gave a nod. With Emily close at his side, he stood and moved as one with his promised family to the kitchen table.

Christopher motioned for Evie to take the chair next to his, and she did so in haste, before Susannah's two energetic children grabbed it first. Looking around at the gathering, she saw that all eyes seemed glued to the two valiant soldiers. How foolish to have thought anyone would so much as notice her flushed face.

Chris claimed her hand under the table and held on tightly.

Susannah brought a tray of cold fried chicken and sliced bread and cheese to them. "It would seem provisions at Valley Forge must have been a bit sparse. Why ever did you not write and let us know? Folks here would have gladly donated grain and other goods. Even in the snow we could have packed supplies out by horseback with the saltpeter we women have been making for gunpowder."

Robert shrugged a bony shoulder. "We didn't want word to get back to the British about how poorly Congress was seeing to our needs. Even the local merchants were leery of honoring the scrip the Congress sent, and they would have had sufficient goods to keep us through the winter." He paused, and a glow came to his eyes. "There was one rather amazing miracle, though. It was on a dark, cold day as dusk approached. The sentinels pacing the outer lines gave a shout— and a cavalcade of kind women came through the snowy valley with ten carts full to bursting with food and other supplies. That sustained our hungry men for several days, and the rest of the time we got by with severe rationing."

"I'd hardly call a starvation diet *getting by*," Emily said, her tone flat.

"Well," he drawled, "after a man from Congress came to inspect the camp in February and saw that General Washington hadn't exaggerated about the desperate condition of the men, things improved somewhat. But enough about that. I just want to enjoy being here with you and the children for this one night." He swept a glance around. "And the rest of you, too, of course."

"*One night?*" Evie's spirit plummeted. She turned to Christopher. "You haven't come back for only one night, have you?"

A guilty look spread across his features. "I'm afraid so. Chandler promised his superiors we'd have Emily at his family's place in North Carolina and return to Valley Forge within one month. That will entail our covering about thirty miles every day."

Evelyn, surprised, swung to Emily. "You never mentioned this to me."

"Robert wrote that he wanted the children and me to spend time with his family after we married," she hedged, then shrugged. "But I . . ."

Robert placed a hand over Emily's and raised a level gaze to Evelyn. "I want Emily and the children to be somewhere safe. North Carolina has been scarcely touched by the war. And this area, as you well know, is quite vulnerable to—" He eyed the little ones and let the thought dangle unfinished.

Evelyn knew well enough that he referred to New York's Mohawk Valley. Not far to the northeast, the valley had been ravaged last summer by Indians, Tory rangers under the command of Colonel John Butler, and his British regulars from Fort Niagara.

"But our valley," Susannah said, obviously catching Robert's meaning herself, "is much more heavily populated. And better organized. No doubt only the more remote settlers and settlements face that sort of danger." She passed a plate to Christopher, then elevated a brow as she set another before Robert. "My dear Mr. Chandler, surely you do not expect me to allow our Emily to go with you all the way to your family plantation without benefit of marriage."

Robert laughed and raised his hands to ward her off. "With the lack of a certified minister in the valley, we spoke to the justice of the peace on our way through Wilkes-Barre. He's coming this afternoon."

"*This afternoon?*" Emily and Susannah gasped in the same breath.

But what about me? Evelyn railed inwardly. *Why can't it be me marrying Chris? Going off with him?* She turned her troubled gaze to him.

Christopher took both her hands in his, not bothering to hide the longing in his own face.

"Chip," Susannah cut in. "As soon as you've eaten, ride to Mary Clare's. Tell her and Prudence to come here posthaste. It would appear our Emily is to have yet another rushed wedding."

With a nod, Chris squeezed Evie's hands. "Come with me, will you? We need to talk."

Gratefully Evelyn rose. Nothing in this entire world could keep her from going.

❦ ❦

"The long winter made me forget how beautiful this country-side can be," Christopher remarked as they turned up the river road toward his sister's, "even before spring has completely taken hold."

Her mind overrun with anxiety, Evie gave only a cursory glance to the view. How on earth would they discuss all that was in both their hearts in a mere half mile?

"I'm not looking forward to facing Mare," Chris went on. "She'll be fit to be tied over the fact that Jon didn't come with Robert and me."

Having witnessed firsthand his sister's reactions whenever Dan had managed to come by during his duties as courier, Evelyn grimaced. "Well, since you know how upset she's going to be, stay objective. Just state the facts. Don't let her ruin the rest of your time here . . . time with me."

Chris turned a loving look her way. "My time with you is far too precious to waste a single minute."

"Then let's make it last longer," Evie blurted out. "Let me come with you to take Emily to North Carolina."

He grinned at first, as if the suggestion had been made in jest. Then, reading the sincerity in her face, his expression softened and became sad. "I wish you could. If only . . ."

"Well, why not? Why couldn't I?" Evie barely suppressed the pleading urgency in her voice.

A wry smirk crimped the corner of Christopher's mouth. "If Susannah would object to a widow leaving here with her betrothed, I wouldn't want to think how she'd feel if I so much as hinted about taking you, a maiden."

"She wouldn't have any objections at all . . . if we were married." Evelyn felt her insides go all quivery and forced the tremor to leave her voice. "We could make it a double wedding."

Chris's eyes widened at her bold notion. But his demeanor remained serious rather than hopeful. "Evie—"

"Please, Chris . . ."

"I'd like nothing better in this world, believe me." He reached across and placed his hand on her arm. "But it's not possible. I want everything to be right for us, do you understand? I want permission, a blessing, the whole of it."

Evie saw her dream fading.

"Of course, asking your parents is out of the question," he went on, "considering they're Tories in a British-held city. But even if they were patriots, what could I possibly offer you that would please them? I've yet to even speak to Morgan. He knows the dangers I face whenever we're called to battle— and he knows I'm an orphan with no inheritance and few prospects unless I complete my engineering course. He knows I'd have no way of supporting you until then."

Everything Christopher said made sense. Too much sense, if the truth were told. But that didn't make it any easier to bear. "I'll have you know I'm doing quite well supporting myself," Evie countered stubbornly. "And now that Emily will be leaving, Susannah will need me to stay here with the horses—at least until the war is over. So you see, supporting me is not really a problem."

Chris smiled gently. "And I'm so proud of what you've accomplished. In fact, I've been doing my best to come up with a way for us to be together sooner. I've asked to be transferred to the engineer corps. That way I could be doing some apprenticing even during this wartime."

The tiny ray of renewed hope enabled Evelyn to return his smile. "As I did with the horses."

"Exactly. But so far I haven't gotten an answer. My commanding officer seems most reluctant to let me go. In time, though, I'm sure I'll wear him down."

But I want now to be the time, Evie pleaded silently. Yet as she looked at Christopher, sitting tall and straight and confident despite his present rawboned appearance, she felt every inch as selfish and spoiled as Mary Clare always implied she was—especially knowing the pride Chris had taken in being promoted to sergeant in the riflemen's brigade. To think he would transfer out of it for her! She tried not to let her present disappointment color her voice. "I'm sure Robert has put in a good word for you."

"Too many, I'm afraid," Chris quipped. "That's why the colonel isn't about to part with me."

Another obstacle. Was there no end to them? "I'll write Morgan, then. My brother hobnobs with the high command all the time."

"No!" Looking chagrined at his own abrupt tone, Chris softened it. "Please, my beautiful Evie . . . you mustn't. If I'm to win your hand, I must prove myself worthy on my own first, then speak to him."

"I declare." Evie pouted. "You men treat a woman as if she were some grand prize to be won or lost."

"As you are." With a half-teasing grin, Chris nudged his horse closer to hers and captured her hand. "A prize I have no intention of losing." Raising her hand to his lips, he kissed her fingertips.

"Evie! Auntie Evie!" little Esther called out.

Evelyn suddenly realized they'd already reached Mary's clearing. And there was so much, much more to say. So many more arguments she could present in favor of their wedding today.

15

Lured by the aroma of fresh coffee, Susannah stopped rum-
maging through her wardrobe for the perfect dress to wear
for the joyous occasion and left her bedchamber.

A few minutes ago the children had persuaded Robert to
go out to the pasture and see the spring foals, and the
household had grown unusually still. Emily stood at the
hearth, pouring coffee into a mug.

"How thoughtful of you to make a fresh pot," Susannah
said. Crossing to the sideboard, she got out a mug for herself
while Emily sat down with her own. "Nothing like a quiet
moment in the midst of a hectic day." Filling her cup, she
crossed to join her sister-in-law at the table. "Is something
amiss? You look a bit pale."

Emily averted her glance as Susannah took a seat across
from her. "I . . . was just thinking about Robert."

"Ah." Nodding, Susannah studied the younger woman over
the top of her cup as they both sipped their coffee. "It was
rather a shock to see the evidence of the privation he and
Chris have endured through the long winter. Still, they both
seem in quite good spirits, considering."

"I suppose."

Susannah watched Emily toy with her mug, circling the rim
with a fingertip. "But . . . something else is troubling you, is it
not? I've noticed you've been rather . . . withdrawn, if I may

call it that, for some time. The endless months with our men so very far away have been hard for all of us, I know."

Emily finally met her gaze, her emerald eyes troubled and unsettled. "That's just it. I've had *two* Roberts to miss. My dead husband and my betrothed. Ironic, isn't it?" Sudden tears welled, rendering her unable to go on. "Sometimes . . . " she murmured at length, "sometimes I still feel I'm being . . . disloyal . . . to my first love. Almost from the very first moment we met, Robby and I seemed soul mates. I had no doubts that he was the man I was destined to marry. We were truly happy. He was a wonderful husband and father. . . ." Emily flicked a tear from her cheek. "And though he's been gone less than two years, I'm beginning to feel as if our whole marriage never happened, as if it was only a beautiful dream. How is it possible I could have loved one man so very much, yet so quickly have grown to love another—even to the point of thinking of becoming some other man's wife? It hardly seems . . . proper."

Susannah reached across the tabletop and placed her hand on her sister-in-law's. "I've no doubts, Emily dear, that you and Robby loved one another deeply. All of us in the family saw that from the very beginning. And it was difficult for us to understand and accept the loss of such a precious part of us. But we must constantly remind ourselves that our loved ones, first and foremost, belong to God. They are only on loan to us. Nothing ever happens that takes our heavenly Father by surprise. He knows each of us by name before we're born, and his Word tells us that all of our days are numbered before one of them comes to be. We might view Robby's life as having been cut short, but in God's eyes it was a life fulfilled. The Lord, in his infinite wisdom, knew the very day Robby's faithful service would be complete and he would be called home to his eternal reward. But that did not stop him from bringing the dear lad into your life and filling both your days with happiness and love. And now the Lord is doing the same thing for you again . . . bringing you a new happiness and love to carry on."

"Do you really think so? As much as I've tried to convince myself I have no right to those feelings within my heart for

Robert Chandler, and that I should be faithful to my first love, there's a part of me that wants to grab hold of this chance, clutch it to myself with everything that I possess. But what if something—"

"Shh," Susannah crooned, giving Emily's hand a comforting squeeze. "You mustn't borrow trouble. Our loving God made you the way you are, you know, and he's aware of the deepest needs of your heart. Just as he brought your first love across your path, so has he brought Robert Chandler."

"You mean . . . Robert is actually a . . . gift? from God to me?"

"As you are a gift to Robert. He, too, had to part with a very dear love, as you recall. But the human heart has a great capacity for love. A great need *to* love. Think of your children. Just because you adored sweet little Kathryn with everything your mother-heart contained when she was first placed into your arms, it didn't mean that when Rusty came along there'd be nothing left to give him."

The confusion in Emily's countenance disappeared, and her lips broke into a smile.

"So it is with the love a wife has for her husband," Susannah continued. "You'll never entirely forget Robby—any more than Robert will completely erase Julia from his past. First loves are incredibly special. But the two of you have been given a chance to move on, now, in a new and different love. Don't waste time comparing this to that, the old to the new. Just accept it, embrace it, be thankful for it. It's another special blessing from the Lord to his faithful children."

"That's beautiful." Emily lifted her eyes to Susannah. "You make a wonderful minister's wife . . . always knowing the right thing to say."

Susannah smiled gently. "Don't start polishing my halo just yet. I'm ever aware of my own faults and that I, too, am still learning to live the Christian life one step at a time. All of us must remember to seek the Lord's will every day of our lives and follow his leading to the very best of our ability."

Emily finished her coffee and rose to hug Susannah. "I

can't tell you how much you've helped me, Susannah. I've been torn so many times. But the things you've said make a lot of sense, and at last I feel at peace about this new step the children and I will be taking. Now I must go and start gathering our things together, before our noisy broods come charging in from the barn."

"Yes. We've a very busy day ahead of us. A least I've managed to unearth those slippers I thought you might like to wear with your gown."

❦ ❦

Christopher eyed the Hayneses' front door impatiently as he paced back and forth before the tiny porch. This interminable waiting for Robert and Emily's wedding to get underway was almost more than he could stand, especially when what he longed for above anything else was to spend this precious time with Evelyn. They hadn't had a private moment together since they'd gone to fetch the women and children at Mary's, hours ago.

Emitting a frustrated sigh, he glanced at Chandler. It was hard to believe the man could appear so calm as he chatted with storekeeper Franklin Meeks, who was also the justice of the peace.

Susannah's son, Miles, darted past Christopher with the other giggling children hot on his heels.

"Hey," Robert chided. "Slow down, all of you, before you fall and get hurt. And keep clean."

"Yes . . . Daddy," copper-haired Rusty said, collapsing into giggles.

"Yes, Uncle Robert." Miles's brown eyes grew solemn as he cast a furtive look at his playmates. "Let's go to the fence and watch the horses." He linked elbows with Rusty and led the way, while the bevy of little girls in a rainbow of ruffles and ribbons skipped happily behind. Katie, her black hair all in curls for the occasion, cast a sweet smile over her shoulder at her father-to-be as she went.

Mr. Meeks pursed his lips, lifting his jowls off his cravat, and turned to Robert to continue their conversation. "What do you think Washington will do to blow those lobsterbacks out of Philadelphia this spring?"

Christopher slid his gaze to the heavens. It was bad enough to have been banished from the house without having to listen to war talk. Why women insisted on this nonsensical trumpery over weddings was a mystery anyway—and something he was certain he and Evie would not be a party to when the day came for them to wed.

So many wasted hours. The slant of the sun was adding noticeable length to the shadows, and the stiff neckband of the borrowed shirt chafed his neck. Chris checked to see if Robert seemed equally uncomfortable in the ruffle-fronted shirt, black frock coat, and breeches Susannah had selected for him from Dan's wardrobe. A lot of good it had done to bathe and shave, anyway, when the women's next whim sent them to gather whatever forsythia they could find. That, of course, had been accepted by Prudence through the cracked door. Far be it from Morgan's Puritan wife to allow them a peek at the goings-on inside.

Christopher glanced at the cabin again, willing the door to open and someone to appear to summon them.

A curtain panel fluttered at the front window, and Evie gazed hopelessly out at him. Then suddenly, as if responding to someone's voice, she looked behind her. A last fleeting glance of disappointment, a wave, and the curtain fell back into place.

Chris sighed. There was more to Evie's disappointment than merely wasted time, he knew. But even if Susannah would have allowed their marriage to take place this day, Chris knew he must remain true to his own convictions. He did not want to cheat Evie out of her family's blessing—he was all too aware of the results in the case of Mary Clare and Jonathan. Not only had they been deprived of a loving relationship with his parents, but Jon ended up being denied his rightful place as first son. Though the couple did their best to act as if it didn't matter, Chris could see the pain in their eyes—especially at special family times.

Cheap land in Wyoming Valley had been all Jon could afford for them after being disinherited of a prosperous farm. It would be some time before he and Mary would be able to afford even the simplest of luxuries. And after years of hand-me-downs and charity, Chris would have preferred to see his older sister a little better established—perhaps like Susannah, who not only had brought some of her own nice things from England but was also surrounded by so many small comforts Dan had been able to provide.

Chris wanted more—a lot more—for Evelyn, who had never known the misery of an existence on scraps. He would not have her risk losing any more of her parents' favor than she had lost already by spying for the patriots.

A tugging on his sleeve captured his attention. "Uncle Chris." Looking down, he saw his five-year-old niece, Esther, her blue eyes huge beneath her flaxen hair. "Miles is trying to pull the flowers from my hair. Make him stop."

Inhaling deeply, Chris switched to a problem more easily handled.

❧ ❧

Susannah surveyed the room one last time—the lace-covered table with its bouquet of bright yellow forsythia, the plates of cookies, the softly glowing candles and beribboned flowers—and smiled. It was fitting for Emily's special day.

"It's all so pretty," her sister-in-law murmured in her airy voice as she came up beside her.

Susannah, determined not to cry, hugged her fiercely. It was hard not to remember another equally lovely wedding she and Dan had held for his youngest sister. That time, however, Emily was scarcely out of her girlhood; now she was a sensitive young woman . . . one who had suffered loss and risen above it, one who had no idea how radiantly she glowed with love and anticipation. The ivory dimity gown upon which Emily had labored so lovingly for months clung to her slender curves, the emerald-edged lace around the neckline and elbow-length sleeves adding depth to the green of her eyes. A crown of forsythia fashioned with trailing ribbons graced the clustered ringlets of golden hair. "Go into the bedchamber and wait until I call you. We don't want anyone to see how beautiful you are until the very last second."

Emily blushed and did as bidden.

Susannah then turned to Evie, who'd been tapping the toe of her slipper for several moments already. "Now, Evie. Now you may invite the others in."

"At last!" Evie adjusted the skirts of her orchid taffeta, one of the new dresses her brother, Morgan, had managed to send to her. She blessed him under her breath—even here in the wilderness she wanted to look nice for Christopher.

Finally satisfied with her appearance, she flew to the door and drew it wide. "Come in! We're finally ready!"

An instant stampede thundered across the narrow porch, and the children burst inside first.

"Not so loud!" Prudence shushed, pointing to her baby sleeping in the cradle. Mary Clare herded the little ones together, and right behind them, Robert and Christopher came through the doorway.

Susannah restrained a nervous giggle as Chris made a beeline for Evie. "Robert," she called as the tall dark-haired groom searched wildly about.

He didn't appear to hear her.

"Robert," she repeated, then catching his eye, motioned to him. "You come and stand right over here by the fireplace."

He repressed an impatient scowl, then complied.

"Chip," she ordered gently. "The best man stands next to the groom."

With some reluctance, Christopher dragged himself away from his own dazzling love and took his place.

Susannah waited for all the shushing and murmurs meant to quiet the children, then nodded to Evelyn to fetch the bride. Only then did she realize that all too soon, Emily would be gone. They had been together constantly in the past year and a half, ever since her sister-in-law had arrived with the horses. And the two had formed a deep family bond. Without Emily around, the place would seem very lonely indeed.

A pity the same sort of relationship had not developed between Evelyn and Mary Clare, she thought. But those two seemed to have little in common. Perhaps one day that would change.

Evelyn returned to the room sedately and fluffed her skirts as she took her position opposite Christopher. Then all eyes turned toward the open doorway of Susannah's bedchamber.

Emily moved into it and paused briefly while she sought her husband-to-be. With a tremulous smile she emerged and slowly came to his side, a translucent flush tinting her cheeks.

In spite of the dozens of weddings Susannah had seen performed since she and Dan had been married, she never ceased to be amazed by the way a man's breath would catch, the look of wonder that would flood his countenance upon first sight of his bride. And Robert Chandler held a special place in Susannah's own past, as the husband of Julia, her closest childhood friend. Susannah could have cried when she witnessed the way his eyes softened as he held out his hand to the lovely vision before him. Their eyes locked and held, almost like a kiss. The fragrant yellow nosegay trembled in Emily's fingers, the only visible sign of nervousness, as her delicate features remained composed. Then she and Robert turned to face forward.

Mr. Meeks cleared his throat and swept a glance over the gathering to signal that he was about to begin. He opened a small black book. "Dearly beloved, we are gathered here in the sight of God and these witnesses to unite in the bonds of holy matrimony Robert Chandler and Emily Haynes MacKinnon. . . ."

As the familiar words were read, Susannah couldn't help but recall her sister-in-law's first wedding, an equally rushed but equally happy occasion. Who could have known how short that union was destined to be? And how marvelous that God, in his great love and wisdom, had provided this second blessing for two of the dearest people in her world.

She turned her gaze toward Prudence and Mary Clare, both of whom were in tears. Susannah's own heart caught, and she had to blink several times to contain her emotions. Prudence had not set eyes on Morgan since the birth of their son, David, and Mary Clare's separation from Jonathan went back even further, to the day he'd gone off to war. Having just been promoted to sergeant of a company, Jon had been unable to obtain leave and had to remain at camp to train a new batch of recruits.

But one young couple at this gathering, Susannah noticed, paid no particular attention to anything but each other. Chip and Evie were gazing boldly and longingly at one another from either side of the bride and groom. So many letters had passed between the two while Chris was away, it was amazing there had been room left over in the freight wagon for supplies. But Susannah felt assured it had been best to keep the lovesick pair apart for most of the day—especially considering Evelyn's reckless nature, not to mention her dreadful lack of concern over her walk with the Lord. Should their feelings for one another last, Susannah felt that spiritually the two were unequally yoked. In the meantime, she would do her utmost to be a proper chaperone until Chris and Robert left to escort Emily and the children to North Carolina.

"Do you, Robert, take Emily to be your lawfully wedded wife?" The words drifted across Susannah's consciousness.

"Yes. I do." The rich timbre of Robert's voice gave added emphasis to the vow.

"And do you, Emily, take Robert to be your lawfully wedded husband?"

"I do." She caught her lower lip in her teeth as she smiled into his eyes.

"Then, by the authority vested in me by this commonwealth, I now pronounce you man and wife. You, er, may kiss your bride."

Their smiling gazes met for a heartbeat, and Robert gathered Emily into his arms.

16

Evelyn closed the gate of the corral, pleased at how quickly she had accomplished the chore of saddling horses to carry the family to Sunday meeting. More than a year of helping Emily look after the strawberry roans had honed her first clumsy attempts to a fine skill. Now, barely two months after Emily had married Robert and gone to her new home, there was almost nothing Evie couldn't do for the horses on her own, from birthing mares to putting down an injured beast. Brushing the lingering dust from her palms, Evie looked down at her hands. Once soft and white as lilies, the tapered fingers now were lean and brown, her palms strong and rough. *Mother would find the change appalling, no doubt—even shocking.*

At the thought of her Tory mother and father still residing in the "Red Brick City" of Philadelphia, Evelyn's brows dipped into a frown, and she gazed off to the southeast. If only she could risk corresponding with them. But Morgan, adamant about how easily a letter could be traced to its source, had forbidden it. Evie wished she could know how they and their merchant friends were faring since last fall, when the prosperous port had fallen under British control . . . whether her and her brother's spying activities had ruined their parents' social standing . . . if things were running smoothly in their business.

Her own position in the Wyoming Valley left quite a lot to

be desired, Evie conceded with disdain. With all the squab-bling going on over who had legal claim to this picturesque river plain—the Pennsylvanians or the numerous settlers from Connecticut—her links to Philadelphia had far from endeared her to the people of Wilkes-Barre. But in truth, Evie hardly cared. The prominent "holier than thou" attitude of the Baptists and Presbyterians chafed against her own High Church upbringing . . . and here it was, the Sabbath *again*. Sometimes it seemed there were two of them every week.

Evie expelled a resigned huff. She had to put up with it—for Christopher. After all the horrendous defeats Wash-ington's army suffered last summer, not to mention Chris's thinness from lack of rations, she had no right to complain. The loss of Philadelphia might have made the patriots give up in defeat, had it not been for the victories of the northern army in upper New York.

A part of Evie harbored the secret wish that General Wash-ington and his force *would* give up. Chris and Robert had been able to spare a mere twenty-three hours here when they had returned for Emily and her little ones.

Even though she did not begrudge the couple their happi-ness, Evie had not been able to overcome feelings of envy whenever she thought of the wedding. Two people who had sustained such heart-wrenching losses deserved whatever happiness came their way.

Well, one day—hopefully soon—she'd be the frontier wife and homemaker she dreamed of being. Besides caring for the animals, she had learned to plant and tend a garden, harvest, and put up food for winter. Now she was concentrating on cooking.

And though she had not been able to wed Chris that fateful day, he had requested a transfer to the engineers. Perhaps he would learn enough that he wouldn't have to return to col-lege, enough to be able to provide for them immediately at war's end.

Evie smiled at the memory of the first sweet moments the two of them had enjoyed in the barn, when they'd stolen away on the pretext of putting away the horses. Her glance flew unbidden to the weathered farm building, and a warm flush crept over her cheeks. Even as he had kissed her, he kept mentioning how much she had changed.

He had changed, too. He seemed taller, with new fine lines beside his eyes. And in those dusky blue depths there lurked painful things he'd likely never share with her. But what they had imparted was incredibly precious. She let herself relive their last tender moments, the wrenching moments just before he rode off. . . .

"Oh, Chris . . . I wish you didn't have to go. I'm so lonely when you're not here."

"I always feel as if you're with me." A small smile played over his mouth as he lifted her chin with the edge of an index finger. "Your letters—I keep them in my breast pocket. A part of you, right next to my heart." Taking her hand, he kissed it lightly, then pressed her palm against his chest.

"And I have you with me always, too." She smiled, and with her other hand, extracted letters from her skirt pocket. Their gazes locked and held.

Chris drew a deep shuddering breath. "I heard talk in the settlement about the local militias being sent back up here."

"It wouldn't surprise me. People in this area are getting more skittish by the day. So much Indian trouble in upper New York. And lately, cows and pigs have been disappearing from the farmsteads closest to the wilderness. No one knows if it's Indians, but they seem to be taking the blame. As I wrote you, some of the Seneca leaders came through Wilkes-Barre on their way to the peace conference down in Easton the winter before last."

Chris regarded her steadily.

"They seemed sincere and all," Evie went on. "Not in the least savage. Wore the grandest robes, with great sunbursts and such, and everything else they had on was trimmed in beads and feathers. They were truly regal looking. Very grand, compared to the homespun folk around here. It's hard to believe they're capable of such atrocities as we've heard."

"We were told at the mercantile that Zeb Butler came home on leave and then left to report the valley's fears to Washington. He's going to request that the Wyoming Valley militias be transferred back here. And if they are, they'll need engineers to direct the building of more fortifications. Now that I've put in for a transfer to the engineering corps, I might return sooner than you think."

"You will? Oh, Chris!" Joyfully, Evie grabbed his arms.

He kissed the tip of her nose. "In the meantime, I want you to keep a lookout. Will you do that for me?"

Nodding, she reveled in the feel of his warmth beneath her hands as she moved them up to clasp behind his neck.

Christopher plucked a piece of straw from her willful curls and slipped it into his pocket. "Another keepsake," he whispered. "This one to bring to mind those shimmery blue eyes of yours, soft and dreamy as they are this moment." His mouth descended to hers. . . .

"Evie!" Susannah's voice came from the porch, interrupting her musings. "Do hurry. Pru and Mary Clare will be here any minute—and you've not even dressed yet."

With a low groan, Evie compressed her lips. If only she could think of some logical excuse to stay home. But over the past year or so she'd already used every single one she could possibly conceive. It was so much more pleasant to be left in solitude to recall those special moments with Chris, to feel beneath her fingers again that lock of sandy hair that fell over his forehead, to breathe deeply of his musky outdoor scent, remember his every . . .

"Evie!"

The rattle and rumble of a horse-drawn wagon caught Evelyn's attention. Up the path, she could see Prudence and Mary Clare emerging from the woods with their children. Here they came to accompany them to church, all of them dressed in their best spring finery. *Already!* Had she spent that much time daydreaming again?

Snatching up her skirts, Evie dashed for the house.

❦ ❦

Evie had hardly time enough for a slapdash scrubbing with a damp rag. It would do little to remove the odor of horses, but nothing could be done about that. Over the muffled yet lively chatter of the women and children out in the main room, she tossed on her newest Sunday-go-to-meeting dress, an apple green linen, then ran a quick brush through her curls. Her good slippers weren't in sight, so she probed beneath the bed with one stockinged foot. They had to be there somewhere— they weren't in her wardrobe.

A toe finally located one. Evie dropped down and pulled them both out, then sat on her rumpled bed to slip them on. She sincerely hoped Mary Clare wouldn't come in and glimpse the complete disorder of her room, with clothes strewn haphazardly about and the bed still unmade. Though Christopher's sister had never actually made any comments about Evelyn's lack of tidiness, Mary's expression more than conveyed her disapproval whenever she popped her head into the room in greeting. At times like this, Evie most missed having a maid, as she'd had throughout her younger years, to look after such mundane chores. Besides, why should one spend time making the bed when the whole thing would only get messy all over again in a few hours, for heaven's sake?

With a last pat to her hair, Evelyn rushed out of the room to join the others, tugging the door closed behind her.

But the women lingering around the table over cups of coffee looked up and smiled. Prudence's arms cradled energetic eleven-month-old David Morgan Thomas to her breast, where he nursed contentedly behind a light blanket draped over the shoulder of her calico frock. She lifted her chin. "Evie, dear, your skirt is hiked up in back."

Evelyn felt a gentle tug, and the gathers fell over her

petticoat. She turned to see Miles walking away to resume his seat on the floor among the other children.

"Miles!" came Susannah's decidedly British reprimand. "A proper young gentleman never touches a lady's gown."

The boy reddened up to his ears. "Sorry, Mum," he muttered, flicking an embarrassed glance up at Evie.

Evelyn had a special fondness for the oldest child, and she leaned down so only he could hear her whisper. "But a young man does eat rock candy whenever possible."

Eyes the same sable brown as his father's brightened at the reminder of the secret Miles and Evie shared—she always slipped him sweet treats when he began to fidget during the seemingly endless sermons at church. His chest puffed out with importance, and he resumed his play with his younger sister and Mary's two little daughters, who looked like wildflowers in their soft pastels.

Evie sneaked a peek to see if any grown-ups had overheard and saw that they hadn't.

Susannah's attention was focused on her guests. "Prudence," she began. "You remember my brother's wife, Jane, don't you? Well, yesterday Nathan Denison came by with a letter from her that arrived in a packet from Connecticut."

Prudence's light gray eyes lit up at the word *packet*, then dimmed as quickly upon hearing the Connecticut source. "Oh. Then there was nothing in it for me. Or Mary."

"No, dear, I'm afraid not. Nor from my Dan. Still, it's the first I've heard from my sister-in-law since last fall's battles up north. According to her, Ted received a bit of a leg wound at Bennington, and while on the mend, he took leave to escort her and the baby out of that back country and down to her sister's in Worcester. I was rather relieved to get word from her. The war has rendered our postal system nearly nonexistent."

Prudence nodded grimly. "We've been more fortunate than most, though, with Morgan being so resourceful in finding men to bring our mail."

"Not resourceful enough to get my Jonathan home since he

left," Mary Clare complained. "Dan, being a courier, has been here several times. And Morgan somehow managed to sneak away for the birth of little David. Even Robert and Chip came." She released a disappointed sigh. "It's not fair. And you heard the announcement last week," she added, her voice rising. "The British and their Tory rangers at Fort Niagara have started south—and may be coming this way aided by a horde of savages!"

Evelyn shrank from Mary's whiny tone. Supposedly the girl hadn't been a crybaby before Jonathan joined the patriot army, but Evie had her doubts.

"Now, Mary," Prudence cajoled. "We heard that very same rumor last year, when the English marched down from Canada. Yet our boys managed to capture Burgoyne's entire army."

Mary pouted. "Well, we don't *have* any of our own boys here. Only old men and lads still wet behind the ears. I wish Jon had never gone away."

"Well, Colonel Butler's men should arrive any day," Evie piped in. "You did write and ask Jon to transfer to Butler's militia, didn't you?"

Mary's thin face scrunched with fear. "How much comfort could there be in Jon's return then, with all of us in dire peril?"

There seemed to be no consoling the girl, Evie concluded wearily. Even the children ceased playing and were staring. Talk of the war was terrifying enough to the little ones without adding the scare of Indians.

Evie snatched the covered plate of cookies from the sideboard and brought them to the table, despite the fact that they were intended to be an after-dinner treat. She whipped off the napkin. "Here, try one of these, Mary. Susannah thought you'd especially like them."

Mary Clare swung her gaze up at her as if Evie had lost her mind.

"They're particularly good when dunked," Evie added,

placing one in Mary's hand. Then she turned to the children. "Aunt Susannah made four extras, too, just for you."

Julia Rose, Susannah's youngest, looked from Evelyn to her mother, and her big blue eyes grew wide. "But—but Mama said we must wait—"

"For company, sweetheart," Susannah interjected. "Each of you may have one."

With a giggle of delight she grabbed the nearest treat from the proffered plate, and Esther and Beth joined into the giggles as they followed suit. Miles took time enough to study the remains before choosing the biggest.

Evelyn couldn't help but smile at the boy. As her own mother was so fond of saying, Wisdom comes with age.

As Evie turned back to the women, Susannah mouthed a silent thank you. "Don't forget our other guest," she said cheerily. "I've never made these before, Prudence. They were Felicia's specialty. And how I do miss her—letters from the Virginia frontier are even fewer than anywhere else. As scarce as—what is that phrase you're so fond of, Mary?" She helped herself to one of the treats.

"Scarce as chickens' teeth."

"Quite. But I also understand Felicia's feelings in the matter. With Yancy off to sea on a privateer, she would naturally experience a need to be with her aging father."

"And a *need* to be near a large fort chock-full of militia," Mary added in a waspish tone. "Even that commander Christopher bragged so much about, General Hand, took a post there. He and the *men* at Fort Pitt will see to it no harm comes to those settlers."

That woman can bring any subject right back to her own fear, Evie thought, turning away before she said something uncharitable. She broke off a piece of cookie and placed the plate back on the sideboard. "Oh, my. It's getting late. If you've finished nursing the baby, Pru, we'd best be on our way to service." She gently wedged the broken treat into the dozing babe's pudgy hand.

Little David stirred and came to life as the cookie and his hand vanished beneath the edge of the blanket.

Prudence tipped her head in resignation and began closing her bodice as the little one bit into the sugary sweet. "Now he's sure to become a sticky mess."

Evie only smiled. Anything was better than listening to Mary Clare's constant griping. She motioned for the kids to get up and ushered them to the door. "Come help me fetch the horses, Miles." On her way out she grabbed her rifle and Susannah's to slide into the saddle sheaths. These dangerous days they were never without them.

The boy grinned and took off running toward the tethered mounts out in the corral. Like the rest of the Haynes family, he had acquired a deep love for the Narragansett Pacers. He reached the fenced enclosure first. "Oh, no! Look at that!" he exclaimed in dismay.

"Where? What?" Mary Clare cried in panic from the doorway. As always.

"Firefly, my colt." He pointed into the big pen.

Evie, not far behind him, moved to the fence rail. The mischievous yearling had somehow managed to slice a long gash directly above his rear hoof, and it was bleeding badly. As soon as she tended the wound she'd have to locate the object responsible before the troublesome colt cut his whole foot off. She wagged her head in disgust.

"What's amiss?" Susannah asked, coming toward them.

Evelyn turned. "It's Miles's colt. He's injured his pastern quite severely. I'm afraid I'll have to stay and tend to it."

"But he will be all right, won't he, Auntie Evie?" Miles asked, his little-boy voice fearful.

Evelyn smiled at the pet name he'd used. His mother disliked having him call adults by their first names, so it was either *Aunt* and *Uncle*, or *Mr.* and *Mrs.* "He'll be fine. I promise." Having stowed Susannah's rifle, she placed the reins of the two saddled pacers into his hands. Her own long-legged hunter she led back to tie to a rail. "Now scoot along, or you'll be late."

Susannah searched the woods beyond the clearing. "I don't like leaving you here all alone."

"I'll work quickly," Evie assured her, "then ride fast. I may even catch you before you reach Wilkes-Barre." Winking at Miles, she patted the rock candy in her pocket.

A few minutes after they had left, Evelyn realized the colt had done her a huge favor, and her anger over his deep cut began to subside. But that didn't stop her from recoiling at the way the injury gaped with Firefly's every step. She led him into a barn stall and looped ropes over his head to secure him on either side, then patted his muscular neck. "Here I've been haranguing at you when I should have been thanking you. If I take my time, I won't have to sit for hours on some hard bench in the town square and endure the droning of yet another tedious sermon. Plus, my pet, you've rescued me from the ride into town with Mary Clare."

Knowing that her voice would help keep the colt calm, Evie continued talking aloud while she went to fetch the medicine box from near the front door. "I swear that woman was whining worse than a Wyoming Valley gale this morning. And you know what those are like. We suffered through more than our share last winter. It's such a relief that summer's here."

Returning, she set the open box down on the straw-covered ground, then reached for the oozing foot.

The leggy animal nervously sidestepped her grasp. She made another attempt but to no avail. "So, it's going to be like that, is it?" Evie eyed the sorrel colt straining against the neck ropes, its nostrils flared. "I see," she said in her most soothing voice. "Well then, I'll have to take this real slow. Slow and easy." Stepping smoothly toward his head, she remembered the rock candy in her pocket. She pulled a piece out and offered it in her palm.

Firefly sniffed the treat, then engulfed it with rubbery lips.

"Good, isn't it?" Evie cooed. She smoothed her hands down his neck and along his sides and flank.

The colt crunched down on the candy.

So far so good, Evie told herself. Her hand continued over the hip and thigh.

His skin gave a nervous twitch.

"That sure was sugary sweet, huh?" she said, moving her hand in circles where it was. "Nice sweet candy." Offering him a second piece, she rubbed a few more circles, then gradually worked her way downward.

Hearing the grinding noises again, she took advantage of the moment to move down to the fetlock. "Nice sweet candy. Sweet, sweet candy." Only inches remained between her fingers and the cut above his hoof. "I'll just try to put a bandage on for now, if you can stay still long enough. Think you can do that for me? Then later, when Susannah comes home, we can medicate it. I'm sure she can keep your attention with a twitch to that lip of yours."

Evelyn kept one hand on his fetlock while she reached for the roll of stripped sheeting with the other. "Then you'll discover how much fun it is to have a hunk of your lip twisted in a noose, won't you," she singsonged.

Firefly kicked.

Dodging the sharp hoof, Evie went sprawling onto her behind, wincing at the stinging in her hand, while the fool horse pranced about unmindful of further damage to the injury.

Evelyn gritted her teeth, stood and brushed off her skirt, flexing her bruised hand. "Yes, it's going to be like that, I see." Her gaze fell upon a loose board, and for a second she considered applying a stout whack to the stupid colt's head. "That would calm your miserable hide," she muttered.

The animal flinched, and she exhaled in defeat. There was no way she could handle the flighty colt by herself. She'd have to ride after Susannah and fetch her back to help.

Taking care not to make any sudden moves, Evie slowly stooped down and tugged from the medicine box the thin, tightly woven rope Emily had taught her to use as a twitch. She began fashioning a loop. As she did so, she heard approaching footsteps crunching across the straw.

She smiled with relief. Susannah must have read her mind. "Over here. This silly colt would rather bleed to death than have me touch him." Finished with the loop, she rose and turned to hand it to Susannah.

But no peaches-and-cream complexion met her gaze. A blackened face striped with vermilion paint peered down at her through malevolent eyes.

17

Evie's heart jolted to a stop, then contracted painfully, hammering against her ribs. Her eyes fixed on the hatchet he held, raised to strike, and she steeled herself against the horrific blow.

The Indian hesitated, his intense gaze fixed on hers.

The rifle, she thought wildly. But it was in the saddle sheath. And she was trapped in a horse stall. *Think. Don't panic. Bluff—and make it real.*

Evie spread her lips in a broad smile. "Oh, thank goodness. Someone to help." She shook her head in a gesture of relief. Trying to dismiss all thought of the poised tomahawk, the odor of bear grease from the sleek painted skin, she pointed at the colt's bleeding pastern.

The young brave's glance darted to the injury on the nervously prancing animal. His eyes widened a fraction.

"Please," Evie said evenly. "It needs to be bandaged." To the Indian, the horse of the white man was a great prize. Surely he would want to save it—if only for himself. But to Evie's dismay, she realized he didn't understand her words. She tried exaggerated hand motions to act them out. When he didn't move, Evie made her wobbly legs take a cautious step backward, still holding his gaze.

The feathers dangling from the tomahawk fluttered. His knuckles whitened on the handle.

Evelyn quickly held out the thin loop of rope, praying that

her hand wouldn't tremble and give her away. "I need you to twitch the colt's lip." She grabbed her own and pinched it in demonstration, then tipped her head toward the pacer.

The paint-slashed forehead scrunched into a frown. Obviously he hadn't the slightest idea what she was saying.

Evie's chest clenched around the rapid thrumming of her heart. How could she bluff her way out of this if she couldn't make him understand what she needed him to do? If she could just move him deeper into the stall. Past her, past the almost grown colt. Stepping back again, she summoned him with a curl of a fingertip.

The black eyes became slits. He did not move.

Dredging up another measure of courage, Evelyn knew she had to convey the urgency of the situation. She turned on her heel, and with every nerve in her body anticipating the crash of the cold sharp blade, she stepped to the animal's head.

Firefly, as if sensing the danger closing in on them both, panted even more heavily and jerked harder against the neck constraints.

The Indian edged cautiously into the narrow space and along the side railing after her.

It took every ounce of Evie's willpower not to take her eyes from the colt, not to stare at the savage's still upraised blade. "Pretty boy," she said softly. "Nice boy." She hated the slight tremor in her soothing tone. With the loop poised in one hand, she grabbed for the horse's muzzle with the other.

Firefly yanked his head away.

A few choice words Evelyn had heard on the Philadelphia docks popped into her mind, but she resisted the impulse to blurt them out. "Be Evie's nice boy," she crooned instead.

The painted intruder loomed closer. A head taller than she, he cast deeper shadows over her. Hatchet feathers fluttered into view at eye level.

With grim desperation, Evelyn snatched a hunk of Firefly's rubbery lip and looped the rope around it, cinching it hard. She tugged with all her strength.

The pacer's eyes bulged, but he froze.

Thank Providence. "Come." Evie tilted her chin, coaxing the near-naked brave closer while she kept the tension taut on the colt's sensitive lip. "Come. Take." She eyed the twitch, then the Indian.

He followed her gaze. Understanding dawned, and his confused expression turned to fear.

Good. Evelyn leveled a look of challenge at him. She'd heard somewhere that cowardice was an Indian's greatest shame. Surely he wouldn't kill her until he'd proven he wasn't a coward. "Take it!"

The black eyes shifted back and forth as if he were the cornered one. He sucked in a breath, then tucked his weapon into the waist of his leather breechcloth. He closed his hands over the rope just below hers.

Firefly, even more frantic now, flared his nostrils and strove to free himself from the painful hold.

Evelyn slipped her first hand away, then the other, and watched the brave's arm muscles flex as he strained against the colt's great strength. She stepped backward toward the open gate of the stall, squelching her instinct to bolt and run. She needed somehow to catch that savage off his guard.

Start doctoring the horse, she told herself. *Then get down low, out of his view.*

Her foot banged against something hard. The medicine box. Stooping before Firefly, she slid it within reach. "Isn't it fortunate," she rambled softly, as much to calm the Indian as the colt, "that a horse can concentrate on only one thing at a time. And right now you and that twitch are it."

Evelyn removed a container of salve from the partitioned medical chest, opened it, and dipped in three fingers.

The pacer lurched and kicked.

The hoof just missed Evie as she dodged out of the way and fell on her backside. "Hold him!" she railed, glancing angrily at the brave.

He muttered something unintelligible, then concentrated his efforts with added determination.

Evie felt a tiny bit of hope. The colt's sole attention was

once again centered on its lip, and the Indian's on his job. *Good.* She just might save herself yet. He would have to let go to charge after her, and when he did, Firefly just might keep him penned long enough for her to get to the rifle.

But she'd better at least make it appear as if she actually was doctoring the horse. She brushed some bits of blood-soaked straw from the left pastern, then gooped on a generous portion of the ointment.

So far so good . . . only she hadn't quite managed to maneuver herself out of the Indian's view. She didn't have to look up to feel his gaze shift often her way.

Returning the tin of salve to the medicine box, she removed a thick roll of bandage. It came to her that the wooden chest, if thrown, would create a pretty good diversion—whether it hit the horse or the brave. It could possibly even cause pandemonium. Firefly happened to be the most jugheaded horse in the herd.

Now, with a solid plan, Evelyn's hands steadied. Carefully she wrapped the injured leg . . . no sense in running before that was accomplished.

Calm now, yet more alert than she'd ever been in her spying days, Evie absorbed all that was happening around her. Horses milled around outside, whinnying nervously—probably no more pleased than she was to have a stranger here reeking of smelly bear grease. If only she hadn't been so preoccupied with the skittish colt earlier, she might have heard their warning.

Evelyn finished wrapping the wound and tore the last length of the bandage into two narrow tying strips. In seconds now, her task would be complete. Willing added strength into her legs, she sneaked a peek through her lowered lashes at the Indian brave.

And met his keen stare.

She didn't dare glance back at the wooden box. Yet Evie knew she couldn't afford to miss when she grasped it. Her heart began to bang fiercely again, drumming in her ears. Her fingers fumbled as she tied off the bandage.

Behind her the straw crunched. Something blocked the light!

Before she could turn, a powerful hand dug into her hair and wrenched her to her feet.

Evie gasped in pain and blind fear. *Another Indian!*

"Mat-tah!" cried the one holding the colt.

The one behind Evelyn yanked harder.

She gave an involuntary yelp. Any instant a tomahawk would split her skull.

The brave holding the twitch barked something in his strange tongue.

The newcomer spewed his own stream of harsh unintelligible words.

The other loosened the rope twitch. Firefly broke free and lunged backward. At Evie.

She lost her footing and fell, only to find herself sprawled on the ground atop her fallen captor. The heavy stench of bear grease hung about him like a cloud, and she almost retched.

Through a tumble of hair, she saw the colt wheel past and charge out the barn door. With all her heart Evie wished she was on his back.

The first Indian now stood above her, the limited light streaming into the barn glistening over the oiled contours of his body. He jerked her to her feet, his fingers digging into her wrist.

His cohort sprang up with the lethal grace of a wildcat and swiftly retrieved his dropped hatchet.

The two of them bandied more harsh words back and forth. The first shook the twitch rope at the other.

They're quibbling over who gets the privilege of scalping me!

As the two argued, her mind raced. She darted a glance out the door to her saddled horse, judging the distance. Her rifle must still be with the mount. Neither savage had it.

The fingers ensnaring her wrist eased their hold.

Now was her chance!

A bloodcurdling scream rent the air. One of the other

pacers burst through the entrance—with yet another Indian astride.

In the chaos, Evie jerked free and ran toward the light, startling the oncoming horse and rider. She dodged the flailing legs as the pacer reared, then dashed past it to the exit.

Two more painted figures blocked the opening.

But she couldn't stop now. She raced onward, determined to plow through them.

With piercing shrieks, they pounced. Rough hands bit into the soft flesh of her arms. Their yelps sliced the air, echoing through the barn rafters.

Evelyn shoved ahead with every vestige of her strength.

From behind, a hand clawed into her hair again, snagging her. The grip tightened on the nape of her neck. She was yanked backward, flush against her tormentor. He released her hair, and his powerful arms pinned hers to her sides.

Faces filled her vision. Painted faces. Vile, leering sneers closed in all around. Like a pack of hungry wolves.

The one holding her grasped her upper arm, dragging her out into the sunlight. Out to her waiting horse, the Thoroughbred hunter she'd ridden into the valley a year and a half ago. Amber Jewel and the fine leather sidesaddle were all that remained of her old life of stylish luxury—the expensive horse she'd ridden always so vainly into Wilkes-Barre for Sunday service. *Why, oh why, dear Lord, didn't I go to church this morning?* Suddenly, she was tossed up onto the sidesaddle like a sack of meal.

Trying to right herself, Evelyn banged her knee against the tall pommel before she could hook her leg over it.

The rifle was still there! She made a grab for it.

The savage caught her hands with a sneer and tied them to the pommel with the same rope she'd used to twitch the colt.

Evie felt her last hope drain away. She was as caught as Firefly had been a scant few moments ago.

The Indian chuckled knowingly.

The darkest despair Evelyn had ever known closed in over her. No one could help her now. Not even God.

18

Susannah refused to allow her anger at Evelyn to ruin this glorious day as she and her little troupe paraded home from church. Mary Clare had been right when she said Evie wouldn't come to Sunday service on her own, that she'd rather risk an Indian attack than sit willingly in humble silence for that short spell each week. Mary never minced words when it came to Evie.

Sighing, Susannah pushed back her bonnet and let it dangle behind her head by the ribbon ties. Summer's kiss had turned the fragile green of spring to a richer hue that spilled across lush meadows and crowned the deep forests. Multicolored flowers filled the air with a fragile perfume, and the landscape brought back memories of the verdant hills and valleys of Ashford, England, and her childhood there. But now, with her marriage to Dan and the arrival of their two little ones, her roots were becoming deeply entrenched in the rich American soil, and over the past two years this valley along the beautiful Susquehanna River had become home.

Inhaling the sweet fragrance, Susannah lifted her face to the sun for the sheer joy of it.

Up ahead, Mary Clare's wagon rattled and squeaked, its wheels crunching over the packed earth as the big farmhorse clopped slowly homeward. The jingle of the harness became lost in the happy giggles and chatter of the three little girls in back. Their exuberance all but drowned out the conversation between Prudence and Mary.

But Susannah was too caught up in the loveliness of the day to mind not hearing what the other women were discussing. She glanced beyond them to Miles, riding straight and tall on his mount ahead of everyone. How like Dan he was—serious one minute, doubling over with laughter the next. And already his young mind seemed bent toward spiritual matters. He could ask surprisingly deep questions for a lad his age. Someday, perhaps, he'd feel the call of God and go off to theological school himself. She smiled at the thought of her son in the Lord's service.

The warm weather had done wonders for the recently planted fields, Susannah noticed as they passed a section of open land. Sprouts of corn were already poking their way through the dirt in the plowed rows, a promise of a wonderful harvest. The only thing that might add to the valley's bounty would be the return of the able-bodied men to help out.

Even her own garden would have been ever so much larger if her husband were here. Four months had gone by since Dan's courier duties had brought him up into the area. Four long months. Endless nights in that big half-empty bed, no cheery whistle as he tended to chores, no lamp burning late into the night while he pored over the Holy Scriptures. An ache of loneliness clogged her throat.

"Susannah," Prudence called out, interrupting her remembrances. "I was just wondering. What did you think of the sermon today?"

From the tone of her friend's voice, Susannah knew they were about to embark on a spirited conversation. "I rather wish there'd have been another choice of topic."

Mary Clare looked back with a wry face and shook her head, the single golden plait moving from one shoulder to the other over her cornflower blue homespun.

"Have you noticed," Prudence went on, "that the elder seems to have a penchant for but one subject—keeping this valley of husbandless wives on the straight and narrow? Last week the story of Ruth, this Sunday that finger-wagging thirty-first chapter of Proverbs. Truly, if there ever was a woman so noble and accomplished as that passage describes, she'd be hard put to find a man remotely worthy of such perfection."

"I know my Jon would never expect me to be that industrious," Mary chimed in. "He's always been so considerate of me, always doing his best to lighten my load. Of course, I have serious doubts that any such virtuous person ever existed in the first place."

A light laugh erupted from Prudence as she swished an errant fly away from the slumbering babe in her arms. "Perhaps that's why old Solomon, the writer of Proverbs, married a thousand women. Obviously he couldn't find her, either!"

Susannah joined in with the merriment, then grew more serious. "I suppose we must remember that those thoughts were inspired by our heavenly Father. If King Solomon had patterned his life after the Proverbs, it's not likely he'd have ended it out of God's favor."

Prudence nodded in agreement.

"I rather consider that last chapter God's special gift to us as women," Susannah went on, nudging her mount alongside the wagon to make it easier for her to converse. "An ideal to strive for . . . even if we can't actually attain it this side of heaven."

"Well, I know one thing," Mary declared. "No matter what, I could never share my husband with a thousand other wives. Having to share him with the army is more than enough . . . and I don't think I can bear that for one more month." She gave a fretful sigh.

"At least you and Jon had some uninterrupted years together," Prudence said pointedly. "I should think you'd be grateful for that much."

Poor Prudence, Susannah thought. She had known but a few weeks at a time with Morgan since the two married during the siege of Boston.

Stricken, Mary flushed. "You're right. I complain far more than I should. I'll try to do better, I promise."

"As we all should," Prudence declared.

"It's just that I can't help hating that my Jon was left to train that new company when Robert and Chip came for Emily. He should never have told his superiors he'd gone to college."

Promise or not, Mary was off on further complaints. Time for another change in conversation. "It's such a lovely day. Why don't we take our Sunday dinner down to the riverside and picnic in the open air?"

"Picnic!" Esther, Mary's oldest, dropped her doll and jumped up. "Please say yes, Mama, please."

"Please, please," Beth and Julia begged, rising to their knees.

Mary Clare turned and regarded the bright hopeful faces with their beseeching eyes of clearest blue. "There'll be a price for it."

Three huge smiles faded. "What?" Esther asked.

"A big hug from each one of you." Mary grinned as the statement registered. Instantly she was swamped by all of them, and a round of laughs and giggles echoed against the grove of trees ahead.

The tender scene brought the sting of tears to Susannah's eyes. This was the Mary Clare she used to know . . . sweet and giving and eager to please. Mary had thrived under Jonathan's sheltering love and had turned from an overtly shy and withdrawn young woman to one far more friendly—and even a little confident. But without her husband, she was becoming pessimistic and uncharitable . . . which hardly endeared her to Evelyn.

The children settled down in the wagon bed, taking up their rag dolls once more.

When the road tunneled through a thick stand of woods, Susannah was saddened by the loss of the glorious sunshine even for the few minutes more it would take to reach her farm in the next clearing.

"Look! A rabbit!" Miles yelled suddenly, urging his horse in chase. A red squirrel scampered up the nearest tree as he cantered by.

His mother watched after him. "Don't go too far, sweetheart. Stay within sight."

The dappled sunlight fell in coin-sized patches throughout the shady grove and played over the leafy boughs and ground ferns. Even the songbirds seemed to worship their Maker as they chirped and flitted about the canopy overhead, seeking food for their nestlings. Such peace, Susannah mused. Such perfect peace.

Mary Clare glanced toward her. "I hardly think we need to invite Evelyn to picnic with us," she said waspishly. "If that colt was so severely injured this morning that she couldn't leave him to attend service, she should probably stay and keep looking after him, don't you think?"

Susannah opened her mouth to speak, but Prudence beat her to it. "I agree. She may be my sister-in-law, but one must be held accountable for one's actions."

"Quite," Susannah finally answered. "But our attitudes must also be tempered with mercy. Evie has had to give up so much for this patriot cause. Home, friends, family, why, every comfort she was accustomed to—not the least of which is Chris."

Mary huffed. "She may say she wants to become my brother's wife, but once this war is won and it's safe for her to go back home, I wouldn't be the least surprised to see her leave all of our everyday hardships behind and reclaim everything she's done without. Things Chip could never give her. Not that I begrudge the girl any of that frivolous nonsense, mind you . . . as long as she leaves my brother behind to find someone far more concerned about his needs than her own."

Prudence looked about to reply, but no words came.

"That sounds mean-spirited, I know," Mary rushed on defensively, "but Chris had a hard life as a boy—you know that, Susannah. And he was finally on his way to making something of himself, studying engineering at the college, and all."

"And you honestly believe Evelyn would hinder him in his honest endeavors?" Prudence asked. "I daresay, they'd be to her benefit as well as his."

Mary released a breath of frustration. "That's just the problem." She glanced back at the children and saw that they were absorbed in their play and not paying the grown-ups any mind. "That spoiled girl will want everything he earns for her own selfish pleasures. I know the two of you seem to feel that the reason she avoids coming to our church meetings at the store, given the slightest reason, is because our services are so different from those of her highfalutin' Anglican church. But I think her motives are much more simple. She doesn't have a vast wardrobe of new dresses to show off. And you know the way she always insists on riding her aristocratic horse with that polished leather sidesaddle. It's obvious her appearance is all that matters to her."

Prudence gasped.

"Well," Mary continued, "you must have noticed the scornful way she views everything we wear. Even now that she's finished sewing her new green dress I wouldn't be surprised if most Sabbaths she drags out that elegant gown she was wearing when she arrived here—no matter how worn the fancy rag is."

Despite Mary Clare's scathing remarks, Susannah could not judge her too harshly. Mary and Chip had lived in abject poverty before the old Lyons couple took them in. The first pretty frock Mary ever owned had been one Susannah made over from her own wardrobe so the girl wouldn't be too ashamed to attend services at Princeton . . . and her drunken father had stumbled into Mary's attic room and stolen it away to sell for more cheap rum.

Nevertheless, this was not a conversation for little Julia's innocent ears, even if the deeper meaning of the words escaped her. "I suppose we all have our faults," Susannah responded. "But I, for one, am pleased to have Evelyn living with me. With Emily gone, I should have been at a loss to take over care of the horses. But Evie stepped right in, and for that I've been most thankful."

"And I heartily appreciate your taking her in," Prudence added. "She's so very patriotic, and as rash as any young daredevil. I'm sure the British would have sent her to the gallows long ago if we'd left her behind in New York when Morgan was exposed as a spy."

Mary Clare looked askance at her and tossed a hand. "See? Another of her many flaws. If Chip has the smallest hope of fulfilling his dreams, he needs to find a sensible wife. One with both feet on—" Her eyes flared wide. "Slow down, Miles!"

Susannah darted a glance up the road to see her son thundering toward them at full gallop.

"Mama!" He reined in with all his might, and his mount skidded to a stop. "The horses! They're gone! All of them!"

"What? It can't be!" But the veracity of his expression eliminated all doubt. "Well, there must be some explanation," she told Mary and Pru as the boy spun and headed back to the farm. "Evie must have left the gate open by mistake." She slapped her pacer's rump and trotted after Miles—and away from Mary Clare's renewed harping on the girl's shortcomings.

Emerging from the copse of trees, Susannah could see that the corral was indeed empty and its gate standing wide open. A wave of anger washed over her. But it ebbed just as suddenly when she noticed an even eerier sight . . . both pasture gates hung open.

Something is very, very wrong. Slowing her mount alongside her son's, she drew her rifle from the sheath. "Miles, dear, ride back to your aunties and stay with them, there's a good lad."

Susannah waited until he had complied before nudging her horse slowly ahead. Tension gripped her as she took mental notes. No mass of tracks coming this way, so they couldn't have taken the road. A tan lump lay on the ground in front of the cabin. *Evie?* Susannah's heart stopped, then thudded again when she realized that Evie had been wearing apple green. She released a breath she hadn't known she'd been holding. What on earth had happened?

A variety of goods were strewn haphazardly outside the open cabin door. "Evie?" she called in a strangled whisper.

Swallowing her fear, she made another try. "Evie? Are you here?"

No response.

Susannah waited a few seconds, then steered her pacer toward the barn. There, too, the door was flung wide. Discarded possessions littered the dirt.

Someone has been in my house! Everywhere! Going through my things! Bile rose in her throat at the repulsive thought.

Then her heart seized up. A trail of blood came from the nearest corral and led into the barn! Cold shivers of terror slithered up her spine. *Evie!* "Please, please, dear Lord, don't let it be Evie!" Flinging herself down to the ground, she raced toward the entrance.

"Mama!"

Susannah stopped dead and whirled around. "Miles, I told you to go back to the wagon."

"But the blood," he said. "It's Firefly's, not Aunt Evie's. He was cut bad, remember?"

At first she couldn't comprehend what her son was telling her. She placed both hands to her temples, trying to think. "Oh. Yes. Quite right." But still, that explained only one thing. What about the rest?

Mustering all her courage, Susannah turned and made herself walk into the dim confines of the barn. The balmy afternoon air was weighted with the odors of manure and straw, and the stench assaulted her nostrils. Her clammy hands wiped perspiration from her brow.

The stream of blood was smeared over in places by kicked-up dirt on the earthen floor, but it led to a stall on the left and on through its open gate. Inching on trembling legs toward the paddock, Susannah was almost too terrified to look inside. She closed her eyes for a second, gathering herself. But it was empty.

"Evie!" she called. No response.

"Evie!" Surely the girl would have answered by now if she were within shouting distance. Susannah left the close confines of the structure and returned to the fresh air and sunshine, but feelings of dread still clutched her heart.

The rumble and rattles of the Bradford wagon announced its arrival as Mary guided the outfit over to the barn. Both women's faces mirrored Susannah's own trepidation. "Where's Evie?" Mary asked, gazing around at the debris and disorder everywhere.

"I've not found her yet."

Without a word, Prudence handed baby David down to Susannah and dropped to the ground. She ran to the house.

Susannah stepped to the wagon, needing to be near her own little girl, praying all the time that Prudence wouldn't find poor Evie lying dead in a pool of blood. She tried not even to imagine the unthinkable possibility.

A multitude of horse tracks had left a trampled path through her young corn, she noticed. They headed northeast . . . away from civilization . . . toward Indian country.

From inside the house came the crash of a chair banging over. Then sounds of swift feet dashing up the loft ladder.

"Are you all right?" Susannah yelled, wanting to make certain the sounds were Prudence's alone.

Moments later, Pru appeared in the doorway. "Evelyn's not in here."

Mary Clare gathered her daughters to herself, her face white as an August moon. "Don't you worry, sweat peas. It wasn't Indians. They always burn a place down when they come raiding." Her expression hardened, and she scowled over their heads at Susannah. "Everyone knows that. I'll bet that worthless girl ran off with the horses herself. Mark my words, she'll sell them off somewhere and use the money to wait out the rest of the war in comfort." Even as she spoke, her eyes took on the conviction of her statements. "Don't you see? That's why her royal highness was ever so helpful, ever so eager to learn about caring for them. Maybe now Christopher will see her for—"

"Mama!" Miles cried, bursting out of the house. Susannah

hadn't even noticed him go in. "My toy soldiers are gone. All of them! They stole every single one!"

Mary caught her breath, and Susannah hugged the baby all the tighter. The figures were made of lead. Lead to melt down for musket balls.

Prudence bolted inside again, then just as quickly came out. "The big hearth cauldron is missing! Who but an Indian would want a sooty old thing like that!"

She's right. It would be a prized possession to a people who had nothing made of iron except for what they got from the white man. The truth could no longer be denied. Marauding savages had come and made off with the herd and whatever else they thought might serve some purpose. And Evie—she had been murdered or taken prisoner. Susannah didn't know which would be worse. Her horrified mind couldn't even form a prayer. She only hoped her heavenly Father could sort through the wordless fears and deepest longings and make sense out of them.

"It's all my fault, dear God," she heard Mary Clare moan. Tears flowed from her eyes as she rocked her daughters back and forth. "Please, please forgive me for saying those hateful things about her. She's a good girl. Truly she is. Please, Lord, don't let this happen to her. Please."

Little Julia dropped down from the back of the wagon and ran to Susannah, flinging herself against her mother's legs, clinging with all her might.

Susannah shifted David to her other arm, then bent and lifted her daughter up to comfort her. Her eyes met Miles's troubled gaze. She should have taken her children and left at the first Indian signs that spring. But she hadn't believed they'd raid this deep into such a populated valley. Last year's ravaging of the Mohawk Valley must have emboldened the British and their army of red men. Their reign of terror in New York's back country had proved Butler's Indians would scalp a baby as quickly as they would a grown man. The age or helplessness of their victims were of no consequence. "Come, Son. Get into the wagon. We're going back to the settlement. Now. Perhaps the men can catch up to the marauders and save Evie."

"Someone should be sent to Valley Forge, too," Prudence said quietly. She took her baby from Susannah and pressed him close to herself. "Morgan must be told about his sister."

"And Jon," Mary added. "I need him to come home. *Today.*"

And Dan. Susannah placed Julia in the wagon bed. *Surely General Washington will stop delaying and send our men home now.* He would have to. No longer was it merely the theft of farm animals. This was the second time in a month that lives had been endangered.

Oh, Evie. Dear, dear Evie.

19

For a timeless moment, no one spoke as they all took a last dazed look at the shambles the raiding party had made of the property. Then, with foreboding, Susannah searched the dark shadows beneath the boughs of the nearby forest. "We mustn't tarry another second. We shall go directly to Fort Wilkes-Barre. Back on your horse, sweetheart," she told Miles, setting Julia into the wagon. "Ride right beside Aunt Mary." Then, gathering her skirts, she mounted her saddle horse.

Without a word Prudence chose a spot in the wagon bed with the little ones, her rifle at the ready.

On the seat, Mary Clare snapped the reins and made a wide turn. The grating of the iron-rimmed wheels over the rock-strewn trail seemed ominously loud in the oppressive stillness, echoing off hard surfaces and trees as the little group started back to town.

Susannah caught Prudence's brave smile and returned it with a thin one of her own as she positioned herself on the other side of Miles. She knew Morgan's wife had been through times of serious danger during her spying days. She possessed the ability to maintain outward calm for the sake of the children. And thankfully, even Mary Clare held her tongue as she guided the farm horse on a straight course.

Susannah kept her eyes open for any unexpected movement on the road ahead of them or among the scattered trees and groves. She gave little thought to the missing herd of

Narragansetts, but her heart prayed ceaselessly. *Keep my children safe, dear Lord. And I beg you to keep your hand upon Evie, wherever she is. Surround her with angels. Shield her from harm. Please, please, don't let those savages hurt her. Bring her back to us.*

The slow pace of the wagon made the trip seem unbearably long, and every mile they covered was one more the rescuers would have to retrace when they began the search for Evie. Finally, unable to hold back any longer, Susannah expelled a rush of breath. "I think I'd best ride ahead and sound the alarm." She whacked the rump of her mount, and it lurched to a gallop.

"Yes," Mary Clare called after her. "Hurry! For Evie's sake."

The sincerity in her young friend's voice touched Susannah as she sped toward the settlement in the distance. Obviously now that the danger had become real, something to be faced, Mary Clare was able to set aside her petty gripes and draw upon some of her inner strength. Instead of panicking, as Susannah had expected, Mary had driven at a steady pace so as not to overtire the horse.

After church that morning, Mistress Gardner had told Susannah that Colonel Zebulon Butler, who had recently returned to the valley, had ordered the temporary militia to meet at the fort after the noon meal. Surely the meeting must still be in progress, or there would have been one or two men along the road by now.

Finally emerging from the last of the trees, Susannah spied the new log fortress built to replace the original fort the Connecticut men had destroyed in a dispute with the Pennsylvanians in 1774. Many settlers and tradesmen of the valley now made their homes within its walls rather than in the town lots. She didn't bother slowing down on her approach but galloped through the open fort gates. "Indians!" she yelled.

Several people burst out of the settlement store.

"The militia!" Susannah cried. "Colonel Butler! Where are they?"

The people only stared.

"The militia!" she urged a second time. "My ward, Evelyn Thomas—she's been abducted!"

There was a collective gasp of horror. "Out the back gate," a man said, pointing with his thumb. "Drilling."

With a nod, Susannah wheeled her pacer and raced toward the opening.

Someone stepped out of the carpenter's shop. "Indians? Here in the valley?"

Everyone ran after Susannah.

On horseback she quickly outdistanced the folks on foot. She could see men marching in ragged formation about a hundred yards away, a number of them lumbering with age. *Old men and lads!* she thought in dismay. *Is this all that's left to protect us and our homes?*

As much as Susannah hated to admit it, Mary had been right. Jon and Dan should never have gone off to war. Last winter General Washington and some of the other leaders had decided that the attack on the Mohawk Valley and other New York frontier settlements the previous summer had been part of a plan to gain control of Lake Champlain and the Hudson. How wrong they had been! Not two months ago word had come that the British, after failing in their Canadian invasion, had kept most of the Iroquois nations in their pay—close to a thousand warriors more than willing to wield their muskets and tomahawks against the sparsely scattered settlements. Savages eager to torture and kill, to plunder and take scalps . . . or slaves.

The straggling formation of men caught sight of Susannah and stopped.

She reined in near the dashing figure in white military wig and blue uniform coat, whom she quickly recognized as Colonel Butler. "Indians," she said breathlessly, "raided our farm while we were at service. They kidnapped my ward, Evelyn Thomas. Please, she needs help."

"Indians?" a militiaman echoed as the settlers converged on her. "Where? How many? Where did they go?"

A pistol shot rang out. "Silence!" The colonel lowered his

smoking weapon as the men obeyed. "Aren't you Mistress Haynes?" he asked kindly. "From upriver? You have that large herd of Rhode Island horses."

"Quite right, sir. They've been taken as well. Please, you must go after Evie. Now. She's young. Innocent. Just a maiden. Get her back for us."

"Do you know how many there were? Which way they went?"

"Must've been a large party," a thin, swarthy fellow said. "Would take that many of 'em to drive that big herd through the forest, that's for sure."

One of the women from the fort pushed her way through the men and planted a fist on her wide hip. "We'll not be riskin' our green lads for some Rhode Islander's property!"

"I don't care about the horses!" Susannah said in desperation. *They've taken Evie.* She's my only concern now."

"Could be that British devil come down from Fort Niagara with those heathens," a male voice rang out in the crowd. "Him and his rangers. Prob'ly want us to follow, to draw us into the woods an' ambush us."

"He could be right," other voices murmured.

Susannah sought Colonel Butler and leveled her gaze on him. "Surely, Colonel, you'll not just stand by and do nothing."

The leader glanced about with indecision.

"This happened during church service," the outspoken matron said. "It's most likely God's punishment on the gal for not bein' where she belonged." She gave an emphatic nod.

Susannah shook her head, unable to believe that this asinine conversation was taking place when time was of the utmost importance. "She would have been, I assure you," she heard herself say in Evie's defense, "but one of the horses was injured, and she remained behind to look after him."

"Mebbe *this* time." The agitated woman indicated a double meaning with an elevated brow. "But how many other times has that prissy Philadelphia *lady* shunned us plainer folk— and our religion—since she arrived here?" She snorted.

A thin-faced woman near her huffed. "Wouldn't surprise me none if the gal's naught but a heathen like them Injuns herself. I'll not have *my* laddie riskin' his life for nothin' but a snooty heathen!"

"Ma-a," a young voice wailed. "I'm a soldier now. I go where my commander sends me."

"Well, Zeb?" the woman challenged, swinging to him.

One of the older men on the fringe gestured in disgust. "I can't wait around for any more jawin'. I sent my daughter an' her young'uns home without me. I gotta go see about them."

"Me, too," another agreed.

The crowd began to disperse.

Colonel Butler grabbed the nearest musket and fired a blast into the sky. "Halt, men!" He handed the weapon back to its owner, then reached for Susannah, dragging her by the waist from her mount. "Begging your pardon, ma'am," he said, swinging up into the saddle. "I can see better from up here." Returning his attention to the ranks, he scowled at the lot of them. "You must conduct yourselves like proper soldiers! All of you! Unless we maintain some semblance of discipline, we'll all be wiped out."

Reluctantly, the men paused.

Obviously understanding their forced effort, the leader motioned to a lad off to one side. "You, there. Go sound the alarm. Those of you with folks at home, go fetch your families as quickly as possible. The rest of you, mount up. We'll ride upriver and warn folks of the danger, see if anyone else has been attacked. Then we'll determine the size of the enemy force that laid siege to the Haynes place."

Astounded, Susannah peered up at the man who'd commandeered her horse. "You must do more than that, Colonel," she begged. "You must go after Evie *now*, before they get too far ahead. So much time has been wasted already—"

"Mistress Haynes," he replied wearily. "I know you're very worried about the young lady. So am I. We'll do as much as we possibly can, I assure you. But there is more at stake here than just one girl, you understand. The thing for you to do right now is go inside the fort and stay calm. Watch after your children and leave the rest to us." With a nod of dismissal, he unsheathed the sword strapped to his side and raised it high. "Follow me, men."

Left in the dust raised by her own departing horse and the pathetic, ragged force that followed it, Susannah trudged resignedly after them and the remnants of the crowd returning to the fort. Her frustration for Evelyn was now tinged with terror, and she had to fight the urge to weep. Dan should be here. If he and Evie's brother, Morgan, were home where they belonged, they'd have gone after her immediately, gotten her back . . . somehow.

Despair overwhelmed her, and she crumpled to her knees in the grassy clearing. "Dear heavenly Father, I beg you to give strength to us all . . . those of us left here wondering, hoping, almost too afraid to think, and most especially to Evie. Dear Evie. Please take care of her. Don't let them hurt her. Please bring her back, I beg you. Please."

After a time, a sense of peace began to flow into Susannah, bringing with it renewed strength and hope. God had never let her down before, even when she was certain all was lost. And if he took note of even a fallen sparrow, he would surely keep watch over his missing child. The awful anguish weighing on her heart felt much lighter, and though she couldn't entirely give it up, at least it was much easier to bear.

She rose and crossed the remainder of the meadow with new purpose. She needed to find someone willing to ride to Valley Forge and tell General Washington of their plight— and even more important, to bring Dan and Morgan back to Wilkes-Barre. And Christopher. He, too, should be told.

The rough ropes securing Evie to her hunter chafed her wrists and ankles as the fierce painted brave she had encountered in the barn pulled her behind him on a lead. She'd begun to think of him as Weasel Eyes. Fearful though she was, she was thankful that he and the rest of the marauding band had been kept so busy by the rambunctious horses that they had no time to give thought to her.

She derived perverse satisfaction from the fact that there had been only limited stable gear at the farm. The inexperienced horse thieves had to make do with three saddles, a few halters, and ropes. Most barely maintained their seats and were forever forced to split off to recapture the confused pacers as the animals crashed through the forest and up steep ridges, chasing off into boulder-strewn gullies on either side of the stream they'd been following this past half hour. Now that she had opportunity to assess her kidnappers, Evelyn realized how young they actually were—and that not one showed the slightest competence in handling the animals.

She watched as a lad who appeared a couple years younger than her own eighteen years lunged his mount up a steep shale rise cluttered with tree branches and underbrush. His naked thighs bled from newly acquired scratches. Evie assumed the string of low mutterings he emitted were Indian curses. She hid a scornful smirk as he almost slid off his mount's back when he veered the faltering pacer around a tree. Evie was thankful she had her sidesaddle, and that Amber Jewel had been bred for fox hunting in rough terrain.

Returning her attention to Weasel Eyes, she noticed his arm muscles twitch. It had to be a chore to lead her much larger horse with one hand, while trying to control his own mount and the herd at the same time. Whenever he glanced back at her, the strain was evident in his brutish expression. They'd been traveling for hours and had yet to stop.

Still, they were making very poor time. The midday sun had passed its zenith hours ago. Trying to keep a mental record of landmarks in case she somehow managed to escape, Evelyn glanced behind herself for the hundredth time. Even a blind man could follow the trail of destruction left in their wake, and that gave her more than a little comfort. Surely her rescuers would be here soon. How could they not?

For a few blissful seconds she allowed herself to picture Chris charging after her, dashing into the midst of this band of painted raiders and making short work of felling the lot of them. That he could do all of that and even more, she had no doubt . . . only he was far away. Unreachable. She tried not to dwell on it.

If she just had the use of her hands, she could get hold of her reins. Her long-legged Amber Jewel could outrun all these other horses put together. Evie gazed down at her wrists, swollen from the tightness of the bonds. She hated being helpless, at someone else's mercy. She looked to the rear. Surely it wouldn't be much longer.

From the angle of the sun, she figured it must be near four or five o'clock. Rescuers would certainly reach her before her abductors made camp for the night . . . before they made her dismount from the safety of her hunter.

But where were they? Evelyn took another backward look.

Then Weasel Eyes shouted something unintelligible, and Evie's heart raced. Had her people come already? Seeing no one behind, she swung a cursory glance at the three captors she could spot out of the seven.

Not one of them pulled out the musket strapped to his back.

Not one raised a tomahawk.

Weasel Eyes tied Amber's reins to a nearby branch as his cohorts gathered around. Ignoring her, they bandied some conversation back and forth. Then Weasel handed them several coiled ropes, which they cut into ten- or twelve-foot lengths.

Another pair of braves rode in just then. They, too, paid Evie no mind. Obviously she was less important than the goods they had stolen from the farm. One thing did maintain their concentration, though—still mounted, they kept sharp watch in the direction from which they'd come as they divided up the lengths of rope.

Evelyn couldn't help but wonder if they were planning to make some sort of trap for the pursuers. Straining her eyes for any sign of approaching horsemen, she saw nothing but the shadows of the forest. At least, not yet.

The braves dispersed, leaving Evie's horse tied to the tree. She watched as each one took a loop of rope and started after a horse.

They've finally realized the folly of this venture, she thought. *They're going to catch and string some of the animals, take only what they can escape with quickly.* That conviction pressed heavily on her spirit. If the men from Wilkes-Barre didn't hurry, the Indians might possibly elude them.

For the next half-hour, Evelyn watched the fumbling attempts of the painted youths to capture their targets. One actually managed to secure three horses, and a few others had each gotten one. If her bound wrists weren't a constant and painful reminder, she might have convinced herself she was watching a troupe of jesters as she had a time or two in Philadelphia.

Just then a pair of strawberry roans shot right past her, clattering into the undergrowth beside the shallow stream. Weasel Eyes, looking harried, charged after them on his mount.

A smile tickled the corners of her mouth.

Something held his attention a second too long, and a low-hanging branch caught him and sent him sprawling into a backward somersault. His mount kept going after the others.

With her nerves strung so thin, a spurt of laughter burst from Evie before she could contain it.

Weasel staggered to his feet. Eyes narrowed, he swung toward her.

Evie sobered instantly. His menacing stare chilled her to the bone. Her pulse throbbed in her ears. "I—I didn't mean to laugh," she stammered, ripping frantically at her bonds as he closed in on her.

He snatched his tomahawk from its leather thong and raised it in one swift motion.

This was to be her end? "Oh, please, dear God," she begged. "I don't want to die. Help me! *Chris!*"

20

On the rampart of Fort Wilkes-Barre, Susannah clutched the stockade poles, her nails digging into the rough-hewn wooden spears. The orange sun was sinking behind the far western ridge, and not one arriving family within the past hour had been able to provide even the most scant information regarding Evelyn. The last shred of Susannah's hope was swiftly diminishing.

Now and then she could make out a militiaman off in the distance as word was carried up and down the valley, but to her knowledge, none had been dispatched to begin searching for Evie. She ground her teeth in frustration. If only she'd been a man, she'd have gone after the girl herself. Immediately.

This dreadful helplessness at having been born a member of the gentle sex brought back similar feelings from Susannah's past, when her deepest desire had been precluded due to her womanhood. The daughter of a country pastor, her bent toward spiritual matters seemed only natural—as did the disappointment that she would never be allowed to enroll in theological seminary to delve into the mysteries of the faith. Upon her arrival at Princeton, a seat of great new theological minds, she would have given anything for the privilege of sitting in on lectures at the College of New Jersey. But that, of course, was unheard of.

Thank heaven for Jonathan and Morgan and their friend

Steven Russell, all of whom had stopped by the Lyons' Den almost daily to discuss their studies over coffee and Mrs. Lyons's pie. Through their understanding and kindness to a young maiden stranded and on her own in this strange new country, the lads had gradually accepted her unconventional thirst for biblical knowledge and, in her stead, diligently sought out the answers to her questions.

And now, Morgan's youngest sister, who had been in Susannah's watch care, had been taken by Indians. If what people had been whispering all afternoon was true, no fate on earth could be worse. Evelyn might have already been butchered and scalped—or at the very least forced to suffer unspeakable torture and senseless abuse.

"The men!" a sentinel shouted from the corner palisade. "They're coming back!"

Susannah swung her gaze northward and saw riders numbering twenty or more. "Oh, please, dear God," she whispered fervently, "let Evie be with them. Please." Climbing quickly down to the ground, she rushed across the square, threading her way through the clutter of neighbors' wagons, horses, and families. She fell in with the throng already heading for the entrance, all of them nearly as anxious as she for news.

A quick glance assured her that her children were safely playing in a corner before she hurried out the front gates. She clutched her hands tightly to her breast as if she could hold herself together by a sheer act of the will, and strode with a score of others toward the approaching militia company several rods down the road.

Prudence and Mary joined her within seconds. "I—I don't see Evie," Mary Clare said, her voice tinged with alarm. "Do you see her, Pru? Susannah?"

Prudence shook her head. "But wait. Let's hear what Colonel Butler has to say. He must know something."

"She could be riding behind someone," Susannah added hopefully.

But Evelyn was not with anyone.

The riders, coming nearer on their sweat-foamed horses, all wore grim expressions.

Susannah's spirit sank like a rock. "Colonel?" She stepped into the path of the lead mount. "Where is Evelyn?"

His bushy brows shelved over his eyes. "Wait till we get inside the fort, Mistress."

"No!" She grabbed his horse's bridle, stopping it. "I must know now. Where is she?"

The leader's face hardened.

His reaction only added to Susannah's ire. Good manners were the least of her worries at the moment. Even before seeing Prudence, she sensed that Morgan's Puritan wife had moved to her side.

"Colonel Butler," the dark-haired lass said with her precise Boston inflection, "this is no time for dilly-dallying. We'll have an answer *now.*"

His gaze moved from her to Susannah and back, then he released a tired huff. "I'm afraid we have no news at all regarding the young miss. We read signs at your place as best we could, saw moccasin prints here and there, but the horses tramped out most everything."

Petite Prudence stiffened to her tallest height. "Leaving a swath as wide as the Susqehanna itself."

He gave a resigned nod. "That they did, madam. Now, if you'll be so kind as to let us by . . ."

"You mean," Susannah cried incredulously, "you made no effort whatsoever to follow and try to rescue Evelyn?"

A hint of color rose upward from his neck. He averted his face and looked straight ahead. "I sent some of my men along the trail for a mile or so. It should comfort you to know they saw no sign of . . . foul play."

Susannah nailed his gaze with hers. "How could you? You should have gone on! Gotten her back!"

"Now, Mistress Haynes," a man said from close behind her. "The colonel can do only so much, under the circumstances. With all the horse tramplings, none of us could determine the size of the raiding party." Deftly he uncurled her fingers from the colonel's bridle. "Last year, if you recall, hundreds of Iroquois swept through the Mohawk Valley, slaughtering and burning everything in their path. There's no way to be certain this wasn't that very same bunch—paid for by that British scalp-buyer up at Fort Niagara."

Susannah could barely restrain herself from wrenching away from that patronizing man even as he pulled her out of the path of the militiamen.

"My thanks, Ripley," Butler said.

Those words enraged Susannah even more. *She'd been handled!* And not a single rider among the lot had courage enough to look her in the eye as the band rode past her in the fading dusk.

"This is not the end of the matter," Prudence announced with determination, her skirts swishing as she passed Susannah. "They will not simply wash their hands of Morgan's baby sister, I'll tell you that."

Susannah sagged against Mary Clare. "Evie has never learned how to draw on God's strength. I fear this will be so much the worse for her."

Mary took Susannah's hand and stared northward with her, in the direction they knew Evelyn had been taken. "We shan't let an hour go by without lifting her up to the Lord in prayer."

"I should have tried harder to show her the heavenly promises. Been a better example. I failed."

"No." Mary squeezed Susannah's hand. "Not you, Susannah. I'm the one at fault. I knew how much she cared about Chip. But instead of welcoming her, making her my little sister, I always treated her as an outsider."

Susannah met her friend's troubled eyes. "I hardly think Evelyn felt that way. She believed you to be merely shy."

Neither spoke for a moment as a draft of the early evening breeze whispered by, ruffling their skirts and hair. Mary tucked a flyaway strand behind her ear and sighed. "Oh, Susannah . . . how are we going to tell the children?"

With a shrug of a shoulder, Susannah tipped her head. "Please, dear, we mustn't give up hope just yet. Mr. Rawlins rode off several hours ago to fetch our men home. He should be able to reach Valley Forge by tomorrow eve. Our husbands could be back within the week. Who would dare to stop them, under such circumstances?"

"A week," Mary Clare murmured in despair.

A tiny dot of light appeared in the otherwise darkened landscape—a solitary glow all the more obvious with the neighboring farms vacant this night.

Hope came to life again in Susannah. It had to be a lantern coming toward the fort down the river road. She squeezed Mary's hand as they watched it move closer.

"Someone's coming!" a sentinel shouted from above them.

"Indians!" a childish voice wailed inside the open gate.

"Inside, you two," Colonel Butler told Susannah and Mary as he and several men ran out of the fort.

Mary obeyed, leaving at once for the entrance. But not Susannah. "I think I heard the rumble of wagon wheels, Colonel. Likely it's another family seeking shelter."

"Or a British cannon carriage down from Fort Niagara," one of the men said warily.

"Alone? I hardly think so." Susannah had lost all patience. This trying day was even worse than when Dan had been arrested for aiding her brother Ted in his desertion from the British army.

The light was now near enough to be easily recognized as a lantern dangling from a horse-drawn wagon.

"That you, Miz Barnett?" one of the men called, jogging out to meet her.

"Aye," came the confident voice of one who'd lived in the wilderness for a good ten years. Since Mr. Barnett had left to join the militia two years ago, she and her youngsters had been on their own several miles beyond Susannah's farm. Even the way the tall, thin woman carried herself gave evidence of her courage. For Mistress Barnett, Forty Fort would have been much closer, but it was across the river.

The colonel moved up the path to her. "What took you so long, Mattie? You should've been here two, three hours ago."

Mrs. Barnett's lined face was now visible, and so were the strained ones of half a dozen children. From their perch atop a pile of belongings, their eyes reflected the lantern glow, making them appear haunted. Mistress Barnett leaned her head toward a freckled lad of perhaps fourteen sitting beside her with a rifle. "Told you, Zeb. I had to wait for my boy here to get back from huntin'. Whoa, there, Belle." She hauled in on the reins. "You know them Injuns you was lookin' for? Well, my Noah seen 'em."

Susannah bolted forward and grabbed the boy's arm. "Was there a young woman with them? Curly dark brown hair?"

"Yes, ma'am," he said with a nod. "That pretty Miss Evie. They had her, all right. Tied to her horse. I wisht I coulda helped her, but we only have this one gun. Sorry."

"I understand." Susannah regarded the skinny youth. "No one would fault you, Noah. I'm most grateful you managed to stay hidden so you could return to tell me."

"I laid low and watched 'em a long time," he went on. "It was one jolly time they was havin', tryin' to keep that bunch of red horses all together. Knowed they was yours right off, I did. Nobody else in these parts has more'n two or three. An' let me tell ya, them lads didn't know nuthin' about—"

"*Lads?*" Colonel Butler frowned. "Thought you said they were Indians."

"Yep. They were, sure as we're sittin' here, Colonel. But they was young. Some weren't much older'n me. Anyways, I didn't think they was ever gonna get by me, the way them horses kept shootin' off, first this way, then that." He switched his attention to Susannah. "Sure do wish I could've saved Miss Evie, ma'am. I surely do."

Seeing a sheen of moisture in his eyes, Susannah realized she was still gripping his arm. She released it and gave it a sympathetic pat. "I know."

"How many were there, Noah?" Colonel Butler inquired. "Did you manage to get a count?"

"Yessir, I did. Seven."

Seven? Susannah railed inwardly. *Only seven very young braves?* Speechless with rage, she swung to the colonel.

He took a step backward, hands raised to ward her off. "We had no way of knowing that, Mistress Haynes. We'll start after them first thing in the morning."

Mistress Barnett reached across to place a hand on her shoulder. "I know this is prob'ly small comfort, considerin'. But not long after we headed out, a bunch of your horses ran by us on their way to your place. If them Injun boys is as inept as my Noah says, most of your herd might come tricklin' back home."

The information scarcely registered through Susannah's mounting fury. Looking from Noah's weapon to the red-faced military leader standing before her, all she could think of was how dearly she would love to grab the rifle and blow a hole clear through the man's head, make room for some sense.

Dear Lord, why didn't they go after her?

21

At Valley Forge, built on the slopes of a ridge overlooking the Schuylkill River, merciless sunshine intensified the humid summer heat. Christopher pined for the shade of the thousands of trees they had cut last winter to build the hundreds of identical log cabins that formed orderly rows in the rolling clearing. On his way to the parade grounds, he wiped a trickle of sweat from his temple and sent a longing look to the wooded hills surrounding the encampment. Just then he spied his brother-in-law coming out of one of the barracks and changed course to intercept him. "Ho! Jon!"

Jonathan acknowledged the call by jutting out his chin. "What's up?"

"No time to jaw at the moment. General Washington summoned me to headquarters."

"Me, too." A curious frown made ridges in Jonathan's ruddy forehead as he fell into pace beside Chris. "That strikes me mighty queer—two lowly sergeants like us having our presence requested by the commander in chief. Oh well, it just better not be something that'll get in the way of my going back home with the Wyoming Valley militia."

Chris shrugged. "Anything's possible. Britain's summer offensive might have begun—in which case, my guess is they want the rifle battalions dispatched to slow them up."

"No." Jon shook his head. "This has to be something else. Orders are always relayed through our battalion officers.

Besides, I have my transfer papers in my pocket. No matter what, I'm leaving with the Wilkes-Barre men. Mary's letters are full of her fear that what happened to the Mohawk Valley may befall ours."

Jon's words made Chris uneasy as the two of them took a shortcut across the grounds.

A newly formed regiment filled most of the open area at the moment, thrusting their bayonets in obedience to a command issued by the Prussian drill officer, Von Steuben.

"Nein! Nein!" the red-faced leader bellowed, adding a few choice swear words in his native tongue. The shiny medals decorating the front of his uniform glittered as he waved his arms, his eyes rolling skyward in impatience. He snatched a musket from the nearest recruit and demonstrated the proper angle of the weapon for thrusting. "See? *Ja?*" With a low belly laugh, he shoved the rifle back at the lad.

Chris chuckled. "Nothing like having the general's drill officer to entertain us day in, day out, rain or shine. Thank goodness none of us can understand German or French."

"Yes, but the man does have his hands full. You have to admit, he's whipped this motley rabble into a functioning army."

"He's something," Christopher conceded. "No debating that. Last winter when I could hardly get my mind off my empty stomach, he always managed to get a snappy step out of me."

Jonathan eyed Chris, then his own rail-thin form. "We've both put on several pounds since Congress finally came through with food and some decent supplies. Mary will think I cut a fine figure in this, don't you think?" He grinned and brushed some fuzz from his new military coat.

With a hint of a smile, Christopher stared at him. "All she'll see is skin and bones, just like she did when she saw me in April." The mention of the leave he'd taken two months ago brought Evie to Chris's mind. He could still see that first look of hers, that rush to want to mother him. He'd basked in every minute of it.

"For a while, I feared most of us would be naked skeletons marching to battle this year," Jon went on. "I truly appreciate these boots you and Robert brought back from Carolina." He lifted a foot and admired his sturdy footwear.

Christopher broke into a wide grin. "Beats those dandy buckle shoes Morgan's been passing out to everyone, that's for sure."

"Let's just be glad he's *got* shoes to dole out."

"To those of us who survived." Chris sobered at the thought of the frightful winter the American army had somehow endured in the bleak hills of Valley Forge, with the bitter north wind seeping through the chinks in their log huts. Hundreds of men, weakened by weeks of half-rations and without proper clothes or blankets, succumbed to all manner of disease. Many died in agony in the pathetic conditions of the camp. "I'll wager that if Adams and Hancock—and Franklin especially—were still serving at the Congress, we wouldn't have starved *or* frozen. Did I tell you about the man in my cabin who lost a foot to frostbite?"

Jon shook his head sadly. "The lads have paid a great price because men like Ben Franklin are away from the Congress. But old Franklin *had* to go to Paris to convince the king of France to join our cause."

Renewed optimism cheered Chris. "You know, if the French send an army even half the size of Britain's, we'll win for sure. Maybe by the end of summer."

"We can always hope." Jonathan expelled a sigh. "Mary doesn't know yet that I got my transfer. Her last letter was not good. The fact that only you and Robert got a furlough last April did not sit well with her. At all."

That was hardly news to Chris. He'd seen his sister's frustration himself. And though he'd been able to spend some time with Evelyn a mere two months ago, he realized he was as eager to see her again as Jon was to be reunited with Mary Clare and his daughters. "For me, transferring has not been so easy a choice. I promised Evie two things—to join the engineers *and* to go home with the militia. And so far the high command isn't sending any engineers with the Wyoming Valley boys."

"Well, I don't believe any of us will be going home until our valley's actually attacked. The redcoats have been making too many forays out of Philadelphia the last few days. All perdition is about to break loose. I can feel it."

Headquarters loomed into view, and Christopher grimaced. "Just pray it's not today." He stopped short. "Hey, maybe they've called us here to present us with medals. We deserve as many as they've got."

Jon laughed and elbowed him back into step. "Then we could stick out our chests and strut around like Von Steuben."

With summer in its glory, the beauty of floral hues and a mixture of fragile perfumes seemed at cross purposes to the starkness of the military encampment with its system of redoubts and entrenchments around its base. The sight of a bush brilliant with bright pink azaleas brought to Christopher the remembrance of the bright spring flowers Evie had woven into her hair for Robert and Emily's wedding.

He paused and plucked a bloom. The scent, when he put it to his nose, brought a sweet ache to his heart. The visit with Evie had been far too short. He recalled standing beside her, seeing those glorious dark curls as they twined all around the flower garland. But he barely remembered the ceremony uniting their two friends.

Chris had yet to seek Morgan's permission to ask Evelyn for her hand. Being accepted in the engineer corps was only a small step forward, not enough to earn a poor man's blessing, let alone one from the heir to one of the richest merchants in Philadelphia. Nevertheless, he treasured the lingering memory of Evie's eyes on him, the feel of her satiny soft skin . . . and he kept hoping.

Over the past year and a half, her letters had been a real comfort to him. But they were no comparison to being with her, hearing her sparkling laugh, watching her put a young filly through its paces. How hard she had worked to become an asset to him. Chris couldn't have asked for any greater proof of her love.

His sister's letters, however, contained only disapproval of city-bred Evie. Chris understood that timid Mary would have a hard time being at ease around someone as self-assured as Evelyn. But the tender words written by Evie's hand, the rough calluses her once-soft and finely tapered fingers now bore, told Chris everything he wanted to know. He loved her strength and determination, her lips. . . .

He pressed the flower to his mouth. Never again would he be able to walk into a horse barn and smell the straw-covered floor without remembering Evie's soft, inviting lips.

A tug on his sleeve brought him back to reality. "I said," Jon whispered, "isn't that General Washington yonder?"

Off to one side Christopher noticed the high hedge surrounding the home of Isaac Potts, a neat, two-story stone dwelling, which was the commander's headquarters. Through a small break in the foliage, the two could easily make out their white-wigged leader as he knelt in a grove of trees, tricorn in hand, his head bowed in private prayer.

"We'd best not disturb him," Chris whispered.

Jonathan nodded. "For him to be praying like that in the middle of the day, I'd guess the British must be marching out of Philadelphia in great force."

The words echoed Chris's own thoughts in a most disturbing way.

The two strode up the front walk, and Robert Chandler, standing within the relative darkness of the open door, gestured for them to come in, then preceded them up the entry hall.

Christopher and Jonathan followed quietly into a side room that had been converted into an office. To their surprise, Morgan and Dan stood there deep in conversation. Their backs turned, they showed no indication of realizing anyone had arrived.

Dan placed a hand on Morgan's arm.

Morgan stiffened and shoved it away. "I should have taken them out of there when Robert went for Emily."

Watching them, a jolt of alarm shot through Christopher. Something had to be terribly wrong.

"I know it's hard," Dan said quietly. "But we must be thankful the Indians didn't sack the whole valley. I just brought news to Washington that they burned the Cobleskill settlement up in New York, butchering and looting throughout the neighborhood."

"I don't care who else the Indians took," Morgan rasped in a choked voice as he clutched Dan's shoulders. "Just my—"

Christopher crossed the room toward them. "What?" He spun Morgan to face him. *Who do they have?*

Morgan's red-rimmed eyes flared. His features crumpled at the sight of Chris. He swallowed hard, then clamped a hand on Chris's shoulder. "Evie, Chip. They've got Evie."

22

Susannah stepped out of the makeshift shelter she and Prudence had constructed between one of the palisades and their wagon. Elongated shadows hailed the end of yet another day, the fourth since Morgan's sister had been kidnapped. Contemplating the wretched uncertainty of whether or not Evelyn might still be alive, she released the flap of the borrowed blanket over the entrance and hurried to the task of fetching wood from the pile beside the blacksmith's for their supper fire—any chore, however mundane, to occupy her mind.

Someone tapped the windowpane as Susannah passed the smithy's cabin. She looked up to see Martha Graham, the assistant blacksmith's wife, beckoning from within the small dwelling.

Susannah didn't want to talk to anyone at the moment, but she felt obligated to the motherly woman who had befriended her and Dan when they were new arrivals in the valley from Boston. Forcing a smile, she waved and turned toward the door.

Mistress Graham's slight form came into view as she swung the door wide. "So good to see you, child. Now that things have settled down somewhat, I've been wanting to tell you in person that you've been in my prayers day and night. Come in, come in. I'll pour the two of us some coffee."

How like the sweet soul, Susannah thought, to extend her

warm hospitality on the spur of the moment. She lost herself momentarily in the woman's hug, relishing the comforting embrace. Then, inhaling deeply, she drew away and smiled into the kindly light brown eyes framed by a coronet of silver braids.

"You haven't been sleeping much, I can tell," Mistress Graham remarked. "Still worried, I expect."

Susannah nodded. "I do try hard not to be, but it's . . . it's just the not knowing."

The older woman smoothed a rough hand across Susannah's brow. "There's nary a body in the fort who wouldn't feel the same if it were one of theirs. You just come right in and sit down at my table, and we two will have some good strong coffee."

Suddenly grateful for the invitation, Susannah allowed herself to be led inside the plain log structure consisting of three cramped but homey rooms. She sank onto a dark pine chair at the rectangular table while Mistress Graham gathered cups and filled them from the coffeepot on the trivet over the coals. She brought them over on a tray, along with plates of warm blueberry pie.

"This is so very kind of you," Susannah murmured. She took the proffered hand while Mistress Graham returned a brief word of grace, then took a sip of the rich coffee.

"Must be truly hard on you and Prudence," the older woman said. "The scattering of the horses, I mean. So many trails to follow. 'Twas such bad luck that old hunter Kinyon has come down sick. We must pray he's well before it rains and washes out the tracks."

Susannah could only shrug as tears welled behind her eyes. It took all her strength to keep them inside, but it was imperative for her to maintain her control and not give in to the fears and sorrow so near to the surface of her emotions. "I'm doing what I can to stay busy," she finally managed. "But it isn't easy. Cooped up here in the fort, there's so little for one to do." She sampled the pie.

A door creaked open and a towheaded tot came out of one

of the bedchambers. Scooping him up, the hostess rose and closed the door, then came back. She offered the child a fat round berry and sat down again.

The little boy chewed the treat and stared at Susannah from the haven of Mrs. Graham's lap.

"I'd forgotten that Bettina was still with you," Susannah said. "She's so easily frightened, I know. It's quite fortunate she's not alone at her farm this spring."

Concern drew the features in the older woman's thin face together. "I doubt her being here has helped overmuch. She's made herself sick worrying over what else might come to pass. Took right to her bed the first day, she did. With this awful business going on all around us, General Washington will have no choice but to hurry our menfolk back to us. If Bettina's husband was with her, she'd likely feel much safer."

"Perhaps I could talk with her," Susannah offered, rising.

The hostess stayed her with a hand. "You're a very gracious lass, dear, and I know you'd mean Bitsy no harm. But it's best she not be reminded about Evelyn's capture, if you take my meaning."

"Of course." With a sigh, Susannah sat back down in her chair. "I can't help but feel reminded of when Boston-town was under siege. The tension was unbelievable, you know, with British soldiers billeted right in some of our homes. Then there was the animosity between the patriots and the Loyalists." She shook her head. "That made it even worse. By the time the patriot army started bombarding the port from advantageous positions overlooking the city, everyone's fear was so real one could almost smell it. After all, cannonballs and grapeshot cannot distinguish between Crown soldiers and civilians, be they Loyalists or patriots."

"I remember hearing about it," Mistress Graham said with a nod. "All of America held its breath."

"The Lord's great mercy, and Dan, of course, sustained me then." Susannah paused momentarily. "I'm doing my best to trust in our heavenly Father's love now, too. But it's hard. So very, very hard."

The hostess didn't respond at first, as though hoping to come up with an answer that would bolster Susannah's fragile faith and tentative courage. "Perhaps at least for now," she said quietly, "we must take what comfort we can from knowing no trace has yet been found of Evie's remains."

Susannah had to swallow. "But I must wonder how hard anyone has actually searched. Evie has no menfolk here to speak on her behalf, and I needn't tell you she didn't fit in all that well. No one seemed to take to her except for a few half-grown lads struck with the first yearnings of love." She raised her cup and closed her eyes while she took a sip. "I should have helped Evelyn more. If anyone should have understood how she felt, it is I. As an Englishwoman married to a patriot, I experienced my share of animosity from both sides while we lived in Boston. 'Twas not in the least pleasant."

"Surely your church folk understood."

"Yes, for the most part. But at one point, I'm sad to say, several of the women actually shunned me."

"You can't mean that!" the older woman gasped in shock.

Susannah gave her a brief smile. "I had befriended some of the young homesick lads from Britain, you see. And before reconciliation seemed hopeless, I introduced a few of the nicer ones to the young maidens in our congregation." She took another mouthful of pie.

"Oh, dear."

"Quite." Her smile turned grim. "Hindsight is ever so much clearer, is it not? Then, to make matters worse, when the Crown forces and the Loyalists evacuated Boston and sailed for Halifax, one of the church lasses sailed away with them. My midwife's daughter, actually, a sweet girl of sixteen with lovely dark hair and huge brown eyes. Liza was her name. She ran off with her young man—without the benefit of marriage."

"Oh, my." A slow shake of the older woman's head set the trailing ribbons of her untied housecap into motion.

"I still pray for Liza every night," Susannah continued. "And the mother she left behind. As far as I know, no one has heard from Liza since. I feel it's my punishment, not knowing where she is or whether Private Blake has done right by her. I don't know if he could afford to marry, being merely an enlisted man. And if he could not, will Midwife Brown ever find it in her heart to forgive them? or me?"

"I sometimes wonder about Bettina's mother, too," Mrs. Graham confessed. "Her family, the Nelsons, have been feuding with her husband's family for years over a property line. She fears neither side would welcome her home—else she'd have sought their comfort and succor when her Buddy left to go to war."

"How terribly sad," Susannah whispered. "She needs all of them so badly just now. Perhaps if she were to contact them by post she'd be pleasantly surprised."

"Perhaps. But the possibility of facing that rejection is about as fearful to her as the threat of those Indians."

The very mention of the Indians brought back Susannah's own uneasiness. She drank the last of her coffee and rose to her feet. "Well, I must go. I was on my way to get wood for our cook fire. Thank you ever so much for the refreshments . . . and for listening."

Setting the little tot on the empty chair beside her own, the hostess rose and enfolded Susannah in another hug. "God be with you, child."

At the woodpile moments later, Susannah couldn't help comparing Evelyn's situation to that of Bettina's and Liza's. Evie was estranged from her family, as they were, but unlike the other young women, Evie had never had the opportunity to plead her case with her mother. Her parents had not the slightest inkling that their daughter's sympathies lay with the patriot cause until British soldiers unexpectedly came to their Philadelphia home to arrest Evie for spying, on the chance that she had returned there from New York. Concerned for her own safety as well as that of her parents, Evie had purposely refrained from writing them once she managed to flee to Wilkes-Barre. Letters were so easily traced.

And now Susannah could only hope her ward's daring and

courage as a spy would somehow enable her to survive. If by some miracle she had not been scalped or horribly tortured, her fate could be equally unspeakable.

As a rule, the people in the fort were careful not to say anything in Susannah's presence that might upset her, but voices carried easily outside. During the still night hours, a mere thickness of blanket walls hardly prevented low conversations from penetrating her crude shelter. Susannah almost wished she hadn't overheard some of the remarks the sentries and other townspeople made to each other when they thought no one was listening. The horrendous tales of wicked and inhuman treatment perpetrated on helpless captives were enough to make the bravest man tremble.

She bent down to pick up a good-sized stick for kindling, and an unbidden reminder of one of the most common forms of torture came to Susannah's mind. Was this rough piece of wood the size some bronze-skinned heathen would use to beat poor Evie as she was forced to run the gauntlet? Susannah slapped her hand with it, causing a sting, and a chill ran through her. How one human being could derive pleasure from inflicting such hideous pain on another was a perversion beyond Susannah's imagination. She couldn't picture an innocent young girl like Evie being stripped naked to run between two lines of laughing, mocking savages while they spit on her and struck her, all the while trying to trip her to gain an added number of licks.

Worse, those who fell before reaching the opposite end would be sent back to the beginning to try again, over and over, until they managed to finish the course—or were bludgeoned to death.

Supposedly, for those they had chosen to keep as slaves, it was some sort of initiation into the tribe. For the less fortunate—Susannah could not bear to dwell on the far more grotesque tortures that befell them. Surely the very heart of God grieved over such barbarity.

In a flush of rage, Susannah whacked the stick against her palm again, wincing at the stinging pain. *Dear God,* she pleaded silently . . . then had no idea what to ask for. It was all she could do to remember that the Indians were merely other lost souls for whom Christ had given his life . . . that only as God's love was given free rein in the human heart could its natural bent toward evil be tempered. But the Iroquois had proven themselves so cruel and ruthless. Should she pray that Evie was still alive—or would death be far more merciful?

Shaking off the disturbing thoughts, she gathered up enough logs for the night's cook fire and hurried back toward her camp, longing desperately for something else to occupy her mind.

"Riders are coming!" one of the lookouts yelled as she neared her shelter.

The men of the fort dropped what they were doing and rushed for their weapons as Susannah flew past.

"Indians?" somebody hollered up to the sentry.

"No. White men. Four, looks like."

Vainly Susannah wished it could be Dan. But there was no possible way he could arrive so soon. By her calculations, the earliest she could expect him would be tomorrow eve. She let out a ragged sigh.

The big gates slowly swung open, and hordes of townspeople poured through them. Susannah caught sight of Mary Clare, Prudence, and the children several yards ahead. She hurried to catch up to them, the awkward load still in her arms.

Suddenly Susannah caught her breath. One of the riders appeared to be the right height . . . and he sat his mount in a familiar way. . . .

"Dan!" She dropped the firewood in a clattering heap and raced toward him.

Reaching her, he swung down from his still-moving horse and caught her to himself, raining kisses all over her face.

Susannah returned his kisses, and the throbbing of his heart against her breast all but made time stand still. She didn't care who witnessed their public display. Prickles from a few days' worth of whiskers mattered not a whit. After a while she realized that her face was wet with tears and that they mingled with his.

Someone tugged on his clothes. Dan dragged his lips from hers.

"Daddy! You're home!"

Dan's exhausted features softened into a smile at the sight of his children, and he swept Julia Rose up into one arm and tousled Miles's hair with his free hand, then tugged him close.

Susannah joined in, gathering her little family into a huge embrace, wishing the moment could last forever.

But discordant sounds gradually intruded on their private joy. She felt a hand on her shoulder and turned to see Christopher's anguished face.

"Evie! Have the men rescued her?" Without waiting for a reply, he turned and searched the sea of townspeople who had already begun to withdraw into the confines of the fort.

Susannah could barely speak around the lump clogging her throat. She shook her head sadly. "I'm so sorry, Chip." Defeat snatched the tiny glimmer of hope from his eyes, and she seized him and drew him close, murmuring wordless, soothing tones.

"Are the men still looking?" Morgan asked, moving toward her with Prudence pressed against his side. Susannah had never seen him more haggard.

"No. The way the horses scattered to the four winds, there was no way to discern any sort of actual trail to follow."

"So they stopped looking for her?" Chris cried incredulously.

From a discreet distance away, Colonel Butler stepped up to them. "I accept full responsibility for our lack of action in the matter. There's talk that the unholy Englishman who bears the same name as I is headed this way with his rangers and his hired Iroquois. I couldn't—"

Christopher lunged at him, grabbing the man's lapels. "Couldn't what? Lift a finger to go after an innocent young maiden? You no good—"

Men immediately dragged Christopher from him.

Ruffled, the colonel straightened his coat. "Tragic as these circumstances are, young man, I am responsible for the safety of all the people now assembled inside this fort—as well as other forts in the valley. We have very few able-bodied men left in the area because of the war, and we are desperately undermanned."

Jonathan came closer. Holding onto the clinging Mary Clare, he placed his other hand on the colonel's shoulder. "We understand your burden. I reckon we'll have a better chance of finding Evelyn if we go on our own anyway."

"You only just arrived!" Mary wailed. "I won't have you going off—"

Christopher glared at his sister, then grabbed her arm. "Don't do this, Mare. It's been four days. They've had Evie four days and three nights already."

Obviously torn at hearing the truth flung so passionately in her face, Mary burst into tears.

Jonathan drew her into a comforting embrace. "Zeb," he said over her blonde head, "where's Kinyon? Garth Kinyon. Is he still here in the valley?"

Butler nodded. "But he's been struck with influenza. Had it near a week. Folks across the river at Forty Fort are looking after him. A man his age and all . . ."

"Sick or well," Jon insisted, "he's got to go with us at first light. No one else in these parts has spent time with the Iroquois. He knows a little of their language."

"Not till first light?" Chris interrupted in disbelief.

Dan met his gaze. "As much as we'd all like to go after her this minute, we wouldn't accomplish anything in the dark. And we must fetch Garth Kinyon. Not only does he speak the Indian tongues, he can outtrack the best of their lot. If anyone can pick out hoofprints from Evie's hunter among those left by our pacers, it'll be Garth." He turned to Susannah. "Your message did say she was on her own horse, didn't it?"

Without taking her eyes from Christopher, she nodded. The young man's expression revealed the same panicked frustration she'd experienced the day Evelyn had been kidnapped. Her own was a mere fraction less sharp. Susannah glanced at Morgan and saw that he, too, was but slightly mollified. She knew that only the fact that his wife and babe were here and safe could temper his anguish for his sister.

But poor Christopher. Susannah stepped away from Dan and opened her arms once again to the young man who had been like a little brother to her in Princeton. *"Chip."*

He moved into her embrace in a flash. Trembling with bottled up grief, he moved into her embrace and clung to her.

23

Christopher resented this added delay—the time it took for him, Jon, Morgan, and Dan to ferry across the Susquehanna and fetch Garth Kinyon at Forty Fort. The man would probably be too sick to travel. Precious time—an entire night of it—had already been wasted in Wilkes-Barre. Now as the eastern sky lightened, Chris urged his mount ahead of the rest and galloped up to the closed gate of the fort.

"Halloo the fort!" he hollered. "Anybody here?"

Scuffling sounds drifted downward from above, and someone peered over the side. "Who goes there?"

"Drummond's the name. Chris Drummond. I'm with Jon Bradford, from over the river. Open up. We're here to see Garth Kinyon. He still here?"

"Aye. Bringin' word about more Indian assaults, are ya?" the guard asked, signaling for the plank securing the gate to be raised.

"Nothing new." But a sick foreboding gnawed at Christopher's insides even as he answered.

By the time the big doors swung open, Jon and the others had caught up. They entered together.

The fort was crowded with people. They crawled from temporary shelters, rubbing sleep from their eyes in the faint light. An older man approached Jonathan. "Bradford. Good to see you. We've been prayin' you fellows would come home where you're needed."

"Hey," someone shouted, "they're soldiers! The militia's back!"

Jon held up a restraining hand. "Sorry, my good man. There's only us. Our two militias will be coming on foot. They're probably already on their way."

"Praise be!" a woman cried as she enveloped a small child in her knitted shawl. "We're saved!"

"How much longer before the rest get here?" a gaunt man in shabby clothing asked above the hubbub. "Won't be a minute too soon."

Hardly caring about the plight of these folk, Christopher swung his gaze to the sky, streaking with the sun's first rays. "Garth Kinyon . . . where is he?"

"Stayin' with the storekeeper," someone responded, indicating one of the buildings making up the outer walls of the fortress.

Chris, with Morgan close on his horse's heels, left his comrades to deal with questions and made a beeline for the store. They dismounted and went right to the door.

It swung open even as Christopher raised a fist to pound on it.

"What's goin' on out here?" the stocky storekeeper asked. Barefooted, he was still in the process of buttoning his breeches.

Chris clutched two fistfuls of the man's undershirt. "Garth Kinyon. Where is he? We need him."

"So do we, lad, so do we, what with those new reports of redskin attacks around the settlements."

"What do you mean?"

"We just got word a couple hours ago that a man was murdered in his field yesterday a few miles from here, and them thievin' scoundrels have been helpin' themselves to whatever they want."

"What about Kinyon?" Chris insisted, unconcerned with matters that could easily turn out to be rumors.

"He's in the back room," the storekeeper replied. But I wouldn't wake him, if I was you. He's been sick."

Christopher brushed right by the half-dressed man to get inside.

"Our business is urgent," he heard Morgan explain behind him.

Chris passed stacks of crates and barrels, almost tripping over a pile of sacks on his way to a small room in back. He could hear loud snoring coming from that direction, and upon entering the stuffy quarters, he made out a form sound asleep on a cot. He crossed the dimly lit room in two strides. "Mr. Kinyon," Chris said in his normal tone of voice.

The bearded man did not stir.

Christopher latched onto his sinewy arm and gave it a shake. "Mr. Kinyon. Wake up!"

Two sunken eyes snapped open. "Wha—? Injuns?" As if in reflex, the older man swung long, stockinged feet to the floor and wavered uncertainly over them as he sat on the edge of the ticking.

A jagged scar through one dark eyebrow stood out in stark relief against the sickly white face. But it was the sight of the grayish circles ringing the older man's eyes that sent a stab of guilt through Chris. He lowered his voice. "Think you're well enough to sit a horse?" he asked tentatively.

"Reckon so." The old man rubbed his bearded chin. "If I have to."

"You do." Spotting a pair of moccasins shoved under the cot, Christopher knelt down and plucked them out. "We have a horse outside for you, all saddled and waiting."

Kinyon's forehead wrinkled in a frown. "Are we evacuatin' the fort?" He looked beyond Chris as more footsteps approached, and recognition eased the puzzlement from his swarthy features. "Jon. Dan. Thought you two was with Washington."

"We were. I suppose you heard my place got raided."

"And my sister was kidnapped," Morgan added.

"I have some recollection of it. Them horses of yours, to boot, if I'm not mistaken. But I was too befuddled with the fever to do anything. How many days has it been now?"

"Four nights," Chris supplied gravely.

"That many." The older man stroked his wiry beard in thought, then came shakily to his feet. "Well, we'd best set out after her." He tugged a hunting shirt on over his head and thrust his feet into the moccasins. "Rained any since she got took?"

Morgan turned a questioning look to the storekeeper waiting just inside the doorway.

"A sprinkle or two, night before last."

Kinyon swayed, obviously dizzy, and steadied himself on Chris's arm. "Prob'ly didn't do too much damage to the tracks."

"Garth," Dan began, "we heard from one of Barnett's youngsters that Evelyn was on her Thoroughbred hunter. He's quite a bit larger than our pacers, so I figure he'd leave a bigger hoof print."

Kinyon's face brightened, and he straightened, letting go of Chris. "Now, that provides more'n hunches an' hope to go on, don't it?" He sat again and hauled soiled leather breeches up over his bony frame. "Best get a move on before we get us a downpour."

The storekeeper held out an arm. "Wait, Garth. That fever of yours just broke yesterday. You ain't really on your feet yet."

The grizzled tracker guffawed and waved him away. "Won't be on foot. They brung me a horse, and we got us a little gal to fetch home." He gave Chris and the others a once-over. "You lads need to shuck them army duds. Seth, round 'em up some huntin' shirts an' plain britches, will ya? Wouldn't do fer them Injuns to think they're bein' invaded."

"Even if they are?" Chris shot back, his rage surfacing again.

The tracker narrowed his shrewd eyes. "Best you put any murderin' thoughts out of your head, boy. If we intend to get your gal back alive, we gotta go in like we're traders, nuthin' more." He swept a speculative glance around the store. "We need somethin' real special. Somethin' that's sure to catch their attention." His gaze landed on Morgan's saber. He reached over and pulled the long blade from its sheath, then turned it over in perusal. "This might just do the trick. Yessir." He sought the proprietor once more. "What else ya got around here, Seth, that'll set them heathens to droolin'?"

The swift, steady pace Garth Kinyon maintained over the rugged, crooked mountain trail astounded Christopher. Without hesitation the tracker followed the distinctive prints left by Evie's hunter in the decaying leaves and pine needles covering the spongy ground. Around noon, they finally stopped in the dappled shade of a thicket, and the scout dismounted.

Chris noted the renewed color in the weathered complexion—apparently the sunshine and fresh air had actually benefited the man. He couldn't help wondering how much more distance they might have covered if Kinyon had been feeling his best at the start.

"This is where the redskins camped that first night," Garth said, eyeing a tramped down area. He brushed a fern frond aside with his moccasin and studied the surrounding area.

Christopher met Morgan's gaze but said nothing. The idea of Evie's being at the mercy of remorseless savages was as unthinkable to her brother as it was to him. But Chris couldn't think about that. He wouldn't let himself. He could only think about getting her home.

"I don't see anything around here but moccasin prints," Jon commented after getting down from his saddle and stepping cautiously through the site. He waved a pesky mosquito from his face as a breeze rustled the forest branches.

"Don't fret, son," Kinyon replied astutely. "After chasin' a bunch of rambunctious horses all the livelong day, them bucks was sure to be plumb wore out. Prob'ly had the gal trussed up so's they wouldn't have to bother with her."

Christopher heaved a shuddering breath. "You telling us those red devils might not have forced themselves on her?"

Garth dismissed the question with a smirk. "Not with their

face paint still on, they wouldn't. Goes against their superstitions."

"But I heard—"

Kinyon interrupted Jonathan. "Not whilst they're on a raid, son."

Whether warranted or not, Christopher felt a surge of relief and gratefully latched onto the slim ray of hope. "How much farther to the Indian villages?"

"On horseback," Garth began, "with nothin' slowin' us up, *and* if these tracks lead us to one of the closer ones, we should get there in three, four days at most. Now that those braves managed to get the horses on strings, it'll take 'em twice as long. Near as I can reckon, they won't beat us by more'n a day or two."

Urgency once more gripped Christopher. Whatever tortures those miscreants had in store for Evie still faced her. "We're wasting time. Let's get going."

Dan, his face grim with understanding, moved his mount next to Chris's and gripped his arm. "Everyone in Wyoming Valley is praying for her, remember? Hold on to that."

Kinyon pointed to tracks farther out. "Looks like the Injuns split up when they broke camp. Each string of horses goes off in a different direction—to throw us off, most likely. They usually meet up again later on." He pointed northeast. "The gal's horse went that way."

Christopher and Morgan immediately spurred their mounts and sped through the forest on the trail before the tracker had time to climb astride his own.

In midafternoon two days later, they crossed a stream and discovered the spot where two other strings of pacers joined the one the men were following. The trail then headed straight north through the rugged hills.

"From the direction they're takin', I'd say our young braves are prob'ly Cayugas," Kinyon remarked.

"Why do you say that?" Morgan asked, obviously disturbed. "You were quite sure earlier that they were Iroquois."

"Don't git all het up," Garth said evenly. "The Cayuga nation is part of the Iroquois Confederation. I did some tradin' with 'em a few years back. They should remember me, so I shouldn't have much trouble dealin' with 'em. They usually treat guests real good. Come on. We should reach the first village by nightfall."

About an hour before sundown, after following a well-beaten path through the dense forest, Garth raised a hand and came to a stop. "We need to wrap our horses' hooves to keep the noise down."

As the scout slid to the ground and took down his blanket roll, Chris and the others did the same. Soon squares cut from their blankets were secured by rope at the animals' niched pasterns.

"No more talkin', either," Kinyon ordered soberly as they remounted.

Dan frowned. "I don't understand. If we're coming to trade in good faith, why are we sneaking up on them?"

A sly smile crept over the older man's face. "Catchin' 'em unawares will gain us more respect. Besides, I don't want 'em to know how many we are. Best not to put all our cards on the table." He bent low and started back on the trail.

Chris and the others also leaned over their horses' heads and followed single file, doing their best to go stealthily through the debris of the woods.

Another hour passed before the guide signaled for them to halt. Silently they dismounted and moved cautiously beside him to peer through the heavy growth at the edge of the forest.

A huge clearing took up most of the view, much of it under cultivation. Young corn, squash, pumpkins, beans, and all manner of other plants sprouted up in long rows. An orchard along one side appeared to have apple, pear, and peach trees, and on the other side was a wide meadow where cattle grazed. In the center stood a fair-sized village.

Christopher perused the assortment of cabins and saw one very long building with a rounded rooftop covered with bark shingles. There was also a sprinkling of dome-shaped huts. Wisps of smoke drifting from holes in the top of the long-house emitted smells of the evening meal, while mostly naked children cavorted about, playing a stick-ball game beside the huge structure.

Movement near a shallow stream drew Chris's attention. A woman was carrying what had to be a white man's bucket.

"Look," Dan whispered, pointing to a split-rail fence housing livestock. "Our pacers."

"And there—see it?" Morgan cut in, staring intently. "Evie's hunter."

The sight energized Christopher, and he started forward. He would find Evelyn, and nobody would stop him.

"Hold up there, boy," Garth Kinyon said, blocking him with his arm. "Nobody's goin' down there 'cept Jon an' me." He glanced at Dan, gesturing with his head toward Chris and Morgan. "Keep them two out of sight."

"What?" Chris demanded in a loud whisper. "I have to go. I need to make sure it's her."

"Quite," Morgan agreed. "And so do I."

Kinyon didn't blink but hiked his scarred eyebrow. "Listen. I don't know fer sure if the two of *us* will be welcome. And don't think fer a minute them redskins can't kill five men as well as two. Fact is, they might find the idea of a whole passel of scalps too temptin' to resist. The Brits at Fort Niagara are payin' a high bounty on American hair, ya know."

Squaring his shoulders, Christopher stretched to his full height. "Well, if you're only taking one of us, it should be me."

"Hardly." Morgan stepped in front of him. "I daresay, she's my little sister. I'll go."

Chris pulled him aside. "Evie's promised herself to me. She's as good as my wife."

Garth released a weary breath and nailed them both with a commanding scowl. "Now ya see why I'm takin' Jon. I need somebody with a cool head. Somebody who ain't overanxious. But first we have to get all the trade goods moved to our two horses. We need to make a good show of it when we walk in."

Gritting his teeth so hard his jaws hurt, Chris fought back the enormous disappointment as he removed a bolt of colorful yard goods from his horse. He piled it atop the new blankets on Jon's mount, aware of Kinyon's gaze on him as he retied the lot.

"I want ya to know I'll do everything I can to get your little gal back," the scout said. "But if they take a notion to keep Jon an' me, the rest of you hightail it out of here as fast as them horses'll take ya."

"What are you saying?" Chris railed.

Dan placed a hand on his shoulder. "How will we know?" he asked Kinyon. "How long should we wait?"

"The tracker slid him a grim smile. "Ya won't have to guess at it; you'll know by the ruckus. Enough said."

Suddenly the full weight of the danger he'd refused to recognize up till this point fell upon Christopher. Now he had not only Evelyn and her welfare to consider but also his brother-in-law and this stalwart tracker—both of whom were about to walk into danger for her. Humbled, he reached out to Garth Kinyon and gave his hand a hard squeeze. "Just know we send you with all our hope and our most earnest prayers. Please, bring my Evie back to me."

24

Leaving the others secluded in the thicket, Jonathan went with Garth Kinyon. They circled some distance away from the rest to enter the Indian village downwind. Should the worst happen, at least his friends would gain a few moments' head start if they had to make a run for it.

Activity in the encampment showed no awareness of their presence. Cooking smells carried on the smoke from the dwellings, and the laughter and shrieks of children at play and the unheeded barking of dogs indicated the rarity of unexpected visitors.

Jonathan's qualms about entering this nest of vipers increased with each step as he and Kinyon led their loaded horses through the field of half-grown corn. The Scriptures clearly warned against the foolhardiness of tempting God and putting him to the test. After all, Evelyn Thomas was neither Jon's sister nor his wife. Why should he be risking his life for her when he had his own family to consider?

It would be some time before he would be able to erase from his mind the vision of Mary Clare's stricken face when he had ridden away with the search party. Jon could still feel his shy, vulnerable wife clinging fiercely to him, could almost taste the saltiness of the tears streaming down her white cheeks—while sweet little Esther clutched her mama's skirt, the girlish face mirroring Mary's pain. But what left an even more jagged and gaping wound inside him was an even dearer price incurred by his absence this past year and a half. His youngest daughter, Beth, no longer knew her daddy enough to care one way or the other. Perhaps it would have been wiser to remain at the fort in case of a full-scale attack similar to the bloody carnage experienced in May up in New York.

Yes, he was needed much more at home in the valley than here in this Indian village allied to the British. He should be looking after his three golden-haired angels, making certain no harm came to them.

Even with those conflicting thoughts warring in his mind, Jonathan knew better than to betray his fears. He tamped them down as best he could. Kinyon had seemed fairly certain the Indians' desire for future trade goods from him would prevent them from lifting their two scalps this day. Jon only hoped the tracker's theory proved true.

In the distance, a small child cried. Very few people were moving about. Most likely the time had come to eat the evening meal or to prepare the little ones for bed. It seemed strange to imagine such routine matters being conducted by a people capable of unspeakable brutality against other people's children—even babes in arms. Yet here they appeared to be living in quiet harmony.

Suddenly a shout of alarm interrupted the tranquility of the village. A young lad bolted for the longhouse, glancing back over his shoulder as he ran.

They'd been spotted. Feeling as if he were walking straight into the jaws of death, it was all Jonathan could do not to hunker down behind Kinyon's horse.

Bronzed men instantly poured out of every structure, their dark eyes and countenances cold, guarded, as they massed together with weapons leveled on the intruders.

Garth Kinyon's pace didn't falter. He raised a hand and greeted them in words Jonathan could not understand.

The answer came in harsh tones.

Kinyon kept up a calm exchange.

A sturdily built Indian in only a breechcloth and beaded

moccasins stepped forward. The sides of his hair were plaited, and the swarthy face showed no warmth. But he lowered his musket, and his tone seemed nonthreatening as he spoke to the old hunter.

Trying to give an impression of confidence, Jonathan drew on his military training and stood tall and erect while Kinyon kept up a stream of halting phrases. Inwardly he marveled at the seemingly relaxed appearance of a man who, mere moments ago, had voiced the very real possibility that neither of them would leave this place alive.

Some of the villagers moved nearer, tightening the circle around the newcomers. A few began rifling through the packs on the horses with pleased grunts and nods.

When Garth spoke again, a weathered, gray-haired man with a splendid robe draping one shoulder stepped through the mob and barked a command.

The crowd respectfully fell back from the horses.

The old chieftain then said something to Kinyon and turned, gesturing for him to follow.

Jonathan gripped the bridle of his horse and followed close behind through a path created by the villagers. Many of the men were armed and in various styles of dress; they stood shoulder to shoulder, muttering to one another as their black eyes darted between the tracker and Jonathan. Jon, seeing no friendly faces among the hostile stares, tried not to think about how the lines of armed savages reminded him of the infamous gauntlet. The stench of tobacco and the heavy odor of bear grease assailed his nostrils.

They passed between a number of log houses and cone-shaped dwellings before reaching the longhouse. As he walked, Jonathan peeked furtively into any uncovered door-way. If Evie were in the village, she would more than likely be tied up somewhere out of sight—assuming, that is, that she was still alive. Still, his eyes searched out the shadows, but he caught no glimpse of her or any other white person.

Upon reaching the impressive rectangular structure, the

old chief turned and uttered a few more words. A youth sprang up and reached for the reins of Jon's horse.

"Give it to him, friend, while we talk," Garth said. "He'll watch over it and our trade goods whilst we're inside."

Jon hesitated, unwilling to relinquish his only swift means of escape.

"Do as I say." The excessive nonchalance in Garth Kinyon's tone contrasted sharply with the urgency in his steely gray eyes.

With great reluctance, Jon complied.

"And do what I do," the tracker went on. He followed the old chieftain inside. Jon entered behind him as a host of others crowded in, closing them off from the doorway.

The longhouse, which had appeared quite large from the outside, caught Jonathan by surprise when he entered its shadowy coolness. The ceiling was two or three times higher than that of a cabin. A few squaws, busy with various duties, ceased their work at once and moved to the sides.

Jon wondered about the huge cavernous structure as he glanced around. Windowless walls roughly eighteen feet wide and over seventy-five feet long were framed of saplings driven into the ground at three-foot intervals and then shingled with elm bark fastened together with a cordage of woody fibers. The only light shafted downward through smoke holes in the rounded roof. A pungent blend of cooking smoke, tobacco, tanned hides, and the ever-present bear grease permeated the interior in an almost visible cloud. Along the dirt floor, shallow pits for cook fires sat under the smoke holes, each surrounded by enclosures partitioned off with hides. Within each alcove they passed, Jon saw a platform about a foot above the damp ground with sleeping pallets of reed or corn-husk mats and blankets of animal pelts.

The chief led the way quite deep inside the building to a large pit at the center—a fair distance from the doorways at either end. He motioned for them to sit on a robe of soft fur pelts.

Following Kinyon's lead, Jon sat down at a fire that had

burned to smoldering embers. The chief and the rest of the Indians silently did the same, circling it.

The women in the background began moving about once more. From the cook fires on either side, they brought gourds and wooden bowls of stew, offering them first to the chief, then to Kinyon and Jon.

After saying something to the tracker, the old leader turned to Jon and uttered additional words Jon could only conclude must be some sort of welcome.

Kinyon responded, but Jon could only resort to a smile and a nod.

The silence broken now, more food was brought for the other Indians, and all began to partake of the stew. Jonathan could not quite identify its smell, but vowed he'd eat politely no matter what. Watching the others, he raised his bowl and tentatively tipped it into his mouth.

At that moment his gaze came to rest on a jarring sight. A gourd-topped stick jutted at a slant from the wall, and from it dangled a pair of long brown braids. Jonathan almost choked. Desperately he tried to recall the color of Evie's hair. Oh yes, much darker—and curly, not straight. The small relief did nothing to restore his appetite, however. He only hoped the horror he'd felt had not registered on his face. Suppressing a shudder, he concentrated on taking another swallow of the odd-tasting concoction. He'd have to ask Kinyon later what on earth it was.

By the time the bowl was empty, darkness had done its merciful best by blotting out the offensive trophy hanging behind the chief. More food was brought, and after that, still more. For two solid hours Jon kept accepting the proffered food, much of which he couldn't identify. Months of short rations at Valley Forge caused his stomach to protest painfully, but he tried his hardest to keep up with the others. He even managed a hearty belch—apparently, among the Iroquois, a compliment to the chef. He had a harder time, however, maintaining a jovial expression. He knew too well that the Indians were fully capable of turning on them at any second.

During the entire time, Garth Kinyon conversed with several of the Indians in the gathering. Jon had no idea what was being discussed, but he knew better than to ask his friend to interpret. It seemed wiser to keep from drawing unwarranted attention to himself. Already he was acutely aware of several hundred black eyes boring holes into him—and no doubt assessing the very hair on his head as well. His mismatched eyes—one green and the other blue—had already captivated the children. They had been sneaking peeks whenever possible, so he purposely kept his head lowered and his eyes averted.

Time dragged miserably. Darkness had descended ages ago, and through the smoke hole of the dying fire, Jonathan could see stars. Were Christopher, Morgan, and Dan still out there in the woods where he and Kinyon had left them? Or had they given up, since the two of them had not yet emerged from the longhouse? The old hunter had never hinted that dealing with the Indians could be such a lengthy business.

Finally the last bowl of food was taken away. But Jon's relief was short-lived when Kinyon remained quietly seated.

One of the Indians took tobacco from a pouch and, in an elaborate ritual, sprinkled some upon the wind, then took more and filled a long, thin pipe adorned by a cluster of feathers. A second brave lit the pipe with a stick from the fire and then, with great ceremony, offered it to the chief.

The old leader drew a few puffs, then passed it on to Kinyon.

Jon concluded that this must be a good sign. He'd heard about this ritual of discussing business over a peace pipe. When it came his way, he gratefully took a puff and passed it back.

At last the tracker began to talk in earnest. Around the fire, the expressions of some of the younger braves turned angry as Kinyon talked, and others grew stubborn. But Kinyon remained unruffled. Unexpectedly he turned to Jon. "Go out to the horses with Gaiwiio, here, and bring back the sword."

He turned to the chieftain. "I want to present it to our illustrious host."

The middle-aged Indian nodded with a grunt, his eyes gleaming.

Suddenly it came to Jon that the chief had some understanding of English, and he wondered how many of the others did, too. Learning the language would certainly have been to their advantage when trading with the English. He thanked the Lord that he hadn't inadvertently muttered something that might have cost him and the tracker their lives.

At a signal from a tall, thin brave whose head was shaved except for one shock of hair running from front to back, Jon rose and followed him outside. The horses had been hobbled, their bridles removed and draped over the animals' backs as they grazed just outside the longhouse. The lad who'd been left to tend them now sat against the side of the building near the center, where he could eavesdrop. Obviously Jon and Kinyon were of great interest to everyone living here.

Withdrawing the saber, Jon walked back inside with his escort. Now that he was aware of the Indians' love of ritual, he bowed astutely to Garth Kinyon and sank to one knee. With the sword lying across both hands, he held it out with utmost reverence as if it were the Holy Grail itself. He made certain that the intricately carved handle was on prominent display.

Kinyon's astonished stare almost broke the solemnity of the act, but Jonathan forced himself to remain composed until his companion accepted the weapon and stood, clasping it the very way Jon had held it. He turned sharply and grasped the handle, whipping the shining sword back and forth with a flourish of his own, the blade swishing through the smoky air. Then he touched the flat of the blade to his nose in a grand bow at the chieftain.

Whatever words he uttered over it as he held it with the handle in one palm and the blade resting in the other were lost to Jonathan, except for the odd phrase—*royal saber, token of peace, welfare of the clan*. But the Indians seemed impressed and murmured with awe, as if the thing were imbued with magical powers.

Much to Jon's dismay, more talk followed, and more time dragged by. Finally three Indians were sent outside, and they returned with the rest of the bundled goods. Kinyon gestured for them to open the blankets and display the wares. Another burst of grunts and nods issued forth over the selection of knives, pots, axes, hoes and hatchets, jars of buttons and glass beads, and bolts of fabrics. Last of all, a jug of rum was lifted high.

Jonathan's spirits deflated. Surely everyone knew how unpredictable the red man became when besotted.

The Indians, however, were overjoyed. One uncorked the jug and gulped a great swig before passing it on.

Kinyon made some forceful comment to the old chief, who in turn spoke to the man now in possession of the rum. Immediately it was plugged again and returned to the blanket on the ground.

Some of the braves who up until this moment had been silent spoke out, each speaking in turn to the leader in what seemed a favorable manner.

Shortly after that, the old fellow rose up and approached the squaws. He conducted several minutes of deep conversation while Jon waited anxiously.

About the time Jonathan was going to give up completely, two of the women left. The chief resumed his seat and nodded to his men, and some dived for the rum again. Others picked through the goods. With renewed optimism, Jon figured Kinyon must have struck some kind of deal. Any second now Evelyn would come walking into the longhouse, and he and Kinyon would whisk her out and get as far away from here as possible.

Sounds of muffled confusion came from outside.

Garth Kinyon stood up while the women came back, returning through the deep shadows and flickering firelight. They dragged a reluctant girl along with them. Thrilled that it was finally happening, Jonathan jumped to his feet.

The jug reached the chieftain, who took a swig and passed it to Jon.

He took a quick gulp. The girl was now near enough to see. Wiping his mouth, Jonathan peered through the dimness at her.

A matted mass of hair covered most of her face. Her dress was in tatters and did little to cover her mottled limbs. Jon's heart cramped with almost uncontrollable rage at the mess of slashes and bruises marring her bare calves and arms. Why, she was little more than skin and bones—yet obviously had been forced to run the gauntlet . . . and heaven only knew what other horrors had befallen her.

The women spoke harshly to the victim, and one yanked her downcast head up by the hair and gave her a shove in Jonathan's direction. As if fearing more abuse, she threw her hands up in reflex as her rigid body crashed into Jon.

Catching her, he could see now that this girl's hair was straight and much lighter than Evie's. "Garth," he whispered. *"It's not her."*

Kinyon ignored him. He faced the chieftain and said a few more words, then turned. "Time to go." Gesturing with his head for Jon to follow, he headed for the entrance.

Jonathan, overcome with confusion and disappointment, supported the girl as best he could as he turned to leave.

She stiffened with fear and would not cooperate at all.

He had no recourse but to pick her up and stride after Garth. "Don't be afraid," he murmured into her ear. "You're safe now." He only hoped it wasn't a lie, that the trade goods would indeed be enough for this frail little thing—and for Evie. Wherever she was.

Kinyon was unhobbling the horses in the faint glow of a torch when the two of them reached him.

"They've given us the wrong girl," Jon repeated in an insistent whisper.

The tracker straightened and grabbed the bridle hooked over the saddle horn. "Heard you the first time, lad. But she's the only white slave they got. Now, toss her up here and get that horse of yours ready to ride out of here. It'd be just like 'em to take a notion to change their mind."

"But—Evelyn's horse is here."

"I know, son, I know. It was brought here without a rider, and the young buck who had it went to join up with Bloody Butler's Rangers. Seems they're headin' down the Susquehanna in force. Hundreds of 'em. Right down to the Wyoming Valley."

25

Flickering specks of firelight were all Christopher could make out from his vantage point behind a broad-leaved maple. Exhaling a shaky breath, he slumped against the trunk in despair and shoved his fists into his pockets. It had been hours. Hours! Without one sign or glimpse of either Garth Kinyon or Jonathan since they'd gone to trade with the Indians. Now in the deep darkness shrouding the woods, every night bird, every animal sound or snap of a twig startled Chris. Would word of Evie never come? For that matter, would Kinyon and Jon get out of there alive?

Chris slid a glance toward Morgan, then Dan, whose silhouettes a few yards away all but blended into the impenetrable black of night. Both heads were bowed in prayer even now, adding to the unending stream of intercession that had been offered throughout the interminable wait. Dan's quiet confidence in the Lord's faithfulness did much to bolster Christopher's wavering hope, but this wretched helplessness, this having to remain virtually motionless and silent for such a long time, was taking its toll.

One good thing had come out of this situation, Christopher thought as he looked at Morgan. For the first time since Chris had promised himself to Evie, he had found the courage to speak openly regarding the feelings he and Evelyn had for each other and his plans for their future. He even explained that Evie had made a point of becoming proficient in handling horses so she could take an active part in those grand dreams. The revelation hardly took Morgan by surprise. No doubt Prudence had written to her husband regarding the growing relationship between his younger sister and Chris. And—thankfully—Morgan assured Chris that if the two of them still felt the same about one another when the war was over, he'd consider Chris's suit. Of course, he'd added, Chris would have her parents' objections to overcome as well.

But all that would have to wait until the war ended. If Jonathan and the tracker ever came back with Evelyn, that is. Christopher sank to his haunches, brushing aside a pesky fern, invisible in the dark. Everything rested on Evie's still being alive.

Suddenly a rustling sounded behind him. Chris sprang to his feet and grabbed his rifle.

"Easy," Dan whispered, shoving aside the raised barrel. "It's only me. Horses are coming."

Christopher held his breath and listened to the muffled crunch of hooves.

Morgan moved to join them. "Do you hear that?"

"It has to be Kinyon," Dan murmured. "Indians wouldn't muffle their mounts' hooves this close to home."

A surge of expectation coursed through Christopher. Following Dan's lead, he and Morgan crouched down to wait.

"You know, Chip," Dan said quietly, "while I was praying, I realized something. We might not have ever had to be here today, had we sent more missionaries into the Indian villages to share the gospel. By now we might all have been able to dwell peaceably together."

Chris shook his head and turned away. Dan might be right about the mission work, but would he have felt the same if it had been Susannah they were waiting for instead of Evie?

Only a sliver of moon pierced the deep shadows in the forest. When the two horses passed through a break in the trees, the form of an extra rider could be seen.

"Evie!" Chris leaped up, barely conscious of Morgan by his

side as he raced to her. He snatched her by the waist and pulled her down into a fierce hug.

She gasped and pushed against his chest, trying to get free.

Christopher held her away in shock, unable to conceive of being rebuffed. *It wasn't Evie! How could it not be her?*

"That's not my sister!" Morgan snapped.

Jonathan gave a resigned nod. "Evelyn isn't there. We spent hours eating and drinking, haggling—only to find out they didn't have her."

Chris barely heard the explanation as his pulse pounded in his ears. Staring incredulously at Jon, he dropped his hold on the girl and moved away from her. "Yes, she is. She's there. And I'm going in. I'll find her if I have to tear the whole place apart twig by twig." He started toward his horse.

Garth Kinyon reined his mount across Chris's path. "No, son. They only have her horse. That's all."

"You're just—"

"Then where is my sister?" Morgan demanded.

The tracker cocked his head back and forth in uncertainty. "Left along the trail, mebbe. Taken someplace else. Who knows?"

Chris grabbed onto the guide's stirrup. "You didn't even try to find out?"

"No point in it." He shook off Chris's hand. "The young bucks who brought the horses went off to join up with Butler's Rangers."

Christopher swung back to the girl and took her by the arms. "Which hut is Evie in? Tell me!"

She whimpered, her eyes wide and dark with terror.

Jonathan pulled him away. "Leave her alone, Chris. This little gal's been through enough already. She doesn't need any more bullying." Gently he wrapped an arm around her and searched her soil-streaked face. "Little miss, we need your help. Can you tell us if there were any other white people at the village with you?"

"Another girl," Morgan prompted, his hand indicating Evie's height. "Eighteen, with curly brown hair."

The waif looked up at him, then at Chris. Her head drooped back down as she slowly shook it from side to side. "Only me." The words were all but inaudible. She took a deep breath, as if gathering strength, and looked up again. "They didn't take no one but me. They killed everybody else. Even—" She sniffed, and glistening tears pooled in her eyes. "Even Baby Joe."

"Where you from, girl?" Kinyon asked.

"Cobleskill." She brushed away the tears with her knuckles.

The name sounded familiar. The entire settlement had been massacred a month ago.

Dan, stepping near, took the girl's hand. "You have our deepest sympathy, dear child. Our very deepest."

At that, she dissolved into tears and flung herself into his comforting arms.

The heart-wrenching scene only made Christopher fear all the more for Evie. "Come on," he said in desperation. "There's two days of backtracking to do before we can pick up another trail to follow."

Garth Kinyon eyed him. "Something else you need to know, son. Butler and that gang of Loyalists of his is headed right now for the Wyoming Valley—with volunteers from every Indian village. A good five or six hundred of 'em, from what the chief said."

Morgan's jaw gaped. He bolted toward his horse. "I have to get back there—now! Which is the fastest way, Mr. Kinyon?"

"Wait a minute," Chris snapped. "What about Evie? We can't stop searching for her."

With a shake of his grizzled head, Kinyon raised a hand. "I didn't want to tell you this, kid, but there's not much hope that gal of yours is still alive. And that's for the best. Believe me, you'll be of the same mind, in time."

"No, I won't," Chris said adamantly. He pointed to the freed girl. "This one survived, didn't she? Well, so will Evie. You'll see."

Dan clamped a hand on Christopher's shoulder and turned Chris to face him. "I'm really sorry, Chip. But you have to try to understand. Our families need us right now. We must get back to them without delay."

Morgan, his voice wrought with emotion, affirmed Dan's statement. "I love my sister as much as you do, Chris. The moment we're sure our families are out of harm's way—trust me, we'll start after her again. You have my solemn word."

Christopher felt as if his insides were being ripped apart. His own sister and her babies were in the gravest of danger right now back in Wilkes-Barre. So were Susannah and her little ones. He loved them all, dearly. There was no question about that. But—Evie. His beloved Evie. Every fiber of his being cried to go after her, to find her. To look for her and not stop searching until he found her and brought her back.

Evelyn, her hands and feet tied, narrowed her eyes and glared bitterly down from her sidesaddle at her two captors. How dare they wash themselves, when she'd had precious little opportunity to do so herself these past nine days? She longed to quench her thirst and wash her filthy, mosquito-bitten face in the cool flow of the stream beside the trace they'd been following. While she stank of grime and horse, those savages preened and adorned themselves and slicked down their greasy hair.

She watched Weasel Eye and the Indian she'd begun to think of as Hawk Nose reach into their deerskin bags and take something out. A chill shot through her. War paint!

Evie's throat closed up. Only by supreme effort did she manage to quell her trembling. There must be a settlement nearby . . . one they planned to attack.

They'd been traveling mostly in a northwesterly direction through dense woods and rugged valleys since splitting off from the others. Surely they must be somewhere in the remote reaches of New York territory, far west of any white settlements such as the Mohawk Valley, which had suffered such tragic losses last summer. She couldn't imagine there being any farmsteads this deep in the wilderness.

The Indians, having finished applying garish stripes of red on their blackened faces, stood and started for their horses, chattering jubilantly back and forth as they strutted past her. Had they done this very same thing in preparation for raiding Dan and Susannah's place? When they rode off for this next unspeakable attack, would they leave her behind in the woods? Or were their intentions even more despicable— would they take her along to witness their bloody carnage?

A wave of nausea ebbed as a tiny ray of hope took its place. There were only the two braves. Perhaps they would be killed this time instead! She would be free!

Evelyn glanced back at the young braves and watched them tie their bags of pigment to the packhorses. Weasel Eyes secured his to the pacer strung just behind hers. The animals were piled high with loot from the Haynes house—including the medicine box.

No doubt if Susannah were here now, she'd be mouthing platitudes about how one must love one's enemies. But Susannah hadn't had the butt of a hatchet slammed down on her leg. Even after all these days a lump the size of a goose egg distorted Evie's thigh. For the first two days, pain from the blow had been excruciating as the prodding steps of the horse jolted it. Now there was a dull, constant ache.

Evelyn pursed her lips. Yes, Susannah would probably be elaborating on the goodness of God because Evie was now riding one of the pacers rather than her Thoroughbred hunter. The Narragansetts were bred for their gentle gait and ease of mounting. With a leg that even now scarcely supported her, Evie knew she'd never have been able to hoist herself up to Amber Jewel's back. She'd barely managed the much shorter pacer. And it went without saying that neither of these two would have helped her. They'd sooner allow a wolf to bite off their hands than stoop to offer her a leg up. And they hadn't liked having her looking down on them from the hunter's height, either.

Her thoughts turned to her finely bred gelding. She hoped

the Indian who'd claimed the horse would treat it with the kindness befitting its nature.

The braves suddenly leaped onto their mounts.

Evie's fears returned as the two started moving. Whatever they were scheming, they must be going to drag her along with them. As her strawberry roan was pulled after them, Evelyn's bruised leg began to itch. Undoubtedly that was a sign that healing was beginning, but along with all the other aggravating itches caused by mosquito bites all over her face and arms, she was helpless to scratch it. Her wrists, chafed by the tightness of the rough hemp binding them, smarted in protest.

The Indians rode ahead of her, the two strings of horses crowding each other as they followed a narrow, ancient path through the woods. What lay at the other end?

Evie glowered at the pair of bronzed backs in front of her. Love thine enemy, ha! Not even Susannah Haynes could be that generous in these circumstances.

But then, Evelyn gloated silently, her abductors hadn't come away entirely unscathed themselves. Because neither of them had a saddle, they had taken a number of hard spills from these horses that were little more than green broke. One brave had a purplish bruise on his thigh just below his breechcloth that all but rivaled her own. New scratches grazed their bare legs with every day of riding through the forests.

Served the heathens right, she decided, for running around practically naked. Then she took note of her own pale green skirt, tattered from rips and jags, shredded in places. If it caught on brambles too many more times, she could easily find herself as exposed as the men.

The braves talked back and forth, and one of them burst out with a laugh. Obviously they were not very close to wherever they were going, or they would have been moving with stealth. To Evie, their laughter sounded as if they were on their way to a party, and it offended her deeply. She was certain that not even the Almighty would expect anyone to love a people who derived thrill and enjoyment from a murderous rampage.

Abruptly the braves quit talking. They turned malicious eyes in her direction, then resumed the chatter.

An eerie sensation slithered through Evie. The one bearable part of this whole sickening ordeal had been the way the pair had ignored her almost entirely until now.

Weasel Eye abruptly halted his mount and flung himself down.

Evie's pacer and the horses behind it bumped to a confused stop.

He moved to her side and began untying her hands.

Edgy as she watched him, Evelyn nevertheless was relieved as renewed circulation burned through her wrists. It would help to rub them, she thought.

But before she could even make the attempt, Weasel Eye yanked her off the horse, scraping her good leg on the tall fork of the pommel before she could lift it over. Evie's badly bruised leg touched ground first, but it couldn't support her full weight. She collapsed in a heap.

Without allowing her time to try to regain her feet, Weasel grabbed her by the arm and dragged her unceremoniously over the rough ground in the direction from which they'd just come.

He stopped beside the last horse of his string and hauled her to her feet. Picking up the rope that had secured her to the horse, he wrapped an end of it around her neck.

The loop of hemp choked her. Evie tried with numb fingers to rip it away.

Weasel backhanded her across the face. The stunning blow brought the metallic taste of blood to her tongue as the brave finished tying off the rope. He started attaching the other end to the cord securing the rear horse.

In dismay, Evelyn snatched at the knot. But Weasel jerked hard on the rope, burning her neck as it whipped her forward, almost throwing her off balance.

The gaudy war paint added a feral malevolence to the

Indian's appearance. When he finished securing the rope, he bared his teeth in a vile sneer and slapped the nose of the horse.

The animal shied away, yanking Evelyn off her feet. She came down hard on her belly, only to be dragged a short distance before the pacer was halted by the length of its tether.

Evie raged in silence at this new humiliation and struggled to her feet. By the time she had regained her footing, Weasel Eye had remounted at the front of the string—and started the horses ahead!

Her fury now lost in mounting terror, Evie ripped at the knot choking her throat. But a violent yank forced her after the pacers. She could only hold on with both hands to keep from strangling and concentrate on each wobbly step through the tangled undergrowth. The back of her neck flamed from the abrasive erratic jerks, while brambles ripped at her ragged skirts.

With dust rising from the pathway to clog her lungs, Evelyn could barely keep her footing as she coughed and stumbled over the uneven ground. A root caught her toe and sent her sprawling. The pacers never faltered, but plodded onward, dragging her behind. Sharp rocks grated against her hands and arms and body. Finally she scrambled to her feet, spitting out grit and blood.

Vile snickers from the front carried to Evelyn's ears, and a dire realization crashed down on her. Early in the trip her skills with the horses had been of value to her captors, but now her usefulness had come to an end. *They had reached their destination* . . . and now the first of the terrible tortures had begun.

The forest growth thinned; then the party emerged from the trees into a huge clearing. The braves whooped and yipped in exuberance and kicked their mounts into a trot.

The trailing horses broke into a faster pace, yanking Evie into a flying run. "Dear Father in heaven, help me!" she cried, holding to the rope for dear life.

Answering yips came from the distance, where Evelyn could make out the clustered cabins and long buildings of a fair-sized Indian village. The structures were unlike any she'd ever seen in her life . . . and whooping savages rushed out of every one of them.

Evie, horrified, lost her footing and sailed forward, hitting the ground hard. With every ounce of strength she possessed she clutched the rope, trying to keep her neck from breaking as the horses dragged her thrashing across the meadow.

It was only a foretaste of what lay ahead.

26

Hauled after her captors, Evie was assaulted by waves of bone-jarring pain as she bumped and slammed over the hard, rough ground toward a blur of rude cabins and cone-shaped huts. There was barely strength enough in her raw hands to keep the rope around her neck from choking the very life out of her. Coughing and blinded by dust, she squeezed her eyelids closed against the abrasive cloud kicked up by the horses.

The piercing yips and hoots of the villagers sliced through her consciousness with chilling sharpness now, turning her blood to ice. How easy it would be to let go, to die. The rope began to slip through her weakened fingers. The noose tore cruelly at her tender skin as she struggled to draw one last breath. She would never see Christopher again.

Suddenly the braves skidded to a halt. Next, the strings of pacers. Then Evie. Gasping for air, she caught the barest glimpse of a huge, crudely built structure as she lay there, bruised and aching. Desperately she clawed with numb fingers at the hemp cutting off her air. Her two abductors vaulted from their pacers to be immediately swamped with hugs and laughter as if they were returning heroes.

Evie watched other men of the tribe clapping the young braves on their shoulders. The women fawned over them with smiles and greetings, totally disregarding her own helpless, battered, and bleeding state. Her skinned hands trembled as she worked feverishly at the knotted rope. A hank of hair fell across her eyes. She stopped long enough to swipe away the tangled curls.

Children and squaws began converging on her, circling her. A tiny speck of hope flickered, then died as leering, hate-filled faces loomed all around. Some of the little ones brandished sticks in her face.

Evie, still fumbling to untie the rope, used the tightly stretched hemp to regain her feet. One of the women shouted something, and the rest fell upon Evelyn, ripping at her clothes, yanking handfuls of hair. She tried to ward off the groping hands and cruel blows, but to no avail. Then an idea came to her—a dangerous idea, but she had nothing to lose. Inhaling as deeply as she could, she leaned back, stretching the rope taut, then hurled herself directly into the pack of horses.

The pacer she was tied to wheeled wildly. Several squaws were knocked aside. The rest of the mob leaped back in fear but kept howling and waving sticks.

Evelyn tugged the packhorses into a circle around her. Amid squealing and kicking and rearing, the attackers fell back again.

Then a man yelled.

The harsh voice sounded like Weasel's. From beneath the muscled neck of a young stallion she could see her captor berating the mob, gesturing angrily for them to move back. Hope flickered in Evie.

The soothing words he uttered as he stepped close, how-ever, were directed not at Evelyn but at the horses. He smoothed a hand down the neck of one of the pacers, trying to calm it. Then, quick as a snake, he pulled out a knife and cut Evie's rope free, jerking on the tether to force her out from the protection of the animals.

Weasel hauled her close and eyed her in disgust. Then he turned and, with derisive words unintelligible to her, tossed the rope to one of the squaws. The woman caught it with glee.

Evie was doomed. Utter despair filled her, tearing from her

mind the beautiful picture she'd conjured up of her and Christopher sharing a life together. All those plans, all their dreams, were over now.

The cruel horde converged on her once more with screeching insanity and clawing, grasping hands. For an instant, Evie regretted not having Susannah Haynes's strong faith. *Almighty God!* she cried from the depths of her being. *Save me! Help me!* But after so many prayerless years, did the Lord even recognize her voice?

One of her sleeves was ripped away, then her skirt. A petticoat went next. Cruel fingers ripped down her bodice.

Suddenly the deep voice of a man cut through the caterwauling. The women froze and stepped back.

Gasping for breath, Evie snatched with fumbling fingers at the remnants of her bodice, trying to hold together her torn camisole with one hand while wrapping the remains of a petticoat around a bare leg. An older man came toward her—but she knew better than to hope now. Whoever it was probably had some other form of torture in mind.

Unaccountably, a splash of red caught the edge of her vision, and Evie raised her head. Uniformed soldiers! White men! She gave a small cry and stumbled toward them, flinging herself into the officer's arms. Profoundly relieved, she could only pour wordless prayers of thankfulness from her innermost being to the heavens.

The tall, stern-faced officer thrust her to arm's length with a grimace. "Take her, Corporal Blake. She's soiling my uniform."

A younger man in red pulled Evelyn away, while the one in charge dusted his immaculate coat with white gloves.

"Well," the lieutenant groused, "get on with it, soldier. Our red brothers have little patience when we interrupt their amusements, you know."

The corporal nodded sharply, then turned a more understanding look to Evie. "We need to know, Miss—" He glanced back at the officer in charge. "Well, I do, actually. Where did these Narragansett Pacers come from?"

Evelyn couldn't believe her ears. Her mouth gaped in shock.

"I thought," the corporal went on, "that the only remaining breeder of the Narragansetts was in Rhode Island."

Seething now, humiliated and violated beyond reason, and on the verge of hysteria, Evie could hardly contain her fury. "These brutal savages," she hissed through her teeth, "are tearing me apart, and all you're concerned with is those blasted horses?" The angry breath she released all but made her collapse. This had to be a nightmare. It had to be.

"Miss," came the young man's urgent voice again. "Please, answer me, will you not?"

Evie swept a glance up to him. For someone with a pleasant face and mild manners, he seemed unbelievably callous. She answered him in clipped, precise tones. "The horses were moved from Rhode Island, out of the war zone. They were taken to a farmstead owned by Dan Haynes, in northeastern Pennsylvania."

"I beg your pardon. Did you say *Dan Haynes?*" The soldier's clear hazel eyes registered surprise. "Mistress Susannah. Have the Indians killed her, then? And her babes?"

Slowly Evelyn realized the young man must be acquainted with the Hayneses. She placed a grimy hand on his arm. "No. Susannah and the children were at Sunday service when the farm was set upon."

"Church." His expression changed to one of vast relief, and a smile spread over his lips. "Yes, she would be. I truly believe God takes special care of that particular lass."

Once again Evie was struck by how very precious and real was the relationship Susannah Haynes shared with the God of the heavens. Tears rose to blur her eyes. "Yes," she could only whisper, "I think he does."

The corporal turned. "I was right, sir. This lass came from the house of an Englishwoman—one who extended great kindness to us soldiers while we were under siege in Boston. I do believe someone should keep better track of precisely whom these Indians ravage."

The officer flashed a disconcerted look at Evelyn, then as quickly hiked his aristocratic chin and peered down his long nose.

His was an intensely familiar stance, Evie decided. Was it possible she had met him before? But even if she had, she knew he'd be unable to recognize her, considering her present state. Uncomfortable under his scrutiny, she gave more effort to trying to cover herself.

Then the arrogant man turned to someone behind him. "Come. Translate."

A figure dressed in the attire of a woodsman, with tanned skin and dark, slitted eyes similar to those of the Indians, slunk forward.

The officer gestured toward the villagers. "Tell these *gentlemen,* here, that this particular female and the horses with her were stolen from our loyal friends—*not* from traitorous rebels. We shall take charge of them now." He turned to the soldier beside Evie. "Corporal Blake, what was the name of that family you mentioned?"

"Haynes, sir."

"Quite." He shifted his gaze to the scout and flicked him away with one hand. "Be about it, man."

The half-breed, with a look of disdain, spoke to the old chieftain who had interrupted the attack on Evie.

Weasel Eye, not far away, broke angrily into the conversation, slanting menacing glances toward her, his words punctuated with wild gestures.

Reminded again that they stood in the very center of this heathen village, Evelyn inched closer to Corporal Blake.

The scout swung back to the tall officer. "Shadow Walker say he raid in valley of the Susquehannocks. He say spoils belong to him."

The lieutenant kneaded his jaw with a long-fingered hand. "Ask who gave him authority to attack a farm occupied by Loyalists—and why he isn't with Butler and his rangers."

Dan and Susannah's loyalties lay with the Americans rather

than the Crown, of course—but Evelyn was not about to correct the arrogant officer in charge.

Weasel—or Shadow Walker, as the half-breed had called him—continued his volatile argument with the scout and the chieftain. His chest puffed with his own self-importance. Though young, he seemed as respected among this tribe as was the officer among his own countrymen.

More nervous by the moment, Evie glanced around. Only two more British soldiers stood near, off to one side. A pittance of a force against an entire village.

Corporal Blake gave her hand a reassuring squeeze.

Turning to the officer once again, the scout gave his report. "Shadow say he gathered his own war party. Is war chief. Attacks where he choose."

The tall redcoat stretched to his full, imposing height and faced the old chieftain. "You gave your word. All sorties were to be carried out under the direction of Major Butler."

When the half-breed finished translating, the old Indian answered calmly. Too calmly, in Evelyn's opinion, considering she was one of the prizes being haggled over.

"Chief say," the scout related, "sometimes a thing too tempting. Young brave sees much wealth, cannot walk away." The dark eyes slid to Shadow Walker. "So many horses he never see."

The British officer scanned the two strings of pacers. "I suppose eleven might seem a large number to an Indian, since the Iroquois have acquired so few over the years. . . ."

"There was more," the half-breed cut in. "This Seneca take up the hatchet with some Cayuga braves. They take many horses."

"Cayugas, Senecas, Onondaga," the officer said flatly with a shrug. "I get them all mixed up. So be it. Tell that fiery young brave he may keep the horses and all the goods tied on their backs. All but the one with the sidesaddle. In return, he must do me a favor—*since he has now encumbered me with a female*. Tell him to take one of his newly gained steeds and deliver a packet of orders to Major Butler. These come directly from

General Carleton. They must not be delayed while I return the girl to civilization."

That information dredged up more arguing; then the translator turned. "The girl. Shadow Walker want to keep. She is healer of horses. Very valuable to man with many horses."

Evie caught her breath.

Corporal Blake stepped forward with a sneer. "We saw how valuable she is to him. If we hadn't stopped them, the women would have torn her limb from limb."

"No, no," the scout replied with a snide grin. "They only strip clothes so she run gauntlet. All slaves do this. Show if heart stout enough to become Seneca." He gave a shrug of nonchalance. "No survive, no good enough."

At this, Evelyn swept a look to the lieutenant.

His gaze remained fixed on the older village leader. "The girl is not negotiable. She comes with us. Corporal, escort the young lady to her horse at once. Cut it from the string and help her mount."

"Yes, sir!" Blake snapped a salute. Without hesitation, he walked Evie through the crowd to her saddled pacer, his hand at the small of her back.

The Indians parted like the Red Sea. For once, Evie applauded British arrogance . . . at least, when it worked this well.

From behind her came mutters and more arguing. She sensed hundreds of malicious eyes on her as the corporal urged her along.

As the other enlisted man cut the horse from the string, the authoritative voice of the commanding officer carried to them. "Tell Shadow Walker that the great chief, King George, will not allow his loyal subjects to be made slaves. If his people want to continue to benefit from the great father's generosity—like those strong hatchets every brave now carries, the knives, pots, and—let us not forget—the muskets they covet so, they bloody well better comply." He pivoted. "Private

Henry. Remove the packet of orders from my saddlebag. Hand it to that belligerent buck."

What audacity! Evelyn thought as Corporal Blake took her by the waist and gently set her on her horse. *What magnificent audacity!*

The officer pulled out a pocket watch and flicked it open, then turned to his scout. "I wish to have the chief's word that this packet will be delivered immediately. I shall hold him directly responsible. Mount up, men! We can make several miles before nightfall."

While the thoughtful corporal guided her pacer over to the other military horses, Evie kept her eyes downcast. After the abuse she had already suffered at the hands of her proud captor, the last thing she needed was to meet his eyes, inflame him any further. His tomahawk could easily be hurled through the air to bury itself in her back.

Evie and the enlisted men had mounted by the time the lieutenant joined them. Only the scout remained on the ground.

"May I assume I have the chief's word?" the officer demanded.

The swarthy-skinned man grunted in affirmation.

"Then convey the proper farewells and mount up."

Corporal Blake nudged his horse to the lieutenant's side. "Lieutenant Conway, sir. Begging your pardon, but I'd like to present Shadow Walker with a token of our gratitude."

Evelyn watched anxiously as the young man dismounted and approached her captor. He drew from its sheath a knife with a gleaming mother-of-pearl inlaid handle and held it out in both hands.

Shadow Walker ran his fingers over the smooth surface, then eyed the young man with menace.

Blake did not flinch.

Evie found herself uttering yet another prayer, this one for the kind man's safety as she held her breath.

Finally the brave snorted and snatched up the knife. Without a word or nod of thanks, he strode away.

As Blake returned to his mount, Evelyn had the strangest feeling he had arrived here in answer to Susannah's prayers for her. She had not the slightest doubt that the Englishwoman had not stopped praying for her welfare since finding her missing. Evie chafed at the way she had made sport of Susannah's faith, her beliefs in God's faithful watch care of his followers. How uncharitable she'd been, especially toward Christopher's sister.

Humbly Evie realized how pathetic her own cries to God must have been. Worth little more than words on the wind. The Lord had placed her in the home of a very godly woman, yet she had refused to see or hear what was right before her eyes. She was nothing but a wretch who had spent this entire journey thinking of little else but taking revenge on her enemies. Evie bowed her head in shame.

Out in front, Lieutenant Conway maneuvered his horse to the center of the path leading out of the Indian village. "Eyes forward," he ordered. He drew his saber forth and raised it. "Move out in pairs."

The translator mounted, and the small party rode past the silent, unsmiling, disappointed people. The back of Evie's head prickled as every muscle and nerve in her body waited for the savages to change their minds and swarm over her again to resume their sport.

She scarcely drew a breath while they passed the remainder of the dwellings and the last log house, then continued beyond several planted fields. Not until they reached the forest did Evelyn feel some of her tension drain away, and then icy tremors began to rack her entire being. She began to weep uncontrollably. She had held herself together for such a long time, and now she was powerless against the flood of tears that poured from her shattered spirit.

Corporal Blake, riding beside her, pushed a blanket into her hands. "Here, miss. Wrap this around you. It'll help keep you warm till you're past the fright."

"I—I don't know . . . what's the matter . . . with me," Evie wailed between sobs as she wrapped herself and the remains of her tattered clothing within the blanket's cocoon. "I'm safe now."

"It's called shock." He smiled disarmingly. "It happens to all pretty young misses when they've just been saved from being clubbed to death. Oh, by the by. We have not been properly introduced. Gerald Blake, miss, at your service. And you're—"

"Evelyn—" Aware of the officer's sudden interest when he glanced back, she feared her real name might be on a list of wanted military criminals. "Evelyn Haynes," she finished.

"Aye." The corporal nodded. "I thought you might be kin to the reverend, rather than Mistress Susannah. With your dark brown hair, I mean."

She was suddenly appalled at what she must look like after more than a week in the outdoors . . . probably every bit as wild as those Indian squaws acted. Evie reached up and felt her tangled and matted curls. And the rest of her had to be even worse—grimy and bloody and bruised, skin torn from her hands and knees, clothes that were little more than a few ragged strips. The added embarrassment provoked a new outbreak of tears. "How many days before I'm returned home?" she finally asked. "Susannah surely must think I'm dead by now."

Lieutenant Conway swung around in his saddle. "Dreadfully sorry, miss. You'll not be going anywhere but to Fort Niagara, up on Lake Ontario. It's much safer there just now."

A British fort! Fresh apprehension filled Evie. She'd met dozens and dozens of Crown officers over the past several years. What were the chances of her not being recognized? She swallowed hard. "But, sir. I cannot have my family thinking I'm dead. They live just outside of Wilkes-Barre. I need to let them know."

The officer's mouth twisted into a smug smile. "Trust me when I say this. The folks in Wyoming Valley are going to be too busy, soon, to give you a second thought."

The chuckle from the privates riding behind her reinforced

Evelyn's ominous premonition. She sought Corporal Blake's face. It had turned ashen.

"You were taken from Wyoming Valley?" he asked, his sun-reddened complexion grim. "That is where Susannah presently resides?"

Evie nodded, her uneasiness intensifying.

He reached across and placed a hand over hers. "It would seem it's our turn to pray for Mistress Susannah . . . and little Miles. And baby Julia. They are in dire need of God's protection."

27

Nellie Parsons was prone to intermittent crying—either from relief at being rescued from the cruel atrocities of the Indians, or from despair that she had neither home nor family to return to. Christopher's heart went out to the waiflike girl of fifteen who, mounted behind Dan at the moment, clung despondently to his back.

But the fact was that it had taken four days to ride the same distance they would have covered in three if the horses hadn't been taxed by the weight of the extra rider rotating among them. And to make matters worse, a spell of driving rain had nearly washed out the last remaining tracks in the area where the Indians had split up. The only hope of finding Evelyn would now involve going from village to village bargaining with any Indian who possessed one of the pacers, until one was willing to divulge information about her. If, indeed, she were still alive.

Chris glanced at Nellie again. Somewhat cleaner than when she was first rescued, her straight, light brown hair hung soft and limp over her fragile shoulders. A strand of it trailed over one of the angry bruises on her upper arm. Since the sleeves had been ripped from her faded, shapeless dress, the remainder of her thin limbs was in plain view, a mass of purplish blue welts and slashes.

Had Evie suffered similar abuse, been beaten and scarred, her beautiful spirit crushed? Forcing aside the gut-wrenching possibility, Christopher tried his best to concentrate on the last time he'd seen her, her face aglow with love, her tremulous lips smiling invitingly. He could only pray he'd find her that way again—and soon. He couldn't give up all hope, no matter how impossible that prayer might be.

Poor little Nellie Parsons.

At least Evie hadn't had to witness the brutal slaughter of everyone dear to her, had their still-bleeding scalps dangled before her eyes by murderous heathens whose hideous laughter would forever mar her soul. No wonder there seemed no end to the frail young thing's anguish. Yet, incredibly, her heartaches seemed to be undergoing a gradual easing with each time she rode with Dan. He possessed a knack for getting her to talk. In time, Chris hoped, the girl would be able to put all her painful memories to rest.

As they came upon a wide clearing, the horses in front slowed to a stop. Garth Kinyon dismounted and began reading the ground in his slow, scrupulous way. Chris guided his horse around Dan and wide-eyed Nellie and halted beside Kinyon's mount. He swung down, and he, too, stared at the tramped earth in earnest.

Jonathan, joining him, pointed to the south. "Looks like a lot of folks headed in that direction."

"More than a lot," the tracker replied astutely. "Upwards of four, five hundred of 'em, mebbe more. Some with moccasins, some in boots."

"Butler's Rangers," Morgan said in an ominous tone from the other side of Jon, where he remained in his saddle.

Kinyon nodded. "Looks like."

Chris saw intense fear pass from face to face, and he knew exactly how each man felt.

"How much farther until we reach the valley?" Dan asked.

Kinyon checked the position of the sun. "Mebbe three hours, if we ride hard."

Without another word, Dan slammed his heels into his horse's flanks, and Morgan did the same. Their animals lunged to a gallop and charged away.

Chris and Jon leaped into their saddles and took off after the others.

"Please," Christopher heard Nellie plead above the pounding of the hooves ahead of him as she held on for dear life. "Please, Reverend Haynes. Just leave me here. I'll hide, I promise, until you come back for me."

Dan shifted his reins to one hand and patted Nellie's arm, tightly clasped around his waist. "We know you're afraid, child. Just hold on to me . . . and to the Lord. We'll see you through."

❧ ❧

When they crested the final hill to begin the downward trek into the valley, the panoramic view they normally would have seen from miles away was masked by a thin layer of smoke. The very air reeked of charred wood—and something even more ominous . . . death.

Neither Dan, Morgan, nor Jonathan wasted so much as a glance at the others. They spurred their sweat-foamed mounts down the wooded trail as if the devil himself were chasing them.

Nellie, now riding with Garth Kinyon, buried her face in his thin shoulder blades and held on, her knuckles white, as he and Chris hastened their laboring mounts after the others. Trickles of perspiration dampened the back of her ragged dress as she clung to the tracker.

Christopher would have liked nothing better than to bury his head, too. The thought that friends and family could all be dead tore at him, but he tried to maintain the same hope for them that he did for Evie. Certainly the women would have stayed within the safety of the Wilkes-Barre fort. Perhaps even at this moment they were valiantly helping to hold off the enemy. The stench of death, which was becoming stronger by the second, could be slain farm animals that the folks had left behind. It had to be.

Not even a breath of wind stirred the heavy humid air of the valley, where the smoke hovered like traces of fog, thin in places, thick in others. The horses snorted in protest and had to be urged along.

Finally the first farmstead along the Susquehanna—or rather, what remained of it—came into view. Christopher started at the horrifying scene, and the nearer they rode, the more intense became his shock. Where sturdy outbuildings had once stood, skeletons of blackened wood now poked up at grotesque angles in charred silhouettes against the darkening sky. "No!" he shouted.

At his baleful cry, a half-dozen crows rose from the ruined stock pens in a frenzy of wings and feathers, flapping away to the treetops of a nearby birch grove. As much for his own sake as Nellie's, Christopher prayed fervently that the blackbirds hadn't been tearing apart human corpses. He didn't even breathe as he and Garth Kinyon guided their mounts toward the incinerated pens. With only slight relief they discovered that the crows had been feasting on slaughtered animals—a cow and her spring calf, a sow and her piglets—all wantonly butchered and left bloating and rotting in the summer heat.

Beyond the outbuildings, a stone fireplace occupied the center of another heap of ashes and rubble where once a fine cabin had graced the knoll. Not even the crops had been spared. Everything lay in utter devastation.

About a quarter mile into the distance, a second farm had been laid to waste in similar fashion. Chris noted that Dan and the others barely slowed at that one but rode past it, galloping for all they were worth. He knew it was still several miles to the fort where they'd left their wives.

Kinyon turned to Christopher with a grave expression. "I, er, think I'll mosey on after the reverend and the others, kid," he said with a significant tip of his head toward Nellie. "Why don't you check around a bit?"

The trapper wanted him to search for bodies or any sign of life. Reluctantly Chris nodded. As the man rode away with his frail passenger's nose still burrowed into his back, Chris became aware of an ominous stillness . . . one that no animal or bird, except for those crafty crows, seemed to intrude upon, as if out of deep respect.

Christopher swallowed and veered his horse toward the second farmstead, making a wide circle around it. Only dead chickens remained here. The heavy silence made him uneasy. Feeling as if he were being watched, he glanced over his shoulder every few seconds but saw neither friend nor foe. Urging his weary horse, he raced after Kinyon.

Chris reached the first of several small forts strung along either side of the river. To his utter dismay, he found the fortress laid to ruin and still smoldering. But there was no sign of life. Apparently the people had all been gathered at the Wilkes-Barre fort and at Forty Fort.

He pressed onward, and each rise in the undulating landscape revealed views of burnt rubble in the fading light. From what he could see, there didn't seem to be a single building still standing on either side of the river. He didn't bother stopping at any more ruined farms, but using familiar hills and groves as landmarks, headed doggedly for Jon and Mary Clare's place.

Theirs, too, lay in ruins, and Dan and Susannah's farm had fared no better. A heaviness unlike anything he had ever experienced filled Christopher. Numb with fear and trepidation, he set off toward the fort at Wilkes-Barre, where he found his worst fear spread before him. The fort was nothing but a blackened shell.

Chris spotted Dan, Kinyon, and the others in the faint remnants of daylight. Leading mounts on the verge of collapse, the men trudged wearily along, their heads and shoulders slumped. Off to one side, Nellie paced alone, her hands clenched in front of her, her gaze faraway.

Dan looked up as Christopher approached. "Everyone has disappeared." He shook his head. "Garth's doing his best to read the signs here, but so far there aren't many clues to tell us where they've gone."

"You think people are still alive, then?" Chris asked.

Kinyon shrugged noncommittally. "All we're sure of, kid, is that there ain't no bodies."

Even that slight hope encouraged Christopher. He latched onto it for all he was worth. "Well, these poor horses are gonna drop if they don't have a drink soon. And far as I can tell, these are the only mounts alive on this side of the river."

Morgan removed his tricorn long enough to rake his fingers through his hair. Then he led his horse over to Chris and handed him the reins. "Would you mind, Chip?"

"Mine, too," Jonathan said, and the others wordlessly followed suit.

Leaving his friends in the rubble of Fort Wilkes-Barre and the surrounding settlement, Chris led all five horses down the slight incline to the Susquehanna River. Twilight bestowed a murky gloom to the dark water, yet it flowed placidly along, as if nothing untoward had occurred in the valley.

Waiting for the thirsty animals to drink, Chris glanced toward the ferry landing. It was obvious the dock had been set afire, but, perhaps due to the dampness of the wood, it had only partially burned. That seemed of little consequence, however—there was not a conveyance to be seen around it or on the far shore. Most likely they'd all been burned or set adrift. A charred farmstead across the river made a black blot on the distant countryside, and Chris released a resigned breath. There was no reason to hope the folks on that side had been spared.

Christopher knelt at the water's edge and washed his face and hands. Melancholy resignation replaced the uneasiness that had plagued him earlier. The enemy had come and done what they intended, then left for other parts to wreak havoc on other defenseless families. Hatred for the British seethed through him, to think they would unleash the savagery of the Indians against helpless settlers.

Where were his loved ones now? Mary Clare, Susannah, Prudence, the babies? Had they all been driven deep into Indian country to be tortured and killed or forced into slavery?

How could God allow such atrocities?

With a heavy sigh, Chris tried to push back the unbearable thoughts. He couldn't lose faith now. God was all they had.

"Chip!"

The sound of Jonathan's call bolstered him. Chris gathered the reins of the other horses and remounted, then returned to the men.

"Hurry!" Jon urged. "Kinyon thinks everyone left within the last day or so and that most everyone is on foot. We should be able to catch up to them quickly enough."

The moment's hope quickly vanished. "You think those butchers are gonna let us just walk up and take our loved ones back?"

"Listen," Jon said, raising a hand. "From the way it appears, the blackguards have marched all the people from the fort toward the road that goes to Easton. Kinyon thinks maybe they were more concerned with throwing the people out of the valley than with making prisoners of them."

"Think so?" Chris was wary of putting too much stock in that possibility just yet. The last time he'd thought something good was about to happen—when he was sure Evie had been freed—it had turned out just the opposite. There was a chance the British had tricked the outnumbered settlers into coming out of the fort just so they could more easily slaughter them. The Iroquois had never been known for their mercy.

Jonathan took the reins of his horse with a strained smile. "Come on. I need to get to Mary."

As the others reclaimed their animals and mounted up, Christopher felt an anxious knot tighten in his chest. Maybe Jonathan needed this hope, but Chris wasn't sure there was still a Mary to get to.

28

Some of the footprints led down to the dock and the missing riverboats. The vast majority headed out of Wyoming Valley and up into the mountains. The narrow road climbed and fell over a succession of steep ridges leading to the trace alongside the Lehigh River, which flowed between more mountain ridges until it would eventually intersect the road to Easton. Chris and the others followed the trail in solemn silence until, with daylight waning, they descended the first ridge.

Garth Kinyon halted the party and dismounted, assessing the evidence left by the travelers. "It would appear Butler an' his cutthroats took the left fork," he finally said, glancing up at the men. "Looks like the settlers kept on this route by themselves. I only see one or two moccasin prints."

"That sounds encouraging." A flash of hope illuminated Dan's eyes.

"Not necessarily." Kinyon rubbed his grizzled jaw. "Injuns like to count coup. Some of 'em might resent lettin' all those scalps just up an' walk off."

Chris let out an exasperated breath. "Well, then, let's not waste any more time. Let's go." He nudged his mount forward through the darkening woods.

The party traveled late into the night with hardly a break, keeping a watchful eye on every side as they alternately rode and walked to spell their weary horses.

The light of a three-quarter moon shone through the trees.

Chris cut a glance at Dan. Clearly, the minister was in constant prayer for Susannah and the children and for the other folk as well. But Chris was unable to seek that same comfort himself just now. From the moment he had ridden into the razed settlement, he had been consumed by intense anger and hatred. With so many of God's faithful followers now in jeopardy, he had to wonder whether the Lord even cared. He directed his attention back to the trail, hoping the moonlight would be sufficient for them not to miss anything significant.

Chris tightened his hold on Nellie's hands where they clasped around him. The girl had nodded off a little while ago, and he didn't want her to fall and get hurt.

A faint pinpoint of light flickered through the deep woods to the left. Could it be his imagination? Chris focused intently in that direction until he sighted it a second time, then halted his horse. He quietly cleared his throat and pointed.

"Someone better check that out," Kinyon whispered as they all reined to a stop.

"We'd better all go," Jon said quietly. "Just in case."

"Wait." Chris tipped his head toward Nellie. "She might cry out, give us away."

"We can't just dump her here by herself," Dan muttered.

Morgan hiked his chin. "Garth, stay with the lass and the horses. We'll—"

"Uh-uh. I'm the experienced one here."

"Right," Dan said. "And you're here because we got you out of a sickbed to help us."

"Don't worry," Chris told Garth. "We've been fighting a very bloody war for over two years. We can take care of ourselves."

The tracker looked from one to the other, then fastened his gaze on Dan and nodded. "Guess I'm actin' like an old mother hen. Well, get your bearings, at least. Check the outline of the ridges on both sides before you set out. Won't be no problem followin' yonder light, but gettin' back is a whole other thing. These woods are black as pitch."

After Nellie was settled, the men headed away on foot. As

the scout had said, it was fairly easy to go toward the flickering campfire. Stepping cautiously over the uneven ground, skirting treacherous roots, they sneaked toward the encampment.

Coming within sight of it, they could make out the slumbering forms of at least six or seven Indians. Not seeing any sign of captive women or children, Chris was encouraged, yet they couldn't leave until they were certain. He glanced at his companions.

Morgan motioned for Dan to reconnoiter to the right and Jon to go to the left. "Chip," he whispered, "edge up a bit. Look for guards. I'll check for horses. Meet here in five minutes."

"Wait." Dan grabbed Christopher's hand, then Jon's. He bowed his head. "Father, be with us now."

"Amen," Morgan and Jon breathed.

But Chris rebelled at seeking help from a God who didn't care, who let his own flock be swept into danger and suffer such horrors. He had serious doubts that any of his prayers up till now had even mattered.

As the others left, Chris uncorked his powder horn and primed his flashpan. He crouched low and moved from tree to tree, testing each step before he took it, avoiding fallen twigs and unseen rocks.

Something glinted and caught his eye. In case it wasn't just moonlight sparking off Jon's rifle, he raised his own weapon and paused, watching . . . waiting.

The silhouette of a lithe Indian figure rose up between Chris and his brother-in-law. Sporting feathers, he had his gaze fixed on Jonathan. A few more rods and Christopher would have found himself in the redskin's lap!

The savage inched stealthily to the left, circling soundlessly toward Jon, his tomahawk raised.

Christopher's pulse rate increased. A shot would rouse the rest of the band and leave him facing them with an empty rifle. Willing his feet to move silently, he drew his hunting knife and narrowed the gap between himself and the Indian.

Just then Jonathan turned and started heading back as Morgan had earlier instructed.

The brave, tomahawk in hand, melted into the inky darkness of a tree trunk.

Christopher knew he had to reach the warrior before he ambushed Jon. With no remaining cover, Chris darted soundlessly through the open, straight for the enemy.

Only a few yards more.

The Indian, still unaware of Chris, emerged from the shadow and raised his hatchet toward his own unsuspecting victim.

Dropping his rifle, Christopher lunged for him. In one fluid move, he grabbed the topknot and sliced with deadly accuracy across the man's throat as they fell with a muffled thud to the spongy forest floor.

Jonathan hastened to Chris's side. With a grateful squeeze to his shoulder, he helped Chris untangle himself and get up.

"My rifle," Chris whispered. "In the bushes."

They made a quick search and retrieved the weapon, then moved warily into the woods a short way before returning to the rendezvous.

Dan already waited for them. Beside him, a young lad of about seven looked up at them and grinned, his smile reflecting the light of the moon.

A crunch came from behind Christopher. He swung around but with relief saw it was Morgan.

Dan signaled for them to withdraw, then led the way with the boy in tow.

"Any more captives?" Chris asked under his breath.

Dan shook his head. He put a finger to his lips.

Even after reaching Garth Kinyon and the girl, much more distance was needed between them and the band of Indians before they dared talk. Dan mounted first and quietly led the way through the dim, speckled light, riding slowly, with the young boy behind him and the others following.

Finally Dan kicked his horse to a trot, and they all sped up and over a hill, stopping on the other side. "I pray we're clear of them. But just in case, keep an eye out. They could still be coming. Tommy told me one of the braves was outside the camp somewhere keeping watch."

"Not anymore," Jonathan answered soberly.

Bile rose in Christopher's throat as he suddenly felt crusted blood on his hand. He shuddered and tried to wipe it on the leg of his trousers.

"Tommy, lad," Kinyon began, "were there any other settlers in the camp with you?"

"I already told the reverend no. I was all by myself when I was took. My ma ain't got no food. I was tryin' to snare a rabbit or somethin'."

"Were you on the road with the people from Wilkes-Barre?"

"Aye. And them what come over from Forty Fort. Them redcoats made us leave with nothin'. Not a single gun to hunt with nor a crust of bread." He puffed out his chest. "Got my slingshot, though. I was gonna get somethin' for Ma and the young'uns."

Cautious relief washed over Chris, and he knew his friends shared it. For once, people were being allowed to leave a settlement instead of being butchered . . . albeit without any of their worldly goods.

"The horses seem rested," Jon remarked. "Let's travel for another hour or so. I'd like to get to Mary as soon as we can."

"And Pru," Morgan added.

Christopher closed his eyes and sighed. None of the men even considered the possibility that their women and children might not be among the settlers on the road.

"Let's be off," Garth Kinyon said, glancing back over his shoulder. "We need to put some space between us and that raidin' party. Pretty soon one of 'em's gonna wake up and discover they got raided themselves."

After several more hours they finally stopped to sleep, although reluctantly. When the dim light of dawn brought them fully awake, they moved on.

About an hour later they came upon a long, straggly line of people. Jon, Dan, and Morgan eagerly spurred their mounts alongside the column, searching faces, occasionally calling out the names of their wives. Chris, following behind with Tommy, couldn't suppress the thin hope that perhaps Evie had been rescued in his absence and was somewhere among the weary travelers. He peeled his eyes for a glimpse of brown curls, a familiar walk.

"Tommy!" a woman cried. Darting through the crowd as Chris and Tommy passed by, she burst forth with three raga-muffin children clinging to her dusty skirts.

"Ma!" He slid off while the horse was still moving and was swamped at once in her tearful hug. "I thought the Indians got you!" She caressed his head and shoulders.

"They did. Him and them other men saved me." He pointed at Chris.

"Bless you, sir," she said to Christopher as she rose to her feet. "Bless you."

"And praise the Lord, you're armed!" a man called out.

How vulnerable they must feel to be in the wilderness without weapons of any kind, Chris thought. He tipped his hat to the mother. "Gotta see about my own family, ma'am."

Ignoring the rush of voices and excited shouts, Chris pressed after Jon and his friends.

Not far ahead, he saw that Dan, Jon, and Morgan had dismounted and now clung to their loved ones. If Evie was here, she'd be with Susannah and the others, he just knew it. Hoping against hope, Chris heeled his mount to a faster pace, dodging past people on the edge of the road.

He met Susannah's eyes as he drew up. Still in Dan's embrace, she brushed away her tears . . . but her smile wilted to a look of pain. "Evie. You've not found her."

That statement was all Christopher needed to kill his moment of optimism.

From out of the crowd, a man emerged and hurried toward them. Chris recognized Colonel Zeb Butler, his clothing soiled, his face streaked and haggard. Butler, the man who had been in charge of the protection of the valley against a British officer with the same surname. Butler, the coward who had apparently surrendered rather than fight. The colonel extended a hand to Dan. "Glad to see you alive, Reverend. Good to see you."

Christopher narrowed his eyes. "We were too late to find Evie. If you'd gone after the savages that first day, you'd have caught up with them easy. They only managed a few miles. Now the tracks are washed over, and I may never find her again."

Zeb Butler's gaze slid back to Dan. "Did you come through the valley?"

Dan nodded. "We saw the devastation. My place and every other one we passed, gutted."

"You came down the Wilkes-Barre side of the river, then."

"Everything we owned is gone," Jon said, stepping up with Mary close at his side. "Everything."

The colonel's shoulders sagged. "I know. But you're alive. When the enemy came down the Forty Fort side, I took some men and went over to reinforce that fort. We had no idea how outnumbered we were. When they started burning everything on that side of the river, we went out and tried to stop them. Before we knew what was happening, they came at us from every direction. The men, inexperienced as they were, were overwhelmed. It was a slaughter. I barely escaped the valley with seventy men—out of almost three hundred."

"You ran," Chris said in a flat voice. "Left women and children to those butchers' mercy." His bare hands itched to vent his anger on the man's neck.

"We knew they'd take any able-bodied men prisoner—at the very least," Butler said evenly. "We couldn't afford to lose any more husbands and fathers. Denison said he'd give us a head start by stalling the surrender of the forts until the next day. We were sure the British wouldn't allow the slaughter of almost two thousand women and children. All of Europe would turn on them. But . . ."

He shook his head in profound sadness. "Those heathen savages made up for it by torturing those they'd captured during the battle. The whole livelong night. Everybody inside

Forty Fort had to stand by helplessly and listen to the wrenching screams until the redskins finally finished the poor souls off at dawn. I'm just grateful my wife was at Wilkes-Barre and didn't have to hear it. Me and the other men only just met up with the folks here a few minutes ago. They told us some of our people took their chances on the river rapids, and some of the Yankees headed back to Connecticut."

Jon tugged Mary Clare tightly to his side. "I'm taking you down to Princeton to the Lyonses. I doubt the war will touch that town again, but even if it does, you'll not have to fear losing your scalp."

"Yes." Dan gave an affirming nod. "That's the only thing to do."

"I rather think the Brits have stopped searching for Prudence by now," Morgan chimed in, taking David from his tired wife. "She should be safe there for a while, too, until I can arrange to take her and our son north and back home to her family."

Prudence frowned. "No. From now on, I don't want to be more than twenty miles from you no matter where the war takes you." She took his face in her hands. "Is that clear?"

Witnessing the looks of love that passed between the couples only added to Christopher's misery. Evelyn should be here. She should be in the loving care of his family in Princeton instead of in the hands of savages.

He had to keep looking. He would not give up until he found her. Dead or alive.

29

Only the breeze from off Lake Ontario made the July heat tolerable as, six days after Evelyn's rescue, the small party neared its destination.

"Look." Corporal Gerald Blake, riding beside her on a tall military horse, pointed into the distance ahead. "Fort Niagara." An easy smile widened laugh lines around his mouth and twinkled from his clear hazel eyes. "We'll soon be there. My Liza will take proper care of you, I'm sure."

Thick forest growth had hampered any previous view of the fortress, but emerging from the trees into a vast meadow, Evelyn glimpsed the earthen walls facing the clearing and the palisades overlooking the shining waters of both the Great Lake and the Niagara River.

"You've done most admirably, under the circumstances," she replied. "I'll be forever in your debt."

Surely here there would be some way to contact her loved ones back in Wilkes-Barre, she mused. She couldn't bear to think about the danger her friends might be in themselves, and she had been in constant prayer for them throughout the ride. If they were safe, they must be sick with worry by now— or else had given up hope of ever seeing her alive again. Sight of the large Indian encampment circling the base of the fort added even more apprehension. Allies of the British or not, she didn't trust them.

Then an even more disturbing thought resurfaced. One of

the officers stationed here might very well have been in New York City when she, Morgan, and Prudence were hosting afternoon teas for that constant stream of British personnel. What if someone recognized her as a spy?

Evie inhaled a calming breath and forced herself to relax. Even if one of those very redcoats happened to be here, it would be next to impossible for him to recognize her. Her own mother would have to look twice. Baked golden as a Thanksgiving turkey where she wasn't scabbed and bruised, she wore the loose-fitting garments of Seneca women. She glanced down at the dark brown skirt and blousy maroon waist the companionable British colonel had secured to replace her own ruined dress.

Evie's glance also took in her bandaged wrists. She would probably always carry scars, but the rope burns were healing nicely, thanks to Gerald Blake's kind ministrations. Though but an officer's aide, he had in many subtle ways assumed the role of her protector.

Lieutenant Conway, riding at the front of the group, swung a mocking leer in Evie's direction.

She lowered her eyes. She would never get used to that man's blatant disrespect. Whether it was directed toward her as a former Indian prisoner or toward her as a woman in general, she wasn't sure. But his ribald comments and insinuations would take a long time to forget—especially one he'd made last evening after dispatching Gerald Blake on an errand. *"I've heard our red brothers are quite clumsy when it comes to pleasing a woman. Did you find that to be true?"* Only the reality of her vulnerable position had prevented her from striking back at the insufferable oaf.

Now as the officer wheeled his mount around and brought it alongside hers, Evelyn felt the all-too-familiar gaze roam over her. She wished she hadn't spent so many hours raking through her curls, untangling the matted mass with the comb the corporal had provided.

"Blake," the lieutenant said.

"Sir?"

"Ride on ahead and see that a bath is prepared for me."

"Yes, sir." The corporal tipped his head toward Evelyn. "And I'll see that one is waiting for you as well, Miss Haynes."

His use of her fictitious name pricked Evie's conscience, but she set it aside at the blissful possibility of a long soak. "Thank you, Corporal."

With that, he spurred his animal and galloped away.

"I should gladly share my bath with you, my dear." The lieutenant peered over his long Roman nose and cocked a dark eyebrow suggestively. Then, faced with her stony glare, he hedged. "But perhaps you'd prefer something less . . . intimate. A private supper for two, once you've bathed and powdered and put on white-woman's attire."

Evelyn did not dignify that suggestion with an answer either. His superiors would put a swift end to such ungentlemanly conduct, she was sure. Or at least, she hoped. But hadn't someone once told her that the British army maintained quite a number of women of ill repute? Camp followers, they were termed. Given stipends as if they were actually wives, though a shocking few had ever taken vows before a minister.

"My good sir," she finally declared evenly. "I am not in the habit of sharing *intimate* suppers with any bachelor, I assure you." His steely eyes narrowed to slits, and she had second thoughts about making him an enemy. She forced herself to offer him a flattering smile. "No matter how dashing and worldly he might be."

His expression softened but only to a smirk. "And I assure you, miss, a woman who has been with Indians for any length of time cannot afford such aversions. She should accept gladly any crumbs that happen to be offered."

Evelyn tucked her chin and looked straight at him. "Lieutenant Conway, I have endured your obviously ill-bred ignorance because fate decreed me your guest. But, thank heaven, I am now relieved of that dubious honor." Giving the neck of her horse a sharp smack with the reins, she raced ahead of the rest. She would love to have threatened that blackguard with the Thomas wealth and their considerable influence among high-ranking Crown officers. But, alas, that would have raised curiosity regarding her true identity.

Behind her, the other soldiers suddenly let out whoops that turned her blood cold as their mounts thundered toward the fort. The sounds dredged up the memory of being dragged into the Iroquois village. Evie's apprehension heightened further when she glimpsed Indians coming out of the cone-shaped bark dwellings on the outskirts of the fortress. She was relieved when, just as she reached the Indians, the soldiers caught up to her shorter pacer and sped past.

Lieutenant Conway grazed Evie with a surly look of arrogance as he took the front position coming up on the gate. She moistened her cracked lips. She had made an enemy of him. Well, so be it. Far less nauseating to have the dolt for an enemy than a friend.

Friend . . . her dear friends. After spending so much effort in not permitting herself more than the briefest thought of the people she'd been torn away from, the very word filled her with intense longing. Susannah and Prudence had to think she was dead by now. How could they not? Were they safe?

And Christopher! Evie's heart ached with anguish. When he learned of her capture he would be beside himself. He'd insist upon setting out immediately to search for her, she was sure. His letters had revealed enough of himself that she knew he'd risk his very life to find her. But it would be to no avail for him to traipse from village to village through the myriad Indian encampments sprinkled throughout the north. He would never even imagine she was with the British.

Then new hope broke through. Corporal Blake had said his wife, Liza, was from Boston. Surely she must correspond with her family there. Perhaps word of her whereabouts might be forwarded via them to Chris.

Evelyn guided her mount through a stone entrance and came out on the parade ground surrounded by an assortment of other buildings—barracks, officers' quarters, storehouses, and the like. Beyond those she saw what appeared to be a stockade within a stockade.

"Miss Haynes?" a feminine voice called out.

Interrupting her assessment of the surroundings, Evelyn saw a rather slight, fine-featured young woman with wavy hair a shade lighter than her own, weaving her way to the fore. A plain, serviceable dress of burnished gold muslin complemented sparkling eyes of rich brown as her lips spread into an amiable smile. "Welcome," she said breathlessly upon reaching Evelyn.

The sight of a friendly person of her own gender and age almost reduced Evie to tears. She made a valiant attempt to maintain her composure as she lifted a leg over the pommel of the saddle and slid to the ground.

The young woman hesitated for a heartbeat, then opened her arms and caught Evelyn in a hard hug. "I'm Liza Blake. I'm so glad you've come."

"I see you've met my wife," her husband said, stepping to Liza's side and wrapping an arm proudly about her slim shoulders.

Liza studied Evelyn for a moment, the hint of a question in her expression. "Hm. I was sure Dan Haynes's youngest sister was Emily, but I must have been mistaken. You've got his dark hair, I see, but so curly—and such light blue eyes. Emily, of course, is the most different, with her blonde hair and green eyes." She shook her head in wonder. "So many different features in one family! But then, it is a rather large one. Oh, dear, I am running on. . . . It's just that I'm so thrilled to see someone I have something in common with. Come along. I've set some water to heating. We won't need to make it too hot, since it's such a warm day." She grabbed Evie and hugged her again.

Evelyn suddenly noticed that a horde of gawking people had gathered, and she was the center of attraction. Surely no one had expected the soldiers to bring back a white woman, particularly one clad in Indian attire. She shifted her stance uncomfortably.

"Lieutenant Conway," an authoritative voice said from a distance. "Report to General Carleton at once."

Searching for the person who had spoken, Evie saw a major who looked quite familiar. She couldn't place him.

"And I do hope you've an answer for this premature return," the major went on. His shrewd eyes then found hers. A slow frown pinched his brows, and he stepped toward her through the gathering, staring intently. He took her hand upon his approach. "Edith? No, Vivian. Is that you?"

Liza Blake, unaware of any danger to Evie, came to his assistance. "I do believe you mean Evelyn, Major. Evelyn Haynes."

He settled back on his heels with a smile. "Ah, yes. Miss Evelyn with the dazzling eyes. New York, wasn't it?"

Nothing would come out of Evie's mouth. It would be only a matter of time before he remembered *everything*. Being duped by a sixteen-year-old girl must have made her the talk of British headquarters. Perhaps there had been broadsides sent to this very fort, offering a reward for her capture.

"Major Norton, at your service," he said, bowing politely.

"So nice to see you again," Evie finally managed. She feigned a smile.

"I must say," he said in clipped British. "Your confusion is apparent in your expression. But then, why should one recall a single soldier among so many, particularly when I had the misfortune of being called away to Canada so soon after your charming presence graced the city?"

Evelyn began to relax. She broadened her smile, and dredging up an old talent, even managed to blush a little. "You're too kind, Major."

He tipped his head. "However, there is another bachelor officer posted here who spent much more time in New York than I. You might recall him, I'm sure. Captain Long is the name. Clayton Long."

Evie's heart leapt to her throat. *Captain Long! The very same scoundrel who had been hounding her brother since his Boston spying days! The man who had set the trap that had ensnared Morgan in*

New York! The one person who would, without hesitation, know her real surname! Her gaze darted about at the bizarre twist of events.

"I can see you're delighted, Miss Haynes," Norton went on. "But, alas, the captain is with Butler at the moment. They've pressing business in the Wyoming Valley."

"I see," Evelyn replied, her lungs compressing at the reminder of the dreadful fate that must have befallen some of the dearest people in her world. A great sadness enveloped her. Her own momentary gain was her family's tragedy.

"You appear to be in dire need of rest and respite, miss," the major said graciously. "I'm sure one of our efficient women here at Fort Niagara will be most willing to attend you."

Liza Blake stepped forward. "Sir, I happen to be an old friend of the Haynes family. I'd deem it an honor to attend Miss Evelyn. In fact, she could abide with us for the time being."

"Yes." Looking from her to Evie, he pursed his lips in thought. "Capital idea." He took Evelyn's tanned, bandaged hand and bent over it with a click of his heels. "Till tomorrow eve, then. With your permission, we'll sup at sunset."

Watching after the man as he whirled and strode away, Evelyn gravitated to Liza . . . her one fragile hope in this most threatening of places.

30

"Ohh," Evelyn sighed, relaxing completely against the sides of the wooden tub in Liza and Gerald's simple barracks. Though far plainer than even Susannah's tiny farmhouse, Liza had made their portion of the single-story structure invitingly homey—and after what Evie had been through, the place seemed like a palace. "I can't begin to tell you how good this warm bath feels." She shifted slightly to ease more of her aching muscles.

With an understanding smile, Liza picked up a decanter of rose water from the washstand of their small bedchamber and poured some into the tub. "Perhaps this will soothe some of those welts and bruises. It hurts me just to see what you've been through."

"Only the beginning of what the Indians had in store for me," Evie replied bitterly. "Until your husband and the other soldiers broke through the mob and intervened. I haven't stopped thanking God for that miracle."

"Yes, I would imagine. I've seen the results of running the gauntlet before. And worse. Last year the Indians brought captives here after . . . well . . ." With a shudder, Liza handed her a cake of scented soap.

Evie lifted it to her nostrils. "Where did you manage to find something this civilized hundreds of miles from the nearest town?" She ran it gingerly down one bruised arm, then the other, inhaling the sweet fragrance that was quickly replacing the smell of horse and grime.

"One of the fort women insists on adding oils from various wildflowers to the lard and ashes whenever she makes soap. Of course, the rest of us are glad of it. A touch of home, and all."

"Have you family back in—Boston, I believe your husband said it was?"

Liza's silky lashes hid her eyes as she nodded sadly. "A mother. But I've never contacted her since I left, I'm sorry to say. She was so adamant about my not consorting with the enemy; I know it must have broken her heart when I actually ran off with Gerald. She probably considers me dead—or wishes I were."

A small flame of hope inside Evie died. So much for trying to contact Christopher through any of Liza's relatives. She would have to think of some other way. "He seems a fine young man."

"Oh, Gerald has been an absolute rock." Liza's finely shaped lips softened into a smile. "He was so considerate of my good name. Determined that no one would think of me as just one more camp trollop, he married me the instant he received permission from his superiors. I may not exactly relish this army life, but I haven't regretted being Gerald's wife a day since . . . though I do miss Mama and wish she could know him."

"I have a sweetheart, too," Evie replied wistfully. "A wonderful young man. And thanks to the providential timing of my rescue, I can go back to him without shame." Reaching over her shoulder, she tried to wash her back.

Liza took the soap from her hand. "Here, let me. I'll try to be careful." Dipping the cake into the water, she gently soaped Evie's sores and scrapes, then rinsed her skin with handfuls of warm water.

"That helps," Evie breathed, sinking lower into the water. "Even just being clean feels better. Thank you."

Liza began to comb through Evie's tangled curls. "What's he like? Your young man, I mean."

"He's everything I've ever dreamed."

"Yes, I hear that in your voice."

"His name is Christopher." Evie tipped her head back as Liza poured water over her hair. "He's written me the dearest letters, all about his dreams for us, his plans for the future. I've treasured every single one of them." She sighed, and her caustic tone returned. "If Butler's Rangers have their way in the Wyoming Valley, all my beautiful letters will be destroyed. I'll regret that loss almost as much as I'd mourn hearing that any harm came to my friends and family."

"Susannah," Liza murmured as she massaged the scented soap into Evie's hair.

"Susannah, Prudence, Chris's sister, Mary Clare, and all their children. When I learned the valley was the next target Butler and the Indians had chosen, I was devastated that I couldn't warn them."

"When Gerald told me that's where Dan and Susannah were living, I couldn't believe it. I just pray there won't be a repeat of what the Mohawk Valley suffered last year."

A breeze ruffled the worn white curtain at the window and wafted over Evie's wet skin.

Liza rose and fastened the curtain together with a hairpin, then returned to rinse the suds from Evie's hair. "You know," she whispered, "I hate what the rangers are doing. Did you know they actually pay the savages for every scalp they bring in from a white settler—be it man, woman, or child?"

"It is true, then."

"The Indians come into the fort with them, flinging them around, showing them off like badges of honor." Liza handed Evie a towel. "I love Gerald, and I know he hates this business as much as I do . . . but I don't know how much more of it I can take."

Evelyn wrapped herself in the coarse towel and stepped out of the tub. She took Liza's hand and squeezed it. "Close the window and pull a chair close. I have something you should know."

Though her eyes were questioning, Liza's movements were graceful as she hurried to do so.

"I hadn't wanted to speak to your husband of this while we were on the trail, but did your last name happen to be Brown before you married Gerald?"

A lock of wavy brunette hair fell over Liza's shoulder as she nodded.

"Then you're the Liza Brown Susannah prays for every day! She asks the Lord every single day to be with you always, to guide and protect you wherever you are."

"She does?" Liza's doe-like eyes grew misty. "She was a very dear friend to me. I know she endured a lot of ill will from some of the church women for introducing me to Gerald. I hate to think how they must have maligned her when I left with the British in the evacuation. But I just couldn't bear never to see him again."

"I know just how you feel. I even tried to convince Chris to let me go off to war with him. He would have none of that, of course." With a giggle, Evie displayed a battered leg. "He thought it would be too dangerous."

Liza joined in with a light laugh, then sobered to a conspiratorial smile. "From what the colonel said, it sounded like you're a Loyalist. Perhaps you can have your wish after all."

"What do you mean?"

"In compensation for being a Tory, wrongfully attacked by his paid Indians, General Carleton just might have you transported to wherever your fiancé is posted. Is he with a Tory company or with the Royal army?"

Evie hesitated. "You do know Dan and Susannah are patriots, don't you?"

"Of course. And so is Mama. That's why my leaving with a British soldier was doubly awful. Of course, if I ever work up courage to write to her, I'll let her know we wed right away, so at least her mind will be at rest that I'm not sullied but well cared for instead."

"My situation is similar to yours, actually," Evie remarked. "Except my parents are Loyalists, and I, like Dan and Susannah, am a patriot."

Liza put her hands to her cheeks. "Oh, my. Well, never you mind. As long as Colonel Travor and the others think you're a Tory, who's to know? I certainly shan't tell them."

"Thank you," Evie murmured, sinking to the chair. "But I'm afraid I'll be exposed regardless when Captain Long returns." Seeing Liza's befuddled expression, Evie made her decision. "I might just as well confess all. I wouldn't want you to be accused of being an accessory, no matter how unwittingly. While I was in New York attending the lavish British and Tory parties and teas, my brother, his wife, and I were spying for the patriots. It was Captain Long who ferreted us out."

"The Reverend Dan Haynes?" Liza's mouth gaped, and her brown eyes flared. "Are you suggesting that the Hayneses were spying too? I could never believe such a thing—not of them, surely! Dan is a true man of God. And Susannah? She simply wouldn't do such a thing."

"You're quite right. Dan and Susannah went to Wilkes-Barre to act as peacemakers between the Connecticut settlers and the Pennsylvanians. They did harbor me; that much is true. But, you see, I'm not actually related to either one of them. I merely chose their surname on the spur of a moment because the Royal army is intent on arresting me for spying."

With a grave shake of her head, Liza met Evie's gaze. "Well, your secret is safe with me . . . but not for long. Gerald went with Lieutenant Conway to deliver a message ordering the return of Butler and the others as soon as they've secured the valley—which they've likely already done, I fear. Gerald told me that between the regulars, the Tories, and the Indians, the force numbered almost eleven hundred."

The revelation filled Evelyn with horror. "My little nieces," she whispered. "My sister-in-law. Surely if God would save someone as unworthy as I, he'd be that much more gracious to his faithful daughters, don't you think?" Evie desperately needed Liza to confirm her hope.

"Yes, I pray. Yes." Liza brushed her cheek against Evie's. "And more, the good Lord sent you to tell me that my pastor and his wife still care about me. You have no idea how much that means. I've felt so alone among the women here. Most of them are such a crude lot." She straightened with a hopeful smile. "We need to pray diligently that one of the supply ships from Montreal docks here within the next few days. We must get you out of here before Captain Long returns."

Renewed hope flowed through Evelyn. Montreal. A real city. Far away from Captain Long and the Iroquois nation. Once there, she could find her way back to the Colonies . . . and Chris.

❦ ❦

Seated at a corner table along the back wall of the Lyons' Den after the noon meal, Christopher cast an irritated glance toward the stairs. Morgan had carried his sleeping son up to his and Prudence's room some time ago, and everyone else had secured rooms for a much-needed rest as well. But Morgan had said he'd come directly back. What was taking so long? He knew how anxious Chris was to solidify their plans.

A few local townsmen lingered to chat over rum or cider after their meal, and boisterous voices and hearty guffaws filled the common room. The confusion only added to Christopher's glum mood.

His morbid thoughts couldn't get past the grim fact that at the very time the men of Wyoming Valley were being duped into leaving the sanctity of the fort only to be savagely massacred by a vast horde of the screaming devils, Washington's army in New Jersey was celebrating a victory over the British. The sickening contrast pained Chris like salt poured into an already festering wound. Now, with summer in its glory, the patriot ranks had swollen to over thirteen thousand men. Surely the general should have anticipated that increase and dispatched the Wyoming Valley militias to their homes weeks earlier.

Now his fellow soldiers were upstairs *resting*, as if their ordeal were over. But the ordeal was far from over. He shot another glare toward the stairs.

"More cider?" one of the redheaded twins asked, plucking the half-empty glass from his grasp.

Chris didn't bother answering the girl, much less acknowledging which one she was. The pair had been underfoot in a most irritating manner since he and his friends had arrived. He averted his gaze toward the stairwell again while she poured more of the amber drink into his glass.

Across the room, one of the locals whacked the tabletop and howled with laughter. "Yessir," he bellowed, "when that coward General Lee panicked and showed his heels, taking our boys with him, Washington rode right out there on his big white horse and turned that army around, single-handed. Then he showed them lobsters what for, he did. By the time he was through, the louts had took off runnin' and didn't stop till they got all the way to New York City!"

A round of hearty laughter echoed through the low-ceilinged room.

"More'n anything," another said, "I'm glad that new British commander took the notion to return his army to New York. Stringin' his whole army out across the countryside made 'em easy as shootin' ducks in a row."

A gravelly voiced man smirked. "Guess Clinton ain't partial to all the party goin' as General Howe was in Philadelphia."

A third fellow snorted. "Well, all I care is, he pulled out of Philly. And by all that's holy, we'll not let the miscreants take it back again."

Hearing footfalls descending the stairs, Christopher turned to see Morgan coming and motioned for him to join him.

One of the twins appeared out of nowhere with another glass of cider.

Morgan accepted it with a nod, absently taking a sip as his gaze gravitated to the noisy townsmen.

Christopher rolled his eyes heavenward. "Well? I'm not hanging around here for one more hour. Kinyon's probably back at Easton by now waiting for us. Raritan, where he took Nellie to her kin, is closer to Easton than we are here at Princeton."

Morgan didn't appear to be listening.

Chris glared at him until he finally noticed.

"As if I didn't have enough worries." Morgan combed his fingers through his thick brown hair. "From what I've heard, the Crown gave the Loyalists in Philadelphia precious little notice they were evacuating. It'll probably be like Boston all over again. Any Tory who doesn't leave will be misused terribly, and all their homes and businesses will be sacked—for fraternizing with the enemy."

One of the twins, hovering nearby, spoke up. "The cowardly Loyalists all left on ships for England. I say good riddance to them!"

"Yes," her sister confirmed. "That's why the redcoats had to march north instead of going by ship. They were obliged to turn over their fleet to those lily livers."

"That'll be all, girls," Christopher said firmly. "Morgan and I need to talk in private."

Both lower lips protruded in dismay, and the twins withdrew to a table on the other side of the common room.

"I'm torn, Chip," Morgan said in all sincerity. "I need to go with you and Garth back to the Iroquois lands. But I also must find out if my mother and father are safe. I've another sister in Philadelphia, too, remember? Tell you what." He reached into an inside pocket of his frock coat and withdrew a coin purse, which he handed to Chris. "You go on ahead to Easton. Buy whatever provisions and trade goods you and the tracker need. I'll meet you there within a week."

"A week!" Chris seized the purse and sprang to his feet. "I won't wait one more *hour!* I let you and the others drag me all the way down here, with Evie at the mercy of savages all this time. Well, no more. Go do what you have to do. Kinyon and I can travel lighter and faster without another person slowing us down, anyway."

"Chris!" Morgan shot to his feet and caught Christopher's elbow. He took a calming breath. "I seriously doubt my sister is alive," he said quietly. "I pray that by some miracle she still is—and I'll not stop praying for that until I know for certain otherwise. But—"

Christopher shoved Morgan's hand away and slammed past him. "Enough! I'll not listen to another one of your doubts. She's alive, and she needs me." Reaching the back door, he flung a scathing look over his shoulder. "Oh, and if it's not *too* much *bother,* bid my family farewell for me."

31

Evelyn, seated at the splendidly set table in the dining room of the bachelors' quarters, straightened her spine as an enlisted man brought in a platter of roasted duck and set it in the middle of the damask tablecloth. She could not wait for this interminable meal to end. It was hard enough to appear relaxed in a borrowed gown far more daring than any she'd have chosen, not to mention its being a gaudy shade of chartreuse, which only drew attention to her healing bruises. But even worse than that, she was having to make inane conversation with Captain Norton and another couple, when what she wanted more than anything was to be back with Liza—or better still, at home where she belonged.

"Eet was—how you say—magnifique!" Denise Dupree gushed through ruby lips, which seemed even bolder in contrast to her elaborate powdered wig. She leaned forward just enough to display the generous swells of bosom bulging precariously from the low-cut bodice of her flounced taffeta gown. "Do you not agree, Jacques?" Her spangled earbobs caught the glow from the candelabra and tossed back an array of sparkles.

Captain Jack Wyatt blotted his mustached upper lip on a linen napkin and gave his mistress a suggestive smile. "But, of course, my pet. Magnificent, indeed."

The plump Frenchwoman tittered behind her fan and batted her eyes.

Evie took a sip of wine from her crystal goblet. It was important to appear amused by this nonsensical banter rather than reveal her aversion to socializing with a common hussy. After all, she desperately needed to leave this place, yet she had no money to secure passage out of this vast wilderness to the seaport of Halifax and then on to Chris. She manufactured a smile as she accepted the platter Captain Norton passed to her and took a portion of duck.

Mademoiselle Dupree sampled the poached oysters in rich buttery lemon sauce and puckered her mouth, emphasizing the beauty patch she'd affixed near her upper lip. She swept a languid gaze between the two officers. "A gentleman friend in Quebec tell to me once that a woman, she ees like a river and needs an experienced sailor to navigate her. You agree, *n'est-ce pas?*" Her mischievous pouty lips conveyed a raft of hidden meaning behind her seemingly innocent remark.

"An interesting thought," Norton said, a gleam in his shifty hazel eyes. "I quite see the comparison. Some lay in tranquil curves for easy sailing, others are tempestuous and wild."

A round of bawdy chuckles followed.

Evelyn had endured more than her share of subtle innuendos during her spying days in New York, but these comments were blatantly vulgar, typical of the irreverent attitude of the British toward the women of the Colonies. Burning with anger, she laid aside her fork and napkin and prepared to rise. But remembering that she hadn't as yet gained the captain's promise to arrange passage for her on the next ship, she reclaimed her utensil and settled back down, viciously stabbing a chunk of meat instead.

"I rather find that some women are both," Wyatt said, lifting his sparse brows at the Frenchwoman.

Her lips slid into a wanton smile, and she leaned to whisper something to both men.

Evie didn't have to hear the comment to blush as Captain Norton smiled and turned his amused patrician face her way. She wished her dinner gown covered her all the way up to her ears.

"And what kind of river might you consider yourself, my dear?" he asked, capturing her gaze with a bold stare.

Clenching her fists beneath the tablecloth, it was all Evie could do to keep from grating out the answer that flashed to mind: *A very high waterfall with great killing boulders at its base,* perhaps, or *one that is poisonous.* But with effort, she controlled her scathing tone. "Considering the horrors of my recent trials, I would have to say I am more like a brook, one too shallow to be navigable."

"Ah, yes," he said smoothly, his thin lips twitching with mirth. "But even a trickling stream can have its moments. Say, after a raging storm, for example."

Evie, swiftly losing her appetite, could not believe she was having to endure this drivel. She would have to broach her own topic soon, before she showed them what a raging storm *she* could be. She smiled at Norton. "Captain, I've been informed that supply ships sail here fairly regularly."

"Quite," he replied, seemingly unperturbed at her change of subject. "They dock here for a day or more while cargo is unloaded for transport down the Niagara to Lake Erie. We are the drop-off point for supplying our other posts as far as Fort Detroit, you see. And speaking of the Niagara," he said after a slight pause, "it contains a most spectacular waterfall. More breathtaking than anything I've ever seen."

"Ees zat so?" Denise Dupree cooed, with a toss of her powdered ringlets.

"Present company excepted," he added with his disgusting leering grin. He flicked imaginary lint from the sleeve of his immaculate red military coat and turned back to Evie. "You said you are an accomplished horsewoman. Perhaps I might take you to see the falls before the men return from Wyoming Valley. 'Tis but a morning's ride from here."

"Perhaps," Evie agreed. "As long as I'm here when the ship arrives. I'll be booking passage to Montreal on its return voyage. My family in . . . New York," she lied, "will be devastated to hear of my capture while I was visiting my brother's farm. *Particularly* if my sister-in-law and her two children have also been harmed in any way. I am most disturbed that your commanders would set Indians upon the innocent women and children of your loyal subjects, Captain, as well as suspected rebels. No one should be subjected to such barbarity."

"The fortunes of war, I'm afraid," he returned with a shrug.

"We do our best to minimize the torturing itself," Wyatt explained. "But the Iroquois insist that as victors they are entitled to a certain amount of it."

"Ah, *mon cheri,*" Denise whined with a theatrical pout. "You promise me when I leave Quebec and join you here that we would not speak of such things. Ees very unsuitable for conversation."

No more unsuitable than everything else that has been bantered about this eve, Evelyn countered silently. "You're absolutely right," she said brightly. "Do forgive me for bringing such unpleasantness to this lovely table." She tipped her head toward Norton. "Captain, the young matron who has so kindly been attending my needs related that a supply ship is due here anytime. Tomorrow, at the latest. I'd deem it a great service if you would see to my travel arrangements. As you know, I am completely without funds at the moment."

He reared his head back in surprise. The idea of parting with his money obviously disturbed him.

"I assure you, my father is a most generous man. He will gladly repay you fourfold."

Norton's expression took on a spark of greed. "We should be most grieved, miss, to lose your delightful company so soon. Perhaps you might delay your departure, say . . . one month. We could forward a message to your family, of course, informing them that you are quite safe and well."

Evie feigned regret. "Oh, I couldn't do such a cruel thing to them. If my departure for home were delayed, my dear father would be most displeased. Most displeased indeed. He'd immediately dispatch a ship of his own to fetch me . . . which, I fear, would cause you to forfeit your own handsome profit."

"Your father has his own sailing ship?" Mademoiselle Dupree asked.

"Ships, my dear," Evie bragged with a smug smile. "Surely you know that no New York merchant can truly prosper without a fleet of his own." Evie almost laughed when Denise suddenly appeared to have lost her voice.

"Norton and I," Wyatt volunteered, "would be pleased to assist you in any way we can. Wouldn't we, Captain?" His tone revealed that he was attempting to wedge into what appeared a very profitable deal. "However, that does not mean we cannot enjoy an adventure or two in the meantime. A jaunt to the great waterfall would be quite amusing . . . perhaps tomorrow or the day after?" He bowed to his female companion. "Would you care to join us, my pet?"

"*Moi?*" She glowered, appalled. "I would theenk sitting atop a horse in the scorching sun while being devoured by mosquitoes would be quite—how you say—not pleasant." She smiled slyly. "I prefer . . . indoor pleasures."

Evie lunged to her feet, her chair scraping loudly over the plank floor. "Forgive me. I find I've acquired an unbearable headache. If you will excuse me."

Captain Norton rose and blocked her path before she could scurry away. "Dreadfully sorry. I'll see you to your quarters."

Wyatt had also come to his feet. "A little rest is just the thing," he offered hopefully. "You'll be in fine fettle by morning. I'll have mounts ready for us to leave promptly after breakfast. 'Twould be a crime to be so close to such magnificence and not take advantage of the opportunity. Plenty of time to see to your passage. Afterward."

Evie caught the thinly veiled threat behind the suggestion. Not only had he inveigled his way along for the ride to the falls without his kept woman, he'd invited himself to be part of Evelyn's transportation arrangements and promised reward *if she proved pleasant company*. Evie had the feeling she was being pursued by a pack of wolves. "You know, as truly wonderful as that sounds, I must confess, I've yet to recover from my harrowing ride here from the Indian encampment. Perhaps it might be prudent to postpone such a delightful outing for another day or so. I bid you good evening," she said politely and turned toward the door.

Evie had no intention of remaining a second longer with this boorish pair of the king's captains. She wished she dared blurt out her innermost feelings, but she did the wiser thing and held her tongue. Far better if Christopher could have been here to put them in their place. Soon, though, she'd see him. Very soon.

A light breeze off the lake cooled the night as she and Norton strolled outside onto the parade grounds.

"Ship ho!" the sentinel called from the lakeside palisade. "The ship's coming."

Evelyn was filled with excitement. The ship! Why, she would be able to reach Halifax and find transport to the middle colonies and Christopher within a matter of weeks. All she had to do was depart this nest of vipers before that despicable Captain Clayton Long showed up!

Through the window above Liza's sideboard, Evelyn spied Captains Norton and Wyatt coming with their aides. An extra pair of horses fitted with sidesaddles trailed behind on leads. "Ooh," she sighed wearily, "it looks like you'll have to finish the dishes without me." She set down the bowl she'd been drying, then wiped her hands on her apron before removing it.

Liza, her wrists submerged in soapy dishwater, leaned over and peered outside. "So it would appear. You've already begged off two days in a row on that outing."

"Yes." Evie giggled. "They seemed able to accept my excuse the day before yesterday as due to being spent from my harrowing experience. My second excuse downright annoyed them. But really, it quite astounds me that even as far from civilization as Fort Niagara is, those British officers would expect me to ride off willingly with them without a *very suitable* chaperone."

Liza tilted her head toward the window. "Well, they must have taken you seriously. They've imposed upon the only woman in the fort who happens to be both an accomplished rider *and* properly wed to her major."

"Nevertheless, I feel guilty for leaving you with the added responsibility of looking after her two little ones for an entire day . . . as if you haven't enough fort laundry and other work of your own."

Inverting a dish onto the drying towel, Liza smiled. "Oh, don't fret. I'm used to it. An enlisted man's wife is put upon much the same as her husband."

When the riding party got halfway across the parade ground, Wyatt and his aide split off toward another building while Norton and the other man continued toward the quarters of the married enlisted men.

"I've cost those officers a hefty sum in pounds sterling," Evie went on, "but I'm pleased they were able to convince the ship's captain to agree to arrange transport for me all the way to Halifax. I should be able to manage quite nicely on my own from there."

"Oh, how I wish I were going with you."

The spontaneous statement and its wistful tone were equally surprising. "Well, come then!" Evie said, placing a hand on Liza's arm. "Come with me. We can easily make our way from Halifax to Boston and your mother."

Liza's long lashes lowered demurely over her dark eyes. "I could never leave Gerald here alone. He's always been a gentle sort. This past year, with all the ugliness he's seen, has been very hard on him."

"Then why hasn't he put in for a transfer?"

"He has. Along with practically all the other men! I'll just have to content myself with the letter I dispatch with you. Perhaps you'll find yourself close enough to hand deliver it to Mother. Maybe even give her a kiss from me." A misty sheen glistened in her eyes, and Liza quickly averted her gaze and blinked the moisture away.

Evie hugged her. "I'll make a point of it. I promise." Then, as Norton swung down and his aide dismounted and gathered all the reins, she tightened her lips.

"Do go enjoy yourself, Evie," Liza said cheerily. "Everyone who's seen the waterfall raves about it to no end."

She'd heard that very thing from several others already, but Evie couldn't ignore her misgivings. "I know. It's just that it seems *indecent* to go sightseeing with English soldiers this deep into Indian country . . . while braves hired by the British from these very same tribes could be attacking my own people as we speak."

Liza, who shared her concern for Susannah and her loved ones, grabbed Evie with her wet hands and embraced her.

A knock sounded on the door, and Evie sighed and went to answer. Liza took her leave then as well. With a polite nod to the men, she hurried over to care for the major's two little children.

"Ready to go, miss?" the redheaded aide inquired of Evelyn. "I'm Corporal Winfrey." He beamed from ear to ear beneath thick blond eyebrows.

"Quite." Forcing a polite smile, Evie plucked her bonnet and gloves from the wall spikes and stepped outside.

His answering smile was far more genuine and was accompanied by a conspiratorial wink.

Evie wondered if Gerald Blake had instructed the aide to keep a watchful eye on her. She would be ever grateful to Liza's dashing husband. Without Gerald, she might not have been able to manage the despicable Lieutenant Conway after her rescue from the Indian village. Shaking off the thought, she walked to a waiting bay Thoroughbred.

Corporal Winfrey immediately sprang to assist her. "Gerald sends his regards," he whispered, as Evie put her foot into his clasped hands.

"He's a fine man," she returned softly.

"I beg your pardon, Miss Evelyn," Norton interrupted,

glancing from her to his aide. "Were you, perchance, address-
ing me?"

Evie determined not to allow the overbearing man's pompous attitude ruffle her. "I was commenting on the gelding,
actually, saying that he has such fine lines."

The major's manner turned to smug pleasure. "I rather
expected he'd suit you."

By the time they had all mounted, Captain Wyatt and the
chaperone joined them. "Good morning, miss," the officer
said with a grand smile. "This is Mistress Patterson, who has
so generously agreed to come with us today. Mistress, Miss
Evelyn Haynes."

Evie extended her hand to the plain-featured woman in the
fashionable summer riding costume, noting her amiable
smile and how well she sat her mount. "So glad to make your
acquaintance, mistress."

"And I you, Miss Haynes," she replied in a clipped English
accent. She gave an elegant tip of her head, and the feathery
plume on her bonnet danced delicately. "I needn't tell you
how seldom we women receive invitations to leave this remote
habitat and get out and about to enjoy the change of season.
I am most grateful for this opportunity."

"And I am pleased you were able to come on such short
notice. I hear the falls are magnificent any time of the year."

"Ladies," Captain Norton cut in. "I suggest you get further
acquainted along the way. We're getting quite a late start." He
scowled at Wyatt. "The sun has been up at least three hours."

As they departed the fort, Evelyn couldn't help smiling to
herself. The private little outing Norton had intended for the
two of them had evolved into a party of six—three of whom
would do their utmost to thwart his every romantic move.

They hadn't even cleared the meadow surrounding the fort
and Indian encampment when a horse and rider galloped out
of the forest toward them.

Captain Wyatt, at the head, raised his hand, and the party
came to a stop. Norton expelled a groan of disgust.

Mistress Patterson craned her neck. "Please, let it be."

Reaching them, the rider halted his horse. "We're back," he panted, out of breath. "The rest of the force is but a mile off."

"My husband, sir," the woman cried. "Is he with you?"

"Yes, ma'am. To be sure."

Evelyn would have liked to enter into her chaperone's joy but felt trepidation instead. Captain Long was certain to be with the army. It was probably too much to hope the man had been killed in battle, and she didn't dare inquire.

"You must forgive me," the British woman said earnestly to the others. "Another time, perhaps." She slapped her reins across her steed's neck and took off in the direction of the returning soldiers.

For a fleeting moment, Evie considered doing that very same thing herself, only in the opposite direction. She resisted the impulse.

Captain Wyatt reined his mount around and faced his fellow captain. "I suppose we'll have to postpone our ride until a later time. Tomorrow, perhaps."

Evie's relief was fortified with the knowledge that the ship would pull out tomorrow. She would have preferred it to be sooner, but since that was impossible, she'd do the best thing . . . stay out of sight until it weighed anchor. But she did have one important question for the wiry rider in uniform. "Tell me, sir. The Wyoming Valley—what has become of it? Did you take prisoners? Did the Indians?"

He met her questioning gaze with a curious expression. "No, miss. We took no prisoners. Those who were left, women and children mostly, we sent packin' before we torched the place. 'Course, the Indians weren't thrilled about that. They might've spirited a few away here an' there. But the bucks won't want us knowin' about it, so 'tis unlikely they'll bring 'em here like they did last year." He closed his eyes and shuddered. "Don't fret. You shan't be kept awake too late by the noise this eve."

His answer was far from comforting. Fearing the unknown horrors that must have occurred in the valley, Evelyn clung desperately to the glimmer of faith that Susannah and Prudence were among those who left in safety. And now she needed to see to her own escape. "Captains," she said with the brightest smile she could muster, "I do thank you for your kind intention to treat me to this lovely outing. However, now that duty is calling you, please feel free to go and take care of what is needful. I shall see that my horse is stabled."

And that I am carefully tucked away until the ship sails, she added silently.

32

Liza's tiny quarters quickly grew stuffy in the sultry dusk once the window was closed and the curtains were drawn, but Evelyn was relieved to muffle some of the noisy celebration of the returning soldiers and the incessant Indian drums. She leaned over Liza's shoulder at the kitchen table, watching her friend sketch a map.

"The streets of Boston curve every which way," Liza said with an upward glance, "but this should give you a fair idea of the basic layout. Just stay on the main road until you get to Milk Street. Then turn here, here, and here." She tapped the feathered quill to indicate intersecting roads. "Mother's house is right on this corner. See?"

Evie nodded. "Don't worry, I'll find it. And I'm grateful for your uncle's address in Portsmouth as well."

"Just ask for the mill pond, and someone there will be glad to point out Uncle Gavin's house. He'll see to it that you get the rest of the way to Boston." Liza blew dry a glistening dab of ink, then folded the map and handed it to Evie. "You might even be able to find some fisherman in Halifax willing to take you across to one of the little Maine settlements. No doubt the British are blocking any traffic between Halifax and Boston."

Sliding the map into the skirt pocket of the durable emerald linen gown Liza had provided, Evelyn smiled into her friend's eyes. "Don't fret. My father has a few business associates in Halifax. There's a good chance they haven't heard about my trouble with the British."

"Well, don't take needless chances, promise? A pretty young miss like yourself shouldn't be traveling alone."

Touched by Liza's concern, Evie bent to hug her. "I shan't do anything foolish. I wish you were coming with me, you and Gerald."

"So do I," Liza murmured wistfully.

"But since it appears that isn't to be, I can't help wishing you hadn't told Gerald about me. If anyone discovers he's aware of my true identity, he'll be accused of harboring me. After all your kindnesses, I shouldn't want either of you to be in danger on my account. Remember how long they kept Dan Haynes imprisoned."

"Yes." Liza clasped her hands tightly in her lap. "That was horrid for Susannah. But I've never been able to keep any secrets from my Gerald. He'll not give you away; I know it. You can trust him completely."

Evelyn was both consoled and encouraged by Liza's reassuring expression and smile.

"Once this war has ended, my husband and I intend to find a church family somewhere in the Colonies that is as loving as the one we knew in Boston with Dan and Susannah. Tell Mother that for me, will you? Tell her I would never have run off with Gerald if he hadn't possessed a burning desire to serve our Lord. His enlistment will be up next year—fourteen months from now. We can hardly wait."

A loud pounding rattled the door.

Evie started in fright.

"Quick, go in there," Liza whispered, motioning toward her sleeping chamber.

While Liza went to answer the summons, Evelyn hurried out of sight. She quietly closed the door of the bedchamber, then crossed at once to the back window. Seeing no one about when she moved the curtain aside, she pushed the window open in case she needed an escape. That done, she tiptoed back to the door and opened it a crack to see if she could discover who had come.

Gerald! He'd returned from loading her horse and saddle aboard ship. With relief, Evie collapsed against the door for a second, then hastened out to join him and Liza. "Back so soon?"

The young man's anxious gaze flew to her. He shook his head, his pleasant face furrowed with concern. "I was a fool to take the animal to the ship before dark. I must ask you to forgive me."

"Why?" A chill ran up Evie's spine.

"Because, of all the rotten luck, who happened to see me but Captain Long. He recognized the unusual breed of horse and inquired as to where I'd gotten it. Before I could concoct a reasonable tale, one of the other men on the parade ground went into great detail regarding the rescue of a young white lass by the name of Evelyn Haynes. Needless to say, that piqued the man's interest to no end." He waved a hand futilely in the air in disgust.

Evelyn felt mounting dread. "How could he possibly suspect me so quickly?"

Gerald ran his fingers through the light brown hair normally concealed by his military wig. "That's just it. He didn't—not at first. He thought you might be Reverend Haynes's sister Jane, the one who ran off with Lieutenant Ted Harrington the night he deserted his post in Boston."

Mulling over that news, Evelyn recalled that Captain Long had been warden of the army's stockade in Boston when her brother, Morgan, had gone to visit Dan in prison. "Oh, yes. Dan had been accused of helping Ted escape. You did inform him I wasn't Jane, didn't you?"

A sheepish expression crossed the corporal's face. "Actually, before I had the chance, that helpful sergeant corrected Captain Long's description of Jane by going into elaborate detail about your dark curly hair and eyes of lightest blue."

His wife's eyebrows flared in distress. "We must spirit her

aboard ship at once and hide her in the deepest darkest nook until it sails from port."

Gerald raised a staying hand. "'Tis more imperative we get Miss Evelyn out of the fort posthaste. Then afterward we'll give some thought on how to get her onto the ship. As it is, I've wasted precious time coming back here. Once the captain learned I was taking the pacer aboard, I was obliged to continue doing just that. I felt all manner of distress when I saw him turn toward the enlisted men's quarters. But providentially, he was summoned to headquarters at that very moment. I quickly handed the horse over to a private with instructions to board him, then hastened home. We may have only a few moments."

"Yes," Liza said in alarm, "before the captain warns the guards!"

Gerald stared at Evie a moment. "Get a bonnet on that mop of yours. If you keep your head down, perhaps no one will notice—"

Sharp rapping rattled the door once more.

Evelyn's heart plummeted.

Grabbing her arm, Liza yanked her to the wood box beside the hearth. "Get in. Fast," she hissed.

Evie peered into the empty depths of the topless receptacle. Not too long ago Liza had complained because Gerald had forgotten to fetch a new supply of wood, and now that memory lapse became a blessing. She climbed in and hunkered down, her heart hammering against her ribs. But still, an open box wasn't much of a hiding place!

The knocking became insistent.

"Coming," Gerald called.

Something heavy dropped onto Evie's back, and she guessed it must have been the sack of flour leaning in the corner. Then another sack fell onto her head, shutting out the light. She felt Liza's fingers stuffing her skirt farther down as the door squealed open.

"I've come to speak with your houseguest," she heard Captain Long announce. She could just picture that imperious ruddy face of his, the cagey eyes and expression of contempt. "It appears we have mutual friends."

"Oh, do come in, Captain," Liza said graciously, moving away from Evie's haven. "Might I offer you a cup of tea? You must be exhausted after that long march."

Liza must have lost her mind! Evie thought wildly as hard leather-soled boots clicked hollowly over the plank floor. She felt her back cramp.

"Thank you, no, madam," Long said. "I've not got the time. A word with Miss Haynes, if you please."

"Oh, dear, how unfortunate," Liza gushed. "She's no longer here."

"*Not here,* you say? That's impossible. There's nowhere else for her to go. Fort Niagara is surrounded by wilderness and Indians."

"Yes, that does give me a fright at times," Liza admitted. "We women are always so relieved when our men return. All the while you're away we have nightmares that the weakened fort will be attacked. Isn't that right, Gerald?"

Astounded by her friend's playacting, Evie heard the young man stammer. "Er—we all feel more secure when the fort is fully manned."

"Yes. Well, we shall discuss your fears at a later time, if you don't mind," the captain said, striding deeper into the room. "I must speak to Miss Haynes at once." The bedroom door opened, and his voice came from farther away. "Tell me now. Where is she?"

"We said our farewells not an hour past, Captain," Liza said evenly. "The young lady left to board the ship. She feared it might depart without her in the morning and wanted to be certain she didn't miss it."

"Is that so?" A significant pause revealed the captain's doubts, but then his tone relaxed noticeably. "How fortuitous. I've been issued orders to take over quartermaster duties in Montreal, to replace that incompetent Fillmore. It seems Miss Haynes and I shall be traveling companions."

Evie felt all the air press from her lungs.

"Why, that is marvelous," Liza said brightly. "Marvelous, indeed. Gerald and I were discussing our concern about Evelyn's welfare. The seamen, you know. But she'll have someone she's acquainted with looking after her. I, for one, will breathe much easier now."

"Quite," Long said in his knowing tone. He crossed to the door again, and it opened. "Well then, rest your worries, madam. I shall be keeping a close eye on the lass. A very close eye."

"We'll be ever grateful, Captain. Do have a pleasant evening, sir." Closing the door behind him, Liza slid the bolt into place. Then her light footsteps scurried to the wood box.

Evie felt the sacks removed from her, and Gerald helped her up and out. But nothing could lighten the hopeless feeling that still weighed her down as she brushed at the wood chips imbedded in her skirt and the flour dust on her sleeve.

"That was close," Liza breathed. "Too close. I'm just glad I didn't have you under the bed. That overbearing man was so rude he actually lifted the edge of the coverlet to peer under it, if you can imagine such arrogance!"

"But you've blocked my only escape," Evie moaned. "You told him I was on the ship."

A faint pink glow rose over Liza's delicate cheeks. "And I'm truly sorry. It was the only thing I thought he'd believe."

"Of course the scoundrel would *believe* that," Evelyn grated. "But what am I to do?"

Gerald placed a comforting hand on her shoulder. "Now that we've more time, we'll find you a more comfortable place to hide until the ship sails. I doubt the captain will come looking for you, but on the odd chance that he might—"

"The chapel!" Liza cried. "It's quite close by and occupied only on the Sabbath."

Her husband nodded. "'Tis a warm evening. I shall put a pallet down for Evelyn in the empty belfry."

"Thank you," she replied without enthusiasm. "But what difference will it make? There's no escape for me."

Gerald met her gaze calmly. "The captain must leave with

the ship. With your name on the passenger list, he'll merely think he can't locate you. He'll sail, thinking he's the cat to your mouse. If you had seen the look on his face, you'd be sure he has no intention of sharing his discovery with anyone. He wants you all to himself."

His words did little to allay Evie's trepidation. "Captain Long is a very patient cat. Rest assured, he'll be waiting on that Montreal dock for every ship that sails from this port. And if he gets tired of waiting, he'll simply sail back here— and it won't be to arrest only me, you'll see."

Liza flicked a bit of flour from Evie's hair and put an arm about her shoulder. "But, Evie, dear. You sailed out of here *with* the good captain, remember? And we'll be quite adamant about finding out why he didn't take better care of you."

"But," Gerald said with a frown, "everyone here will know she remained behind."

"Not if we don't tell them," Liza said. "Forgive the inconvenience, Evie, but you'll have to stay inside and out of sight for awhile."

"You and Gerald will be putting yourselves at too much risk."

"Not at all." A spark twinkled in Liza's eyes. "We'll leave our watch care in the Lord's hands, won't we? Surely if he can bring you through hundreds of miles of hostile wilderness just to comfort me in my despair, he can easily lead the three of us to safety."

33

A blast of January's icy breath whipped over the snow-covered landscape of Princeton, swirling loose snowflakes into shallow mounds and drifts. Christopher, bundled against the frigid weather, rode listlessly toward town, his mount and the four pacers trailing behind him leaving hoofprints in the new-fallen whiteness. Their muffled clomping over Stony Brook Bridge set the neighborhood dogs to barking, but Chris paid them no mind. Six fruitless months of searching for Evelyn had left an emptiness within him that nothing could lessen, and he took the defeat personally.

At the racket of the dogs, lamps were lit hastily in the houses along the road, and doors cracked open. What used to be a common sound when the stages came through Princeton on their way from Philadelphia and New York now made the town residents nervous.

The long war had changed so many things, had exacted such a high cost, and Christopher's ever present despair surfaced to darken his thoughts. He no longer had any trouble understanding how Robert Chandler could have mourned his deceased wife for so many years. But Chandler at least had been spared the torment of not knowing if Julia was dead or still alive and living in unspeakable torment.

Dragging his mind back to the present, Chris observed the silhouetted dwellings on either side of the road. At one time he had known the name of every family in Princeton, yet now everything had changed. The two and a half years he had been in the military might well have been a lifetime.

But as the Lyons' Den came within view, the sight of the golden shafts of light streaming from the windows of the main floor flooded Christopher with warm memories. However dark and cold the rest of the world might seem, it was gratifying to come home. Home to Ma and Pa Lyons.

Nearing the three-story coaching inn, Christopher's gaze wandered past it to the outline of Nassau Hall's bell tower, jutting black against the night sky. For so long he had entertained grandiose dreams regarding that beloved school. Dreams of coming back to complete his studies once the war was finally over, to find the means to provide for Evelyn in a way more in keeping with her upbringing.

Now it didn't matter one way or the other if he ever earned that coveted degree. Without Evie, nothing seemed to matter. Besides, he conceded with a shrug, there was much to be said about becoming a hunter and tracker, a frontiersman. Six months with Garth Kinyon had taught Christopher almost everything a man needed to know about surviving alone. Being alone, *unencumbered,* seemed ideal—particularly at this moment. Living by himself he wouldn't have to endure the hundreds of questions he'd encounter once he went inside the inn. Some answers were far too painful to be put into words, and after all had been said, questions would remain in the eyes of those dearest to him.

Reaching the horseshoe drive of the establishment, Chris bypassed it and rode around back to see to the horses before facing anyone.

The back door of the ordinary swung open, emitting a stream of light over the barnyard. A great shadow loomed across it. "Who goes there?" Pa Lyons's gruff voice asked.

"Just me, Pa. Chris."

"Chris!" he bellowed. "Esther! Our boy's back! Christopher's come home!" Setting down his lantern and musket, he rushed outside. Other men quickly poured out after him, calling good-natured greetings.

Chris, dismounting, recognized the excited voices of the townsmen even though it was hard to distinguish individual features with the faint lantern light behind them.

He felt himself crushed in his old guardian's massive arms. Just then a shutter flung open on the second floor, and a plump figure in white nightclothes leaned out. "That you, Chip?" Ma Lyons cried.

Small clouds of steam burst into the frozen air as a collective shout from the men affirmed his return.

A round of hugs and thumps about took Chris's breath away. The excited greetings of familiar faces seemed little more than a blur in the scant moments before Ma Lyons and Susannah rushed outside with arms open wide. Arms to hug him and love him. Arms he needed so badly to feel around him.

Yes. He was home. Truly home.

❦ ❦

Susannah smoothed the down quilt over the blankets on the bed she shared with little Julia. Concern at spoiling her daughter by permitting Julia to sleep with her these past several months had taken second place to helping erase the nightmares the terrible ordeal at Wilkes-Barre had brought on.

She moved to the window and peered outside. The children had been playing in the snow for hours already, and Christopher had yet to emerge from his room. That anyone could sleep with all the noise and laughter of the rambunctious little ones was nothing short of amazing. But then, Susannah had never seen Chip appear more haggard than he'd been last eve. From the look of the young man, he needed whatever rest he could get.

Susannah returned to the bed, picked up a pillow, and hugged it to herself with a shuddering breath. She had never once allowed herself to doubt that Chris and Mr. Kinyon would find Evie. Now that Chris had returned without her, the defeat etched into his face made Susannah's own hope dwindle. She would never give up entirely, but still . . .

Burying her nose in the downy softness, Susannah inhaled the scent of her young child. Only God's grace had kept her little family alive through these trying times. Had the British officers not shown the residents of Wyoming Valley some Christian charity—however belated—and controlled the rampaging Indians, it was likely the townspeople would have all met their deaths or been taken into captivity.

She fluffed the pillow and patted it into place, then started for the twisted tumble of Miles's cot, across from the big bed.

Whispers drifted from the hallway through the partially open door. "Yes. The excitement woke me up last night. But I was too sleepy to get up."

"All the same, Sissy, you know what Mistress Lyons said."

"But he's been sleeping all morning! How tired could one person be? Maybe we could just take a peek."

Susannah opened her door and peered at the redheaded twins huddling outside Christopher's room. "Do be quiet, won't you? And go about your chores."

Sarah and Selina turned beet red and stared at their feet. Then they shoved each other. One twin grabbed the other's hair.

"Ow!" That twin reached for a handful of her sister's locks.

Shaking her head, Susannah tugged the pair apart and stared pointedly toward the stairwell, giving them an encouraging nudge in that direction. But at that moment her son clattered noisily up the steps.

"Mama!" Miles cried, catching sight of her. "My colt! My colt's back!" Pausing for no more than a second, he blasted past his mother and the twins and burst into Christopher's room, throwing himself onto the bed. "Thank you, Uncle Chris! Thank you!"

Christopher sat up, groggily rubbing a hand over his sleep-dulled eyes. "Huh?"

"Firefly! You got him back from the Indians!"

A slow grin spread over Chris's lips, and he grabbed Miles

and fell back with him in relief. "The colt, you say. Actually, buddy, I just happened to find him at the end of one of the many sets of tracks I followed."

"Well, I don't care. He's back, and I'm glad!"

Not to be left out of things, the slim redheads vied with each other, each trying to be first into the chamber.

Susannah had to smile. With all the young men off to war, and these fetching lasses approaching marriageable age, it was evident that the sisters had cast their affections upon the only eligible bachelor at hand. He was all they had talked about since the day she and the others had arrived here destitute and seeking shelter. Susannah had lost count of the times the pair had related the tale of Christopher's heroic bravery in saving them from British soldiers.

"Good morning, Chris," they said sweetly in unison, then wrinkled their freckled noses at one another.

Sarah jabbed her sister in the ribs, switching her gaze the same instant to Christopher. "What would you like for breakfast?"

"I'll fix anything you wish," Selina affirmed, aiming a gloating nod at her twin. "You can even eat it in bed."

"And then we can go for a ride on our horses," Miles chimed in.

Susannah took over. Pulling her son from the weary hero's bed, she swatted his behind. "Everyone out. Now. Give the poor man a chance to wake up. Sarah, go fix that breakfast you offered, and Selina, bring up some hot water and soap shavings. I'm sure our friend would appreciate a nice clean shave."

"I'll even help you shave," the second twin offered eagerly.

"Thank you, no." Christopher waved her off with a smile—the first Susannah had seen since his arrival. "If it's all the same to you, I'm quite competent at doing it myself. I've already had a sample of your work with a pitchfork."

The lass scrunched her freckled face. "That wasn't me. It was Sarah."

"Well, whoever it was," Susannah cut in, "off with the lot of you. Give Christopher a chance to get dressed."

"Then could we go riding?" Miles asked, peeking around his mother's form.

Susannah lifted one eyebrow. *"After* he has dressed," she said in her no-nonsense tone, *"and* shaved, *and* eaten; *then* you may ask him. Now, scoot out of here."

As the noisy troop scrambled to do her bidding, she turned to Christopher with an apologetic smile. "'Tis rather pointless to say welcome home. They've certainly said it loud and clear."

"That they have," Chris replied, straightening the blankets across his midsection. "Odd that my sister's kids weren't swarming over me right along with Miles."

"Oh. We must have neglected to tell you last night. Mary Clare and Prudence have taken over your parents' old house and are staying there for now. With so many of us arriving so suddenly, we required too many of the rooms available for paying guests."

"So Mare's gone to that old wreck?"

"It's not quite as bad as you remember, actually. The poor old place just needed a woman's touch . . . and the willing help from some of the inn's regulars, which they most generously provided. Now it's quite sufficient, and there's plenty of room for the children to run. When the weather permits, my two go over during the noon rush to play. I suppose you already know Washington's winter camp is scarcely twenty miles away, so Jon and Morgan manage to come home at least once a week."

"That must be a great comfort to Mary."

"Yes. She's ever so much better. She's back to her old sweet self again—and I rather think she'll be thrilled to see you."

A bitter grimace flattened Christopher's lips. "And how is Morgan . . . the brother who had more important matters to tend to than going after his sister?"

The young man's terse tone was not lost on Susannah. "You really mustn't blame him, Chip," she said gently. "Not three days passed before he hastened after you to Easton . . . but you'd already left. He had no idea where you'd gone."

Chris shrugged a shoulder in disgust. "No matter. It was probably much easier for him to think of Evie as dead than to leave his wife."

Concern washed over Susannah in a wave. She gathered her skirts and sat down beside him. "Chris, Morgan has not given up hope on Evie, I assure you. He and Prudence have held both of you up to almighty God in their prayers day and night, and so have the rest of us."

Averting his gaze, Chris tightened his mouth. "*God.* Don't speak to me about God. If he was the loving Father the Bible says he is, he never would have allowed this to happen. Didn't I suffer enough as a child? Wasn't that sufficient to satisfy him?"

Susannah was stunned at the hardness in her young friend's countenance, the stark brittleness in his blue eyes. She sent up a swift prayer for wisdom, then reached and took his hand, tightening her hold when he attempted to pull away. She waited for his gaze to return to hers before she spoke. "I'm more than aware I may never know all that has befallen you since last we met. But I do know that there's hardly a soul in these Colonies who hasn't endured more than a fair share of trials while we've been engaged in this difficult struggle for freedom."

"Precisely," Christopher hissed.

"And can you not see the hand of God evident in the very fact that we've survived every hardship my former country-men have thrown at us? We've endured starvation, been victorious over tried and proven military strategies even though our numbers were but a fraction of theirs, and sur-vived all sorts of other deprivations. . . ."

"Evie hasn't been victorious, though, has she." It was more statement than question, asked in a flat voice.

"That is something none of us knows for certain," Susan-nah admitted quietly. "But the very fact that there's been no proof of her death provides reason to go on hoping. The Lord knows where she is, and in his time, I believe she will be returned to us."

Christopher huffed and looked away. "That's easy for you to say, sitting here in these cozy surroundings. Last autumn when I heard that Colonel Hartley and some of the Wyoming Valley men had gone into the southern end of the Iroquois lands and had rescued sixteen white captives, I thought my constant prayers had been answered at last. Kinyon and I nearly killed ourselves getting back to the valley because I was so sure Evie was among them."

"I know how very hard that must have been. And, oh, so difficult to understand. Perhaps if the two of us pray together, the Lord will rekindle and strengthen our faith. That must be of great importance to him, testing and refining our faith until it shines like purest gold. After all, if everything always worked out exactly the way we hoped and asked, vast hordes of the world would trip over themselves to come to God and accept the sacrifice he has provided for our salvation. But that is not his way. He desires a people who will trust him with their very lives, accept his will even when it's the last thing we would choose, and be faithful until our very death. And in return, he will hold us up when we cannot stand and carry us when we cannot walk. And, one day, usher us through the very portals of heaven, where no evil shall ever touch us again."

Christopher's expression remained unchanged, but at least he hadn't interrupted. Susannah appreciated the encouraging sign and went on.

"Job, in the Bible, was a good and righteous man, as you recall. Yet he suffered much for his faith, just as have so many of us."

"My *faith* was not in question."

"Neither was his."

A muscle twitched in Chris's jaw, and his eyes grew hard again. "Well, I guess I'm not the saint old Job was. Sometimes I—I even wonder if there truly is a God. There. I've said it." His angry gaze rose to Susannah's. "Maybe we've all just been fooling ourselves into believing God exists because we like the thought of someone up there watching over us. Well, after the horrors I've glimpsed these last several months, I find it harder and harder to believe that's possible. No true God would have allowed such terror or suffering."

"Why? His own Son suffered, and did so willingly, for our sake. If the Father could permit that, could endure the pain of a broken heart himself, who are we to expect a life free of trials?" She paused for a moment, then recalled Christopher's last statement. "Where God is not acknowledged, the prince of darkness prevails."

"Interesting you should mention that." A corner of Chris's mouth lifted sarcastically. "According to Garth Kinyon, those same savages are just as loving to their own as we are. They are gentle parents. They don't raise a hand to their children, and within their own villages they live quiet, orderly lives. *Until they bring in captives to provide a bit of entertainment and diversion,* of course. You might even appreciate hearing that their women have a council of their own and must be consulted by the men before any decisions are made that will affect the village."

"That may very well be. But Matthew wrote in his Gospel that even the evil know how to give good gifts to their children. God, however, has given his children a much higher calling. We are to love our enemies enough to pray for those who persecute us."

"Hmph." Chris shook his head disparagingly. "Forgive me, but I could never do that. Never. The very thought is repulsive to me. I've seen far too much."

Susannah searched his pained expression. Bitterness and sorrow had altered the guileless face of the Christopher she had known. Her heart grieved to think of the anguish he must have borne all alone, pressing ever onward in his quest to rescue the woman he adored. But Susannah loved him too much herself to accept what he was becoming. She prayed that God would speak through her somehow and draw him back, restore the peace he once knew. "It would seem," she finally managed, "that the more righteous the anger, the harder it is to forgive."

"Oh, it's righteous, all right. Never doubt that."

Placing her hand on his shoulder, Susannah smiled thinly. "I only wish I had more comfort for you. But I must confess, I struggled with this myself, just as you have. At first I couldn't pray for the souls of those who'd stolen Evelyn away from us. I lacked even the desire to do so. But slowly I came to realize that none of us is guiltless before a holy God. As he forgave us our trespasses against him, so must we forgive those who wrong us. If we do not, even our most fervent prayers are for naught."

Christopher took Susannah's hand in both of his and looked straight at her. "You wouldn't be talking like this if you'd been forced to lie in hiding and listen to the screams of a captured man while those heathens skinned him alive, one strip at a time. Or when they cut his belly open and pulled out his entrails for him to see—right before they gouged out his eyes."

"Enough. Please." Cringing at his horrid word pictures, Susannah lowered her eyes.

"But that was only the beginning. There was more. Much more. And I lay there helpless to stop it."

"It was the same at Forty Fort," she said softly, tears rising in her eyes. "The people who remained inside the walls had to endure an entire night of hearing the screaming agonies of their men who'd gone out to fight. No one knew who lay dead on the battlefield and who was forced to suffer the tortures of knife and fire. I can only thank God that the children and I were at the Wilkes-Barre fort and were spared such horror. Without the Lord to lean on, to draw comfort from, the desire for revenge could easily consume us. But the Bible says that vengeance belongs to the Lord."

"Since you're so fond of quoting Scripture, Susannah, let's not forget 'an eye for an eye, a tooth for a tooth.'"

She met his cocky smirk. "And let us not forget that Jesus brought us a better law, one of grace. We are to repay unkindness with kindness. Those who refuse the sacrifice on Calvary and the salvation afforded by the shed blood of Jesus will be judged by the old law. They will be condemned by their own deeds and by what is in their hearts."

Chris did not appear entirely appeased but did not attempt to counter what she'd said. Susannah again took heart.

"Another thing," she added while he remained silent. "If and when you do find Evelyn, don't betray her by turning into someone she never knew—and would never wish to know. She's yearning for the same man she fell in love with . . . and she's going to need all the love you ever had for her, and even more."

A slight softening in Chris's demeanor dispelled a measure of the former hardness. He inhaled a long, slow breath. "That is asking an awful lot."

"Yes, I'm aware of that. But God still loves you as much as he ever did. With his help, I have every confidence you'll find your way back to him. We'll pray night and day for him to give you the strength and the will to let go of this hatred. Will you do this with me?"

Chris cocked his head back and forth in uncertainty but gave her the hint of a smile. "Very well . . . for however much good it'll do."

A surge of hope warmed Susannah. She leaned to kiss his cheek above his whisker stubble. "I happen to love you, Christopher Drummond, as if you were my very own brother. As well you are, you know—in the Lord." With a smile, she rose. "Now, you'd better hop out of that bed. Your sister and those little nieces of yours will likely be here soon. Prudence, too. You'll find fresh clothes in the wardrobe." She turned to leave.

"Susannah," he said, snagging her hand just before she moved out of reach. The intense anger no longer burned in his countenance, and he spoke quietly. "It was Garth Kinyon who made me stop looking for Evie. He said if we didn't, the Indians would track us in the snow, and then she might never get rescued. He didn't want to chance our getting caught. But I don't know—we managed to escape capture all these months."

"Yes. Another answer to my prayers." Susannah gave his hand a squeeze. "I shall always be grateful for the months you've remained safe while searching for our dear Evelyn. And thank you for listening to Mr. Kinyon."

"He had Indian friends in some of the Iroquois villages," Chris went on. "So we risked going into several. But everyone was closemouthed. They're being paid by the British to make war against the Americans, so their loyalties are with the Crown. No one would admit to anything. Whenever we happened upon one of their villages that had a Narragansett Pacer, we'd spy on it for days, hoping for a glimpse of Evie."

"You needn't tell me how hard you tried, Chris. It's written on your face, in your eyes. But for now, rest until the snow's gone. Regain your strength for the next effort." With a last squeeze, Susannah released his hand. "Now, don't you think you should dress before those twins come up to help you?"

Gratified that she could at least draw a chuckle out of him, Susannah departed his bedchamber. But it was with the knowledge that one of her deepest concerns remained unanswered . . . the unequal match between Christopher and Evelyn. Evie had only displayed a cursory interest in spiritual matters. Other than saying grace before a meal, she had never expressed the least passion for learning about the Lord. If by some miracle the girl had managed to survive, perhaps she had been victorious in her crucible by fire as well.

Please, dear heavenly Father, keep your hand upon Evie and bring her closer to your Son. That same fervent prayer had been uttered countless times, but Susannah offered it again, out of the deepest longings of her heart. For Chris and for Evie.

34

"Think we'll get more snow, Uncle Chris?" Miles asked as he mounted Firefly outside the dry-goods store. He rolled the rock candy in his mouth from one cheek to the other, sucking it with a puzzled expression.

Chris eyed the sky, leaden with clouds, then set fair-haired Julia in front of his own saddle and climbed up behind her. "Wouldn't be surprised." He grinned when he saw Miles wave to a passerby. The lad was so proud of sitting astride his young horse. His face positively glowed when someone took notice.

"I like snow." Julia leaned her head back on Christopher's chest and peered up at him as he clucked the horse homeward past the assortment of business establishments on either side. "Mama lets us make big snowmen."

"Well, she won't if you don't start keeping that stuff in your mouth," he chided gently, wincing at the sticky peppermint on her cheeks and mittens. "You're getting it all over you."

A frown made a dip in the delicate brows above her huge blue eyes. "There's fuzz on it."

"Because you keep taking it out to play with it."

Miles gave his sister an I-told-you-so snicker, and Julia popped the treat back into her mouth with a pout.

Christopher squeezed her shoulder. "That's better. Leave it alone this time, so your mother won't give us all a good talking-to when we get home."

As the child settled down, Chris thought about the letter for

Susannah he had picked up at the post. It would divert her from fussing at her sticky daughter. She'd be thrilled to hear from Jane, all the way up in Massachusetts.

"Hey! Now I remember," Miles said with a big smile. "This candy tastes just like the kind Aunt Evie used to sneak to me in church when I was tired of sitting still. She sure was nice. I miss her a lot, don't you?"

"Me, too," Julia chimed.

Chris swallowed down the rush of emotion that Evie's name always caused. He nodded. "Yes. Very, very much."

Julia gave an exaggerated nod and tilted up her sticky face again. "Are you sad, Uncle Chris?" Spitting the peppermint into her mitten again, she shoved it within inches of his mouth. "Want some? It helps you to not be sad."

Chris reared back a little at the sight of the melted, fuzzy candy. "No thanks. I bought it just for you."

She smiled, much relieved. "Oh, goody." Unperturbed by its sorry state, she plunked it back into her mouth and turned forward.

A thin, white-haired man sweeping the stoop of his leather shop glanced up as they went by. "That you, Chris?" He stopped working and laid his palms on the top of the broom handle.

"Yes, sir. Got home a few days ago, Mr. Madison."

The gaunt man nodded, his small blue eyes atwinkle as he walked alongside for a few yards. "Them folks of yours are glad of that, I'll wager."

"Sure are."

"Too bad ya didn't have any luck findin' that little gal."

Chris blanched. First the sympathetic look from the proprietor at the mercantile, now this. Did everyone in Princeton know about it? But most folks around here had known him since birth. He should have waited out the winter someplace where he could be anonymous.

"Headin' on over to Middlebrook to take up with Washington's army again, are ya?" Madison asked.

"No. Soon as it thaws, I'm going out again. Nice to see you."

With a polite nod at the merchant, Chris nudged his mount to a faster pace. "Let's trot, kids."

Within moments the welcoming smoke from the chimneys of the inn beckoned to them. As he and Miles slowed the animals and guided them around back, they passed several horses tied at the hitching rail. Ma and Pa Lyons were doing pretty good business for the middle of the afternoon. Christopher quickly put the pacers into the stalls and started for the inn.

"Carry me, carry me!" Julia pleaded, reaching up as her brother raced ahead and went into the inn.

"A big girl like you?" he teased with a withering look. His hands were already sticky as a pine tree just from lifting her down from the saddle.

She stepped into his path. "Please, Uncle Chris? *Please?*"

Gritting his teeth, he swept her up into his arms, and she giggled. Her stiff hair brushed his cheek. Chris shook his head. All this from one little chunk of candy! Scolding or no, he'd be more than happy to have Susannah reclaim her little princess.

When Christopher entered the kitchen door, he could hear several voices engaged in a lot of busy talk, plus the scuffling of children cavorting about the ordinary. He set Julia on her feet and followed as she ran into the common room.

Ma and Pa Lyons were seated by the big fireplace at the other end of the long room. Across the sea of linen-covered tables, light from the wall sconces cast a warm glow over the family gathering. Susannah, Morgan, Prudence, Jonathan, and Mary Clare had drawn chairs into a semicircle between the Lyonses and the hearth. In the fire glow, the women's winter-hued frocks looked like rich jewels. Chris's gaze settled on Morgan's back—and the arm he had draped over his wife's shoulder. The sight struck him with both irritation and envy.

As everybody turned to see who'd come in, Morgan and Prudence's little toddler hustled to safety between his daddy's long legs. Morgan lifted him into a loving hug. "Well, look who's here, Davey. Uncle Chris. Let's go show him how big you've gotten." Helping Prudence up with his free arm, he drew her close, and they stepped from the arc of chairs to greet Chris.

"Chip!" Mary raced to hug him with Jonathan close at her heels. With her shining hair loose, framing her face, she looked years younger, soft and fetching as she smiled up at Chris. "It's so good to see you, to have you back."

"Chris," Jon said, clasping his hand warmly as Mary stepped beside her husband.

Morgan, coming near, tentatively offered a hand.

Chris took it with surprising sincerity. He'd been prepared to dwell on what had seemed a betrayal by his two friends who had not shared his overpowering need to search for Evelyn. But seeing the couples together, witnessing the tenderness of their love, he could understand in a new way how they felt. He had experienced the unfathomable depth of emotion and need that drew one person to another, and suddenly all the ill feelings he'd harbored inside for so long faded to nothing. "You're looking fit," Chris managed, then laughed. "I take it the army has a better food supply this winter."

"So sorry I wasn't able to catch up to you last summer at Easton," Morgan said earnestly, handing David over to Prudence.

Christopher dismissed the apology with a toss of his hand. "It's forgotten. You had your concerns, and I had mine."

"Well, I don't reckon the Indians will be running amuck on the frontier next summer," Jonathan announced. "Washington is serious about sending an army into New York's back country to deal with them once and for all. Colonel Clark, out of Fort Pitt, has shown us it can be done. He took a measly hundred and twenty-seven men down the Ohio all the way to the Mississippi, and they've been capturing the Shawnee villages where redcoats are posted, one after another."

Morgan nodded his dark head. "The general says the Iroquois have had free rein over the frontier long enough, killing and looting without fear of reprisal—and getting paid for it, to boot. It's past time for the war to be taken to them."

"Washington is talking about dispatching an entire army," Jon said. "I've already put in to go."

"So have I," Morgan declared. "I want to be there when we enter every one of those villages." He clasped Christopher's shoulder. "This time, if my sister is still alive, we'll find her."

Susannah moved quietly to the edge of the group. "And I do pray you'll do no more than is necessary to get them to desist."

An unbidden smile spread across Christopher's face. His spirit had risen measurably with all the news, and with the lightened mood came the memory of their talk. "What Susannah is trying to say is, we're to attack them with love in our hearts."

She gave him a playful scowl, then tilted her head up to the others. "As the Bible says, 'Vengeance is mine; I will repay, saith the Lord.'"

"Rest assured, Susannah," Morgan told her. "'Tis far from army policy to torture prisoners."

Jonathan snorted. "We'll likely have a problem restraining some of the Wyoming Valley boys, but we'll do our best."

"Mercy me!" Ma Lyons exclaimed, coming from behind with little Julia in tow. "A body'd expect a lad to know better than to give a four-year-old candy when she's all bundled up!" She glared expressly at Christopher as she took the child to the kitchen. The line of squealy girls skipping among the tables chased after her, leaving surprising quiet in their wake.

A twinkle rose to Prudence's light gray eyes, and she flashed Chris a spirited smile. "Why don't we all go back over by the fire, where it's not so drafty."

"We were having hot cider, Chip," Mary said, brushing a lock of her long hair over the shoulder of her russet gown. "I'll get you some." As the rest reclaimed their seats, she returned from the bar with a mug for him. Then, picking up her own, she snuggled beside her husband as if they hadn't been apart a day since they'd wed, and smiled up into his face.

It'll be like that for Evie and me when I find her, Chris assured himself as he laid his coat on an empty chair and took a gulp of the cider. He glanced at Jon and Morgan directly across from him. "If I haven't found Evelyn by the time the army comes into the back country, I'd like to hook up with them again—if I'm not considered a deserter, that is. I could be a lot of help. I know my way around in there now."

"Put your mind at ease about that," Morgan said with a grin. "Chandler saw to it you were placed on an extended leave."

The mention of their friend's name perked him up. Thanks to Robert, Chris had learned how to be a soldier. "Too bad he didn't come with you. I'd like to have seen him."

"You're a few days too late, actually. The war has taken a southerly turn. Savannah was attacked in the last half of December. Chan asked to transfer down there so he could be near Emily and the kids in case the British decide to move into North Carolina."

Chris nodded solemnly. "That's good. He needs to be near his wife. In fact, I . . . have an announcement I'd like you all to hear, and this is as opportune a time as any." He watched interest mount on everyone's faces as they turned his way. He inhaled a strengthening breath. "Soon as I find Evie, and the minute we locate a justice of the peace, I intend to marry her. If she'll still have me," he added with a sheepish glance at Susannah.

"I don't know about that." Morgan folded his arms.

"Well, I do." Chris met his gaze straight on. "I wasn't asking. I was informing you. You can do whatever you think fitting in regard to telling your parents. Their approval would've been nice, but I've had plenty of time to think during these past several months. I've come to the conclusion that the Bible's advice about marriage, how a man should leave his father and mother and cling to his mate, is what's truly important. As for dowries and inheritances and the like, well, we've all seen how quickly that can be wiped out." His glance around the circle included his sister, Jonathan, and Susannah.

Morgan frowned. "Whether you want it or not," he began

sternly, then broke into a grin, "you have my blessing. As for our parents, they left Philadelphia when the British pulled out, and they've gone to stay with my oldest sister in England. I've written them several times, but only one reply made it past the British to me. So, I'm afraid their blessing—or lack thereof—would be difficult to come by. I've not even informed them of Evie's capture. I felt it best not to keep them in needless suspense for months on end until we've received definite word of her rescue."

"They would want to know, Morgan," Susannah said softly. "I'm sure they would want to add their prayers to ours."

Somewhere along the way, Christopher noticed, everyone had stopped referring to Evelyn's rescue as *if,* and replaced it with *when.* Their new faith cheered him.

Morgan, obviously chagrined, raised his thick brows and turned to Susannah. "You're quite right, of course. As always. My parents have endured enough dishonesty from their only son as it is. I shall write them a long letter this eve."

"Oh! Speaking of letters—" Chris picked up his greatcoat from the chair beside him and reached past the sticky lapel to the inside pocket—"a letter came from your sister-in-law Jane."

With a cry of delight, Susannah hardly gave him time to offer it to her before she took it and broke the wax seal.

The front door opened just then, and the twins came in on a frigid blast. They wiped their boots on the mat and hung their cloaks on the pegs. Two pairs of green eyes sought Chris at the same time.

Miles, who had been playing with some wooden horses and soldiers at the fireplace while the grown-ups talked, sprang to his feet and rushed over to them. "Guess what?"

"What?" they chorused.

"Uncle Christopher's getting married," he said in a singsong. "The soldiers are gonna go get Evie, and then Uncle Chris is gonna marry her."

The rosy flush from the cold fled their cheeks. They turned

in different directions, one running to the kitchen, the other bolting upstairs. The room fell silent.

"Oh," Mary Clare crooned. "Now look what you've done, Chip."

"Me? What did I do?"

"Can't you see those two are sweet on you? You should be more considerate of their feelings."

"But I didn't—"

"Oh, my!" Susannah looked up from her letter.

"What is it?"

"The most marvelous news!" Susannah rested her arms on her aproned lap. "You remember Liza Brown, that lass I've been praying for since I left Boston? Well, she's written to her mother! What an answer to prayer! She's married and well. According to Jane, Liza's up in Fort—" Her gaze returned to the missive, and she gasped in shock. "Evelyn? *Evelyn?* Oh, thank you, Father! Thank you! Thank you!" Jumping up, she waved the letter about. "She's alive! Our Evie's alive!"

Chris sprang to his feet and seized the paper from her hand. He tried to read, but tears blurred his vision.

Morgan took over. Taking the creased parchment from Christopher, he scanned down the page, then began reading aloud:

> "Mistress Brown was asked to forward to me news that an Evelyn Haynes has been rescued from the Indians. Liza's husband, Gerald Blake, and a number of British soldiers came to her aid at a most opportune time and escorted her to their post at Fort Niagara. I can only assume this refers to Evelyn Thomas. I knew I must relay the news to you at once."

"But, why would she call herself Evelyn Haynes?" Mary Clare interrupted.

"Because, dear," Prudence replied, "Evelyn *Thomas* is wanted by the Crown for spying, and she's in a virtual hotbed

of the Crown's men!" She placed a hand on Morgan's sleeve.
"Go on with the letter, sweetheart."

> "I was to tell you that she was harmed very little and that
> she is doing splendidly. The letter to Mistress Brown was
> dated the fourteenth of August."

Chris finally found his voice. *"August fourteenth!* That was
only five or six weeks after she was taken. How on earth could
a letter take so long to get here?"

Morgan glared at the lot of them. "If you'd all stop cutting
in and let me read the whole thing, quite likely most of our
questions will be answered."

"Go on, then. Read!" Chris clamped his lips together as he
clenched the arms of his chair.

With a cautious look around, Morgan returned his attention to the written words:

> "It seems that any correspondence should be directed to
> Corporal Byron Winfrey—"

Christopher's resolve to be silent lost out to a stab of
jealousy. "Why not directly to her? or the Blakes?"

Morgan did not raise his head as his eyes glanced impatiently up from the letter, then back down:

> "—because of the unusual circumstances which might
> result in the tampering of their own mail."

Morgan ceased reading and perused the next paragraph.
He whitened. *"He can't be!* Captain Long. Stationed at Fort
Niagara! Or at least, he was." His hand holding the paper fell
to his side while he explained the rest. "Apparently, the man
was transferred to Montreal before he actually saw Evelyn, but
he strongly suspected her true identity. The Blakes led everyone at the fort to believe she embarked on the same vessel
with Long, for Montreal, then hinted that her disappearance

had to have been Captain Long's doing. In the meantime, they are keeping her hidden. We are not to worry. No one suspects that Evie is still with them, and they're trusting the matter to God, sure that he will provide a means of escape for her."

"Praise the Lord!" Susannah breathed.

"The gal has spunk," Pa Lyons said, finally getting an opening. "Saw it in her from the first, I did." He smacked the tabletop in emphasis.

Christopher frowned. "That letter is five months old. How are we supposed to know what's happened since it was written?"

Prudence reached for his hand and gave it an empathetic squeeze. "Mr. Lyons is right. Evelyn's always been fearless. It's one of her strong points. And she's also smart."

"And determined," Mary added. "She spent an entire year and a half learning everything about horses—all to snag you, Chip. No shipload or fort full of lobsterbacks will stop her."

Morgan raised the missive and scanned the final words. "Oh, yes. Here at the bottom, Jane writes that Evie hopes to hear as soon as possible that all her friends from the Wyoming Valley reached safety. And—" he grinned at Chris—"she sends her very deepest regards and love to one Christopher Drummond."

Chris released a pent-up breath. No longer able to be polite, he yanked the letter away to see the words for himself. They truly were there. Evie's very thoughts. He ran his fingers across the ink, wishing her hand had written them instead of Jane's. But he'd settle for getting them this way, for the moment. Looking up, he found everyone staring at him. He cocked his head with a silly grin. "Well, now that I know where she is, I guess I'll head out tomorrow."

"And what?" Jonathan asked.

"Go fetch her home."

"Do you propose to travel through hundreds of miles of Indian country to get there?" Morgan asked. "To sneak her out of a heavily guarded fort? And if you make it, will you then risk my sister's life on your return? To say nothing of natural hazards such as blizzards and ice-choked streams, rivers, and swamps."

"Morgan is right," Jon said gently. "Washington is providing us with the way to get Evelyn out of there. And he's one man who always does his best to stay within God's will. You know that, Chip."

"But that will take forever. How can I wait that long?"

Susannah moved closer and put an arm around his waist. "Write to her, as you did before. I'm sure Dan will find a much faster way to get a letter to Halifax and beyond than this one took. He's sure to have contacts up in Maine. Fishermen, perhaps, who could get it to the Canadian port."

"Forget Dan." Pulling away, Christopher stood and started for the stairs. "I'll take it to Maine myself. I can be out of here in five minutes!"

Mary Clare giggled. "Don't you think you ought to write the letter first, little brother?"

He didn't even slow down, just tossed a happy grin over his shoulder. "I'll write it on the way."

Nine long, endless months of hiding were taking a toll on Evelyn, and the first spell of warmer weather only added to her claustrophobia. If she didn't get outside to breathe some fresh air and go for a walk soon, she'd go mad. Sometimes it seemed to her that the prayers for patience and peace of mind did little more than bounce back from the ceiling of the attic room Gerald had prepared for her above his and Liza's quarters. There she could never walk about or make the slightest noise. Her only consolation was the relative freedom she was permitted in the Blakes' two rooms for a good portion of every day. Behind locked doors and drawn curtains, only her voice was restricted. She hadn't spoken above a whisper for so long she'd forgotten what her own voice sounded like.

If only she could know Christopher was alive and well. Was he still searching, or had he given her up for dead? Sitting at the kitchen table, she folded her arms and rested her chin on them, moodily watching Liza kneading bread dough. Gerald, seated at the other end of the table, smeared fuller's earth on a stain on his white uniform trousers and rubbed the soiled spot against his knuckles.

"Oh, blast. Another weevil," Liza said, picking the creature out of her mixture. "I'll be so glad when the supply ships start coming again so I can get some fresh flour."

"I'd rather contend with weevils than have that unholy pack of Tories around," Gerald said consolingly. "The first ships will bring them back from winter leave. I heard that the company under Butler's son Walter was even more vicious than the Indians were, if you can imagine that."

"Perhaps they think that with all the war paint, no one will know who they are."

"God will." Gerald held his breeches at arm's length in perusal, then, satisfied, went to put the light-colored clay away in the larder. "It's one thing for heathens to torture helpless souls. They've never heard the teachings of the Bible. But for supposed Christians to do so . . ." He went to wash his hands in the basin on the sideboard.

Liza's gaze followed her husband's movements while she worked. "As much as you dislike being aide to Lieutenant Conway, I'm so thankful he's a member of General Carleton's staff and that you haven't been ordered into the field."

Evelyn's thoughts flew at once to Christopher. She was sure he'd never stopped looking for her . . . as sure as she was that he'd never find her. *Just please, dear Lord, don't let the Indians catch him and torture him the way they have so many others.*

Out of the corner of her eye, Evie saw Liza hand her husband a clean towel, and the movement drew her back to the present. "I think the loss young Major Butler took last fall, when he and his devils encountered that expedition from the Wyoming Valley, knocked them down a notch or two. His Tories certainly couldn't wait to leave for the winter. With any luck, they won't come back."

"I wouldn't count on that, my love," Gerald told his wife. "They'll come. And when they do, I want you to stay clear of them whenever you must cross the parade ground on your own." He turned his head and looked at Evie, concern in his hazel eyes. "There are actual advantages, you know, in your not having to go out and deal with the sorry lot of ruffians stationed here."

"Or socialize with them," Evie conceded, remembering her one and only dinner party.

Liza gave her an affirming nod. "Thank goodness we have one kind soul we can trust. Without Byron Winfrey to brighten our winter evenings, life for you in particular would have been ever so much more unbearable."

Evie knew she should also sing the copper-haired corporal's praises, but she couldn't bring herself to do so. She knew Byron was taken with her, and she didn't quite know how to deal with his growing ardor and still keep him as a fellow conspirator. Plus, he was a dear friend of Gerald and Liza—their only true friend here, aside from her.

To their everlasting credit, they had been wonderfully unselfish about her imposing on them day and night for the past nine months. She could never have been that charitable—particularly to someone sleeping in the attic right over her head. How much more trying it must be for a married couple. Married. That was another struggle she had to endure—watching this loving pair, when it had been twelve interminable months since she'd seen Christopher. "What day of April is this?" she asked.

"The eleventh, I believe." Gerald raised the water bucket and held it poised above the tea kettle. "Shall I pour enough for you ladies to have tea as well?"

"Yes, darling, please do," Liza returned. Shaping her dough into three loaves, she rounded them up in pans and covered them with a towel for the second rising. Then she set about clearing the excess flour and dough from the surface of the table.

"In two days," Evie sighed, "it'll be a whole year since I last laid eyes on Chris. And almost a year since his last letter."

Liza's delicate features softened with understanding. "Evie, dear, we've spirited out three of your letters, and mine as well, with the help of our kind Byron. Surely when the ship docks there will be answers for us both. You know the tremendous distance and the difficulties of sending mail in and out of blockaded territory, especially during the winter months."

"I could have sent *myself* out of here," Evie all but snapped, "if it wasn't for that dreadful Captain Long. I am so weary of waiting for a letter, and of these four walls and that dark attic, that I'm about ready to take my chances crossing Indian lands on my own. I'd wager that with a good horse and a map I could slip right past them and make it at least as far as the settlements in the Mohawk Valley."

"It would be crazy to even try," Liza said, arching her brows.

As much as she hated to admit it, Evie knew her friend was right. Ruefully she dropped her gaze and turned to Gerald instead. "Please, as Lieutenant Conway's aide, you must have seen a map or two at the commandant's headquarters, haven't you?"

"Right. There's one on the wall right by his desk. Why do you ask?" His forehead dipped into a frown.

"Well, every day when you're there, you could memorize a section of it. Then you could come home and draw it."

Gerald's eyes grew thoughtful. "Quite right. I should do that—but not so you can just run off half-cocked. In the event something should go wrong and my superiors become suspicious, it might be to our advantage to have some idea of the terrain. Liza and I would be sent to the gallows right along with you for our part in all this, if we're discovered. And that Captain Long has never given up. He's positive we know where you are."

Evelyn looked from him to Liza and back, then gestured helplessly with one hand. "Another reason I should leave here—and soon. It's just a matter of time before we forget to lock the door when I'm down here and someone barges in to catch us. We'd have no chance to escape then, would we? And even if we did, you'd be pursued as a deserter as well."

He chuckled. "I hardly think it would matter one way or the other. I've no plans to reenlist, as you well know. Liza and I hope to make our home here in the Colonies—colonies that I'm sure will one day be independent. The Crown seems to have lost their zest for this war. Our army didn't launch a single major campaign all last summer."

Gerald had mentioned earlier that the only decisive British victory had been one in which they'd retained possession of territory they already held. According to him, the other soldiers had laughed at General Sullivan's attempt to take back the Rhode Island town of Newport last summer. Not having the promised naval support from their alleged French allies, the general had ended up beating a swift retreat.

"So in five-and-a-half more months our ties to this fort will be a thing of the past," Liza murmured, her eyes shining. She switched her attention from her husband to Evie. "And if you're still here, we'll put you in a trunk and take you with us, wherever we may go."

"There's a thought," Evie said with a droll smile. "Too bad Captain Long is at the other end, checking everything that comes through. The man's as tenacious as an old bulldog."

A musket report sounded from the north redoubt. A second followed, this time from the south. Muffled shouts filled the parade grounds, and when Evelyn peered through the crack in the curtains, she saw men running out of the buildings.

Gerald moved quickly to the door and opened it enough to step outside. "What's happening?" he yelled.

"Ship's in. Supplies, old man."

Liza wiped her hands on her work apron, then untied and removed it from her burgundy calico dress. "Evie, when the bread has risen, would you please put it into the oven?" Donning her cloak, gloves, and bonnet, she rushed with Gerald outside to join all the others on their way out of the fort and to the boat dock.

Evie locked the door behind them, barely restraining herself from racing outside herself and going along. She had almost forgotten how wonderful it felt to have the sun warm her face, to feel the breeze feathering across her skin and through her hair. An intense longing for freedom rose up within her.

She moved reluctantly from the door, dragging her feet. Then a wild thought came to her. Everyone at the fort was too caught up in the arrival of the supply ship to notice anything else. Perhaps she could at least steal some fresh air. She peered through the window and saw no one nearby. Cautiously she unlatched it and shoved it open, careful to shield herself with the curtain. The muslin billowed with the breeze. Evelyn inhaled deeply, filling her lungs with the wind's breath, fragrant with the scent of new pine and other pungent woodsy smells. What a treat it was to smell something other than the musty fireplace! She closed her eyes in bliss, breathing slowly in and out with no regard for time or anything else.

When she opened her eyes, Evie spied one of the few children of the fort, walking hand in hand with his mother in the distance. He was jumping up and down in the excitement of the day as they neared the Gate of the Five Nations, as someone had ceremoniously named that entrance.

The kettle was steaming over the hot coals, so Evie went to toss some tea into the pot and set it to brewing, then checked the bread. It had completed its second rising, so she popped it into the oven before returning to the window. If only everyone at the fort would go down to greet the ship, she could lean all the way out and raise her face to the sun. But this time she saw some soldiers milling about.

A shouted greeting carried from the gate. Evie saw a man in a green uniform rounding the long hospital building. One of Butler's Tory rangers. She ducked back inside. Gerald had been right when he'd said they'd start returning with the first ship. According to Liza, these men, mostly Loyalists from New England, were very bitter about having been forced to leave their homes when the patriots ran the British out in the spring of 1776.

Evelyn couldn't help wondering about her parents once again. Gerald had informed her that all the Loyalists in Philadelphia had sailed to England when the British pulled out of the city. For all she knew, she could be hanged for spying and her mother and father might never learn of it. Nor anyone else, if Liza and Gerald met the same sad fate.

It just wasn't right, the jeopardy in which she had placed this dear couple. For their sakes, she'd better stop taking foolish chances like this. Drawing in one last breath of the clean, fresh air, she checked to see if it was safe to close the window.

Then she saw him. Captain Long, coming around the corner of the hospital. He was heading straight for her building.

Evelyn caught her breath and ducked behind the curtain. The drape insisted on flapping to one side, making it easy to see inside.

Would that man never give up? He had returned twice last fall, looking for her, but the long winter had prevented any further investigation. Why did he have to come back?

Evie knew the door was bolted, but the window stood wide open, and she could not chance pulling it closed and latching it. How easy it would be for the captain to stick his head through and have a look around.

She ran to the bedchamber and closed the door. Gerald had positioned a chair beside the commode to enable her to climb atop it and then to the taller wardrobe in order to get into her little attic haven. Evie quickly did just that, careful not to disturb the bowl and pitcher on the commode. She moved Gerald's tall uniform hat and Liza's fancy feathered bonnet from the middle of the wardrobe where they were kept as decoys.

The door handle rattled sharply. Obviously the captain wasn't bothering with such mundane courtesies as knocking first. No doubt he had seen Gerald and Liza down at the ship.

From her perch atop the wardrobe, Evie heard more rattling. She reached up and pushed open the trapdoor Gerald had cut for her, then carefully, silently laid it down on the ceiling floor.

From outside she heard footsteps. Three of them. He had to be looking in the open window. If only she'd kept it closed, *as she was supposed to!*

She heard scratching and bumping sounds, and her heart thudded. Captain Long was actually climbing in the window!

Holding her breath, Evie crawled through the opening to her haven and lowered the door. Then she remembered she hadn't put the headwear back in the proper places. She raised the door enough to reach down and pull the tall hat to the middle again.

Footsteps clomped toward the bedroom door.

Evelyn's hands shook as she frantically moved the bonnet into place. Then very carefully, she let the trapdoor come to a soundless rest . . . just as the latch rattled and the door swung open.

Her heart thundered in her ears. Surely the captain could hear it as audibly as she.

In the dim light provided by small openings at each end of the attic, Evie reached for a blanket from her pallet. Spreading it across the door to buffer her noise, she slowly slid onto it. Even if the captain found the trapdoor, he wouldn't be able to push it up with her sitting on it. Hopefully.

Below, she could hear him walking. Stopping. Walking again. The doors of the wardrobe closet swung open with a bang. He cursed. A few more steps. He stopped again.

Evelyn was afraid to breathe. It would be only a matter of seconds before that keen-eyed bulldog would spot the trapdoor. Though it had been cut with irregular lengths on the opening side, the hinged side had necessitated a straight cut.

He'd find it for sure. And when he did, even if he couldn't shove it open on the first try, he'd find a way . . . even if he had to break another hole in the ceiling.

His steps returned to the wardrobe.

Dear Lord, Evie pleaded silently, *help me to remember I am in your hands.*

36

Evelyn did not move a muscle. She waited, her pulse roaring in her ears.

Below her hiding place, Captain Long's feet shuffled slightly, but he remained at the wardrobe.

Evie could envision his gaze boring into the ceiling. Any second now, he—

Another noise. This one from farther away. Someone rapping at the front door.

Long swore under his breath but did not respond.

The knocking came again.

The captain groaned and stepped away. "What is it?" he finally asked.

A pause. "Captain Long?" came a muffled voice. "Is that you, sir?"

"And whom, I might ask, is peeking in the window?"

"Me, sir. Corporal Winfrey."

Evelyn let out a slow breath of relief.

"What do you want, Corporal?" Long asked gruffly, plainly annoyed.

"Begging your pardon, sir. I've no business with you, actually. It's just that I come by every day at this time for tea. With Corporal Blake and his wife."

"Surely you're not so woodenheaded that you failed to notice the ship's arrival in port." The captain's irritated voice moved farther away as he spoke. The bedroom door closed.

The voices became harder to make out. Evie slid from the trapdoor and raised it a fraction.

"Yes, sir. I happened to be at the dock when the ship came in. I retrieved the mail pouch and delivered it to headquarters. I've a letter for Mistress Liza, a long-awaited letter from her mother."

A jolt of fear shot through Evie. Liza's mother would most assuredly make reference to her, and then Gerald and Liza would be arrested.

"I'll take it, Corporal. Pass it through the window."

Another pause. "Mistress Liza's personal mail, sir?"

"That's right," the captain said, his tone flat. "As you well know, this couple is still under suspicion of aiding the spy, Evelyn Thomas."

"But, sir, the young miss in question departed from here last summer—on the same vessel you took to Montreal. As far as the Blakes knew, the girl was one Evelyn Haynes, sister to Liza's pastor in Boston."

"*Presbyterian* pastor. *Rebel* pastor," Long grated. "Pass the letter through the window at once."

"Through the window, sir? If you'll but open the door, I shall bring it in and await the return of the Blakes."

Despite her fear, Evie had to smile. The corporal had put the officer on the spot. The lock was operated only by a key, and Long had none.

"Just hand me the blasted letter, and be off with you!" Captain Long ordered. "Or I'll have you brought up on charges."

"Yes, sir. Very good, sir."

In seconds, Evie heard the sound of ripping paper. The captain had torn the packet open. She was doomed for sure. They all were.

"Oh. How fortunate," Byron said cheerily. "Here come the Blakes even as we speak, Captain."

The officer did not respond. Evie concluded he was determinedly reading the missive. She had to do something. Get

the thing from him! Warn Gerald and Liza! *Do something! Now!*
She swung the trapdoor all the way open.

Byron Winfrey's voice carried much more easily from outside. "Gerald. Mistress. Captain Long—from Montreal—has
come. He's here, in fact. In your quarters, waiting for you."

"How did he—" Gerald cleared his throat. "Oh, I see." His
footsteps approached the door.

Evelyn couldn't let her friends simply walk in like lambs to
the slaughter. She quietly eased herself down to the top of the
wardrobe closet, eyeing the water pitcher—the only possible
weapon she could wield.

The key rattled in the lock. The door squeaked open,
followed by more footsteps.

"You might as well have this, Mistress Blake," Captain Long
said unceremoniously. "I found nothing incriminating."

"Why . . . thank you."

Nothing incriminating? With her foot stretched midway
down between the wardrobe and the commode, Evie stopped.
She retreated into her hiding place once more, with the
trapdoor cracked and her ear low.

"Nevertheless, Corporal Blake," the officer went on in his
booming, self-important voice, "you and your wife are not as
yet absolved of all suspicion. You two were the last to see
Evelyn Thomas before her . . . mysterious disappearance,
shall we say."

"May I assume, then," Gerald responded, "that your in-
quiries among the Indians have also proven fruitless? That
the young lady in question was not discovered on any of the
wilderness trails?"

"Not entirely fruitless." The curtness of the reply revealed
that he wouldn't have volunteered the information unless
asked. "I've been informed by the Indians that a pair of white
men, hunters, have also been looking for a woman of her
description. Therefore, I must conclude that she did not
return to Wyoming Valley. And one thing is certain, no Indian
would keep the girl. The reward offered for her return is far
too generous."

Evelyn's heart warmed. One of the two white hunters surely had to be Christopher. But the encouragement dwindled with another disturbing thought. He had placed himself in all that danger for naught. She wasn't among the Indians.

"Might I offer you some tea, Captain?" Liza asked. "I left the kettle on hearth coals when we went down to the ship. Of course, my going served no purpose, since Corporal Winfrey had already brought my mail. I've been waiting for word from my mother for quite a long time."

"Thank you, no. I'll be off to see to other matters. Good day." His purposeful strides echoed to Evie's ears as he took his leave.

The door closed behind him, and the lock clicked into place.

"I say," Byron remarked as the window was also closed and latched. "Can you believe such nerve? The utter gall of the man to break into one's home and insist upon opening personal mail."

"I'm not surprised about anything pertaining to that particular officer," Gerald said scathingly.

Byron came into the bedroom just as Evelyn was climbing down from her haven. "Here, let me assist you," he said, offering a hand. "A bit of a close call, eh?"

Evie smiled thinly and gave him her hand. "You have no idea how close. You have my eternal gratitude."

"I shall treasure it." Raising her fingers to his lips, the corporal kissed them.

Evelyn wished he wasn't quite so smitten. She'd done her best not to encourage him, but with so few women at the fort, she knew his attraction to her was almost inevitable.

Byron's gray eyes lingered longingly on her face, then he cocked his head with a grimace of disappointment. "I, er, have some mail for you, too." He withdrew three letters from inside his breast pocket and held them out. "They were inside packets addressed to me."

Evie wanted to sing, to shout for joy, as she took them from him and rushed out to her friends. "Did you hear? Byron brought me some letters!"

Liza sat in her rocking chair poring over her own letter while Gerald read over her shoulder. Tears were streaming down her face when she looked up at Evelyn. "How wonderful," she whispered with a watery smile. "I hope they bring you news as good as mine."

Gerald, too, had tears in his eyes. "And thank Providence, Mistress Brown was wise enough not to mention you in her letter to her daughter." He bent to hug Liza's shoulders. "You two read your mail. I'll see if I can manage the tea."

"I'll help you, old chap."

Byron's offer eased much of Evie's discomfort. The last thing she needed at the moment was to have the corporal hanging over her shoulder. She had three blessedly thick letters, all in Christopher's handwriting, just waiting to be read.

She hugged the precious envelopes to her chest, then turned and hurried back to the privacy of the bedroom.

❧ ❧

The soft tapping on the bedchamber door was an unwelcome intrusion. Evelyn looked up from the second letter to see Liza peering around the open door.

"From your Christopher?"

Evie nodded.

"And look at all the pages!" Liza exclaimed, her gaze taking in the abundance of papers scattered around Evie on the bed. She closed the door and came over to her. "You probably wanted to be by yourself, but I thought I'd let you know the tea is ready. We mustn't snub dear Byron. Without his help, your letters would not have slipped past that ogre, Captain Long."

"You're right, of course." With a sigh, Evie smoothed the pages still in her hand and put them aside with the rest. "There's so much to tell you," she whispered, getting up, "but I think it's best to spare Byron. He's been burdened quite enough as it is." Smiling, she swiped at her tears with the corner of her apron, then caught her friend's hands. "This is such a happy, happy day."

Evelyn did her best to give the impression that there was no place on earth she'd rather be presently than having tea with her friends, but in truth, most of her thoughts were still in the bedchamber with the rest of Christopher's letters. Seated around the table with the others, she forced a smile and bit into a cranberry tart.

". . . and best of all," Liza was saying blissfully, "Mother has begged Gerald and me to return to Boston as soon as his enlistment is up. Not only has she forgiven us both, but she wants to be a part of our lives. She says that with so many people gone from the city because of the war, she's managed to purchase a larger house, one with a spacious shop below. There'll be plenty of room for us all *and* the cobbler's business Gerald has dreamed of starting."

"That is wonderful," Evie said. "I'm so happy for you both."

"Yes. Truly splendid news," Byron affirmed.

"And what did Christopher have to say?" Gerald prompted.

Out of respect for Byron, Evie decided to be brief. "That he, indeed, had been one of the two hunters Captain Long mentioned. At least until the winter snows forced him out of Indian country. He was quite relieved to learn I'd been rescued by the British."

"I'm glad no harm came to him," Gerald said. "Would you care for more tea, Byron?"

Byron smiled distractedly. He blotted his mouth on his napkin and stood to his feet. "I think not. I must be off—I'm scheduled for guard duty this eve. Thank you for the hospitality, Liza. And Evie—" he turned to her and took her hand— "I'm glad I was able to deliver the mail from your friend. Take care. Until tomorrow?" Bowing over her fingers, he brushed them with his lips, then left.

Gerald accompanied him and locked the door after him before returning to the table.

"Since he's no longer here," Evie began, "I have information that will affect all of us greatly. And, I fear, some difficult decisions will have to be made."

"You needn't tell me," Gerald said, retaking his chair. "Your young man wants you to escape into Indian country, doesn't he? To some rendezvous."

Evelyn shook her head. "No, not that, though it might be simpler than what he has in mind."

"What is it then?" Liza asked, her eyes dark with concern.

"Chris says General Washington has ordered an expedition into Iroquois country this summer. They plan to retaliate by destroying the Indian villages . . . and taking Fort Niagara."

Liza looked fearfully at her husband.

He patted her hand. "You knew, my darling, they would eventually have to take some sort of action. That's been our primary objective—to pull fighting men away from their main force."

No one spoke for a moment. Evie couldn't help the apprehension she felt for these two dear friends. As much as she wanted to be with Christopher, she also wanted Gerald and Liza—and even Byron—to be unharmed and well. "Anyway, Chris wants me to be patient and to stay hidden until the time comes for the rescue. And he asked me to convey his heartfelt thanks for all you have done for me, for the risks you've taken. And speaking of risks—" She looked instinctively toward the window. "Today Captain Long came within seconds of discovering the trapdoor."

"I feared as much," Liza said. "That must have been terribly frightful for you."

"I was far more concerned for you. Knowing that you and Gerald would be incriminated along with me—for nothing more than showing me kindness—was a terrible burden. And there I sat, trapped, with no possible way to warn you."

Gerald shrugged nonchalantly. "Well, personally, I think since the man's had his opportunity to search our quarters, he'll not make any further attempts to do so." He chuckled. "I must say, catching the snoop red-faced was rather gratifying. He couldn't quite bluster his way out of his embarrassment."

"Especially since he didn't find a single clue," Liza added with a giggle of her own.

Evie nodded soberly. "Thanks to Byron's intervention."

"Byron has reasons of his own to help us," Gerald replied. "He, too, wishes to make a life for himself here in the Colonies once his enlistment has ended. And after Liza's mother's letter about the shop, he'll be even more eager to see us succeed."

"He does have a good heart, Gerald, dear," Liza said, leaning her head against his shoulder. "That's why the two of you became such good friends in the first place."

Evelyn stacked her cup and saucer with Byron's and folded her hands. "That's all well and good, but we need to be better prepared. Especially if the fort is going to be attacked. I, for one, don't want to get caught here for some long siege. I've been thinking, Gerald. I've kept that Indian garb you got me when I was first rescued. Would it be possible to trade with the Indians for some more clothing? We could travel past them much easier if we blended in, if you know what I mean. We need a plan in case something happens to cast additional suspicion on you. The first of October, when your enlistment is up, is still quite far off."

"Yes." He rubbed his jaw in thought. "Clothes. And that map. I shall bring home a big piece of parchment and get started on that right away. Even if I must stay to defend Fort Niagara, I'll want both of you safely away from here."

"I would *never* go without you," Liza said emphatically. "Never."

He looked beseechingly at Evie for support, then turned back to his wife. "Well, as Evie said, that's still a long way off. Let's just see to today. And speaking of that—isn't that bread I smell?"

"My bread!" Liza jumped up and ran to the Dutch oven.

Yes, Evie thought, watching her, *do take care of today. But plan for tomorrow, and dream about the day after.* She believed more than ever that the day would come when she would reach out and Christopher would be there, in her arms, to kiss away all the rest of her lonely tomorrows. Pray, let it be soon.

But doubts insisted on niggling to the fore. Captain Long would never give up. And there were still a few more months to go. Weeks and weeks.

Evelyn inhaled slowly. She'd heard from Christopher at last. She could wait. He'd written hundreds and hundreds of words for her to devour, words to fill those weeks. All of them teeming with hope.

Thank you, heavenly Father, for the renewed hope. After that close call with Captain Long, I really needed the reminder that you're still in charge.

She rose. "If you don't mind, I think I'll go finish reading my letters."

37

Christopher mopped sweat from his brow in the steamy August heat. He wished for the coolness of one of the spring-fed waterfalls he and Garth Kinyon had passed on the hundred-mile march to Tioga country in western New York. The foam-whitened waters roaring over a high cliff and plunging downward in cool mist brought a few minutes of blissful reprieve from the stickiness of the day. But the falls were behind them now, and at the present time he could content himself only with the limited comfort provided by huge buttonwood, rock maple, pine, and hickory trees that shaded the thick forest.

Coming up on Newtown, the large Indian settlement located along the Tioga River, he and Garth emerged stealthily from the sanctity of the woods and crouched down in the underbrush along its outer edge. The prosperity of the village was amazing. Here the Indians lived in a sprawling assortment of well-built wooden houses with glass windows. Lavish crops grew in vast fertile fields and orchards, and hundreds of farm animals grazed placidly in meadows and pens.

"Hmph," Kinyon muttered. "Hasn't hurt 'em a bit to have their hand in all the plundering the king's puppets have been doing against the white settlers."

Chris nodded. From this distance, a spyglass would have aided the two of them greatly as they tried to get a fair idea of the size of the enemy force gathered in the village. He narrowed his eyes, straining to calculate the number of canoes inverted along the riverbank.

They could see hundreds of men in the green uniforms of Butler's Rangers milling about, plus twice the number of Indians one would have expected in a settlement this size. Most were clustered in large circles watching their painted and feather-bedecked *shamans* dance and stomp to the pulsing rhythm of Indian drums.

"Only a preview of what'll be going on come nightfall," Garth remarked. "They'll sit at a war council and feast on platters of dog meat. Then after the leading warriors are presented with the heads of the dogs, the real dancing will start, a mock battle. 'Course, they offer up tobacco to the war spirit hoping for success, too."

Christopher pointed to a flash of red at the entrance of the longhouse. "Lobsterbacks."

"Just like we figured. I've been lookin' at that rise over yonder, too. Above the trail comin' from the south. See it?"

Chris nodded.

"Notice anything strange?"

"Now that you mention it, the leaves on those shrubs are wilted. Half dead. They must be hiding something there. Breastworks, maybe."

Kinyon gave him an approving grin. "You're turning into a right fine scout, know that? It appears to be the spot where they'll make their stand. They have to know the expedition is headin' this way, and they're takin' it real serious."

"I'd take an army of four thousand men seriously myself," Chris said quietly. "Especially if I were an Indian. There probably aren't many who've ever seen a force so large. Our packhorses and baggage are strung out a good two miles, to say nothing of the artillery. If Sullivan had left that blasted heavy equipment behind, this march wouldn't have taken twelve days. Sticking to every twist and turn of the rivers, poling those big guns upriver, then having to portage them over rocky ridges and through mucky swamps has us crawling like snails."

"Well, time for us to do some crawlin' of our own." Still keeping low, Kinyon began scooting backward, deeper into the brush.

With an eye out for possible enemies patrolling the vicinity, Chris followed the tracker's lead.

Inside the much denser forest growth, they came to their feet and silently made their way to their tethered horses.

Once they'd put a fair distance between themselves and Newtown, the hunter picked up the conversation from right where it had been dropped half an hour ago—a peculiar habit of his that always amused Christopher. "I know you got your own reasons to wanna hurry up north, son. But the roar of them cannonades has been all that's needed to clear out every village along the way. Ain't been much loss of life on either side yet, and our boys have been free to get on with the task of destroyin' crops and buildings."

"That may be the general's plan, but some of the men with us have lost a number of loved ones to Butler's butchers. Jonathan told me it's getting harder all the time to keep the men in check. They were fit to be tied when they came upon those long blonde scalps adorning the wall of that last long-house."

"Aye. That was odd." Garth kneaded his frizzy beard as his mount plodded over the rocky trail. "The heathens must've been pretty spooked to go off an' leave their prizes behind."

"Prizes." Christopher grimaced bitterly. "You talk about them as if they're medals of honor."

"They are, son, and you know it. Why else would the savages decorate 'em and flaunt 'em before their company?"

"All I can say is it's too bad for them they didn't take all those bones and mangled skulls they left behind at Forty Fort. Our men had plenty of time to ponder those grisly trophies while waiting for the march to start."

The tracker eyed him with a sidelong glance. "Well, looks like our own boys'll get a chance to get in on some killin' soon enough."

Chris winced and lapsed into a short span of silence before

replying. "Susannah Haynes is always talking about how we should love our enemies. But ever since I was a kid that's been one of the hardest things for me to do. I suppose it's fortunate I'm not sergeant to a company of men this time around. I might not be so willing to keep them in line."

Garth suddenly held up a hand, signaling he'd heard something. He dismounted.

Chris, too, swung down from his mount. He bent low and moved silently from cover to cover beside the tracker.

Garth jutted his chin in the direction of two men nested alongside an empty forest trail. "Some of ours," he said under his breath, then straightened and stepped into view. "Don't shoot, boys. We're comin' in."

Caught off guard, the pair wheeled in surprise. Their expressions of panic eased upon seeing familiar faces. Several small parties on this march had already been set upon by Indians. Scalped and murdered.

"What company are you with?" Chris asked.

"General Hand's Brigade, sir," one said with an unwarranted salute.

"Where is he, soldier? We need to make a report." Despite all the drawn-out delays, it encouraged Chris to know that the very capable General Hand was here and in charge of the advance guard, just as he had been when Chris was in his rifle battalion.

❦ ❦

After delivering their report to the general, Christopher and Garth Kinyon squatted on the spongy forest floor to wait for their news to be forwarded to the other commanders and a plan to be formed.

"Might as well get a little shut-eye," Kinyon said, stretching out with a yawn. "Could be a spell before we get another chance like this." He laced his fingers together and propped his hands behind his head.

"Right." Chris unslung his gear and propped his rifle against the tree trunk. He, too, lay down and closed his eyes, even though his mind was far too active to sleep. If all went as expected, by day's end the scourge of the frontier would be vanquished. Then nothing would stand between this force and their trek to Fort Niagara, and Evelyn.

If she was still there. And still alive. Her one and only letter had been written more than a year ago, and he'd never received another. Whenever Dan Haynes came with a message for Washington, he always made certain Chris got any mail addressed to him. And Chris had no idea if Evie had actually gotten the letters he'd written. He'd been careful to address hers to Miss Haynes, and to place them inside packets to Byron Winfrey. He'd even attempted to word the letters so as not to expose her. But despite his efforts, they might have been confiscated and cost her her life.

How could anyone manage to remain hidden for such a long time? And so far from civilization, the fort's General Carleton would probably dispense with such mundane matters as a trial. Any man who would encourage the massacre of women and children would have no qualms about hanging a young woman.

Raising up on one elbow, Christopher looked to see if the messenger had returned to where General Hand sat with his officers some distance away. If Robert Chandler were here instead of down in the Carolinas, he'd have informed Chris immediately of what was going on. Would have assured him what a resourceful young woman Evie was. . . . Evie, who had begged him to take her along that lifetime ago when they were last together. The thought tore at his heart, and he closed his eyelids against the picture.

After a while, someone shook his shoulder. "Time to go, son."

Chris awakened to the tracker's voice, surprised that he'd fallen asleep.

"The cannons have been poled past us upriver. Hand wants us to lead his men into position behind those Indian breastworks and pin the enemy down while the rest of our boys sweep wide and outflank them and the town."

Checking the position of the sun through the canopy of boughs overhead, Chris saw that considerable time had passed. It had to be nearing three. He lunged to his feet and grabbed his equipment. It wouldn't be long now. Their numbers easily doubled the enemy's, for once. If the Lord was with them in this effort, victory would be swift.

❦ ❦

The Indians, aided by the British, displayed fierce bravery as they tried to protect their homes in the battle. Whooping and hollering, they made a number of sorties from their lines out into the open, trying to provoke the patriots into the frontal attack for which they were prepared. But then the cannons were rolled into firing position and powerful blasts echoed through the surrounding hills. Within thirty minutes the paint-streaked braves ran for the deepest woods, with the green-uniformed Rangers right behind them.

Christopher exchanged a grin with Garth as the two of them stood up. From behind the safety of a boulder, they had been firing down on the pine-log breastworks. Below them, hordes of shouting and cheering Continental soldiers poured into the open fields.

"It seems we run out of purty feathers to shoot at," Kinyon declared.

"I only pray we've done enough damage so the British can't convince their red brothers to make war on us again."

"Well, that's somethin' we won't know for a spell. The Injuns always tote off their dead and wounded, so we won't get a count."

At that moment, sporadic musket fire started from the rise above them.

The tracker's scarred eyebrow hiked in puzzlement. "Thought you an' me was the farthest out."

A man below them crumpled and fell. Then another.

"Come on," Chris said. "Let's circle around and see what kind of force we're dealing with."

Bending low, he and Kinyon moved along the hillside.

Several patriot soldiers, full of the exuberance of victory, charged recklessly up the incline, fully exposing themselves. "Take cover, lads!" an officer shouted, but musket balls claimed a few of them before they could heed the order.

Christopher watched in dismay. There hadn't been a single patriot killed during the battle. To see senseless losses resulting from nothing but foolishness was hard to accept.

By the time he and the tracker had reached a spot where they could observe their attackers, artillery pieces had already begun blasting the enemy position. Shortly, a company of rangers and a handful of redcoats could be seen fleeing into the dense forest.

Garth nudged Chris. "Look. Under that big walnut tree yonder."

Turning toward the spot the scout indicated, Christopher spied a redcoat sprawled motionless on the ground. A second, obviously wounded, dragged himself and his musket toward the cover of tangled vines.

"Go around," Kinyon said quietly. "I'll sneak up behind."

With the British force in swift retreat, Chris bolted down the hill and through the shadows of mature cornstalks, his moccasins making no sound.

Victory shouts and cheers took up again in the distance. Through an occasional break in the rows of stalks, Chris caught sight of thin columns of smoke and knew the men had started torching the town. It seemed such a waste to destroy cabins with glass windows, a luxury unheard of by so many white settlers. But he tried not to dwell on it.

At last he reached the far side of the meadow. He was now a mere few rods away from where he'd seen the wounded man crawling into what appeared to be a wild gooseberry patch. The poor fool would likely be a scratched up mess from all the brambles, but even injured, the soldier might be capable of firing a round from his musket.

Chris stopped and loaded his own weapon, then dropped down to make his way around the back side of the prickly vines. But once there, he discovered nothing but a bare sandy stretch sloping gently down toward a shallow stream, no place to hide. He turned back toward the cornfield.

"Aaaah!" came a sharp yelp.

Peering into the berry brambles, Christopher could make out the red of a military coat amid the dense growth. He might do well to put the poor soul out of his misery right now. Crouching down, Chris raised his rifle and took aim. He put his finger to the first trigger.

Another groan drifted from the gooseberry thicket.

The sound made Chris hesitate. Something about shooting a man who was wounded and caught in brambles seemed too much like murder . . . even if that man happened to be a villainous blackguard of a British soldier.

I'll let him make the first move, Christopher decided. *Then I'll kill him.* He had no doubt that as a professional soldier the fellow wouldn't spare Chris the second he caught sight of him.

There came scuffling sounds and movements. Several seconds of silence. Then a low groan, a catching of breath.

Chris knew the man must be suffering. The man needed help. Then he berated himself for such compassionate impulses. That little bit of pain was nothing compared to the tortures inflicted by the Indians and rangers on their helpless victims.

"Oh, Lord, help me," the voice begged softly. "Please."

Susannah's beseeching gaze flashed before Christopher, her blue gray eyes luminous in their plea. He exhaled. "Toss your musket my way, soldier," he said. "I'll help you out of those thorns."

No one answered. Chris prudently moved back several yards.

"I'll keep a bead on him, son," Kinyon called from the other side of the berries.

The redcoat had to know he was surrounded, but he still did not respond at first. "I . . . can't," he said with effort.

"Can't what?" Garth asked, clearly suspicious.

"Throw out my Bess. I'm caught. My coat."

Christopher laid down his rifle and pulled his hatchet from the loop in his belt. He stood up. "I'm going to trust you're telling the truth." Moving to the vines, he began hacking away at the tangled growth.

"God bless you."

By the time he'd managed to reach the wounded soldier, Chris had snagged his own skin and clothing and suffered a number of scratches himself. The fellow was indeed hopelessly caught. He was also bleeding from the head and the leg. Still, one couldn't be too cautious. Picking up the redcoat's musket, Christopher tossed it out of the berry patch. "How bad are you wounded?" he asked, chopping at the vines surrounding the man.

"I've no idea. I was a bit befuddled for a while. My leg must be shot, but I can't think past the pain in my head. My lieutenant . . . is he dead?"

Christopher glanced at Garth. "Better check that other one."

"No need," the tracker returned flatly. "He ain't drawn a breath for some time."

Smoke from the fires now filled the sky as bright orange flames licked upward in fury. The smoke began drifting their way. "Better get you out of here before the fields are torched." Finally he disengaged the last vines and gingerly peeled them back from the wounded corporal. He bent to help him stand, then, seeing how shaky the man was, picked him up and carried him.

Garth came over and pulled a kerchief from his pocket as Chris lay the man down. He began staunching the bleeding wounds. "This'll have to do till the sawbones can see to him."

"Wonder which way the surgeons are set up," Chris said as he and the tracker hoisted the redcoat between them and started toward the rear, away from the swarms of men who were slashing and burning the fields.

Kinyon wagged his head at the destruction. "A pure shame, it is, ruinin' all them harvest-ripe foods. A pure shame."

"Sergeant Drummond!" one of General Hand's aides

called, running toward them. "The general wants you to report to him at once. You and Mr. Kinyon." He stopped, his gaze taking in the wounded Englishman.

"We're kinda busy here, lad," Garth replied. "Did he say what he wants?"

"No, sir. He just wants you."

Christopher felt a subtle stiffening in the injured man as he tipped back his head and squinted through pain-filled eyes. "Drummond, did he say? Your name isn't perchance Christopher Drummond."

Chris came to a dead halt. "Yes. But how could you know that?"

Still staring, he sagged and had to be hoisted up again. "Evelyn's talked so much about her handsome, daring young man. But somehow I expected . . . well, someone at least a bit . . . tidier."

38

"I just can't believe it! I won't! Not my Gerald!"

Evelyn, hiding behind the closed bedroom door, felt her heart wrench as she listened to Liza sobbing in the other room. Her eyes swam with tears as the weight of the dire news Captain Wyatt had brought pressed heavily on her spirit.

"I'm afraid it was just one of those unfortunate accidents of war, my dear," the officer explained patiently. "Your husband and his lieutenant were caught in an exchange of fire. They died valiantly and honorably in the service of His Majesty."

Liza sniffed. "But—but they—weren't even combat soldiers," she cried between sobs. "They were just—messengers." Her voice broke on the last word. "My Gerald, he—he was hardly more than a—a postrider."

"Yes, my dear. 'Tis one of the great sorrows of war," Wyatt droned on, his feeble attempts at comfort useless in the face of Liza's grief. "Corporal Blake and his ready smile will be sorely missed by all who knew him."

"His . . . smile," Liza murmured, obviously trying to compose herself. "Yes. He—he did have a wonderful smile." Then she broke down again.

Evie felt helpless, shut up as she was in the bedchamber. She wished the captain would leave so she could at least go to her dear friend and offer whatever sympathy she could. It had been two weeks since Gerald and his lieutenant had gone to check on Butler's Rangers for General Carleton—merely to check and return to report. It was hard to conceive the possibility that he had been killed. Evelyn had grown so close to the amiable British corporal and his sweet wife during the long months they had lavished their friendship on her and made their home her refuge. Now to hear this! It was incredibly unfair.

Wyatt's voice cut across Evie's thoughts. "I know this must be quite a shock to you, my dear. And quite likely you've not the slightest idea which way to turn just now. But I've come with assurance that you needn't feel pressured in any way to pack up your belongings for departure on the next ship. Quite the contrary, we've been most pleased with your services here among us, helping out with the laundry and mending as is required of the wives of our enlisted men. Your faithfulness has not gone unnoticed."

As well it shouldn't, Evelyn railed silently with a bitter smirk. *With me to help her, she's been able to do twice the work of the other wives.*

An immediate silence followed, as if Liza was stunned by the realization that without her soldier husband she no longer had a right to dwell on a military post. "I—I don't . . ."

Then came the scrape of a kitchen chair on the plank floor. Liza must have dropped onto a chair, present worries warring with her despair. By now, Liza, with her unselfish nature, was probably already looking beyond her own pain and considering the predicament leaving the fort would place Evie in.

"As I said," Captain Wyatt continued, "don't worry your lovely head about the matter. I shall be more than happy to look after you for as long as you need me."

A chair scooted again, sharply this time. "I do thank you, Captain. But I'm afraid I must ask you to leave. I need to be alone for a while. I've much to think about."

"Of course. I shall come by this eve and look in on you, in case you're in need of anything."

"Thank you. That is very kind. Now, if you'll excuse me."

"Quite. Again, the staff at Fort Niagara is at your service. You have our deepest sympathies." He crossed the room.

Barely had the door closed after him and the bolt rammed into place when Evelyn rushed out to Liza. "Oh, my dear, dear friend," she whispered. "I'm so sorry. So very sorry."

The slight woman's composure shattered with renewed anguish as she collapsed into Evie's embrace. "It can't be true. Please, don't let it be true," she pleaded as the floodgates of her tears burst again.

Evie hugged Liza close, and the two sobbed on each other's shoulders until the wave of pain subsided.

Finally Liza took a shuddering breath and eased away a little. She lifted her apron and blotted her puffy face.

"All this time," she said quietly, "all this time, we lived in fear of being hanged. Together. Never once did it enter my mind I'd be left here alone, without my Gerald."

Evie, not knowing what to say, placed a hand over Liza's and gave an empathetic squeeze.

"It happened to Maudie Snow last summer. Remember?" Liza went on, raising moisture-spiked lashes to look at Evie. "Maudie's husband was part of Walter Butler's raiding party. But—" She fluttered a hand in a helpless gesture. "Gerald and I have been faithful to God . . . or at least, tried to be. It wasn't supposed to happen to us."

Evie leaned to hug her. "Yes, you have. Both of you. You've been a shining beacon in this darkest of times for me. A light of hope and promise. A spot of humor. I can't count the times you and Gerald made me laugh when I thought I'd go mad from this confinement."

Liza made a heartbreaking attempt to smile, then, with a ragged sigh, looked away.

Evelyn wished for all the world that Susannah were there to offer comfort to Liza from the Bible. Evie rued the hours she'd wasted daydreaming through Susannah's words of wisdom. Little had she known then that the time would come when she'd appreciate that loving Englishwoman's priceless example and testimony, when she would reach out to that very same God herself and accept his Son as her Savior. Thankfully, Liza and Gerald had put their own worn Bible at Evie's disposal—their one and only book—to read to her heart's content.

Searching her memory, a passage from the Gospel of Matthew came to Evie's mind. She had committed much of the fifth chapter to memory because its verses reminded her to pray for her enemies. She found that hard to do, since she was virtually imprisoned in a British fort with hostile Indians camped outside its palisades, but she tried—she truly did try. "As the Lord told the multitude on the mountainside," she said to Liza, "'He maketh his sun to rise on the evil and on the good, and sendeth rain on the just and on the unjust.'"

To Evie's surprise, quoting Scripture rather than voicing her own wisdom hadn't felt in the least pompous. She lifted a corner of her apron and wiped a smudge from Liza's face. "Gerald was a sterling example to me of many of the blessings of the Beatitudes. Most of all, he was pure of heart. And just imagine . . . this very day he must be basking in God's very light, wrapped in the shining glory of all the Bible's promises."

Liza's eyes welled with moisture. She blinked it away, and with a nod took Evie's hands in hers. "The Lord couldn't have sent me a kinder or more loving friend, do you know that? I felt from the first you would be a blessing to us, and now I'm more sure of it than I ever was. I don't know how Gerald and I would have been able to endure this past year without you."

The sincerity of the statement rendered Evie speechless. In her whole life, no one had ever called her a blessing. And in all truthfulness, this period of forced seclusion had benefited her more than she could have imagined. All those empty hours with nothing to fill them but prayer and Scripture and reflection. Oh, for the chance to ride to church with Susannah once more, to pray with her! She would hang onto every word uttered by the pastor next time she had that precious privilege.

Evie squeezed her friend's slim fingers. "A lot of people

have been praying for the two of us for a very long time. Hold on to that . . . and to me. Hold on tight, dear Liza."

Light footsteps sounded on the planks from outside, and there came a soft rapping on the door.

Evelyn exchanged a worried glance with Liza, hoping they hadn't been overheard. Quickly putting her glass out of sight, she hastened to the bedchamber while Liza went to answer the summons. Evie glanced up at her route of escape, but remained near the cracked door to try to determine whether there was cause for alarm.

"We hope ye don't mind a bit of an intrusion," a woman said, in a precise British accent. "We've only just heard the sad news. We brought some stew, in case you might not be up to cooking for yourself."

"Thank you, Miss Townes, Miss Newberry. Might I offer you some tea?" Liza asked politely.

"Well, perhaps a drop. We shan't stay long."

Folding her arms, Evelyn shifted her stance alongside the slice of an opening.

"Have you made any plans yet?" the first voice continued after the briefest pause. "Is there a place you might go?"

Liza's rattling of dishes at the sideboard ceased. "Captain Wyatt assured me there was no need to rush. He said I may stay at the fort as long as I like. But—he had a look that made me uncomfortable."

"Oh, aye," a coarser, less cultivated voice said. "Ye needn't explain that look, I'd say. The captain's a rake, after anything in skirts, he is. Don't seem to care overmuch about a lady's age or circumstance either, that one."

Evelyn's jaw fell open. That worthless bounder couldn't wait a decent five minutes before taking advantage of a comely young widow? Seething rage began to gather inside her.

"Aye, lass," the first confirmed. "Even us older ones keep a sharp eye out for him when our gentlemen are away on campaigns. We found out, early on, the truth of the adage about safety in numbers. If you've family that will take you in, I'd not delay returning to them."

"On the next ship, if 'twas me," the second added.

"Well," Liza began, returning to the table and drawing out a chair. There was the sound of tea being poured and china cups being set before the visitors. "Truth is, I have been lonely for home, for my mother, for some time."

"'Tis lucky you are, then, to have a body who'd welcome you. I'd set sail for England myself, if 'tweren't for the mess I made of things."

"Perhaps things have settled down by now, Miss Newberry," Liza said gently. "If you wrote first, you might discover that the people you left behind miss you every bit as much as you do them."

"Aye, wouldn't that be a lark?"

"Time does have a way of healing," Liza said.

"Quite true," the other one said. "And Harriet and I trust you'll remember that as well, in the lonely days to come."

"I'll try." A short pause. "It was so thoughtful of you both to bring this food," Liza said a little more brightly. "It seems we never found time to get to know each other very well."

"Well," Miss Townes replied, "folks such as us feel a mite uncomfortable around decent folk like you and your corporal. Ye might say ye remind us of what we were like before we traded our precious innocence for a bit of cheap excitement. Promise ye'll be on the next ship out, will ye? Harriet and I and the others will make certain one particular *gentleman* keeps his distance till then."

"Some of us'll be goin' too," Miss Newberry confessed. "It wasn't just your own husband who got killed, ye see."

"It wasn't?"

Evelyn's curiosity increased. She pressed her ear closer to the door.

"Oh, aye. Our force suffered dire losses, but they weren't able to stop the rebels. Now thousands of them are on the march here. Thousands. Like locusts, destroyin' whatever's in their way, they are."

"When are they expected to arrive?" Liza asked in alarm.

"Three weeks. Four at most."

"Don't fret, however," Miss Townes said placatingly. "Even if a ship hasn't arrived before then, we've been assured that the fort is impregnable."

"But, Millie, remember the cannons," Miss Newberry cut in.

"Oh, yes, quite. No sense risking our lives in this backwater to nowhere. I, for one, would dearly love setting foot back in civilization again. Preferably where no one knows me."

"Won't your . . . Sergeant McIver, isn't it, be concerned?" Liza asked.

"Not to worry. If he survives, he'll know where to find me."

"Well, in any event," Liza said earnestly, "I thank you once again for coming by. You've been a comfort. I do find that I'm quite tired, though."

"Of course. We've overstayed our welcome, I'm sure." The patter of feminine feet moved to the entrance. "Thank ye for inviting us in. Rest well, Mistress Blake. We'll likely meet again in the days to come. May the Almighty comfort ye in your loss."

"Thank you. Take care now, both of you. Good day."

Evelyn exited the bedchamber immediately after the two had departed.

Liza turned to her with an anxious expression clouding her features. "It would appear we have some serious decisions facing us, Evie."

"So I heard. You'll be sailing for Boston, and I'll be seeking a hiding place somewhere in the woods until Christopher finds me."

"No!" Liza clutched Evie's shoulders. "Please, don't say that. I can't lose you, too. I couldn't bear it."

Chris wheeled about in his saddle and waved to the corporal. It was good to see color back in Gerald Blake's cheeks again.

Gerald, having recovered sufficiently from his wounds to

ride in a wagon with other casualties, grinned and waved cheerily in return.

For weeks, however, the British corporal had hovered between life and death while the surgeons stood by, helpless in the face of raging fever and delirium. The puncture wound in his thigh became infected, and if not for Kinyon's knowledge of some Indian methods of doctoring, Gerald would most certainly have lost his leg. Thankfully, the addition of native herbs to the surgeons' poultices on both the head and leg wounds brought marked and swift improvement. Within a day of the treatment his fever broke, and he began regaining strength.

Personally, Christopher attributed a good portion of the recovery to prayer. But at the same time, having witnessed the startling effects of the Indian treatment, he would never discount the fact that God could use nature's bounty to work some of his miracles. It would have been ironic for a man who dreamed of being a shoemaker to end up with only one foot himself.

After riding into camp with Garth on this sixth day of October to deliver their scouting report, Chris had spent the better part of an hour talking with Gerald about Evelyn. The corporal felt certain she remained hidden away at Fort Niagara.

The assurance of her well-being throughout the endless months of their separation made Christopher extremely lighthearted. It seemed that the whole countryside rejoiced with him now in his happiness. The first bright hues of autumn appeared in the trees, and there was a hint of fall in the air. Best of all, every mile along the trail brought Chris closer to Evie.

Chris rode toward the head of the long column comprising General Sullivan's expedition force. As he passed a string of packhorses, Chris spied Garth Kinyon riding toward him. He reined his mount off the trail and stopped.

The tracker motioned with his chin in the direction of Gerald Blake. "How's the lad's leg doin'?"

"Great. Really great. He's been able to get up and walk around a little already. Even though the surgeons think complete bed rest is the only tried-and-true method, they haven't dissuaded him from getting an hour's exercise every day."

"Good. I'm right glad to hear that."

Chris nodded. "He wants to continue on with us till we're only a few days shy of Fort Niagara, then return to the fort on his own, as if he escaped our clutches and trekked all the way back himself. He is desperate to get his wife and Evie out safely before those two decide to take matters into their own hands."

Tucking his grizzled chin, the tracker looked askance at him. "Now that would be a fool thing, wouldn't it? Them gals might could sneak out of the fort, but to get past the Indians?" He shook his head.

"Gerald says they have a map and that he bargained with some Senecas for various articles of clothing. Knowing Evie, she'd be daring enough to try an escape if she felt we might be within a few days' march."

"And with all them redskins on the British side—and who knows how many other spies—the lobsterbacks would know just when that would be. Did I tell ya they were so sure we were on our way to Newtown they had those breastworks dug an' covered with branches a full eight days afore we ever got there? That accounts for the wilted leaves."

Someone whacked the rear of Chris's mount, startling the animal, and Christopher had to fight to regain control.

"Some Indian scout you make, Brother," Jonathan laughed. "Don't see a grown man walking up in broad daylight."

Chris took the ribbing good-naturedly. "At least I'm smart enough to be riding horseback instead of walking on my blisters."

Jon could only grin. "Happen to locate that Indian village along the Genesee you were looking for awhile back?"

"Aye," Garth answered. "They're already pullin' out, hauling their *whole* harvest, they are. Picked every last field and tree clean."

"Well, I reckon that kept them too busy to attack any more defenseless settlers." He switched his attention to Christopher. "From what I overheard you saying when I was sneaking up, you must not have gotten the latest word. Sullivan plans to head back to Wilkes-Barre as soon as we destroy this next village."

"*What?*" Christopher was positive he hadn't heard right. "Tell me you're joking."

"I'm afraid I'm not. You know we've been on half rations since Newtown."

"Who's fault is that? You men could be harvesting those crops instead of burning them."

"Trust me, Chip, we carry as much as we can along with us before we torch the fields."

"Look, son," Garth piped in. "With four thousand hungry men an' fourteen hundred pack animals besides, those few village fields could never feed us all for long. Them cattle the army brought have already been put to the knife, remember?"

"But the fort! That's been our main objective all along, right?"

Jonathan shrugged. "It was. But apparently plans have changed."

"Well, my plans haven't changed. Evie's been waiting all these months for us to come get her. And I can't just turn around and leave her. I won't."

39

"Every time I think our circumstances are improving," Evelyn complained, burying one of Liza's dishes amid the straw in a wooden packing crate, "something happens to spoil everything." Then recalling how fragile her friend's good spirits had been since the recent loss of her husband, Evie softened the tactless statement with a chuckle. "I can just hear Susannah. *'Tis not what happens to one, but rather how one handles oneself which matters most.*"

To Evie's relief, Liza giggled too. She placed a large pot from the tabletop in the bottom of the next carton and added another layer of clean straw. "I've often wondered how many pearls of wisdom that English lass actually has tucked away in that memory of hers. As I recall, there was one for every occasion."

"So true." Evie straightened to ease a kink in her back. She swept a glance around the bleak room, now more bare than ever with most of Liza's possessions packed for transport. "Well, I would imagine that's what becomes of a young woman who spends so much time in the study of the Scriptures. Everyone knows that particular endeavor is supposed to be the exclusive province of our more learned men. But perhaps no one ever informed Susannah about that. My brother, Morgan, told me that when the lads from the college in Princeton would frequent the inn where Susannah worked, she asked them so many questions they were compelled to study doubly hard in order to come up with proper answers for her. She's the chief reason they knew enough to pass their examinations!"

Liza smiled wistfully. "Mistress Haynes was such a lovely lady. So kind and thoughtful to everyone, whether patriot or Royal soldier. It's been my dearest quest to follow her example."

Arranging handfuls of straw to separate a stack of bowls as she worked, Evelyn mulled over her friend's remark. "It seems whether I wanted to or not, I've certainly done a good share of Bible study myself this past year or so. The truth is, had it not been for the comfort I found in reading of King David's own struggles in the Psalms, I doubt I'd have survived these many months of confinement." Evie frowned. "Speaking of confinements, I do hope the crate Byron is building to house me won't be awfully cramped and dark."

Liza smiled. "I promise to get you out of it the very second everyone is occupied with the business of sailing."

A new flood of emotion overwhelmed Evie. "Oh, Liza," she wailed. "Why? How could our army come this close and then turn back? Only a few weeks more and I could have been with Chris. This is too much. Too much. My hopes are constantly raised only to be dashed again. I'm so very weary of it."

"When I think of the amount of work my Gerald put into that map," Liza murmured. "The raft of questions he risked asking about the terrain and everything."

"Not to mention all his bargaining to obtain the Indian clothes." Evie looked down at the comfortable moccasins adorning her feet beneath her gathered homespun skirt. She'd worn them since the day he brought them home. "Thanks to him, the map is ever so detailed. Every last trail in every direction is clearly marked." She paused and idly plucked a straw from the edge of the crate. "I could have easily avoided the Indians for the few days it would have taken to reach the military column. I just know it."

Liza regarded her steadily. "Don't be disheartened, Evie," she said gently. "You'll get to your Chris yet, you'll see. It will just take a little longer, is all."

"We mustn't forget about that fox, Captain Long, waiting as always in Montreal."

"You mustn't worry. Byron told me to go in where the animals are kept and collect armfuls of straw to cover the box just before we dock."

The remark far from cheered Evie. "How delightful! My new quarters will be devoid of light, space, *and* air."

"Oh, Evie," Liza chided. "You know it'll only be during the times of loading and unloading. Now that the danger here at the fort is past, very few of the other women will be coming with us, so you'll be able to stay right in the cabin with me."

"That's all well and good," Evie replied, unconvinced. "But when we reach port and Captain Long catches the fervently awaited sight of you disembarking, you can wager he'll tear apart every crate aboard ship. My only hope would be to jump off before we anchor . . . if I knew how to swim, that is."

A curious expression clouded Liza's features, and she looked away. "Actually, there is one other small obstacle."

Evie prickled with uneasiness. "How small?"

Liza grimaced and nibbled her lip. "This particular ship only goes as far as the head of the Saint Lawrence River. There are rapids—"

"Rapids?"

"We'll have to portage around them, then board another vessel. You know, the way they do at Niagara Falls when cargo is taken up to Lake Erie."

Evie's mouth fell open. *"Are you trying to tell me I'm to be carted for miles inside a sealed crate? Over a bumpy trail?"*

"Well—" Liza flicked a hand futilely in the air. "It's not that far. Really it's not."

Clamping her mouth shut, Evie rolled her gaze heavenward. "This is too much." She shook her head. "I'd rather take my chances in the woods. If I could just steal a horse—or, better yet," she added bitterly, "if my own horse hadn't been already shipped off to Montreal. . . ."

Liza held up a hand for silence and directed her attention

outside, toward the distinct sounds of a commotion. She put a finger to her lips, then went to the window and opened it.

"What's the fuss?" somebody hollered across the parade ground.

"Rangers!" a man answered. "Four of 'em. They escaped the rebel force and are ridin' in now."

"That's a bit of good news for the fort," Liza said, turning to Evie.

"I wonder where it was that they left the column. Liza, go find out the details. I need to know more. Much more. Maybe you can learn exactly where the American army turned around and started back. Please! Do it for me!"

Her friend scalded her with a glare.

More desperate than ever, Evie took Liza by the shoulders and turned her for the door, giving her a little push. "Please. What can it hurt?"

Liza's forehead crinkled with a troubled frown, but she released the bolt and left without a word.

Please, let the army be closer than previously reported, Evie pleaded. *Someplace marked on the map.* The more she thought about being nailed inside a wooden crate and carried aboard some vessel, the more Evie doubted she could go through with such a plan. Who knew what horrors might befall her—if indeed she could endure being in such a state to begin with!

Mentally, Evie reviewed the items Gerald had collected in the event they could arrange an escape for her—and themselves, if it became necessary. They were now piled in the attic—more than sufficient supplies.

As usual, a celebration would take place in the fort this eve for the return of the rangers. Perhaps while everyone was occupied, Evie could slip out unnoticed. With her mind fixed on this plan, she rushed into the bedroom and closed the door, then hurriedly climbed up to the attic. She tossed down the loaded haversacks and knapsack, a heavy shawl, and some blankets. There was no way on earth she could simply sail off in the morning. Crate or no, the vessel would be going hundreds of miles in the wrong direction!

Barely had Evie gotten back down from the attic when the front door crashed open. She dived behind the bed.

Footsteps ran toward the bedchamber, and the door was flung wide. "Evie!" Liza whispered with tremendous urgency. "Evie!"

Raising her head, Evelyn peeked over the counterpane.

Her friend gave the door a shove behind her and dropped down to the floor beside Evie. She seized Evie's forearms, her face absolutely white. *"He's alive, Evie! My Gerald. He's alive!"*

"What?"

"It's true." Liza's dark eyes shimmered with tears of joy. "Gerald was gravely wounded and captured, but the rangers say he was doing fine when they left. They said he was being treated well, that one of the scouts visited him frequently, bringing him things as if they were old friends. *He's alive!"*

Overcome with joy for Liza, Evelyn rose to her knees and grabbed her friend in a hard hug, alternately laughing and crying with her. When at last the shock subsided, Evie eased back and sank down on her heels. "Will you still take the ship now or wait here until a prisoner exchange can be arranged?"

Liza heaved a sigh. "According to the rangers, they have no prisoners to exchange." Her gaze fell to the belongings scattered about the floor, and she sobered. "So. You'd already made up your mind to take your chances in the forest before I even walked out the door."

Evie felt a flush creep up her neck. "I have to try, Liza. Please understand."

"I more than understand. I'm coming with you."

❦ ❦

Evelyn could not believe she had relented and allowed herself to be sealed up inside the rough wooden crate after all. Liza's reasoning had made sense at the time—that it would provide the easiest, safest way for Evie to be spirited out of the fort. And she couldn't deny it would be much easier to leave the ship in the middle of the night.

She and Liza had decided it was best not to tell Byron their true plan. He had taken on so much responsibility for them once Gerald had mistakenly been reported dead. Surely he'd try his utmost to stop them from undertaking such a dangerous venture. So they allowed him to believe they were going to sail as previously arranged.

But now, hunched inside the fathomless darkness of this airless nailed-shut box, Evie realized this was far worse than any prison could ever be. Perspiration gathered on her forehead and upper lip. She would never erase from her mind the sound of the succession of nails . . . one after another . . . being driven into the lid of the crate. Or worse, being hoisted to the men's shoulders and carried none too gently up the loading plank. It had made her dizzy, and she'd bumped her head when the crate had been set down with a thud. The rough interior provided virtually no room to move or change position, and Evie's hysteria began to mount as she waited an interminable forever for Liza—or anyone—to open this confounded thing and get her out. She tried to calm herself with shallow breaths, forcing herself to relax.

The thud of heavy footsteps came down the steps. The muffled voices of men, of other crates being set down nearby.

Evie barely suppressed the need to cry out as an annoying cramp started in her lower leg. As a last resort she clamped a hand over her mouth and pressed hard until the men went above. Then she drew a deep breath. Finding it more fetid than satisfying, she wondered grimly if this supposed hiding place would turn out to be her coffin.

She wanted out. *Out!* Now! Evie knotted her fists and started rocking from side to side. If she hadn't been hunched over her knees and facing downward, she would have banged on the lid until somebody came.

A Scripture, she told herself. *Think of a Scripture.* Racking her brain, she wondered if the basket the disciples used to lower Saul from the city wall to keep him from being discovered by the authorities had been this confining. At least he must have been able to breathe, she decided glumly. Then a phrase from the Psalms drifted to her. *"Hope thou in God."* She had to hope.

It was all she had. "'What time I am afraid, I will trust in thee,'" she said under her breath.

"Hush in there," came Liza's fevered whisper. "I'm here. I'll get you out." The claw of a hammer wedged beneath the edge of the lid, and a nail groaned. Evie arched her back to press against the wood.

"What'cha doin' down there?" a loud male voice rasped from the deck above.

Liza hesitated a second. "I . . . um, need something I packed."

"Oh. Well, I'll help ya with that big ole crate, missy."

Liza was alone down here, Evelyn knew, as fear over her friend's vulnerability shot through her.

"Mistress," Liza corrected firmly, even as his boots clomped down the steps. "Mistress Gerald Blake. And thank you, no. I wouldn't want to trouble you. They're just some of my . . . unmentionable things."

"No trouble a'tall, ma'am. I'm known for bein' able to help a damsel with her *frilly undertrappings.* Whenever, wherever I'm needed." Evie could easily picture the leer his tone implied.

"My husband," Liza said calmly, moving to the opposite side of Evie's crate, "always said one of my screams could rattle the rafters of a big barn. I'd be most pleased to demonstrate that considerable talent."

"Er, if it's all the same to you," he said, his voice receding, "I'll take yer word for it."

Liza's ability to handle the tense situation amazed Evie. She dearly loved the young woman and had been surprised a number of times at her quick wit.

After a few moments of silence, Liza set to her chore again.

When she finally lifted the lid away, Evie came with it, gulping great draughts of fresh air, revelling in the light the single wall lamp provided. "Byron needed to make more air holes," she gasped between breaths. She pushed a damp braid over her shoulder and sagged against the lip of the box.

"Soon," Liza said, helping her out, "you'll have all the fresh air you want. Most of the seamen have gone ashore to get in on all that free-flowing rum at the celebration. We'll have little trouble sneaking off."

Her words filled Evelyn with hope and vigor. "You see? God *is* with us!"

"Evie," Liza said, placing a hand on her shoulder, "there's still the matter of all those hundreds of Indians the two of us will have to pass before we ever reach the woods. They're camped right up to the dock, you know."

Evelyn only smiled as she straightened the gathered skirt and belted tunic of her Seneca attire. "You jest! As soon as you change into your own Indian clothes, we won't have any trouble at all."

40

Evelyn tapped the toe of her moccasin impatiently on the rung of the ladder leading out of the hold of the two-masted schooner. With the top of her head still below the main deck, she could see naught but a mast and some stars, but after having endured seclusion for fifteen long months, she drank in those sights and hungered for more. Where in the world was Liza?

The night breeze rustled through the ropes, tinkling the rings against the mast and spars. Gentle sounds, against the occasional creak of timber as the docked ship rode the lapping waves of Lake Ontario. From far away came shouts and laughter and the even fainter muffled celebration noises from inside Fort Niagara.

Wait, wait, Evie railed silently. It was all she'd done these past two years. Patience would never be considered her finest virtue. She shifted the considerable and cumbersome bulk of a musket, the two stuffed haversacks, and Liza's blanket, all hidden beneath her own blanket, which she now wore like a hooded shawl. Evie felt like a traveling squaw.

"Psst!" came Liza's urgent whisper.

At last! Grasping the ladder tightly, she struggled up to the next rung and peeked out.

"Hurry!" Liza beckoned with swift motions. "The watchman is at the stern."

The cumbersome burdens hindered any ease of climbing, but Evie managed another few rungs.

Liza grasped her hand and pulled with all her might.

With her friend's assistance, Evie hauled herself and their gear out of the bowels of the ship, and her feet finally gained the deck.

"Quick! Step to!" Liza muttered frantically, tugging on her again. "The gangplank." She drew Evie toward the sloping bridge leading down to the dock.

Evie's blanket slipped off her head, exposing her and the assortment of strapped-on bundles. "Look what you've done," she groused in a loud whisper. She stopped and reached behind her for the cover.

"Shh." Her friend tried to lend a hand, but the woven wool caught on the musket. Liza gave a fierce jerk, and the weapon knocked Evie's other burdens off-balance.

One of the shoulder packs slipped down her arm. "Stop. Will you just stop?" Seething, Evie unslung one of the haversacks. "Here. Take this. Put it under your cloak."

"I can't. The ship's officer will notice the bulge when I walk down the gangplank."

Evie stiffened. She shoved Liza into the shadow of one of the tall masts. *"The ship's officer?"*

Liza shrugged. "From what the man on watch told me, the officer won't leave. It's his duty to monitor who comes and goes."

For a moment Evie entertained the delightful thought of strangling her best friend. Then she rejected the notion. "You got me on a ship with no possible way to get off except to jump? And with all this truck?" She was so overloaded the straps cut into her shoulders. She pushed the haversack at Liza. "Take your bag now, or I'll chuck it overboard."

"Oh, all right." Liza's lips flattened into a line. "But there's no need to get so upset. I have everything figured out."

"No need to get upset, you say?" Evie's voice was quickly rising above a whisper.

"Who goes there?"

Startled by the deep male voice, Evie flung her blanket over her hair.

"'Tis merely I, sir. Mistress Blake." Liza stepped toward him. "This squaw has been giving me a difficult time. She wants everything we've traded for, but she's too lazy to carry it by herself."

The officer's boots made hollow reports over the deck as he approached. "Squaw? What squaw?"

"Why, this one, of course." Liza grabbed Evie's arm and nudged her forward.

"I don't recall her coming aboard."

Liza looked at him, then swung to Evelyn. "And I don't recall saying I would help you carry all this back to that camp of yours. If you hadn't been so greedy . . ."

Evie could tell from Liza's stare that she expected some sort of answer, but she also knew opening her mouth would reveal she was anything but an Indian.

"Oh, very well," Liza said on a weary breath. "But I'll carry this bothersome bag only until we come to another Indian. Is that clear?"

Evie uttered a deep grunt.

Liza hung the haversack over her own shoulder. "Come along, and be quick about it. I've a celebration to attend back at the fort." Elevating her nose, she swept past the officer and down the gangplank.

With pounding heart, Evie ducked her blanketed head and followed meekly after her friend.

The officer snagged her arm as she passed him. "Wait just one minute." He raised the back of the blanket. "Mistress Blake," he called. "Are you actually trading a musket to a heathen? Does General Carleton know about this?"

In his viselike grip, Evie was powerless to move. She held her tongue and stared at the deck beneath her.

Liza, having reached the landing, whirled around. "There's nothing to be alarmed about, my good man. The b-a-r-r-e-l happens to be c-r-a-c-k-e-d." She smiled disarmingly. "The perfect musket for trading, don't you think? Especially for the exquisite mink furs she had with her."

From beneath the edge of the blanket shawl, Evie caught the greedy smirk that widened his full lips. Then she nearly lost her balance as he propelled her forward with his boot. "Off with you, then. And don't think this means you can come aboard my ship anytime you please."

Evelyn's feet barely touched the gangplank as she ran down to Liza and hurried with her toward the campfires of the Indian encampment. Inwardly she marveled over the way Liza had handled herself throughout the crisis. Obviously Evie had underestimated this Boston lass.

"Now what?" she asked after they'd gotten out of the man's earshot. "He's probably still watching us. How are we going to get away?"

Liza pointed through the darkness to a giant oak. "See that big spraddling tree? I'll take off my dress there, then we'll both have on just our Indian clothes. With such a mix of tribes in the area, we should be able to simply walk right past them all without anyone being the wiser. So much better than trying to sneak, wouldn't you say? *That looks so suspicious.*"

"Are you quite sure you've never done this kind of thing before?" Evie asked in wonder. "For a novice, you're quite adept."

Her friend giggled under her breath as they reached the inky shade. "I got a lot of practice, if you recall, sneaking out to see Gerald when I was still with my mother in Boston."

"But this is life or death." Dropping her load, Evie began helping Liza out of her cloak and dress.

"If you'd met Mama, you'd understand that the danger was no less then. I suppose when it comes to being with the man I love, I dare to be much braver."

"Don't we all." Evie lifted the dress over Liza's head.

As her friend adjusted the garb she'd been wearing under her regular clothing, Evie untied the wrapped blanket, then rolled the discarded items in it and tied them. She passed a haversack to Liza. "Here. Put this on and turn around." Then she lashed the bulky roll onto the bag and picked up her own things, along with the musket and ammunition box.

Last of all, they dropped their blankets over their heads and clutched them tightly under their chins.

"Ready?" Evie asked, trying not to dwell on the fact that if they failed their next test, the consequences they'd suffer at the hands of the Indians could be much worse.

Liza's hand trembled, but she reached for Evie's and gave a firm squeeze. "Yes. Time's awasting."

Looking neither right nor left, their blankets pulled taut around their faces, Evie mentally ordered her feet to start moving. A rod, then two, and nothing happened. With growing confidence, she kept going, conscious of her friend's footsteps at her side. They walked past many an evening fire, many a spread blanket where men tossed a form of dice, past women stirring cauldrons over a fire or squatting to chat. And no one paid them any mind.

Soon they reached the outer edge of the wigwams and started across the wide swath of clearing beyond the temporary camp. Evie tried to dismiss the feeling that a thousand eyes were on their backs. After all, it would be difficult for someone near the brightness of a fire to focus into the deep darkness outside the rim of light. But reaching the forest and entering its blessed ebony sanctuary eased her mind. "I can't believe how easily we just walked right by all those campfires."

"Yes," Liza said with a nervous giggle. "We made it."

"This is only the beginning, though, you know. We must walk all through the night. Put as much distance between us and them as possible. If we're lucky, no one will discover you're not aboard the ship until after it sails. We'd best not count on that, though."

"Which way are we heading?"

Evie peered up at the sky, then back toward the lake. They would shortly be leaving the body of water, which indicated a northerly direction. And the moon and stars would constantly change position. Navigating in the darkness would be a challenge. She'd heard stories of grown men who had lost their bearings in the dense wooded areas surrounding the Wyoming Valley, only to become hopelessly confused within a mile of home. But she had studied the map of this area very intently. And she needed to convince Liza she could find the way for both of them.

"Well?"

Father in heaven, what should I do? An incredibly simple answer came to Evie. "We're going to walk to where the trail cuts into the woods. The one that leads down to the Genesee River. We'll take that. It *was* the last place the Americans were before they turned around."

"But I thought we were going to stay off the trails."

"We will." Evie patted her friend's shoulder reassuringly in the dark. "After it's light. Until then we can cover a lot of ground . . . providing my back doesn't break from this load, first."

With the sprawling camp still in sight, the two picked their way gingerly over the uneven, debris-scattered forest ground until they reached the packed surface of the trail. Then they turned onto it and headed into the dense wilderness.

The last specks of light from the fort quickly disappeared after the first curve in the trace, rendering them more alone than they had ever been.

A surge of exhilaration filled Evelyn. This was her first walk in freedom since she'd sought refuge within the four stifling walls of the Blakes' quarters a lifetime ago. Despite the nippy air, she let her blanket slip from her head and lengthened her stride, allowing the air to waft across her face. She inhaled the piney fragrance, the cool freshness.

Beside her, Liza jumped. "What was that?" She latched onto Evie.

"What?"

"I heard something."

"Probably a small animal, is all."

Liza's nails dug into Evie's forearm, right through the blanket. "How can you be sure?"

The pensive hoot of an owl broke the stillness as its great wings flapped noisily through the treetops.

Liza shuddered and inched closer.

"It's harmless, really," Evie assured her.

"Why aren't the animals and birds sleeping? It does happen to be nighttime. Or don't they ever sleep? We could be eaten by a wolf or a bear."

"You've never been in the woods at night before, have you?"

"No. Why would I? I went by ship from Boston to Halifax, then to the fort."

Evie smiled to herself. Liza was a city girl, just as she had been a long time ago. Unslinging the musket, she cradled it in her arms. "Stick close to me. If anybody does any eating, it's going to be us."

❦ ❦

Evelyn stirred, rousing from her sleep beneath the prickly, drooping branches of a fir which fashioned a kind of den around them. Her head ached, her shoulders ached, and her back and neck were so stiff she could barely move. Struggling to open her eyes, she recalled the reason for her misery . . . lugging those ungainly bundles and the heavy musket through the forest trail. Her shoulders felt as if the skin had been rubbed away by the coarse straps of the bags. Lying on one of the blankets with Liza, with the other spread over them, she exhaled and snuggled closer to her friend for warmth.

In what seemed only a few moments later, Evie came fully awake. She sat up and peered through the fronds of the tree to decipher the position of the sun. In the dense wood, however, it was unaccountably hard to tell what time it was. She eased onto her tender feet and raised a branch enough to step out from its shelter.

The day was overcast, but Evelyn surmised it must be mid-morning. Through a break in the trees, she made out some heavier clouds to the north. Blast! That's all they needed. Rain to blot out their only means of finding direction, plus soak them clear through. She glared down at her feet. The moccasins whose thin soles had seemed so exceptionally comfortable inside Liza's quarters left much to be desired when crossing rock- and twig-strewn ground in the pitch dark of night.

Evie strained her ears to make out distant noises. Men's voices! The guttural tones were coming from the south, the opposite direction of the fort, thank heaven. Still, one could not be too cautious. Shrinking back beneath the cover of the tree, she knelt beside Liza and shook her shoulder.

Her friend came slowly and grumblingly awake.

"Shh," Evie warned.

Liza's brown eyes popped open.

Evie pointed toward the southerly trail, where the approaching voices were growing clearer and closer by the second.

Liza started to rise to a sitting position, then with a stifled moan, fell back. Obviously Evie's muscles weren't the only ones making a loud protest after the unaccustomed labor.

Evie placed a staying hand on Liza's arm, and the two of them remained completely still under the heavy branches of the fir a mere rod off the trail.

Five Indian braves came into view, loping along at a slow but steady run. Their easy conversation indicated that they weren't the least out of breath.

Evie peered at the ground directly beyond the perimeter of the tree. As careful as they'd tried to be leaving the trail for the sheltering tree, she couldn't be sure that she and Liza had left no telltale signs of their presence. As far as she could tell, everything appeared normal, but she was no tracker. She hardly breathed until the small band had moved completely out of sight and beyond their hearing.

"What were they saying?" Liza asked.

"I have no idea."

"But you spent lots of time with them when you were captured, didn't you?"

"Only a week or so. And I could never discern a single word.

Once I thought I'd figured out the word for water, but when I used it, they just looked confused. Their language is different from any other I've ever heard. Not at all similar to French or German."

"Oh, well. I suppose it makes no difference, as long as we don't actually run into any of them. You did say we would stay off the trail today, didn't you?"

Nodding, Evie began rolling the blanket they'd spread over themselves during the night.

Liza snatched it back. "We don't have to get up already, do we?"

"Why not? We're awake."

"Tell that to my poor body," Liza moaned.

Evelyn offered a hand. "You'll loosen up once we get walking again."

"I'm not so sure." She struggled to her feet, groaning as she alternately flexed and straightened. "I thought doing all that army laundry was keeping me limber, but I declare I hurt all over."

"Me, too." Evie handed Liza a chunk of beef jerky from one of the haversacks. "I'm the one who spent the better part of endless months in an attic where I couldn't even stand up. But take heart, old girl. We can do this. We'll just keep putting one foot in front of the other, remembering that every single step will bring us closer to Christopher and Gerald."

Liza, her wavy brunette hair a mat of pine needles and sappy twigs, wrapped the blanket more snugly about herself and bit into the meat with closed eyes. "One foot in front of the other," she chanted. "One foot in front of the other."

A pang of guilt assaulted Evie. She shouldn't have brought her friend along. Liza would have had little trouble making her way back to Boston by herself. Gerald would have had the peace of knowing she was safe and waiting until he was free to go to her. But the chances of the two of them ever making it through Indian country were very slim. Gerald's friend Byron had been against the venture from the start. *"Even if you do elude the Indians,* "he'd said with that cocksure look of his, *"the wilderness itself is as wild and treacherous as any painted brave."*

The image of the redheaded corporal's smug expression and tone brought Evelyn's stubborn streak to the fore. She had experienced both of those things before and managed to survive. This time she had a map. She turned a satisfied glance down to the haversack in which it was neatly folded.

No, it was too late to turn back. Liza would be arrested right along with her. Like it or not, they had chosen this course. Now they had to stick to it. "Let me braid your hair, dear heart," she said soothingly. "Then we'll be on our way."

41

The cloudy sky prevented getting directions by the sun. Regardless of the potential danger, Evelyn and Liza were forced to stay close to the trail all that day. They took each other's hand and moved in tense silence, keeping their eyes and ears open for unusual sounds or movement.

All around them, the glory of autumn was fading. Red, yellow, and gold leaves swirled and fluttered downward on the cool air, creating a brilliant carpet on the forest floor. But Evie scarcely appreciated the season's colors as she focused her thoughts on the task at hand. She felt especially responsible for Liza's well-being and vowed that her friend would come to no harm.

A little before noon, something huge and dark stirred in the path a dozen yards ahead. Evelyn's breath caught. A black bear! She stopped in her tracks and wordlessly squeezed Liza's hand.

Her friend, following Evie's gaze, gasped and turned rigid. They stood absolutely still and watched the beast raise his nose to sniff the air. He grunted and swung his massive head back and forth, then lumbered away and out of sight, fallen branches and twigs snapping and cracking beneath the massive paws.

Liza's knees buckled, and she crumpled to the leaf-strewn ground, her dark eyes woeful.

Evie sank down beside her friend. "Thank Providence there was no wind to carry our scent to him," she whispered.

"What else must we face?" Liza cried in despair. "What else? Three more parties of Indians we had to hide from this morning—then those on horseback. Now a bear. I've never been so frightened in my life."

Evie leaned closer and hugged the young woman's slim shoulders. "So far, the Lord has taken care of us," she reminded Liza gently. "And I don't think he's brought us this far to desert us, do you? Let's trust him to keep us from peril the rest of the way too."

Liza held Evie's gaze for a full minute. Waves of emotion crossed her expressive oval face like storm clouds across a sky. Then she gave a thin smile. "Yes. You're right." Gathering herself, she stood up.

Her friend's renewed optimism cheered Evelyn. She rose and joined Liza, and they continued on.

The days were growing shorter, and the impending darkness was a greater threat than Evie had counted on. When late that afternoon they made a wide circle around the first Indian village, one the map indicated was barely twenty miles from Fort Niagara, her original optimism vanished. She had to fight hard not to let her friend know that after stumbling along a good part of one whole night and most of the next day, they had made so little progress.

"Hey, that tree should make a good shelter for tonight," Liza murmured, pointing to a hemlock with low-hanging branches, thick ferns around its base, and a rocky outcropping just behind. "Don't you think?"

Evie nodded. "Right now, I'm so tired I could probably sleep up on the rocks themselves."

They wasted no time in spreading out their blankets and settling down for the night. Evie's eyelids had never felt heavier. She welcomed the chance to close them and sleep.

Suddenly a piercing screech rent the night.

Liza bolted upright. "What was that?" she hissed, clutching the blanket to her throat.

Evelyn felt around for her musket. "I would guess a cata-
mount. Go back to sleep. I'll sit up for a while and keep watch.
Later, you can take a turn while I sleep."

Evie wasn't as confident as she sounded, but having assumed the role of leader in this venture, she knew better than
to reveal her misgivings to her jittery companion. She patted
Liza's upper arm. "Go ahead, lie down. We'll be fine."

With a resigned moan, Liza finally complied.

Evie tightened her lips and grimaced at the cruelty of fate.
She had no idea how she'd keep her eyes open half the night,
but she leaned back against the gnarled tree trunk and stared
into the black void.

Not once did the wildcat make its presence known again,
but the night's rest was ruined nonetheless.

The dawn of the next morning brought more leaden
clouds, more cold gloom. Despair crept into Evie's soul as she
ate a ration of jerky. Tired before she started, it was only the
second day. They would have to spend yet another day close
to this Indian trail, constantly on the alert, hiding from pass-
ersby, and skirting Indian settlements, wasting so much more
time. But it would serve no purpose to complain about it, so
she forced a smile and stood on her throbbing feet.

Liza swallowed her last mouthful of dried meat and struggled to her feet. The two of them shook out their blankets and
wrapped them about their shoulders.

Evelyn slid a glance down at the packs. She couldn't bear
the thought of strapping them to her raw shoulders again, but
their survival depended upon the dried food and other neces-
sities. There was nothing that could be eliminated—not the
musket, flour, clothing, rope, tools and utensils, bedding,
flints, or the cartridges Gerald had made for the musket.
Everything was essential. She looked at Liza. "This is not
going to work."

"Are you suggesting we turn around and go back?"

"No. Never. But I do have an idea. You stay here with our
things while I backtrack to the Indian village. If I could

manage to steal a horse from a pasture—or even a cow—we'd have an animal to carry our supplies. We could go a lot faster."

The color fled her friend's face. "Do you know how risky that would be? What if you were caught? I'd be stranded here by myself." Then her jaw set. "Besides, that would be stealing."

"Taking one horse from a people who stole sixty from the Haynes farm?" Evie looked askance at her. "The Iroquois culture is built around stealing from other tribes, not to mention from white settlers."

"But was that the tribe who stole your horses?"

The young woman's simple logic bordered on being maddening, and as tired as she was after the practically sleepless night, Evie was in no mood to argue. "Tell you what," she said with an exasperated sigh. "I'll see if there's a Narragansett Pacer in the pasture. If so, that's the one I'll take."

Liza's mouth drooped as she shook her head and placed a hand on Evelyn's forearm. "Please, don't go off and leave me. We must stay together. For both our sakes."

Evie could not bear the pain in her friend's eyes. "Oh, very well. For now."

❧ ❧

After crossing a frigid stream shoeless, the two removed their gear and sat on a log to rest while they dried their tender feet.

"I wonder which would have been worse," Evie droned in a monotone. "The blisters I would have gotten from wearing my hard-soled shoes, or the bruises I'm getting in these paper-thin moccasins."

Liza raised an eyebrow. "That is something we'll never know since our proper footwear is on its way to Montreal with the rest of our worldly possessions."

"Well," Evie said with a shrug, "maybe we're better off in the long run. Most frontiersmen around Wilkes-Barre seem to prefer these."

"But is it by choice? Is there a cobbler in Wilkes-Barre?"

"Come to think of it, no."

"Hm. Perhaps Gerald would be wise to set up shop in some

more remote location like the Wyoming Valley. Boston, like so many other cities, has more than its share of shoemakers."

Evelyn chuckled. "After these past few days, I'd think you'd have had enough of life in remote regions."

Liza bubbled into a laugh.

Somehow, the unexpected touch of merriment made the dreary day less gloomy, their circumstances less terrible. But the moment of humor faded, and they slipped into their plain moccasins again.

"You'll probably think I've gone mad," Liza admitted with a wry smirk, "but when we're making our way through the woods, I feel a certain . . . thrill, for want of a better word. I mean, here we are, the two of us, setting foot in places where it's likely no white man has ever trod before. Oh, I know they've walked the trail over yonder. But away from the trail, making our own way, well—maybe even the Indians haven't seen everything. That meadow we circuited not too far back, for instance—the one with the knoll rising up in the center, remember?"

Evie nodded, enjoying the sound of her friend's pleasingly low voice again after so many long silent periods.

"It was so inviting," Liza went on wistfully. "Surely if anyone else had ever seen it, people would be living there. I could picture a snug little cabin on that rise, a roaring fire in the hearth, a grand glass window I could gaze out of and know that all I surveyed belonged to Gerald and me."

"You did see our Drummond coach horse grazing out in the pasture, didn't you?" Evie teased.

"Yes. Right beside Gerald's cobbler shop," she returned brightly, then seized Evie's hands. "We are going to make it, aren't we? We've enough food to last us three weeks, and the more of it we eat, the less our packs will weigh. God willing, all we have to do is keep out of sight, keep dry—and try not to think about our miserable feet."

Evie squeezed Liza's hand and nodded, preferring not to add another very real obstacle to the young woman's list. The shallow brook they had just waded was one thing . . . but much deeper, much swifter rivers lay ahead of them. What then?

Suddenly Liza stiffened and jerked out of her grasp. Eyes wide, she put a finger to her lips.

Evie, motionless, strained her ears, but the only other sounds in the whispery stillness of the woods were the babbling stream and the few birds flitting among the trees.

Easing off the log, Liza knelt behind it and pointed through the thick undergrowth ahead.

Evelyn signaled for her to stay low, then crept forward, testing every footstep for sound. She wondered what had frightened Liza. Very carefully she made her way through a tangle of leafless vines. Then she heard it.

A whinny.

Her heart leapt. A horse! *Please, let it be alone!* How incredibly wonderful it would be if one of her very own scattered pacers had wandered this far north and happened to be grazing nearby! Surely no one could fault her for reclaiming an animal that was rightfully hers. Of course, the odds of that kind of miracle were less than slim; they were almost nonexistent. Still, she and Liza were in dire need of a horse.

Evie dropped onto her belly and edged toward what appeared to be a small glen.

A dollop of rain plopped onto her nose, then two more. The storm was about to break, and they would need to chop branches for a shelter. *Dear Lord, please let that horse be alone. I must hurry back to Liza.*

Coming to the end of the log, she ignored the gathering intensity of the pattering droplets and scurried to the cover of the next bush, then the next tree trunk, and the next. At last a break in the sparse autumn foliage permitted a view of the swampy area beyond.

A bay mare grazed among the tall reeds and grasses. Oblivious to the harder rain out in the open, she munched contentedly.

A second horse stood not ten feet away from the first.

Snaking forward a few more inches, Evie saw more—four

in all—and at least one was the distinctive sorrel shade of the Narragansett breed. Then she spied the reason for their apparent lack of movement. Hobbles.

Evelyn's spirits sank. The owners had to be close by.

Then she heard new sounds, chopping and hacking noises that carried over the pouring rain. Whoever had hobbled these horses must be building a shelter to wait out the storm. Her heart sank. Obviously, she and Liza couldn't stay here.

Then her hope returned with a flash of an idea.

The horses' owners were occupied. They'd soon be inside their haven—and hopefully, confident that they'd already seen to their mounts. Then they probably wouldn't bother to check on them for some time. After dark, perhaps. Maybe not until morning.

If she took two horses, she and Liza could be far away by then. A little soaking wouldn't hurt them. They were both strong and healthy.

Evelyn glanced heavenward and smiled. No, better take only the pacer. *Thank you for sending him,* her heart sang. *It has to be a sign that we're doing the right thing.*

A wave of quiet confidence warmed Evie, and she slid through the tall grass, snaking slowly toward the hobbled pacer.

All four animals' heads came up and turned her way, but they merely paused in their chewing.

"There's a good boy," Evie murmured to the pacer. She hoped he still remembered her and wouldn't spook.

He moved a few inches away, watching her, but didn't whinny.

She took heart. "That's right, I'm the one who used to give you your oats." She slowly reached out and began working the hard knots loose. "Let's just take off this mean old rope, shall we?" she crooned under her breath, willing her cold, stiff fingers to function. Her knife would have made the job easier, she knew, but having that piece of rope intact would be better for leading him away.

The horse shifted again, tugging out of her grasp.

Blast. Stay still! Scooting ahead a little, she resumed her chore. The first leg finally freed, Evie rose to her haunches and started on the other with more nimble fingers. The knot loosened more easily.

Then something sharp jabbed her spine, and a harsh voice rasped something in the Indian tongue.

Evelyn's heart stopped beating. The rush of her pulse echoed in her ears. Only a fool would have exposed herself as she had just done. And Liza! Poor Liza! What would become of her now?

The prickling point nudged again. More quiet, lethal words.

Desperately hoping that a tomahawk would not be the first—and last—thing she saw, Evelyn swiveled around.

Her gaze took in moccasins, then crept up leather leggings, right to the barrel of a rifle aimed at her nose. She choked down her rising fear and looked up into the face of a . . . a *white man?*

The weathered, grizzled face showed its own surprise. "Confound it, you're no redskin!"

Remembering her braided hair and Seneca attire, Evie knew that from behind she had to resemble an Indian squaw. She also realized that the man before her wasn't wearing the green of Butler's butchers. A rush of hope washed through her, then ebbed. She couldn't count that much on his attire.

"You an Indian captive?" A scarred eyebrow arched. "That why you're bent on stealin' our horses?"

Evie wasn't sure how she should answer. She could easily find herself being handed over to the savages or taken back to Fort Niagara.

His glower turned to steel. He grabbed her arm and hauled her to her feet. "What's the matter? Been with the redskins so long ya can't remember how to talk English?"

"Who've you got there?" a man asked from behind Evelyn.

"Horse thief," he answered over her shoulder. "The white Indian kind."

As running footsteps came near, Evie whirled around.

The tall, bearded hunter stopped dead. His mouth gaped in shock. "Evie?" He took a step closer. "Evie?"

It can't be! "Chris?"

For a breathless instant the world stopped spinning.

A whoosh of movement, and she found herself crushed in Christopher's arms. "Evie, Evie," he was saying as he rocked her back and forth. Then his lips claimed hers.

Evie felt her feet leave the ground as Chris swept her up in his strong arms. She could do little more than hang on and kiss him back. *Christopher had come. He'd come for her.* Warm, salty tears joined the cold raindrops streaming down her face.

"What's all the commotion?" another voice asked—one strangely familiar.

Evelyn eased away enough to glance past Chris toward the soggy newcomer. "Gerald!" she cried. "It's me! Evelyn! Liza's back in the woods!"

His whoop echoed through the forest, and he took off in the direction she pointed.

Evie laughed through her tears and gazed up again into the loving blue of Christopher's eyes.

His expression was a portrait of wonder and awe, caught somewhere between an almost-smile and his own joyous tears.

"You came," she whispered, reaching to palm his bearded cheek. "You came for me."

"Oh, my dearest, dearest love." He crushed her against himself so tightly she could scarcely breathe. "I've been coming for you for a long, long time."

42

Christopher knew it was important to listen as Garth Kinyon related the safest direction to take on their return to civilization. But hard as he tried to concentrate on the man's prattle, he could not prevent his mind from straying to Evelyn. How deliciously sweet it was to have her snuggled close to him inside the limited bounds of the storm shelter. He loved feeling her next to him as she leaned against him, sharing the warmth of his blanket while the lot of them waited for the pot of water on the campfire to come to a boil.

Evie had untied the leather thongs from her braids, and her soft mass of curls framed her face. Chris could hardly believe she was here with him. The driving need to find her, to rescue her, was all that had kept him going for what seemed half a lifetime. Now he felt as though they'd never been apart—and yet it was like a dream.

His arms encircling her, he couldn't resist hugging her every few minutes, kissing her head, her cheek. And the pleasure doubled each time he did, for she smiled and pressed closer. The touch of her hand smoothing up and down his arm was heaven.

"Well, Gerald," Kinyon remarked, "it appears things worked out for ya after all."

"Quite. I couldn't be happier."

Christopher looked over at his British friend, snuggled under his blanket with his petite, dark-haired wife. It was obvious they were deeply in love. Liza's dark eyes returned her husband's adoring gazes with equal fervor.

"I'd have preferred, however," Gerald continued, "to have left your rebel camp when we first planned. The very thought of my wife wandering about in the wild these past two days, subject to all manner of danger, is most distressing."

Liza swept a glance up to her husband. "You could have returned to me sooner?"

"That's debatable," the tracker answered before Gerald had a chance to reply. "Took me and Chris four days to convince General Sullivan to release him to us and let us come for you. After all, the corporal was a prisoner of war. But Sullivan finally agreed that your husband was to be trusted and that the plan had a fair chance of succeeding."

"That plan of yours wasn't too dangerous, was it?" Liza asked, concern in her delicate features.

"Nothing of the sort, my love," Gerald told her. "Mr. Kinyon and Christopher were to wait in the woods with the horses while I returned to Fort Niagara saying I had escaped the rebel army. Then we were merely going to go out to meet them."

"Merely?" Evie repeated in a dubious tone. "You're saying I was to merely walk out of the fort with you?"

He cocked his head. "Well, we did have those Indian clothes. I was going to have you make an exit with some Indians when they came in to trade. As it is, it's quite a miracle we ran into each other. Come to think of it," he added, eyeing her sternly, "why *were* you on that trail? As I recall, you were supposed to stay far off the traces, away from the Indians."

Chris felt Evelyn's back go rigid. Obviously she had never lost her spirit. And thank the Lord for that, since without it she might not have survived all she'd been through.

"We weren't *on* the trail. Merely parallel," she answered evenly. "A calculated risk. One I'd take again rather than getting lost for good. As you must have noticed, there was no sun to guide us."

Chris barely managed to keep his grin in check.

"As it turns out," Evie continued, "it's a good thing you were delayed. Had you arrived two or three days earlier, you would have found us there, all right—along with several other soldiers who actually did escape the Americans. And they'd brought news. Not only were you alive and recovering from your wounds, but you'd received *very special* treatment from your alleged enemy."

At that disturbing implication, Chris glanced from Gerald to Garth and back.

"Oh, my!" Liza gasped. "I'd never thought of that."

The tracker kneaded his chin thoughtfully as he focused on Gerald. "Well, boy, looks like we plumb lucked out again. From what ya told us about the cloud of suspicion hangin' over that head of yours because of Miss Evelyn, I reckon they'd a strung ya up right proper for bein' a rebel agent."

Liza blinked back tears. "I wouldn't call it luck, Mr. Kinyon." She turned and flung her arms around her husband's neck. "Oh, Gerald, I'm so thankful for the mysterious workings of the Lord."

Chris watched them, profoundly grateful but just a little jealous. He wished Evie could feel as free to embrace him in front of their friends, but until they were wed, it would be improper.

Kinyon cleared his throat. "Water's boilin'." Leaning across the saddle behind him, he fetched a cinched bag, scooped out a handful of ground coffee beans, and dropped them into the pot.

The burst of rich aroma smelled better than ever to Chris. He listened to the rain against the trees and realized that all his senses seemed heightened now that Evie was with him. Chris pressed his face into her hair. "I'm never letting go of you again," he whispered at her ear.

She turned in his arms and lifted her beautiful eyes to his. "And I'll never allow you to let me go."

He took a ragged breath. "I'm sure glad to hear that. I, er, took the liberty of doing something. Saying something, actually . . ."

Evie tilted her head and stared questioningly. "Yes?"

Chris shot a quick glance around at the others, then scooted back a bit with her. The cramped space inside the spruce-and-pine shelter was woefully inadequate for gaining the privacy he might have preferred, but with the rain pelting down outside it had to suffice. "Last winter I told your brother that when I found you, we'd be married by the first justice of the peace we came to. I also told him he had no say one way or the other in the matter."

Her blue eyes flared wider. "You did? That couldn't have set very well with him. He was always a prankster himself, but when it came to his sisters, he was as heavy-handed as any father."

Chris ran the backs of his fingers over the curve of her cheekbone. "Actually, once Morgan rehinged his jaw, he agreed. I gave him no choice."

"My," Evie murmured, "you must have been forceful, to shut Morgan up that way." Her smile pleased him immensely; then it wilted suddenly. "But what about my mother and father? How much do they know?"

"Around the time you were captured by the Indians, the British evacuated Philadelphia."

"Yes, I'd heard that from Gerald."

"Well, your parents feared reprisals from the patriots, so they sailed for England to join your sister there. Morgan wrote to them last winter, informing you were at Fort Niagara, and stressed that it was imperative the information be kept secret. He also wrote that we would see to your safe release. He didn't want to cause them further worry."

"Good. Good." She nodded in thought. "But did he tell them about our betrothal, sweetheart?"

The endearment washed over Chris in a warm wave. "I doubt it. I don't think he truly believes it'll come to pass himself."

Her chuckle was music to his ears. "The poor, poor dears. I have been a bother. But with everything that's transpired, I'm sure my family will be glad just to know I'll finally be settling down. By the way, my love—" her fingertip toyed with his wiry beard—"with all the planning you've been doing, have you decided exactly where that will be?"

A shadow loomed over them, and Kinyon, on his knees, held out a steaming tin mug. "Thought ya might like to share some coffee."

"Thanks." Chris offered Evie the first sip, noticing that Gerald and Liza were engrossed in their own conversation. They must have been as worried about one another as he had been about Evelyn. His gaze returned to her as she blew on the hot liquid, then tasted it with caution.

"Mmm," she sighed. "I've been longing for something to warm my insides." After another sip she handed the cup to him. "You never answered. Where will we be going?"

There was only one place they could go. "Back to Princeton, for now. You'll be safe there. In your absence, the British gave up trying to whip us northerners. The conflict has moved mostly to the south. Georgia, the Carolinas." To keep from elaborating, he took a gulp of the hot brew.

"And you, sweetheart," she prodded. "What about you and the war? A few minutes ago, you told me you never wanted to be separated from me again."

"I don't. You know I don't. I'll stay as long as I can, I promise. And return every chance I get. But our freedom is far from won. And—" he brushed her tempting lips with his—"I've been neglecting my duty for a long time while I was chasing all over the countryside after my blue-eyed angel."

The hint of a smile played over her mouth as she searched his face. "I know. That's what kept me alive, knowing that you'd never give up. Not my Christopher Drummond." Her index finger twined around a lock of hair lying on his brow. "Princeton," she mused. "Your letters said Susannah and Mary were there."

"And Prudence."

"Christopher's been kind enough to invite Liza and me to stay with his family until we can make arrangements to travel on to Boston," Gerald said from across the fire.

Evie looked over at them and smiled. "Oh, you'll love his guardians. They've been such a cheery haven in these hard times. I think their coach house should be renamed. The Good Samaritan Inn, maybe. It's much more fitting."

Liza reached up and touched her husband's face. "Oh, Gerald, I just realized. You'll be a wanted man now. A deserter."

He kissed her nose. "Not really, my sweet. My enlistment was up November first. Five days past."

"November," Evie breathed dreamily. She gazed up at Chris. "Another month and it'll be three whole years since we celebrated our first Christmas together. You, me, our dear families and friends. A memory I shall always treasure." She paused, studying his face. "Would you mind terribly if we waited until we got to Princeton to marry, sweetheart? I'm so full of love and joy, I couldn't imagine not sharing it with everyone who's special to us."

It wasn't particularly what Christopher wanted to hear, but as he drank in the love shining from Evie's glorious blue eyes, how could he refuse her anything her heart desired?

❦ ❦

"I'm gonna feel awfully silly standing before everyone I know in all these ruffles," Christopher grumbled as Ma Lyons fluffed out his cravat.

The old woman finished fussing with it and stepped back to admire him. "Pshaw! You're as handsome as one of them English aristocrats. Handsomer. The sun has turned you a golden brown, a beautiful contrast to this new lace."

"*Beautiful,* huh? I should have kept my beard. I look like a kid."

"Nonsense." Smoothing the nap on the sleeve of his frock coat, she turned her hazel eyes up to him. "Fact is, this war's put too many years on that face of yours." She touched his cheek lightly. "Life's been mostly hard for you, hasn't it, Son? But I see the love you and your Evie have for each other. Things'll be much easier when you're together with the woman you adore. That's what life's about, you know. Being a help to one another, a comfort when there's pain. No joy is quite as sweet as it is when there's someone to share it with."

Her voice cracked as she went on. "Jasper an' me, we're pleased as punch that this day has come. Pleased as punch. And such a fine one it is, too." As tears pooled in her eyes, she grabbed her apron and dried them. "Oh, my. Now I'll have to go wash my face again, and it's time to get on over to the church."

The little woman had lost some of her plumpness of late and was beginning to show signs of frailty. And when had so much white crept into the thin crown of braids beneath her bonnet? The change caught at Christopher's heart, and watching her retreat, he felt his throat tighten. How like a mother she'd been to him. "Ma?"

She turned back, revealing the unchecked tears flowing freely now. "Yes?"

There was so much inside him that he wanted to say, but he figured that she really would start bawling then and stain her good meeting dress. "Uh, don't forget to take off your apron before you go," he said instead.

She glanced down, then wagged a finger at him. "And don't you be late. Susannah and Mary have already taken Evelyn to the church."

"Don't worry. Wild horses couldn't make me late."

The door closed behind Ma, and Chris turned to assess himself in the looking glass. *A dandy. A real dandy,* he decided with a grimace. He just hoped Evie would appreciate this expensive clothing her brother had insisted upon. Chris had never dressed in such elegance before. Even the color had a fancy name. *Cafe-au-lait,* Morgan had called it, a hue that seemed all the more rich against the cream brocade waistcoat. But those ruffles at his throat and wrists! Only love could make a man dress like a fop.

Might as well finish the picture, he reasoned. No sense being half a peacock when he could go for the whole bird. He plucked the new feathered tricorn from the washstand and plunked it on his head, then rolled his eyes at the stranger reflected back at him. He'd better hope Evie recognized him!

His droll smirk died as he wondered what his bride would wear. Even in that oversized Indian sack with her curls pulled into braids, she was the most beautiful woman he'd ever seen. Had she really promised herself to him forever?

A knock sounded at the door.

Chris removed the hat and tucked it under his arm. It was one of the twins, her face flushed and downcast. Her glum demeanor made Chris groan inwardly. Would he ever stop feeling guilty for unwittingly encouraging those redheads in their infatuation? He'd never been able to figure out a proper response without sounding conceited. "Yes?" he asked.

"There's somebody waiting to see you out in the barn. Says he has a wedding present for you." She turned away with a shrug. "Might be a horse. He brought an extra one."

"He didn't give his name?"

"No." She turned her back and started downstairs.

Chris checked to make sure all the proper papers for the wedding were inside his breast pocket, then stepped out into the hall and closed the door. Only a few more minutes now.

Who could be wanting to see him that the girl wouldn't recognize? And for that matter, who would bring an expensive gift like a horse? Perplexed, he hurried down the steps and out the back door.

The coaching yard was vacant, but then Sarah—or was it Selina?—had said the man would wait in the barn. *This had better not take very long,* Chris thought, and lengthened his stride. He entered the big open door.

A sudden blackness enveloped him, and the rough texture of a gunny sack scratched his face.

"Hey! What's going on?" Christopher tried to throw the thing off, but strong hands—several, from what he could tell—held his arms down. Someone bound something across his mouth, stifling any attempt to yell. Kicking and thrashing, Chris struck out at the unseen attackers, but to no avail. The gag was tied tightly behind his head. Then his arms were bound to his sides.

This couldn't be happening! Not today, of all days!

Christopher's breath left him in a whoosh as his legs were swept out from under him and he was lifted bodily up onto a horse. Though the men grunted with the effort, not a word was spoken. Before Chris could even kick, his legs were tied to the stirrups.

Who would be doing this? And why? Unable to do anything to help himself, Chris searched his brain trying to come up with names. Motives. This didn't make sense.

The other men scuffled about. The groan of a saddle. The horse Chris was on pranced nervously beneath him, then started forward with the others, obviously being tugged after them.

The twins, Chris concluded. They'd always been unhappy about his affection for Evie and their impending marriage. But no, that was stupid. They'd have nothing to gain by this. And they certainly wouldn't have had the means to hire five or six ruffians—the number he'd deduced from the sounds.

Chris could tell that he and his abductors had left the barn, and as the horses sped into a gallop, he suspected they were heading for the cover of the woods so no one would be able to apprehend them. Despondency settled into his spirit. After all the time he'd been searching for Evie, hoping to find her, this was insane.

The horse he was riding turned this way and that, making it hard for him to keep his seat, let alone determine any direction. Chris tried to focus on who might be the instigator of this kidnapping.

Morgan, maybe. But that, too, seemed crackbrained. Evie's brother had been unusually quiet, true. But he *had* accepted the wedding plans. He'd even bought the whole outfit Chris would wear for the ceremony, for heaven's sake. No, it had to be someone else.

Who might be so completely opposed to this union that he'd pay the price to see that the wedding never took place?

The Thomases! Of course! That had to be it. Evie's parents must have had their spies here watching Morgan and Prudence all along, waiting for the very moment when Evie returned. Spies with specific orders . . . *to take their daughter to England!* Had they already gotten to her? Spirited her away? After all she had been through—*all they'd been through!* Christopher's heart felt ready to explode.

Suddenly his horse skidded to a stop. Chris all but flew over the animal's head. He heard the creak of leather as the men dismounted and moved about. Then someone tore at his leg ropes.

There was one advantage. Christopher could tell they hadn't gone much of a distance. They couldn't be more than half a mile from town.

Hands latched onto him and hauled him from the saddle, then held him aloft, his feet never touching ground as they climbed some wooden steps. He'd be inside some building! Completely out of sight! No one would find him! He fought fiercely to get free.

The grips tightened on him as, mumbling and grunting, his abductors carried him across a plank floor. Both the restraints binding the sack around him and the gag were removed.

His arms now free, Christopher ripped at the ungainly covering, frantically lifting it off.

Dan Haynes's face was the first thing he saw. "Don't blame me!" Susannah's husband said. In his ministerial robes and clutching a Bible, he grinned sheepishly at someone behind Chris.

Chris whirled.

He met a raft of impish mugs. Morgan. Jonathan. Pa Lyons. Gerald Blake. Even Garth Kinyon, who, as he stood a little apart from the others, sported a toothier grin than the leathery old hunter had ever displayed in all the time Christopher had known him. All of them were decked out in their best clothes.

Morgan stepped closer and straightened Chris's tricorn. "Ah, yes. Much better, old chap."

Chris knocked his hand away. "Mind telling me what all this is about? *Brother?*" he added murderously.

In a look of supreme innocence, Morgan arched his brows. "I daresay, we were just helping out. With you being so reluctant, the lot of us thought we'd better get together and make sure you got to the church on time. After all, what are friends for?"

The church? For the first time since he'd been relieved of the sack, Christopher took in his surroundings. Sturdy wooden desk and chair. Shelves of books. He was in someone's study.

Morgan bowed, and with a sweeping gesture, indicated a door off to one side. "Your family and friends await. Not to mention a lovely lass who happens to be an absolute vision in white."

Chris felt some of his anger begin to dissipate.

"If you're to be part of this madcap family," his soon-to-be brother-in-law went on, "you'd best get a taste of it right off. I shouldn't want you calling foul later on. Yes, 'tis rather time I acquired myself a little brother, actually. Someone to blame when things don't turn out and all that. Someone who'll stand between me . . . *and Mother.*"

Realizing he'd been the victim of a harmless wedding prank, Chris felt his humor slowly returning. Then he shivered. From what he'd heard, Morgan and Evie's mother was quite a formidable woman.

Laughter erupted all around, and en masse, the men thumped his back and shook his hand in congratulations.

"Time to go, Chris," Jonathan, his best man, said. "Shall we?"

"Wait!" Morgan blocked the way as he brushed debris from the sack off Christopher's frock coat and tweaked the ruffle at his throat. "I can't allow you to go off without my saying . . . you've my wholehearted blessing. Of course—" he quirked a mischievous smile reminiscent of his school days—"a dowry is quite another matter entirely."

Jonathan tugged Christopher to his other side and eyed Morgan. "Oh, I reckon there'll be a dowry, all right. A fine one—or a whole raft of secrets will come flying out of the closet."

"Not about me, I hope!" Morgan fell back in mock horror.

"I think that's enough, lads," Dan said in his most authoritative voice, stepping forward. "I've a wedding to perform, one that's been waiting much too long." He opened the door to the sanctuary.

Christopher knew he'd always remember these few zany minutes. These men, his best friends, had concocted a silly prank, and in doing so, managed to restore a small measure of the normal frivolity of youth that the war had stolen from them all. It was a glimpse of tomorrow, a tomorrow bright and shining with hope, when the war would finally end and they could all live in the love and freedom God intended.

Filling his lungs with a calming breath, Chris walked out onto the dais of the small, homey church. It seemed that every citizen of Princeton had come to his wedding. Him, Christopher Drummond . . . son of the town drunk. *No,* he amended, *son of a renewed man, a forgiven man, thanks to the power of almighty God.* Chris's one regret was that his father had long since gone to his eternal home and could not be here for this special day.

He looked out over the assembly, picking out so many familiar faces, all here to wish him well. Art Bentley, Asa Appleton, Hiram Brown—townsmen and tradesmen who had frequented the inn throughout his growing up years. A few of his former professors. So many others. And in the front row, Ma Lyons, beaming from ear to ear as Chris took his place beside Jonathan.

Susannah pumped the opening notes from the pipe organ.

Then from the vestibule came Mary Clare, her blonde coloring contrasting the olive beauty of Morgan's wife, Prudence, right behind her. Then Liza Blake, petite and confident, smiling.

After a slight pause, an angel moved into view. On Pa Lyons's arm, she hesitated only an instant in the doorway.

As Evelyn, in a gown of pure white, started slowly up the aisle, Christopher forgot that anyone else existed in the world. And as each step brought her nearer to him he was lost in the wonder that such a beauty was coming to him. A socialite daughter of wealth, floating down the aisle to a penniless orphan . . . an Anglican bride coming to her Presbyterian groom.

A mismatch made in heaven.

When she reached the front and Pa Lyons placed her hand on Christopher's, Chris couldn't have spoken if his life had depended on it. But a radiant smile glowed at him through her veil, and glorious promise filled her eyes.

He answered with a promising smile of his own, and hand in hand, they turned to face Dan and repeat the solemn vows that would make them man and wife forevermore.

Chris felt Evie tremble slightly . . . or had it been himself? It didn't matter. Whatever came their way now, they would face together, as one. After all, as Ma Lyons had said, the sharing of things . . . that's what life was about.

Epilogue

December 1783

A weight of sadness came over Susannah as she watched Evelyn fussing about in the kitchen of the Lyons' Den, bringing tea and cake to Susannah and Mary Clare at the table.

"Would anyone care for sugar?" Evie asked. "Cream?"

"A bit of cream," Susannah said, forcing a smile. She smoothed a hand absently over the tablecloth. "Did you know that come this spring it will be fourteen years since I first sat at this table? Fourteen years since dear Esther Lyons put her comforting arms around me while I wept on her shoulder."

Evelyn, heavy with child, passed the small pitcher and eased herself onto a chair across from Mary.

Susannah poured a dollop into her cup, then returned her glance to Evie and Mary. "I had just been informed that my dearest friend, Julia, was dead, and her grief-stricken Robert had returned to North Carolina." She shook her head. "Here I was, stranded in a strange country, a strange town. No funds to speak of. And there was Mistress Lyons, happy to take in one more stray."

"Just as she did Chris and me," Mary said, reaching to catch her hand. "She and Pa Lyons saved Chris and me when we were in the most desperate straits. No amount of love or money in this world could ever repay their kindness."

Susannah nodded thoughtfully. "Quite. She just took us all in and treated us as if we were her children."

"Me, too," Evelyn put in, refilling her own cup. She glanced around to see if anyone else needed more before continuing. "And 'Little Chip' was the apple of her eye, right up until she passed on. Our son still asks for her, even after two months. And, of course, Grandpa Lyons must feel a stab in his heart every time he overhears. I can't tell you two how thankful I am you've come for the holidays."

"We could hardly stay away, knowing what a sad time it was likely to be," Susannah replied.

Evie's eyes misted, and she fluttered a hand. "Well, all of us know what a fuss Mother Esther always made over Christmas."

With a grave nod, Mary broke off a chunk of pound cake and took a bite. "Pa's so quiet. In just the few months since Jon and I went back to take up our life again in Wilkes-Barre, he's really changed."

"I can't help noticing he's lost weight," Susannah added. "I'm glad Emily and Robert will be coming up from North Carolina. Emily's always had a gift for making the old dear laugh."

Mary smiled. "I'm anxious to see their new baby. It'll be grand to see Robert as the proud papa of his own son. He was already so crazy about Emily's other two. They've probably grown like weeds since last we saw them."

"Well, the more little ones running through this place, the better," Evelyn remarked. "It'll keep Pa Lyons too busy to brood. Now that Chris is preoccupied with his engineering studies and I'm trying to keep up with our growing tot while running this inn, we've had precious little time to give Pa."

"Not to mention my little niece or nephew on its way," Mary teased lightly.

Susannah smiled at the light banter between the two as she watched Evelyn place a hand on her bulging abdomen.

"I just wish I had this one's energy!" Evie confessed, tucking her chin. "And I thought Christopher Junior was lively!" She sobered. "But all that aside, do you know what my most trying chore has been since Ma's passing? Keeping those serving girls and the hired boy hopping. They pay me less mind than my two-year-old does. I never dreamed I'd miss Pa Lyons's gruff growl."

Mary giggled. "Well, after this huge invasion of children Susannah and I have brought on the old place, with my four and her three, I'm sure our gruff lion will find his growl again."

"There'll be even more running about than you think," Susannah informed them. "I just received a post from Dan's sister Jane."

"She's married to your brother?" Evie chimed in. "I have trouble keeping them all straight."

"Yes. She and Ted went back up into the Green Mountains—or I should say, Vermont—when General Washington began issuing furloughs to the troops after the cease-fire. Jane wrote that they're still trying to convince the Congress to grant the territory its own statehood. Anyway, once she heard Emily was going to be here, she implored Ted to come, too. They'll be meeting Ben and Abigail in Rhode Island, then sailing down by packet with all their youngsters."

The sound of scraping feet came from the back door.

"Did someone mention Ben?" Christopher asked, entering with Jonathan and Dan behind him.

Susannah nodded. "Yes. He and his family will be joining us here for Christmas, along with Ted and Jane."

Chris grinned. "This is turning into quite the reunion! Morgan and Prudence said they'll be coming up with their boys on the twentieth from Philadelphia." Bending over his wife, he kissed her, then put a hand on her stomach. "How's Junior doing?"

"Junior number two, you mean," she said with a blush, then pushed his hand away. "Not in front of company."

Susannah smiled at Chris's impish laugh. There were some things men would never understand. "Dan," she said in an effort to ease Evelyn's discomfort, "why don't you go into the common room and give Mr. Lyons the news about the extra guests?" She turned back to the others. "I suppose we'll have to turn the entire attic into one giant bedchamber."

Dan started to comply but stopped at the door. "Speaking of news," he said, glancing at Chris, "it's been months since the cease-fire. Has there still been no word at military headquarters about Yancy Curtis?"

Jonathan shook his head. "I sent another request up to Newburgh just last week when the stage came through. But all I ever hear back is that the British are slow in telling us anything. Especially regarding all those seamen of ours that were imprisoned in England."

Dan frowned. "But we do know exactly when and where the *Providence* was sunk. You said 1779, right? Off the coast of Maine."

Christopher just shrugged in resignation. "Last I heard, the British are still refusing to release most of the American naval prisoners of war."

Jon moved to stand beside Mary Clare. "I reckon they're still smarting over our sailor boys taking the war to their own waters. They may not let them go until the treaty is signed, sealed, and delivered. And you can bet they won't give them free passage home afterward, either."

"That may be," Chris replied, "but Morgan has sent word to his father in Britain to offer a free ride to any and all released American seamen."

"I just hope for Felicia's sake Yancy is still alive," Susannah said quietly. "In the nine years of their marriage, I doubt they've been together a total of a year."

Mary gave an empathetic nod. "And poor Felicia has yet to be blessed with a child to comfort her."

"I'd better warn Mr. Lyons about those added visitors," Dan said, winking at Susannah.

As the men left, Susannah poured herself more tea. "Felicia continues to hang on to her hope, but there's been no word from Yancy in four years."

"So many have suffered loss," Mary said quietly. "Our freedom has come at such a high price."

"I trust that in the years to come, our children will appreciate all we've sacrificed for their future." Evie passed the plate of sliced cake around. "I've been meaning to ask, Susannah. How are Dan's parents getting along? I haven't seen them in years. I know his father was shot when the British tried to take Providence, and they eventually moved back to their farm, but . . ."

Susannah met her gaze. "His mother seems to be holding her own, but sad to say, Papa Haynes has never fully recovered the use of his leg. Since Ben's back at the farm, things are much better. By the way, Evie, do you happen to remember Alex Fontaine, Ted's army friend?"

"Hm. Rather thin, with straight blond hair? Jane would drag him and Ted to our house whenever they came to Philadelphia."

"Quite right." Susannah laughed. "Needless to say, when Ted deserted the king's army, he and Alex had a serious falling out. But all that's been righted. They've been corresponding for some time now. Alex was rather fond of Dan's father. When he learned of the loss of the Narragansett Pacers, he sent three Thoroughbred mares and a fine stud from his family's breeding farm. He might even come for a visit himself, if the peace treaty is signed before next summer."

"Visiting back and forth," Evie mused, "just like before the war. That would be a sure sign the conflict is over. I know Mother is on tenterhooks waiting for me to sail to England with Little Chip—and the new baby, when he or she arrives. In the meantime, she sends us huge boxes filled with all manner of niceties. She wants to ease my *unfortunate circumstance.*" She gave a wry grimace. "Mother will never change, I'm sure. She shows little regard for sending Chris anything to ease *his* circumstance."

Susannah looked at Evie over the rim of her cup. "Aside from the sadness here at the moment, how have you and Chris been? Seems I recall you had a more adventurous life planned than keeping an inn in Princeton."

Evelyn laughed. "Having babies has a way of taking the

place of most other adventures. But someday, when our little ones are older, we still hope to go and see what's out there beyond the frontier. Just the wilderness I saw seemed so vast. And from what Christopher said, there's so much more waiting to be discovered. So much beauty."

"Ah, the adventure that has lured so many," Mary said. "Now that peace has been restored, hundreds of families came through Wilkes-Barre over this last summer."

The door from the common room burst open, and eleven-year-old Miles galloped in with little Christopher perched on his shoulders. His younger sister, Julia, and Mary's daughter Esther were close behind. "Mother. Julie and Essie won't stop mimicking everything I say."

"Mother," they chorused, "Julie and Essie won't stop—"

"See?" he bellowed.

"See?" came the syrupy echo.

"See?" young Chip chimed in.

Miles winced. "Oh, no! Now they've got *him* doing it."

"Now they've got—"

"*Girls!*" Susannah said, placing her hands on her hips. "It would appear you need something to occupy you for a while." Rising, she handed them folded tablecloths. "Go change any that are soiled from the noon meal. And be sure to put them on straight. It won't be long before holiday travelers will be stopping for evening lodging. And then, Miss Julia," she added, "check on your baby brother. He might have awakened from his nap by now."

They groaned as one but took the cloths and obeyed.

"Serves them right," Miles muttered with a snicker.

"And you, young man," she went on. "Hand me Little Chip. You go out and bring in logs for all the wood boxes."

The lad's jaw went slack, but only for a second. With his very favorite person in the world watching, he caught himself. Aunt Evie winked conspiratorially, and he returned it with one of his own as he skipped out.

Little Chip reached up for Susannah's cheek, and she

gazed down into eyes the same startling pale blue as his mother's. "Cookie?" he asked.

Not about to refuse, she handed him a piece of cake from the plate.

"Thankee, God," he said.

Caught by surprise, Susannah and Mary laughed.

Evelyn stood and wet a corner of her apron with her tongue, then began wiping the tot's face and hands. "Our Chip takes the giving of thanks for food quite literally."

As she watched, Susannah wondered how she could ever have worried that Evie wouldn't make Christopher a good, practical Christian wife. To look at her today, one would never guess she'd been born to a life of wealth and ease. She'd become truly one of them, a sister in Christ.

A ruckus broke out in the common room.

"What now?" Mary groaned, rising. "The kids again, no doubt." As she headed toward the commotion with Susannah and Evelyn following, the howling and stomping became even more fierce.

The men and children had apparently surrounded someone, and everyone was yelling at once and grabbing at him.

"Shiver me timbers, mates!" came the jaunty voice. "Give a poor sailor some wind for his sails!"

"Yancy!" Susannah gasped, catching sight of a wild shock of flaming red hair. She squealed and ran to hug him. Little Chip, still in her arms, let out a huge wail. Quickly she thrust the tot to Chris, then included Dan in her hug. "Oh, sweetheart, our dear, dear Yancy has come back to us. Is this not the most marvelous Christmas present ever?"

"None better." Dan slipped an arm around her waist and hugged her to him while he pumped Yancy's hand with the other. "It's been a long time, my friend."

The seaman's lopsided grin hadn't changed much. "Ye know how some folks are. Ye drop in for a wee visit, an' them Brits don't want to let ye go home."

"Felicia," Susannah prompted. "Have you brought her with you?"

"Nay. Since me ship anchored in Philadelphia and wasn't to sail down to Yorktown for another four days, I couldn't pass up comin' to find out how ye all are. Sure didn't figure I'd be findin' so many of ye here, though." Clamping a big hand on Dan's shoulder, he yanked him and Susannah both into another big embrace.

"Oh, Yance," Susannah murmured, "Felicia is going to be beside herself with joy. Do give her lots of hugs from me, will you? And first thing after the thaw, you must bring her to visit us in Wilkes-Barre for weeks and weeks."

"You're headed for Yorktown?" Christopher leaned around Evie to peer at Yancy. "I'm afraid you'll find that city a little worse for the wear."

Jonathan nodded in agreement. "That's where we finally convinced the British once and for all that we weren't going to go home until *they* did."

"Aye. We did hear word ye lads quit playin' cat and mouse and captured their main force there. Ye never heard such celebratin' as went on in that pest hole of a prison. But what I'd like to know is why it took a whole year, ten months, and fifteen days after that to sign a treaty to let us go!"

"You weren't counting, were you?" Jon quipped.

"Wasn't much else to do, ye might say!"

Mr. Lyons, looking more alive than he had since laying his wife to rest, finally entered the fray. "They've signed a treaty, you say?" he asked Yancy. "The war is over at last?"

The seaman's grin spread from ear to ear. "I was on the very ship that brought the news. Never had more fun in me life than I've had since arrivin' in Philly. The paper was signed in Paris on the third of September."

Pandemonium broke out, and without stopping to gather their coats, everyone ran down the road, yelling the news to all of Princeton.

When they trickled back inside a short time later, Dan glanced around at the roomful of jubilant faces. "We have much to be thankful for. So much." He spread his hands and grasped Susannah's and Yancy's, and everyone linked on to form a huge circle.

"We fought long and hard," he said, "for the freedom to govern ourselves, the freedom to call no man king but King Jesus."

"And the freedom to worship our God free of the heavy hand of the Church of England," Yancy supplied.

Susannah recalled how Yancy's father-in-law had once been arrested for preaching without the Church's ordination. She squeezed his hand.

"In the middle of the century," Evelyn said, "they called us *new lights*. I like to think of us still as bearers of the eternal light of God. I pray that this holy flame will never go out. That we'll remember the cost of this triumph as we pass the blessed torch to our children." Her gaze fell to her son in Christopher's arms. "And our children to their children."

Tears clogged Susannah's throat as she thought about the maturity and wisdom Evie had gained over the past few years. Her gaze met Jasper Lyons's faded blue eyes across the circle, and he gave a poignant smile of understanding. "And they to their children," she finally managed.

Beside her, Dan lifted her hand and kissed it. "Amen," he murmured, and the word was repeated around the circle . . . this circle of God's love, which Susannah hoped with all her heart would grow and grow until one day it circled the world.

Dear Reader,

We highly regard your interest in our series, and we would be pleased to receive your comments and answer any questions you might have.

> **Sally Laity & Dianna Crawford**
> **P.O. Box 80176**
> **Bakersfield, CA 93380-0176**

P.S. Your self-addressed stamped return envelope would be appreciated.